I Give You Oscar Wilde

I GIVE YOU
OSCAR WILDE

a biographical novel by

DESMOND HALL

AN NAL-WORLD BOOK

PUBLISHED BY THE NEW AMERICAN LIBRARY

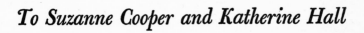

To Suzanne Cooper and Katherine Hall

PART *1*

MR. OSCAR WILDE

1   FOR MY LAST STAY IN LONDON I RESERVED A ROOM AT THE
Cadogan Hotel, on Sloane Street. It was a quiet time of a quiet
year, 1931, and as I signed the registration book, *Lawrence Young,
New York City, N.Y.*, it occurred to me to ask if by any chance
Room 53 was unoccupied. Yes, the clerk replied after consulting
his records; would I prefer Room 53 to the room they had given
me?

He paused, and then, leaning forward with a nice smile, and in a
slightly louder voice, he asked the question again. I wasn't deaf,
despite my gray hair and other tokens of a good deal more than
middle age; the prospect of actually staying in Room 53 had set
my mind wandering in the past, and it took me a minute to return to the present.

"Yes, please," I said. "I should prefer it."

"Very good, sir. Porter."

The Cadogan's old-fashioned lift gave a gentle wheeze as it carried us up, or so I thought until I realized that the sound was the
asthmatic breathing of the porter. "Down 'ere, sir," he said as we
got out of the lift. "Mind the step."

I had an absurd pang of suspense, looking at the door. "Is Room
53 still the same?" I asked.

The porter put down my bags and smiled uncertainly. He had a
good-natured, rather puffy face; the corners of the mouth were
stained with nicotine. "It's Room 53, sir, right enough."

"I really meant, has anything been changed in the last thirty-five
years?"

"No, sir, I wouldn't say so." Reflectively he passed his hand over
his thin hair and added, "Except the decker."

"The—?"

"The decker—decoration, sir; painting and so on." He unlocked
the door and pushed it open. "And of course it's a bedroom now,
whereas it used to be a sitting room, with bedroom attached. It
was Lord Alfred Douglas', in them days."

It seemed to be a comfortable room, with one broad window
and a fireplace. "Were you working for the hotel then?"

"Oh, yes. I was in this 'ere very room, sir," the porter said, bringing in my bags and closing the door, "when the police officers

3

came to arrest poor Mr. Wilde. 'E 'ad a great thirst that afternoon, I remember, couldn't seem to get enough to drink, and 'e was always calling for me. 'Chester,' 'e'd say, 'where's Chester? More 'ock, Chester,' 'e'd say, 'and another siphon.' Of course Lord Alfred never kept anything like that on 'and, not if others was going to drink it, not 'im. But I beg your pardon, sir, perhaps the subject doesn't interest you?"

"It does, very much."

"Do you mind if I smoke, sir?"

"Please have one of mine."

"A Yankee fag? Ta." I lit the cigarette for him; he drew in deeply and coughed. "The wife says I oughtn't because of me bronchitis, but when you've got the 'abit, you've got it, and if there's any 'arm to be done it's done by now. Mr. Wilde was a tremendous smoker; favored cigarettes with gold tips. I've always remembered 'is last remark to me—been proud of it, you might say. 'E said it as 'e was walking out the door. I can see 'im and 'ear 'im as if it was yesterday."

"Do you mind telling me what he said?"

The porter chuckled. "Bless you, sir, I don't mind, except that you'll never believe me."

"Was it something amusing?"

"No, I wouldn't say that, though you might think so now. But you'd never guess, not if you was to try a 'undred years."

4

2

IN SEPTEMBER OF 1881, WHEN I WAS TWENTY-TWO YEARS
old, my father summoned me to his office. He was a small, brisk,
tidy man to whom time was supremely important; only the rare
visitor could manage to stay for more than five minutes.

"Lawrence, you're not happy with me, I believe?"

"I'm not happy in the office, Father." I cleared my throat and
added, smiling, "My soul isn't fettered to an office stool, you see."

"What's that?"

"Gilbert and Sullivan, *H.M.S. Pinafore.*"

"You want to write, eh?"

"Yes, Father."

"If you took half the day off, mornings or afternoons, would
that do?"

"Writing can't be a— I mean to say, one must devote all one's
time and thought to it. One must burn with a hard, gemlike flame,
as Walter Pater wrote."

"Was he burning with a hard, gemlike flame when he wrote
that? Never mind. What if you left the office for the next six
months?"

"That's very kind of you, Father, but the atmosphere in America
isn't really congenial."

"Where would it be congenial?"

"In Paris or London."

"A ship is sailing tomorrow—the *Arizona.* Here's your ticket."
He pulled an envelope out of the desk. "A reasonable allowance
will be paid over to you on the first of every month through my
London bank, Messrs. Coutts. If you don't, inside six months, discover your gemlike flame, admit it and come back. Now I suppose you will want to start with your packing."

He saw me off. We shook hands. I wondered if he knew what
was in one of my bags. My mother's photograph was the first
thing I had packed; then I had gone downstairs and found a small
photo of him and packed it too.

During my few months in London I saw a good many plays
(one cannot burn with a hard, gemlike flame all the time). The
most notable, I thought, was a revival of *She Stoops to Conquer;*
not because I liked the play. It didn't amuse me; I don't think I

5

laughed once. I was lost; spellbound, breathless. For there before me was beauty: Lillie Langtry, in her first stage appearance. The critics said it was a pity, because she wasn't an actress, she was simply beautiful, and beauty should never be forced (by financial difficulties, in this case) to make a fool of itself. Stupid little men; had they seen Aphrodite rising from the foam they would have criticized the production.

I learned from my landlady, a human encyclopedia devoted to royalty and the smart world, that the Prince of Wales himself had come to see *She Stoops to Conquer.* "Which would be sufficient to turn any young lady's head," Mrs. Wolstonholme continued, "but not Lillie Langtry's. Hers had been turned already."

"Is that so, Mrs. Wolstonholme?"

"Do you know her history, sir?"

"I know she was married when very young, sixteen or seventeen, I believe, to Mr. Langtry, who is old enough to be her father."

"The poor gentleman. It is said"—Mrs. Wolstonholme was partial to the expression; tolled out in her deep voice, it gave an authoritative, House of Lords air to her most casual remark—"that he soon bitterly regretted it. A pretty dance she led him. It is said that his Irish estates were mortgaged to the hilt to pay for her whims and that even so it was all he could do to get a cup of tea in his own house. But her head was turned, you see."

"What turned it, Mrs. Wolstonholme?" It was a joy to pronounce these grand syllables, and I indulged myself as often as I decently could.

"Why, all the attention that was paid to her by that Oscar Wilde. Always at her feet. Slept on her doorstep one night, it is said. Armloads of lilies and fancy speeches for a country parson's daughter. It cannot be wondered at that her head was turned."

"Did she—do you think they were in love, Mrs. Wolstonholme?"

"Ah. One cannot be blamed for thinking *the worst* where people like that Oscar Wilde and Lillie Langtry are concerned."

Hopelessly smitten as I was, I had tried to comfort myself by reflecting that the adorable girl could not love her ancient husband and no doubt had married him for the sake of an impoverished family; this was a blow. And yet—Oscar Wilde; Lillie Langtry's lover? That mincing idiot? Just the other evening I myself had laughed at him until my sides ached, or if not at him in the

6

flesh, at the stage figure that was generally supposed to be modeled on his, the ultrapoetical, superaesthetical Reginald Bunthorne. With his knee breeches and mouse-gray silk stockings and velvet coat and long curled hair and simpering face, Bunthorne had only to step in front of an audience to evoke a great wave of feminine shrieks and masculine guffaws; and he was doing it every night in Gilbert and Sullivan's new comic opera, *Patience*.

Bunthorne is a fraud. As he confesses:

> Am I alone and unobserved? I am!
> Then let me own I'm an aesthetic sham!
> This air severe is but a mere veneer!
> This cynic smile is but a wile of guile!
> This costume chaste is but good taste misplaced!
> . . . affectation!
> Born of a morbid love of—admiration!

Lillie, Lillie, how could you lose your heart, or even one precious beat of it, Lillie, to such a fellow?

"I do not hold with poets, sir, of this new-fangled kind," said Mrs. Wolstonholme. "Lord Tennyson was good enough for my father and he is good enough for me. *He* does not wear knee breeches, I think!"

"I've never read any of Mr. Wilde's poetry. Has he really written any, Mrs. Wolstonholme?"

She did not know. I inquired at a bookshop and learned that he had published a slim volume several months before. Because, surely, of all the attention he had received in *Patience* and the pages of *Punch*, which doted on him as a perfect butt for ridicule, *Poems*, by Oscar Wilde, had sold very well, and I had to visit half a dozen shops before I could find a copy.

I opened it expecting to be amused (and reassured) by posturings in print as absurd as Bunthorne-Wilde's on the stage; but I found this:

REQUIESCAT

Tread lightly, she is near
Under the snow,
Speak gently, she can hear
The daisies grow.

7

All her bright golden hair
Tarnished with rust,
She that was young and fair
Fallen to dust.

Lily-like, white as snow,
She hardly knew
She was a woman, so
Sweetly she grew.

Coffin-board, heavy stone,
Lie on her breast,
I vex my heart alone,
She is at rest.

Peace, peace, she cannot hear
Lyre or sonnet,
All my life's buried here,
Heap earth upon it.

I acknowledged defeat. He was a poet, qualified to love and be loved by the most beautiful woman in the world. Granted, nothing else in the book approached this level, but how many poets could claim twenty lines so arrow-swift, so clean, so sure, so heartbreaking?

I wondered who the girl was who lay under the snow, with all her bright golden hair tarnished. She could be no mere invented sorrow, not in the face of the poem's sovereign grief.

In December in London I received a cable from our family doctor: YOUR FATHER GRAVELY ILL RETURN FIRST POSSIBLE SHIP. The first possible ship turned out to be the same *Arizona*, sailing on Christmas Eve. There could not be a more melancholy time to depart on a melancholy journey. English rain, the gloomiest, the grayest in the world, enveloped the day. The passenger with whom I was to share a cabin had preceded me to it; he was, in fact, snoring and giving off a great beery smell on the lower of the two berths. As I stared at him he hitched himself around, leaned over, vomited, and fell asleep again. He had a fat red face. I went in search of the purser.

He agreed to move me, and found an empty berth in a cabin on A deck. "But perhaps you will object," he said, looking up from his

8

papers with raised eyebrows and a smile, "to sharing a cabin with Mr. Oscar Wilde?"

"Mr. Oscar Wilde. Do you mean the Mr. Oscar Wilde who is— who is——"

"Surely there is only one?"

"He is *really* on board?"

"If he is not now, he will be, I am sure, before sailing time."

"Going *to America?*"

Abroad I never carried in the front of my mind the most attractive aspects of my native country; I always thought of the worst. I did not think of Mr. Wilde in my own New York of Gramercy Park, or Boston, or Philadelphia; I thought of him in the savage west.

"To give lectures to the American ladies, I believe," the purser said.

"You asked if I would object to sharing a cabin with him. Good heavens, no. On the other hand, he may very well object to sharing it with me."

The purser felt confident Mr. Wilde would not. I hoped this was not merely professional optimism.

A steward rescued my bags from the cabin of the slumbering drunk and led me to the cabin on A deck. I waited nervously as the steward knocked on the door, but there was no answer. "The gent'man can't be on board yet," said the steward, and he opened the door.

It was a pleasant cabin. After the steward left, I unpacked some of my things, expecting each moment to hear behind me the sounds of Mr. Wilde's arrival. Perhaps it would be a point in my favor if he should find me reading his book. I took it out but promptly put it back. It had been a ridiculous notion, the way an infatuated schoolgirl would behave. I must come down to earth. Probably meeting him would be a disappointment. There must be *some* truth in that cruel portrait of Bunthorne, silly, fattish, la-de-da Bunthorne. It was possible, wasn't it, to write a few beautiful lines and still be thoroughly objectionable? Yes; but then how could the sublime Lillie have loved him? Ah, he had a clever tongue, an artful tongue—even *Punch* admitted that. He must have flattered Lillie until her darling head was in a whirl.

I came across my father's photo. I hadn't thought about him for the last half hour.

"Good evening," someone said, and I turned to see a perfectly enormous, smiling man.

I am no more certain today than I was that first evening in our cabin (and how small it had become after his entrance) of the color of Oscar Wilde's eyes. Gray, blue, green; I don't know. His hair was brown. He wore it long when I first saw him; here the Bunthorne caricature was accurate enough. It curled gracefully into a loose, light mass at his neck and of course this was not a natural curl but the product of the hairdresser's art. I think the style became him; it complemented the rather heavy lower part of his face; the upper part was handsome. It was noble. The eyebrows were dark and full and beautifully curved.

His mouth, flowing and easy, seemed designed for smiles. A slight dark line barely marred a few of his upper front teeth near the top. I wondered how someone otherwise so immaculate could neglect it.

"Good evening," I said in return, astoundingly at ease. "My name is Lawrence Young, Mr. Wilde. I hope you will not mind my sharing a cabin with you?"

"I think it is charming of you to ask. Are you American?"

"Yes, sir; New York City."

"And a seasoned traveler?"

"Not very, I'm afraid. I've only crossed the Atlantic once."

"And I, never. Was it a disturbing experience?"

I smiled. "I wasn't sick."

"Excellent," he said. "Then I can turn to you for support and encouragement. When I give signs of disgracing myself you shall murmur to me, 'Be brave, Oscar. Remember Lady Icklesham.' But of course you don't know about Lady Icklesham. Lady Icklesham is eighty or more and a most precious person, but she cannot spell. Last year she was obliged to travel to Canada. She wrote to a family friend in the Cunard Company asking if he would be so kind as to make sure that she would have a good cabin and a comfortable berth; but here poor Lady Icklesham went astray and spelt berth with an 'i.' The friend, therefore, could hardly be blamed for replying that although Cunard would provide her with a splendid cabin, alas, despite the best will in the world, they could not guarantee Lady Icklesham against *mal de mère*."

His laughter was irresistible. As was his voice. Bunthorne's voice was comically exasperating; high, affected, effeminate, it could not have been more unlike these melodious tones. Wilde's voice, though, was not at the mercy of melody. The meaning, the clear understanding of words, came first with him in print and in speech.

He took off his coat; he was not wearing knee breeches but respectable tweeds. He wore no silk stockings, no frilly lace at sleeves and collar either. The Bunthorne caricature was outrageous.

"I am proud of this coat," he remarked, holding it off from him at arm's length. "Isn't it handsome?"

A child might have said it as ingenuously.

The coat was long, down to the ankles; the material, bottle green, was thick and soft, like an expensive rug; the most striking feature was the enormous pelt around the neck, a great swatch of fur. The coat itself was fur-lined as well.

"Yes, very," I said.

"I don't think you really mean that, Lawrence. I may call you Lawrence, mayn't I? And you must call me Oscar. After all, we must be very much of an age. How old are you, Lawrence?"

"Twenty-two," I said, adding, hesitantly, "Oscar."

"And I am twenty-seven. Yes, I think you didn't want to hurt me and were being kind. That was very sweet of you and it makes me like you more than ever, but you must always tell me what you really think."

We had been friends for years. I had never been happier.

"Isn't it perhaps a little—strong?"

"Strong, Lawrence?" he said with a humorous look. "My coat —*strong*?"

"I mean, perhaps a little—overpowering?"

"But that is it *precisely*," he cried. "It *is* overpowering. That is why I had it made. It is my armor, my suit of mail. It is intended to daunt people—not people in general, but Americans, and I speak to you now not as to an American but as to a brother—take them aback, so that they will think, 'There must be a *remarkable* man inside this remarkable coat, for who but a *most* remarkable man would have the courage to wear it?' "

Tenderly, he hung up the coat. "In this superb coat I feel bold enough to grapple with America, I feel myself equipped to withstand the icy blast of the American winter and the copious expectorations of the American male. Are you torn between a smile and a frown, Lawrence? Smiling at my coat, I fancy, or at me, or at both of us (because this coat is an individual, as much as I am, and

11

we are linked together in a passionate friendship), and frowning at my mention of the expectorations of the American male. But he *does* expectorate, doesn't he?"

"I suppose he does," I said, "or some of him."

"*You* don't, of course; but you are a gentleman. Not even Dickens said that *all* Americans expectorate, although in reading his *American Notes* and *Martin Chuzzlewit*, which I did to prepare myself for this trip, I gathered that life in the United States is one long expectoration."

"He wrote those books thirty or forty years ago," I pointed out.

"To be sure he did. And I dare say most of it was grossly exaggerated. But I mustn't criticize Dickens," he added solemnly. "He has brought sunshine and cheer into my life in some of its gloomiest moments. One must have a heart of stone to read the death of Little Nell without laughing."

That completed his conquest of me. When I was able to speak again, I said that it made me indignant to think how he was caricatured in *Patience*. The lace, the knee breeches, the silk stockings, the velvet jacket, the effeminate air—why, it was a libel. Couldn't he sue?

"Sue, my dear Lawrence? I wouldn't dream of it. In the first place, to sue for libel in an English court is to enter the lion's den, and a vicious, cowardly animal he is."

"Excuse me," I said, "but aren't you English?"

"Lawrence, really. There are limits, my dear chap, to the insults friendship will tolerate."

"I beg your pardon. I thought——"

"I am an Irish gentleman, the son of a long line of Irish patriots. To resume. In the first place, never tackle the English lion in his den, which is a lawcourt. In the second, I owe this trip to the delightful Bunthorne. In the third, he wasn't, originally, supposed to be me. It is my peculiar triumph, and I shall never tire of congratulating myself upon it, that I have made the public think Reginald Bunthorne *is* Oscar Wilde. I have even befuddled his creator, Mr. W. S. Gilbert, into thinking that he had me in mind when he invented Bunthorne, whereas in fact I suspect he wasn't thinking of anyone in particular but of the whole tribe of aesthetes. I saw Bunthorne, Lawrence, and at once realized that here there could be a very good thing. If I had never worn knee breeches before, I would have rushed to wear them."

"But you *don't*." I protested. "Wear them, I mean."

"My dear boy, they are in my luggage. I shall put them on for my first appearance as a lecturer in the States, and the ladies will swoon and the gentlemen will gnash their teeth and foam at the mouth—between expectorations. Knee breeches *can* be quite devastating if one has a well-shaped leg. And all this will bring rapture to the hearts of Mr. Gilbert and Mr. Sullivan, and most particularly, Mr. Carte, their producer. It is not only your compatriots who are devoted to the almighty dollar, Lawrence."

"How do you owe this trip to Bunthorne?" I asked.

"Because *Patience* is playing in New York and before long touring companies will be traveling throughout the States. A certain Morse, a colonel—are all Americans colonels, Lawrence? Are you? —who is Carte's American representative, suggested that it might very well drum up business if the newspaper reporters and the public were to see the supposed original of Bunthorne. And so these lectures were arranged. Does that distress you?"

How quick he was to sense my feelings. But I suppose it was written all over my face.

"It does," he answered himself, "and I am very pleased, because it shows that in this half hour since we met we have come to be rather more than chance fellow passengers. You are concerned to think that I should be debasing myself for money, whereas half an hour ago you wouldn't have cared twopence, would you? Or, rather, the disclosure that I am going to America as the willing pawn of commercial interests would merely have confirmed your darkest suspicions about that mountebank Oscar Wilde."

"No," I said.

"It wouldn't have?"

"I didn't think of you as a mountebank. Oh, I did, yes, when I saw *Patience* and the cartoons in *Punch*. But then I read your poems."

He looked at me earnestly. He had done so before. There was no polished performance in the attention he gave me; I could be myself with him.

"And they changed your opinion of me?"

"It was the poem called 'Requiescat,' really."

He sat down on the berth. "It's an odd thing," he said. "I set out on this trip in fear and trembling, and not only of the Atlantic, although the thought of it, that monstrous beast lying out there, has haunted me ever since I knew I had to cross it. Bad enough. Worse—who would be in the cabin with me? I couldn't afford to pay for a cabin to myself. And oh, good God, to think of it. A storm at sea—desperately sick—and some absolute stranger, some vulgar Philistine, some moneyed brute from Birmingham or Manchester, being sick a few inches away from me. And I would have to sleep in the same cabin with him for nine interminable nights. Hear his horrid snores. See his disgusting socks. Witness him putting on his obscene undergarments unless I kept my face turned to the wall or pretended to go mad. And then I come into the cabin and find—" he smiled at me "—this quiet, gentle person who I know at once is to be my friend. Very odd, and very wonderful, that I should meet him here."

I had been smiling at the picture of the disgusting socks and obscene undergarments and thinking, I confess, that no doubt the "vulgar Philistine" would have rushed to the purser to demand another cabin—anything rather than share one with the lunatic Wilde, who according to *Punch* was content to sit for hours in rapt contemplation of a sunflower or a lily, which he found *too, too utterly consummate*. With his last words I said seriously, "Thank you. I am very fortunate."

"But still distressed, Lawrence?"

"You said yourself," I reminded him, "that you were debasing yourself for money."

"No, dear boy; I said that was what you thought. I don't consider for a moment that I am debasing myself. The promoters—I think that is a good American word, Lawrence? Colonel Morse used it repeatedly in his tedious communications—the promoters of my tour believe that I am going to come prancing out on the stage in knee breeches and velvet and lace and eat a dish of sunflowers and lilies and perform God knows what other antics. Well, I *am* going to wear the knee breeches and velvet, because they are not unattractive and I have no reason to be ashamed of my legs, but otherwise there will be precious little Bunthorne about me. I propose to educate my audiences, not amuse them. I am going to show them that those of us in England who are called aesthetes are simply people of intelligence and good taste who wish to introduce beauty into the everyday world and everyday lives. In short, Lawrence, I shall be spreading the gospel of the New—the English—Renaissance. And for this I shall be paid. Could there

14

ever have been a luckier missionary to the heathen? Provided of course that they don't eat me alive. But, then, your red Indians aren't cannibals, are they? And I dare say your society hostesses are no more ferocious than ours."

"Are you really going to the far west?" I asked.

"If I am successful in the east."

"Not just to see it, but to lecture on the English Renaissance? In knee breeches and silk stockings?"

"Yes, of course."

"Candidly, Mr. Wilde——"

"Oscar," he interrupted, smiling.

"Oscar, the prospect fills me with alarm. They're not really civilized out there, you know. It wasn't so very many years ago that General Custer was scalped, and as for the cowboys, they may be all very well in their proper place, looking after cows, but when they come into town, where presumably you would be lecturing, I understand they turn into drunken, vicious mobs."

"Dear me," he murmured.

3

THE ATLANTIC WAS CALM AS A MILLPOND. "LIKE BUN-
thorne," Oscar remarked, "it is a sham. Or do you suppose that
hardy old salt Captain Murray has lost his way and we are really
in the Mediterranean? Perhaps he turned to the left when he
should have gone to the right? Do be a good boy and ask him,
Lawrence; it would be better to bring it to his attention before
we have gone too far. I dare say he will thank you humbly. Oh,
and while you are about it, please give him my compliments and
say I was profoundly moved by his exquisite rendering of the
Christmas services."

Funny to hear our fat, pompous captain called a hardy old salt.
On Christmas he must have taken a glass too many; he had a terrible time with hiccups during the prayer for those in peril on the
deep.

There we were, the first-class passengers, hailing our merciful
Saviour and wishing peace and plenty to our fellow humans when
at each end of the ship, far forward and aft, several hundred men,
women, and children were packed together like beasts. They were
immigrants: Russians, Poles, Hungarians, Romanians, Bohemians,
Italians, following the earlier tidal waves of Celtic and Teutonic
stock to the promised land, the thought of which sustained them,
no doubt, in their present misery.

We could look down on them, if we cared to, from our superior
position on the promenade deck, but the sight (and the smells)
upset Oscar. "I hate poverty," he said, "and squalor and disease
and all ugliness. I pity it, I wish to solace it, but from a distance,
if you please. Nevertheless, there is one absurdly slim feminine
creature down there—a gypsy girl, I dare say—have you noticed
her?"

I hadn't.

"Are those blue eyes of yours blind, Lawrence? She has a leopard
look about her. Her skin is tawny and her hair incredibly black and
her teeth marvelously white. I dare say they are very sharp. How
red her lips are. Her breasts seem very small and very firm, and her
eyes—honey-colored, are they? But I should have to look closer to
be sure—are not altogether devoid of interest as she glances up

in this direction. I wonder if she would care to join us in a glass of champagne in our cabin this evening?"

"Wouldn't that be against ship's regulations?"

"That is why the idea is so attractive. Does it horrify your law-abiding Yankee soul?"

Hurt, I said, "I don't have a law-abiding Yankee soul. I only meant that they'd stop us if they saw us bringing her there."

"The eagle-eyed Murray and his officers and men? Ah, but we would disguise her. We would have her braid the black torrent of her hair and hide it under your cap, Lawrence, and since you are almost as slim as she, one of your suits would do very nicely to cover the rest of her. I am sure she is a passionate little thing. Her mouth is really quite exciting. If it should turn out to be you she has been glancing at (for we can't really be sure at this distance, can we?), I shall modestly withdraw and leave you alone with her to have your fortune told, which I am convinced she does very prettily, with all sorts of fetching little arts and graces. If on the other hand she should prefer to tell *mine*— But we are crossing our bridge before we come to it."

We continued our constitutional around the deck. We took it every morning, a full mile; at least it had started as a mile (ten circuits), but was rapidly growing shorter, and I foresaw that by the end of the voyage we would have cut it down to a dozen steps. It was not that Oscar disliked the exercise; it was the other promenaders, and the faces of passengers who lay wrapped in steamer rugs in their deck chairs and stared at us as we passed. Their faces, he declared, made him ill. How ugly they all were; the avarice, the stupidity. The great middle class—how he loathed it.

"Some day it will be the death of me, Lawrence. I feel it in my bones."

"We could take our constitutional at night," I suggested.

"No, it is too cold then. And I refuse to cut my jib (pray note the nautical expression; how proud Captain Murray would be of me) because of these Yahoos."

But cut it we did, walking less and less, although Oscar pretended we weren't. To tell the truth, I was relieved; he was not a graceful walker, indeed he had a clumsy, rather shambling look, but his long, powerful legs devoured space, and I, several inches shorter than he and slight, had my work cut out to stay abreast, and ended up panting.

Of course his long hair and the mighty fur coat—and for that matter the contrast between us as we raced around the deck—were enough to make anyone stare; added to this was the curiosity his name aroused. He loved to be recognized and to hear his name whispered back and forth. Many of our fellow passengers read *Punch*, the official jester to the English middle class (and protector of its interests); I could see a copy here and there on those well-wrapped laps, and although Oscar's name wasn't used in its cartoons and jokes about him (he was called Jellaby Postlethwaite), the figure and hair were unmistakable. I dare say the most aesthetic of all aesthetes never spoke as Jellaby Postlethwaite spoke, and I dare say too that most of those who laughed at him really believed that it was a fair approximation of Oscar Wilde's speech.

Captain Murray, at any rate, believed it; I could almost feel him bristle when we came near. But then, I suppose he was jealous. His waxed moustache and dandified roosterish strut testified to his opinion of himself as a ladykiller, but he suffered a total eclipse in Oscar's presence. For Oscar was attractive to women. Those in first class on the *Arizona* had long since said farewell to youth, but the sourest spinster among them would brighten up in his presence. Two dear old ladies, friends for a lifetime, quite fell out over him.

I knew, therefore, that he was the reason for the gypsy girl's glances. I hated to think of her visiting our cabin, but not (as I truthfully protested) because steerage passengers were forbidden to set foot on the sacred first-class territory. It was the thought of Lillie Langtry that dismayed me. I had worshiped at her shrine; so had Oscar. We must do nothing to sully that precious privilege. I didn't dare explain this to him; for that matter, something would have been lost if it had *had* to be explained. Surely in his heart of hearts he must feel as I did. Surely he would change his mind.

"Lawrence," he said that evening, "I do hope you won't be annoyed, but I've rather cooled on the gypsy charmer. After all, we would have to give her a bath, and I fear it might be awkward."

"A bath, Oscar?"

"Of course, dear boy; she simply can't be entertained in an unwashed state. It is all very well to speak of the delights of living next to nature, but filth is filth and heaven alone knows when she last had a bath; no doubt she looks back on the event, if indeed it ever took place, as a somber and disturbing episode and would fight tooth and nail to avoid undergoing it again. And we don't have a private bath, and the bath steward has the key to the bathroom, and the whole thing is really somewhat squalid. Do you mind?"

Indeed, he was finicky as a cat; it took him a good hour in the morning to make his toilet, first the bath and then the elaborate ritual of shaving, combing and perfuming his hair, brushing his teeth (extraordinary that they should be stained), rinsing his mouth with pink mouthwash, and dressing in underlinen of a quality soft enough for a baby's skin and outer clothes fit for a lord; and two or three times during the day he would go back to the cabin to see that all was well.

"You really don't mind?"

"I really don't."

"Good. What shall we do instead? I have it: you shall tell me your history. I am anxious to learn everything, Lawrence. All I know, really, is that you are young and charming and American and returning to New York because of your father's illness. Now you must tell me the rest."

"It's very ordinary, Oscar. I'd much rather listen to yours."

"We have done nothing but talk about me, I think."

"That isn't so. Anyway, the subject is fascinating."

He laughed. "Well said, Lawrence. And I agree. But it is dangerous to become too interested in oneself, for fear of being swept into a love affair that might last all one's life, and that would be boring. Still, since you insist— You *are* insisting, aren't you?"

"I am."

"Very well. Where shall I start? With my birth? No, this is too much like *David Copperfield*. Rather than talk about me, I shall tell you about my father and mother."

His manner changed. *He* changed. I heard a small boy talking innocently of great people, people without fault, so grand, so brave, so brilliant, so stunning, and so involved in tremendous affairs that surely when they slept the world must pause and sleep too.

Yet there was a magnificence to William and Jane Wilde, if it was only their contempt for public opinion, all too often agitated by William Wilde's behavior. William was a surgeon. It was audacious in those days to operate on the eye; he did, and so successfully, inventing his techniques and instruments as he went along, that by and by he could take his pick of patients if he wished to. It must have been extraordinary to see, in his thick, strong fingers, fit for a shovel, tools the size of a doll's butter knife, honed to a savage edge, scrape and plunge into the eyeball. He was reckoned to have moved with corsair boldness when he cut one one-hundredth of an inch; extraordinary, too, to think of that leaping energy of his leashed down to the execution of a task so infinitely delicate that the finest needlework is gross in comparison. It was beyond me how he managed it, because I gathered that he was a rude, impulsive, rather vulgar man who drank far more than was good for him, seldom bothered to wash (*Why are Dr. Wilde's fingernails dirty? Because he scratches himself*—this joke followed him on his rounds; since antisepsis was still unknown, one marveled that his patients survived), and took his audacity and vigor with him from the operating room into the bedroom.

He must have had charm; Dr. William Wilde was ugly. His forehead was too high for the in-sloping chin, his nose too long, his eyes too small for the great melancholy overhanging brows. And his legs too short to suit the powerful body.

But he was passionately loved. Once seduced by his freebooting spirit, women would not leave him alone. I had a picture of him skipping from window to window over the Dublin rooftops, constantly pursuing, constantly pursued, interminably ruttish, squalling his defiance of all and sundry. Uproars and alarms followed in his wake; his bastards were said to be legion; and at last, when Oscar was nine or ten, a Vesuvius of scandal broke out, fiery enough, one would have thought, to consume Dr. Wilde (now Sir William, such was his eminence) on the spot and scar his family for life.

Tiring of one of his loves, Sir William had moved on to fresh fields; but the lady refused to wither by the wayside—she insisted on following and ferociously blooming all over again, so to speak, at his heels. She was a Miss Mary Travers, and when it became evident even to her that her ugly, adored lover could not stand the sight of her, she set out to destroy him. She had come as a patient to his door, Miss Travers said, and he had promptly administered chloroform and violated her virgin body. She not only said it, she printed it in handbills and had them distributed up street and down. As a final blistering touch, she signed the handbills with a penname used by Oscar's mother in her frequent contributions to magazines.

A proud woman, as energetic, in different directions, as her husband, Lady Wilde could not tolerate the slur; she denounced Mary Travers, whose object, she said, was solely to extort money. Miss Travers sued for libel and won. True, the jury awarded damages of only one farthing to indicate that they put precious little stock in her story, but it was spread throughout Ireland and England and no doubt reached the ears of Sir William's most august patients. He stayed in practice.

Three years later a worse blow fell; the death of his youngest child, Oscar's sister. In another few years two more daughters, who were not legitimate but whom he loved no less, died too. After this he had heart only for solitude.

"Toward the end he spent more and more time at our country place in Connemara," Oscar said, "but he came home to die. There are few women who could behave as my mother did then. She knew he had not been the most faithful man in the world, but she is a wonderful woman and such a feeling as vulgar jealousy could take no hold on her. He lay ill in bed for many days before he died, and every morning a woman dressed in black and closely veiled used to come to our house, and unhindered by my mother would walk upstairs to his bedroom and sit down at the head of his bed and stay there for hours, without speaking a word or raising her veil. She took no notice of anybody in the room, and the servants and my older brother and I were instructed not to pay any attention to her. Not one woman in a thousand would have tolerated her presence, but my mother allowed it because she knew that my father must have loved this woman and she felt that it must be a joy and a comfort to have her there by his dying bed. And I am sure that she did right not to grudge that last happiness to a man who was about to die, and I am sure that my father understood her apparent indifference, understood that it was not because she did not love him that she permitted her rival's presence, but because she loved him very much. And therefore I am sure that he died with his heart full of gratitude and affection for her."

"Did you ever discover who she was?" I asked.

"No, never. Perhaps she was the mother of those two poor young beautiful things, my half sisters, who died when the bright new dress of one of them was set on fire by accident at a party. Her sister tried to smother the flames and was devoured too."

"How horrible."

"There, there, Lawrence, it's all over and done with, and my father's life was by no means entirely tragic. I remember him best on those grand occasions at home when the house would be full of friends and there would be talk and laughter and dancing and storytelling all the night through, and Willie and I—my older brother—wouldn't be packed off to bed like children but allowed to watch and listen until our heads dropped over on our shoulders. We were never really aware of *being* children with my father."

"Did his death make a great difference in your life?"

"It brought great shocks. First there was the shock of losing him, although of course we had been forewarned; and then there was a shock of which we'd had no warning whatever, and I can tell you it took some time to believe it was really true. You see, we had never wanted for anything, our home was in the best part of Dublin, my parents entertained splendidly, and Willie and I took it for granted that we were rich, but in fact my father had lived up to the hilt of his income and the estate he left was modest. Kind friends said it was all for the best. They said Willie and I would be forced to buckle down to work and that it would make men of us if we could stand the gaff and put our noses to the grindstone, and similar vulgar expressions. What nonsense. There are never such changes in people unless they are trivial and empty-headed in the first place, in which case they can be shoved off in any direction, like clockwork toys, and I most certainly did not buckle down to work—that is to say, I worked no more and no less.

"But I have never been idle. Of course I do not count it as idleness, whereas your grindstone and standing the gaff people do, to watch the throbbing flush of the dying sun stain the clouds, to observe the dew clinging to a rose's cheek, to note how the wind leaves the print of its tumbling body on a field of tall grass; I *do*, on the other hand, count it as idle to spend hours playing cricket; besides, the attitudes are indecent. And, of course, to pore over ledgers and do sums and prove equations, if that is what one does to equations. Do you follow me?"

I did.

"Then how does it happen that I was considered an idle fellow as a boy and not at Oxford after my father's death? Because things I did not enjoy doing became less important at Oxford and things I enjoyed doing, more. And also there was a certain amount of luck. Oh, I have come to believe in my luck; I quite depend on it now. I am convinced—I am *rather* a mystic at times, Lawrence; try not to mind—that luck will be a sweet bedfellow of mine for years and years until at some terrible crisis in my life it will entirely desert me. I was lucky enough to find great men at Oxford, Ruskin and Pater, people who showed me beauty, who wedded me to Greece, a marriage that will last until I am dead. I won the Newdigate Prize. The Newdigate is for a poem, I should explain; the subject is given out at a certain time every year. In my year it happened to be Ravenna, in Italy. It was a great piece of luck, because I had been in Ravenna not long before and soaked its sun and shadows into my skin."

"I'm sure writing a prizewinning poem is more than a matter of luck," I said.

"Oh, certainly," he said, laughing. "There is genius too, but one takes that for granted. Well, I began to be noticed. Along came another piece of luck. There was a fancy-dress ball in my last year at Oxford and I went as Prince Rupert—Rupert the dashing cavalry commander of the civil war, you know—but I see you are puzzled. I mean the *English* civil war, Lawrence, which after all does antedate yours. It was a charming costume, lots of lace and velvet, and of course I wore my hair long, a la Rupert. I created a splash and improved on the occasion by saying that I thought a reformation in dress was long overdue and much, much more important than a reformation in religion. Martin Luther's neckties, I said, must have been quite horrid. This got into the press; pious people were dreadfully upset. It identified me with what was coming to be called the aesthetic movement, and when *Patience* was produced nearly everyone thought that I was that silly ass Bunthorne who walked down Piccadilly with a poppy or a lily in his medieval hand—a ridiculously simple thing to do, by the bye, Lawrence. I did the difficult thing—made the public *believe* I had. And there you have my story."

"May I ask for a little more?"

"Well?"

"Who was the girl in that beautiful poem?"

"Which poem? I have written poems to several girls—beautiful girls, beautiful poems."

" 'Requiescat.' "

The laughter left his face. "She was my little sister, who died when she was ten."

23

4

THE CLOUD ON THE HORIZON THICKENED INTO LAND, AND Oscar said, "Ah, America. Where once they fired the shot heard round the world and now shoot their Presidents."

"Not invariably," I said.

"Quite so. But the rate seems to be increasing."

Five months ago President Garfield had been shot by Charles Guiteau, who thought the President had deliberately and wickedly deprived him of a job to which he was entitled. It had taken Mr. Garfield two long months of agony to die.

"That isn't really fair, Oscar. Besides, it can be argued, as many people have, that it wasn't Guiteau's bullet that killed the President, but the doctors."

"My dear Lawrence, you are quibbling, although Voltaire would have agreed with you; he said on his deathbed, when told that the doctor was waiting in the anteroom, 'No, no, send him away; I am too ill to see him.' I understand your Mr. Guiteau has become very hoity-toity, signature much in demand by fashionable ladies attending his trial. Do you think he ever will be punished, or has the trial become such a popular institution that it will go on forever?"

"Charles Guiteau will be hanged," I said; my tone must have been sharp.

Oscar murmured, "I'm sorry; I didn't mean to hurt your feelings."

But I was in a nervous state. There was no wireless then and I had had no news from New York since leaving London. I blamed myself for having thought so little of my father during the eight-day crossing. At this moment he might be dying. Or he might have died days ago, at a moment when I was doubled up over one of Oscar's sallies. I couldn't wait to get ashore, but I knew that the ship was bound to be held for a long time in quarantine while our hundreds of immigrants were examined by the medical authorities. And customs would still remain to be got through.

Oscar continued, "I'm sure all is well; I have a sixth sense in these things. Now, you must begin to point out interesting features to me. What are those heights on the left?"

24

"Staten Island," I said.

"Is that where they are going to put up the statue the French are giving you of Liberty Enlightening the World?"

"No; that's to be farther inside the harbor."

"I think the whole thing is a charming idea. I've seen a sketch of the model for Liberty; her profile is adorable; I do hope it will be turned toward incoming ships. Do you think I should mention this in my first lecture, Lawrence? Better not, I dare say. What have we here?"

"The port authorities."

"All those people? How many authorities do you have? They sound quite savage. Look. One is expectorating. An historic moment, Lawrence—my first American expectoration."

No doubt two or three of the people who had come out to meet the *Arizona* were officials, but the rest were reporters. We had not realized how famous Oscar already was in America; the most outrageous stories about him had been circulated, and also reproductions of the *Punch* cartoons, in the interest of more business for *Patience*. Perhaps he had expected a reporter or two after we landed, but never that this wild throng would meet the ship in midharbor.

For the first time I saw him at a loss. The crowd of jostling men and the shouting bewildered him; as he struggled to get his bearings and regain his customary poise, the reporters must have wondered if this really was Oscar Wilde. They didn't hesitate; they were looking for a man with long hair, extravagantly dressed, perhaps holding a sunflower. And there he was. No sunflower, and much taller than anyone had suspected—shoulders like a prizefighter's—but "Look at that hair." "And that coat."

"Hey, *Oscar!*"

"Oscar, how many times a day you take a bath? Three, four times, Oscar? Five? You put perfume in the water? Oscar, do you curl your own hair or does someone do it for you? You use any rouge, Oscar? Oscar, is it true you wear silk underwear with your initials embroidered on the drawers?" A great guffaw at this. "And gorgeous lace nightgowns? You let your toenails grow long like the Empress of Japan's, Oscar? Oscar, why aren't you wearing the knee breeches? What you think of America, Oscar? Oscar, you like your eggs fried on one side or over? Oscar, no joshing, did you say you never went in swimming because you hated to see yourself foreshortened so dreadfully in the water? And did you sit up all night with a sick peony, hey, Oscar? Oscar. *Oscar.*"

A more civilized voice asked:

"Mr. Wilde, will you tell us, please, what exactly are aesthetics?"

Oscar gratefully singled out the questioner.

"Aesthetics are the science of the beautiful. The word, you know, comes from the Greek, meaning 'perception by the senses'; today, as we interpret it, it is a search for truth, an attempt to live gracefully, beautifully. Aestheticism is a correlation of all the arts. Keats was an aesthete, and so was——"

A voice bawled, "Hey, Oscar, are you the prize horse's assthete?"

The crowd exploded with laughter. Oscar fled.

Burning with shame, I followed him to our cabin. "It appears," he said, "that in America bad manners make the journalist."

"Oscar, you mustn't think they're all like that. They were the barbarians from the sensational press, except for that one."

"I shouldn't have turned tail on them. Never mind, I shall make up for it; I'll give them something to talk about." He shook his head. "Gorgeous lace nightgowns. Toenails as long as the Empress of Japan's. Dear me."

Since the initials of our surnames, W and Y, are so close together, I was not far from him in the customs shed. A few reporters were still tagging at his heels.

"Have you anything to declare?" the inspector demanded in the gruff, suspicious manner that sets American customs inspectors apart.

"Nothing," Oscar replied. He paused. "Nothing, that is, except my genius."

5

MY FATHER WAS DEAD. HE HAD DIED MORE THAN A WEEK before, on Christmas, of pneumonia. "Once he came to the crisis," Dr. Mellish said, "it was very fast." He smiled mournfully. "Your father was never one to delay things, Lawrence."

My mother had died in our respectable brownstone house on West Twenty-first Street when I was a child. I hadn't liked it from that day; now I hated it. An older cousin who had worked in the family business for half a dozen years would be glad to assume full control. There was no one to keep me at home, or in New York for that matter. If Oscar would let me, I was going to accompany him on his American travels, make notes as an observer and friend, and later on write some sort of record of the trip.

In fact, of course, that was an excuse. Never before had I enjoyed myself so much as during the eight days on the *Arizona;* I wanted to continue with this best of companions, to bask, if you will, in his reflected glory and in that radiant light to forget the shadow of my father's death and other disappointments—among them the discovery, in London, that when I got down to it I had precious little stomach for the lonely hours in which the hard and gemlike flame must burn.

Oscar agreed. "I am delighted, Lawrence. You will be my guide in darkest America."

"I'm not qualified to be that, Oscar. I hardly know my own country myself."

"At least, then, my interpreter. I have already observed that the English and Americans have everything in common except, of course, the language."

I think that it was only his kindness—he was always kind, even in his most wretched hour—that led him to agree; God knows he had guides and advisers to spare. He knew that I was alone and, in my own eyes, pretty much a failure. Surely he must have smiled, privately, at the idea of my playing a junior Boswell to his Dr. Johnson.

6   AFTER OSCAR'S FIRST LECTURE, ON THE NIGHT OF JANUARY
9, he forgot the reporters, who grotesquely exaggerated his words
and conduct when they didn't lie outright. "America," Oscar said,
"is marvelous—New York, anyway.

"Glorious," he cried. "A glorious, glorious success. They say
there's been nothing like it since Dickens. My dear Lawrence,
d'you know what's going on in there?" He pointed to the next
room. "Three secretaries. One answering letters. Another writing
my autograph as fast as he can. The third clipping off locks of
his hair to send to all the ladies who have begged for a strand or
two from my head. He is almost bald by now, incidentally, and
will have to be replaced; we are wondering if the Bearded Lady
from Mr. Barnum's would be interested. Also I have a charming
Negro servant (it appears that in a free country one *must* have a
slave), rather like a blackface minstrel except that he does not
tell jokes and has yet to burst into song about his relatives. Dozens
of receptions, invitations galore, mobs outside waiting for a
glimpse of me. Cherishing virtuous obscurity as I do, you can
imagine how I detest it all."

And yet the response to the lecture itself, in Chickering Hall,
could not have been called overwhelming. True, his appearance
was satisfactorily elegant: black-plush knee breeches, silk stockings,
patent-leather pumps with large bows, dress coat, white vest, gleaming shirtfront, white-muslin tie (no sunflowers or lilies); but his
manner was sedate, almost shy; he cut no antics and didn't look in
the least languid. He was simply a tall, earnest young man. If he
hadn't been Oscar Wilde, if people hadn't been able to remind
themselves that this was the original Bunthorne, it is doubtful if
many would have stayed beyond his opening remarks. He said such
things as:

"Among the debts which we owe to the supreme aesthetic fac-
ulty of Goethe is that he was the first to teach us how to define
beauty in terms the most complete possible. So, in the lecture
which I have the honor to deliver before you, I will not try to give
you any abstract definition of beauty, still less to communicate to
you that which in its essence is incommunicable, the virtue by

which a particular picture or poem affects us with a unique and special joy."

And:

"For the poet all times and places are one. The stuff he deals with is eternal and eternally the same; no theme is inept, no past or present preferable. The steam whistle will not affright him nor the flutes of Arcadia weary him; for him there is but one time, the artistic moment; but one law, the law of form; but one land, the land of beauty—a land removed indeed from the real world and yet more sensuous because more enduring; calm yet with the calm which dwells in the faces of the Greek statues, the calm which comes not from the rejection but from the absorption of passion, the calm which despair and sorrow cannot disturb but intensify only."

Heaven knows it was not to this austere disquisition that his social popularity was due but to his wit and cool nerve, which hostesses soon discovered. The word spread: Mr. Wilde is *enchanting*. Perhaps some of his bon mots, his ripostes to the rude and the pushing and the merely fatuous had seen service before in London (and were to see service again; Oscar was never one to disdain using a good thing twice). What matter? They were all brilliant, they were audacious, and the manner of their delivery was superb. Most of them were inspired by the moment; they came fresh-minted from those smiling lips.

People fortunate enough to get near him in the crush hurried home babbling the glittering words they had heard, repeating them to envious neighbors. "Do you know what Oscar Wilde said last night? 'Nothing succeeds like excess.' And 'Give me the luxuries and I can dispense with the necessities.' And 'I can resist anything except temptation.' Did you *ever?* Isn't he *wicked?*"

One lady informed him, in a superior voice, that she looked forward to seeing him kiss a sunflower—where was it? "At home, madam," said Oscar, "with your manners." A celebrated bore feared by all approached him. "My dear chap," Oscar said, "I've been simply *longing* not to see you. There is *so much* I'm dying not to talk to you about." Widening rings of laughter spread out from his tall person, the center of the drawing room, as he scattered more bright flakes of his diamond wit: "Morality is simply the attitude we adopt toward people whom we personally dislike." "It is always silly to give advice, but to give good advice is absolutely fatal." "Consistency is the last refuge of the unimaginative." "He hasn't a single redeeming vice." "The public is wonderfully tolerant. It can forgive everything except genius."

In the glacial atmosphere of the Century Club, at which, somebody said, a laugh was heard once a century, Oscar observed: "Perhaps man can best be defined as a rational animal who always loses his temper when he is called upon to act in accordance with the dictates of reason." "The only difference between the saint and the sinner is that every saint has a past and every sinner has a future." "Work is the curse of the drinking classes." "People have asked me if I don't get tired of talking so much, and I have answered, 'Not at all; the great trouble is that sometimes I have to listen.'" "The English have a miraculous power of turning wine into water." "She loved him with such a simple, singlehearted, perfectly unselfish love that it made his life a burden."

Major Mulroyd, a robust pillar of New York society, famous as a fox-hunter, marksman, yachtsman, and general evangelist for the masculine virtues, had been heard to say at the Century Club, before Oscar arrived, "Where is she? Isn't she coming today? She is a she, isn't she, with her long hair and lace nightgowns? And isn't her name *Charlotte-Anne* Wilde?" The major glared from a corner of the room as Oscar set everyone else laughing, but later came up and with an appearance of manly good humor, said he wished to apologize for having been unfair in certain remarks to Mr. Wilde, and would Mr. Wilde signify his forgiveness by accepting an invitation to dinner with a few other good fellers the night after next?

Oscar, the soul of affability, replied that he would be charmed, an expression which deepened the steely glint in the major's eye.

The plot was to get Oscar so drunk that he would blurt out whatever secrets he had to tell and then to set him loose in the streets to make a spectacle of himself. The major and his cronies had done something like this to other victims.

As Oscar talked and told stories, the conspirators drank more and more, in an excess of good fellowship, enjoying themselves so much they forgot their purpose. Oscar kept up with them; indeed, he egged them on.

Toward midnight the conspirators began to disappear, a couple under the table, others in the direction of the lavatories, from which they did not return; another was found feebly grappling with his coat and hat in the cloakroom. The major was by now almost hopelessly plastered but remained upright in his chair, with one arm around Oscar's neck; with the other he intermittently shook Oscar's hand. He had conceived a tremendous liking for him; when the major thought of the depth and force of the friendship established this evening between them, it brought tears to his eyes.

"By God, you're a good feller, Wilde," he muttered. "But ought to cut your hair."

"You don't care for it?" Oscar asked politely.

"Gives wrong impression," said the major. "Makes you look like Charlotte-Anne—Charlotte-Anne—a pun, d'ye see—Charlotte-Anne, charla-TAN. But you're not, are you? Doan mine fy call you Woscar, Oscar?"

"Pray do."

"Call me Jack."

"Jack," said Oscar.

"Jack-Oscar. You're *not* a Charlotte-Anne, Oscar?"

"Certainly not."

"Not a sissy?"

"No, no."

"No, by God," shouted the major, "you're *not*. Shoot any son of bitch what says so." And he glared at the innocent tablecloth. "But must cut hair. Oscar"—his head swayed closer; he grinned and with infinite labor produced a ponderous wink—"you know the story of the old bull and the young bull, Oscar?"

"I believe not."

"Listen," said the major. "You *will* listen, Oscar?"

"Certainly," said Oscar. The major's mouth was an inch away from his left ear.

"Old bull and young bull on top of hill. Cows in valley. 'Look at all those dum-dum-dum cows,' says old bull. 'What say, sport? Shall we go down and have us each a cow?' 'Have us each a cow?' says young bull. 'Let us go down and have us the whole God-damn fiddle-umpty herd.'"

Oscar rewarded this jest with a barely audible laugh. When the major had recovered from his own laughter and seriously burned

31

his moustache in a struggle to light a cigar, he proposed that they should follow the bulls' example and wander down into the valley. "Round off jolly evening, Oscar, eh?"

"I'm afraid I don't follow you."

"Hah. Leave it to me." And the major called for a stirrup cup. Oscar did not see how his host could contain it without grave internal injury, but he did not protest. The major ordered a cab and directed it to a shuttered house. He then collapsed on the doorstep. A large, powerfully perfumed woman opened the door. "Good evening, madam," said Oscar ("And you will grant, won't you, Lawrence," he inquired, telling me this the next day, "that in so addressing her I was impeccably correct?"). He steered the major into her arms. "I bring you herewith one old bull." And he bowed good night.

7   OSCAR'S SUCCESS DID NOT FALTER, AND IT SEEMED CERTAIN that the tour would be extended to the far west. I still hated to think of the possible consequences. But he was having a grand time.

Philadelphia. "I am delighted," he observed, "that, after listening to me, these gentle Quakers are not prevented by their creed from employing the amount of physical violence necessary to bring the palm of one hand sharply against the palm of the other."

Washington. "This city has too many bronze generals. Everywhere the eye turns it is greeted by some dead statesman or extinct warrior with a live pigeon on top of his head. To see the frock coat of the drawing room done in bronze or the waistcoat perpetuated in marble adds a new horror to death."

Niagara Falls. "Every American bride is taken here, I understand, and the sight of the stupendous waterfall must be one of the earliest, if not the keenest, disappointments in American married life."

St. Louis. Oscar's room at the New Southern Hotel had been appointed by the management with many dainty touches, including tasselled drapes and tiny satin pillows. The manager called to present his compliments and ask if his guests would care for a little refreshment, some *petits fours*, perhaps, and a cup of tea. Oscar thanked him; yes, that would be delightful, but before the *petits fours* and tea, could he have a tenderloin of beef, rather rare, three or four lambchops, a few boiled eggs, toast, and onions?

Omaha. Muddy streets, wooden sidewalks, cowboys driving cattle to the stockyards, and sad, lost-looking Indians. "The life seems to have gone out of them," Oscar said. "I don't believe they'd be able to muster up the energy to take my scalp. I feel sorry for the poor things. Perhaps I should donate a few locks to encourage them?"

San Francisco. The city gave him an out-and-out triumph. "I love this city," he announced. "Adore it. I have yet to meet an unfriendly Californian. They are so hospitable. So generous. They have opened their hearts and homes to me, a stranger. Everyone is kind, everyone is courteous, from the street cleaner who paused in his labors the other afternoon to doff his cap, to the group of select young gentlemen who have invited me to dinner at the Bohemian Club and afterward to the celebrated Cliff House. I look forward to a delightful evening."

He reported later. "I have mentioned, I believe, that this is an innocent, happy land, full of innocent, happy people?"

"You have."

"I repeat it. My young Californians could not have been more appealing in their boyish simplicity. They innocently urged on me one cocktail after another and drank as many themselves to keep me company—even more, I fear, for when we arrived at the Cliff House and began drinking champagne, some of them were forced to retire. Those of us who remained played an innocent Californian game called dollar ante——"

"For goodness' sake, Oscar, that isn't an innocent game, that's poker, for cutthroat stakes. These innocent young Bohemian Club rascals 'suckered' you into it—played you for a boob. I hate to say I told you so, but I must say I've been waiting for something like this. I suppose you've lost your shirt?"

"My dear boy, what extraordinary expressions. 'Sucker,' 'boob,' 'lost my shirt.'" He pulled out a bundle of wadded greenbacks. "Innocent, happy people—innocent, innocent, innocent."

From San Francisco we backtracked to Denver. After lecturing at the opera house, Oscar was addressing himself to a vast meal, with a bottle of Burgundy, when the hotel manager called to say that Mr. Tabor wished to present himself.

"Who is Mr. Tabor?" Oscar asked.

The manager smiled indulgently. "Mr. Horace Austin Warner Tabor, sir."

"I see. And who is Mr. Horace Austin Warner Tabor?"

"You do not know who Mr. Horace Austin Warner Tabor is, sir?"

"I do not. Who is he?"

"Surely, Mr. Wilde, you have heard of Mr. H. A. W. Tabor, the owner of the Matchless Mine, the First National Bank, the Calumet and Chicago Canal and Dock Company, and the Tabor Investment Company? Why, he is one of the richest men in the world."

"And he wishes to meet one of the poorest, eh? Then by all means show him in."

Mr. Tabor was as tall as Oscar himself, and broad to boot. His longhorn moustache captivated Oscar; the diamond shirt studs, preposterously large, fascinated him equally.

Mr. Tabor had come with an invitation for Oscar to lecture at Leadville, the mining town up in the Rockies, and to visit the Matchless Mine. Oscar said he would be delighted; he had always longed to go down a mine. "Provided, of course, that I may be quite sure of coming up again?"

"If you don't, I'll know the reason why."

"In that event, my dear Mr. Tabor, you must promise to shout the reason down to me so that I can suffocate with my mind at ease."

We got on the train the next morning for the trip to Leadville. The friendly conductor told us colorful stories about our destination. Leadville was the gol-dangest, rip-roarinest town on the face of the earth. Every man carried a gun. There were more saloons than in New York and Chicago put together. The red-light district was noted for its opulence and variety. Shooting went on twenty-four hours a day; the big saloons hired brass bands to render the noise less disagreeable. The town bootblack wore two six-shooters and owned a bullterrier that had been trained to answer the call of nature on gents' boots. Last week, in the middle of Main Street, a newspaperman had been horsewhipped by the lady he had described as a notorious demimondaine, when everyone knew, she shouted, that she was a good honest whore. The Leadville Opera House presented *Macbeth* with a convicted murderess in the part of Lady M., and the gravediggers in *Hamlet* were professional gravediggers on Leadville's Boot Hill.

There at the station stood Mr. Horace Austin Warner Tabor, in white tie and tails, a top hat, and even more immense diamond studs, waiting for Oscar with a gorgeous carriage drawn by two milk-white bullocks. Hundreds of miners surrounded him, all in red shirts, all enormously energetic. A brass band played; the fire brigade was in attendance, as were the mayor and his lady, about three quarters of the population of Leadville, and dogs, horses, pigs, chickens, and goats galore, all enthusiastic. Off we went with the brass band blaring, the crowd shouting, dogs barking, and Oscar waving his hat with one hand and shaking the mayor's hand with the other. Mr. Horace Austin Warner Tabor drove the two milk-white bullocks with an aplomb that befitted a man whose income was five million dollars a year. The procession toured all Leadville, paused outside the most famous gambling hells and dens of vice, cheered and yelled and danced while Oscar was taken on tours of the interiors and showed the lovely young lady hostesses how to dance the latest London steps as performed by His Royal Highness the Prince of Wales in the most elevated society.

Then, as dawn found the mountain peaks, the milk-white bullocks pulled us up a rocky road to Shaft No. 3 of the Matchless Mine—"the most comfortable shaft," its owner explained. Down we went, in the plunging, swaying buckets, to find below, in the light of lamps stuck in the ore-webbed walls, a palatial supper and a dozen miners who joined with a cheer in Horace Austin Warner Tabor's toast: "Gentlemen, I give you Mr. Oscar Wilde."

PART 2

CONSTANCE

1 MUCH AS I WISHED TO RETURN TO ENGLAND WITH OSCAR, MY
father's death had brought forward creditors of whose existence
we had known nothing, and the family business was going to have
a hard struggle to survive. It was indicated to me that the least I
could do would be to lend a hand at my old desk, and I was in
no position to refuse.

When I met Oscar again, he had a great deal of time to spare,
and he talked to me more freely, I think, than he would have if I
had continued to see him often throughout the intervening years.
I remained a friend, but there was not between us the barrier
constructed by the very sameness of day-in, day-out friendship. I
don't think that in the normal course of events Oscar would ever
have talked with complete freedom about himself to anyone; he
always wished to please, and he considered that others were
more interested in themselves than in him. But the normal course
of events had disappeared when I saw Oscar again.

2

EVERYONE SAID IT WAS IMPOSSIBLE TO LECTURE IN AMERICA without lining your pockets with gold and marrying an heiress. I have achieved the impossible, Oscar thought. Now and again his bank balance had climbed to heights never previously dreamt of, but then the altitude had seemed to frighten it and it had gone rushing back to the familiar valley below. The expenses were to blame; they were damnable.

He had no complaint with the actual cost of things. It had always seemed miraculous to him that the slip of paper called a bank check could be exchanged for gold; therefore the best of everything was absurdly cheap. He scarcely glanced at prices, they were so unimportant. America had been no trouble at all in that respect. The waiter brought the bill and Oscar pulled out some of those curious green things and put them on the tray and asked if they would be enough. Usually the waiter said they would, went away, and returned with mounds of silver—cartwheels, simoleons, and smaller coins called two pieces, or perhaps it was two bits.

As for heiresses, Oscar supposed he had met many in America at all those receptions, and no doubt some were attractive, even beautiful; but to go to America and come back married to an heiress would be to behave like the common herd. Besides, he hadn't fallen in love.

So far he had been in love twice. With Lillie Langtry, though, it had been mostly make-believe, on both sides; beautiful Lillie, who was nobody's fool—and who was a nice person indeed. When he had read her the poem she had inspired, the look on her ravishing face had puzzled him. "My poor poem seems to have upset you," he had said at last, a little stiffly. "That is not, to be quite frank, the effect for which it strives."

"Oh, no, it's all lovely," she had assured him, "and I am so flattered and pleased and proud, but—that bit about death and the lotus leaves and the silver trumpet, and I think there was a wheel in it too somewhere——"

"Is this what you mean?" he had inquired, still stiffly, and had read the lines again:

"The lotus leaves which heal the wounds of Death
            Lie in thy hand; O, be thou kind to me,
                While yet I know the summer of my days;
        For hardly can my tremulous lips draw breath
                To fill the silver trumpet with thy praise,
            So bowed am I before thy mystery;
        So bowed and broken on Love's terrible wheel,
                That I have lost all hope and heart to sing,
                Yet care I not what ruin time will bring
        If in thy temple thou wilt let me kneel."

"Yes," Lillie had said. "That's it."

"Well?"

"Well, but, it seems so— Oh, goodness, how can I say it. I only mean, I only mean—you *don't* really—you aren't really, are you? I mean, all that about being bowed and broken on the terrible wheel?" And she had peered at him anxiously, as if wanting to poke a finger in here and there to make sure.

"My dear, sweet Lillie," he had cried. "My precious Lillie. No, I'm not, but I should like to be. All poets should be. So let's pretend I am, shall we? And I shall sleep on your doorstep to protect my darling Lillie from harm."

"You will not."

"Yes I shall, for five minutes or so. I have always wanted to know how it feels to sleep on one's lady-love's doorstep. Quite too ghastly, I should imagine."

After that they got along together extremely well, and occasionally she had permitted him to kiss her and stroke her, and occasionally, he had thought—

But of course not. He could never lose himself in a mad passion over Lillie; she was too matter-of-fact. She was not going to stay young forever, she said, and so while she was what she was she intended to make the most of it, and Oscar could help her.

"My dear," he pointed out, "that is precisely what I have been doing, with my poem and my armloads of lilies and what will become a popular legend—that I sleep on your doorstep."

He could help her in something else, she said. Oscar said he couldn't think what it might be but she had only to name it.

"You can write my letters for me. They give me the most horrible time, not the business letters but the ones where I have to be all romantic and gooey."

"In short, a superamanuensis."

"And teach me gorgeous words like that. What does it mean?"

Lillie would never starve—she knew which side her bread was buttered on. Making love to her, it would be impossible not to think that in one way or another you had paid for it or shortly would be paying for it. On the other hand, she would never break your heart, not if it could be avoided by a kindly inquiry.

But that vastly different girl, Florence Balcombe, the one girl he had really loved, for two sweet years, and had wished to go on loving forever—she, the well-bred Miss Balcombe, had felt no such concern. One week he had believed himself secure in her love; the next, he learned that she was to be married. Never again, he hoped, would he fall in love with a beautiful, misty-eyed, soft-voiced, impeccably brought-up, cruel Irish girl.

He found, when everything was totted up, that he had come back from America with rather less than a thousand pounds. His brother, Willie, said, "Salt it away, my dear chap, salt it away. Otherwise it will be gone before you can say Jack Robinson."

"Nothing of the sort," Oscar said.

"You are deluding yourself, my dear boy. The Yankees have been up to no good with you, I can see that. They have put some very rum notions in your head if they have led you to think you can keep a thousand pounds in your pocket."

"When I said nothing of the sort, I meant that I had no intention of trying to save it. I am going to spend it as luxuriously as possible. It will be gone in a month or two—say three at the outside. But by then I shall have finished my new play."

"What sort of play?" Willie asked cautiously.

"A five-act tragedy in blank verse."

"Good God," Willie said. "I don't know, Oscar; at times I despair of you. You're a thousand times cleverer than I am and yet things that are plain as a pikestaff to me seem to elude you. Any producer in his right senses knows he'd be cutting his throat if he put on five acts of blank verse. No one can be amusing in blank verse, not even you."

"This is a tragedy, Willie, not a farce. I'm not setting out to be amusing."

"So much the worse for you. Chuck your blank-verse monster

into the dustbin, I beg you, while it is still a little monster, before it eats you out of house and home."

"Nonsense," Oscar said good-humoredly. *The Duchess of Padua* will make us all rich. I've never been surer of myself; the lines fit together so beautifully it's a joy to work on them. Here, I'll read you a few."

"Where is the whisky?" Willie found the decanter and did not stint himself. "A few, mind."

"The scene," Oscar said, going to his writing table and picking up a manuscript, "is the marketplace of Padua; the time, the latter part of the sixteenth century. In the background is the magnificent cathedral, and to the right the public fountain, with a stone seat around it. Two people are on the stage, one an elderly man, Count Moranzone, the other a handsome young man whose name is Guido Ferranti."

"I know," Willie said out of his whisky glass. "You don't have to tell me. Guido is a distinguished waiter disguised as a nobleman. It will all come out in the fifth act, when he serves the macaroni with an inborn grace nothing can conceal."

Oscar read from the manuscript:

> "Guido says eagerly to Moranzone: 'Now tell me of my father?' (*He sits down on the stone seat.*) 'Stood he tall?
> I warrant he looked tall upon his horse.
> His hair was black? or perhaps a reddish gold,
> Like a red fire of gold? Was his voice low?
> The very bravest men have voices sometimes
> Full of low music; or a clarion was it
> That brake with terror all his enemies?
> Did he ride singly? or with many squires
> And valiant gentlemen to serve his taste?
> For oftentimes methinks I feel my veins
> Bent with the blood of kings. Was he a king?'
> "Moranzone speaks, in a low voice: 'Aye, of all men he was the kingliest.' "

Willie stared at the drop or two of whisky left in his glass. "Frankly, dear boy, I think it is very poor stuff."

"Apparently you have no ear for blank verse in the classic style, Willie."

"Perhaps not; but," Willie said, filling his glass, "mark my words, no one will touch it. Put it in the dustbin."

"Dear Willie," Oscar murmured, "what a rotten critic you are." Willie was the most agreeable person under the sun, a roly-poly, big-brown-bearish sort of man who had started out to be a lawyer but had turned into a newspaperman.

"I'm not a critic at all," Willie said, "I only know no one will touch it, unless he's an idiot."

"Then that makes Miss Mary Anderson and Mr. Hamilton Griffin idiots."

"Who are they?"

"Mary Anderson," Oscar said, with relish, "is a magnificent American tragedienne. I saw her in New York after I returned from my far-western tour. She was playing Cordelia in *Lear*, a performance of such nobility that she held the audience spellbound, and New York audiences are hard customers. I wrote to her afterward to say I had been deeply stirred and asked if I might call to pay my respects to an actress who I had no doubt was destined to be remembered as one of the greatest of the age. She responded very graciously and when we met introduced me to her stepfather and manager, Mr. Griffin. He is a shrewd Yankee, and so in case you are thinking that my praise of her was bound to ensure an enthusiastic reception for anything I had to propose, you are mistaken."

"I was thinking nothing of the sort," Willie said. "I'll tell you what I was thinking, though: if you'd talked like that to some American heiresses, you'd have come back married to one."

"I've brought back something better than an American heiress— Mary Anderson's faith in *The Duchess of Padua*, her faith that it is to be an artistic triumph, and her stepfather's that it will be a financial one. And he paid me a thousand dollars to show he was in earnest."

"How much is a thousand dollars in pounds?"

"Two hundred. But that is only a starter. Our agreement is that Griffin will pay another four thousand dollars, eight hundred pounds, upon satisfactory completion of the play, and I am to have a royalty of twenty-five dollars on every performance in large American towns and ten dollars in small ones. You can see how that will mount up. For a great success you can count on two or three hundred performances in New York alone, and a hundred each, I dare say, in Boston, Philadephia, Chicago, and San Francisco. And then there are the touring companies. You have no idea how large America is, Willie. There are enough small towns to keep two or three touring companies going for ages."

"My boy," Willie said, "I withdraw my remark about despairing of you. If you got two hundred pounds and are going to get another eight hundred for the tosh you read to me, you are a wizard."

"It's quite simple, really, Willie. It isn't tosh, you see."

"Bless my soul," said Willie, sighing; "perhaps it isn't, then. Perhaps you're another Shakespeare. But I still think the only certain thing in the theater is a play that makes people laugh, and God knows you could write one, Oscar, whenever you put your mind to it. In fact I don't think you *would* have to put your mind to it. Whereas with this tosh I suppose you do."

"It is not tosh, dear old boy," Oscar said gently.

If he was to do justice to the play, he must not be distracted. He must take the *Duchess* to a cloistered atmosphere, at least a place where he wouldn't be surrounded by friends. It was only too easy to lose yourself over a delightful luncheon with charming people and find that the whole afternoon had gone shimmering away into the silvery shadows.

Oscar decided to go to Paris for the two or three months the *Duchess* would require. He thought of three great names linked with Paris: Honoré de Balzac and Victor Hugo and Sarah Bernhardt. Sarah was young, Hugo very old, Balzac dead; but at this moment, his was the significant name—the stupendous Honoré, who so often had been faced with just such a task, so much work to be finished in a short time, and who had got it done by wrapping himself in his cowled monk's robe and driving away at pen and paper in the frosty candlelight while all Paris lay beneath his windows and called in vain. Honoré would be his guide.

3   WITH THE THOUSAND DOLLARS IN HAND, AND FOUR THOUSAND
to come, and thousands upon thousands after that when the *Duchess* would be gathering gold and glory up and down America, it was not necessary to live in the proverbial Paris garret or even a solitary room in a second-rate hotel.

Oscar took a suite of rooms at the Hotel Voltaire. The rooms needed fairly extensive refurnishing. While the work was in progress, he spent hours in the Louvre; this grandeur from the past could not fail to help him create the proper atmosphere for his beautiful, doomed heroine; she came close to him in the silence of the tall chambers. Suddenly he knew—her name would be Beatrice. He whispered it often, "Beatrice, Beatrice—Beatrice, Duchess of Padua."

A marble head caught his eye. It was the famous bust of Nero. Now, there, exactly, was the model for the duke, the tyrant who was to die at Beatrice's hand but who in death would be no less than he had been in life, the author of lovers' woe. The hair was superb. "Veritable Neronian coiffure," Oscar said to himself, smiling; the massive head so incongruously crowned by those dainty curls seemed to give him a smile in return.

He left the building and took his reflective way to the hairdresser around the corner from the Voltaire. "Oh, Monsieur Raoul," he said, "do you know the bust of Nero in the Louvre? I wonder if you could reproduce its coiffure upon me?" The old Oscar was associated with *Punch* jokes and Bunthorne; the new Oscar would be the lover of *The Duchess of Padua*. Monsieur Raoul said the idea was enchanting and he would visit the Louvre to inspect Monsieur Nero's coiffure; he could ensure that in duplicating it upon the head of Monsieur Wilde no nuance, however subtle, would be lost.

Excellent; Oscar was pleased with the New Oscar who regarded him from his mirror. And the suite's new decor was satisfactory, in the opulent style Balzac had always favored. There on the chair next to the writing table lay the monk's-cowl dressing gown, tailored to Oscar's order, and on the table were the massive candelabra, the quill pen, and the sheets of paper.

But perhaps the *Duchess* wanted some amusement. She was not, after all, a creature to be sequestered for hour after hour of the enchanting Parisian nights.

Oscar put aside his monkish robe, his pen and paper and went out. Lights and laughter greeted him on his emergence from the lonely room. He visited the pretty, loving young ladies of the rue Blondel and drank absinthe with a group of new friends at the Café François Premier. One of these turned out to be famous—the poet Paul Verlaine. By rights he should have been as comely as a Greek youth; in fact he was atrociously ugly—he couldn't have been much at his peak (though there was something fawnlike in the cast of his head) and since then he had gone steadily downhill, ending, rather, in a swamp.

The young man next to Oscar, Roger, said that this sad deterioration of Monsieur Verlaine was due to his fatal friendship with Rimbaud. "That beast Rimbaud," he said forcefully.

Monsieur Verlaine raised his head. "He was an angel." Half his teeth were gone and there was a sickening crust at the corners of his mouth; the skin was like a patchwork quilt of tiny red veins. His clothes were an abomination. Oscar ordered more absinthe; Monsieur Verlaine spilled half the milky-green liquor in his eagerness to get it down. "An angel," he repeated.

"A devil, you mean," said Roger.

"A beautiful boy, beautiful as the morning."

"Bah," Roger spat out. "Do you know what your beautiful boy said when he was taken to meet the divine Victor Hugo?"

"What did he say?" Oscar asked.

"He said the divine Victor Hugo was an old fart."

Monsieur Verlaine cackled in a spray of absinthe. He drew out a filthy handkerchief and obscurely wiped the top of his bald head rather than his dribbling mouth, then offered the handkerchief to Oscar. Oscar declined, with many thanks.

"One would not consider it possible, would one," Roger continued, "for an individual of exquisite perception like our friend here, or as he was then—sober, respectable, the happy husband of a beautiful young woman, the father of an adorable child—to see in this clod of a peasant, this Arthur Rimbaud, this pig, this mouther of obscenities, reason for turning his back on domestic tranquillity and becoming as revolting as he now is?"

"He was beautiful, and he was a genius," Monsieur Verlaine said. "Do you know his poetry?" he asked Oscar.

"I'm afraid I am not so familiar with it as I should be."

"My congratulations," Roger said. "Avoid it as you would the plague. Arthur Rimbaud is not the name of a poet; it is a stench."

Monsieur Verlaine chanted:

> "Il prit âme et corps,
> Est dispersa tous efforts.
> Que compendre à ma parole?
> Il fait qu'elle fuie et vole!
> O saisons, ô châteaux."

"Still infatuated," Roger said sourly. "He will never be cleansed of the disease."

"Where is Rimbaud now?" Oscar asked. Verlaine seemed not to hear; he was peering with a smile into the vast depths of his empty glass. Oscar had it refilled.

"That stuff is killing you, you know," Roger said.

"I forgive it," Monsieur Verlaine said.

"Where is Rimbaud now?" Oscar said again. "In Paris?"

"No, no," the poet said. "He is in Africa, surrounded by ivory and gold and peacocks and cockatoos. The primeval sun kindles fierce fires in his eyes and beautiful naked black creatures bow down before him."

"And give him syphilis, one hopes," Roger added.

"Why are you so bitter about him?" Oscar asked.

"Should I not be? Look at Verlaine. Rimbaud did that. I was not joking when I said he was a devil. Beautiful, it is true; Lucifer was beautiful. And malicious and spiteful and vindictive. Those he kissed, he destroyed. The good God rot his body."

"Pouf, pouf," Verlaine said with a jocular air, and then his eyes went cloudy and he fell forward on the table.

"Ah, poor master," the young man sighed. "The same every night. Now I must get him to the lavatory before he dirties himself."

"May I help you?"

"Thank you, but no. It is a disgusting task, and I don't know why I continue with it."

Evidently absinthe was more potent than other drinks. Oscar walked slowly through the cool, rain-smelling air.

Presently he paused and leaned against a tree. His perceptions had been refined to an edge of unbearable sharpness. A thin, ragged shape came seesawing down from above, and he swiftly dodged, feeling that should it brush his skin it would bruise him painfully. He picked it up. It was a rain-soaked leaf; when he sniffed at it a sodden, melancholy forest seemed to rise around him.

"Dreams are the only reality," he said in a loud voice. "I do not believe that," he said.

Music bloomed in the night; a waltz; violins. Oscar gently placed the leaf on the ground and walked on tiptoe away from the tree, trying to trace the music to its source. Almost as palpable as water, a wave of moonlight tumbled through the broken clouds. He saw the house the music was coming from and knew that it was a harlot's house. He had a glimpse inside of chandeliers as gaudy as planets.

A man in evening dress came out of the house, smoked a cigarette, and went back in; at that moment the music stopped, the moonlight faded, and all was dark and still. A new, shy radiance crept down the street.

After this night the *Duchess* gave him no more trouble. Oscar finished the play on March 15, a red-letter day. He had the precious manuscript beautifully bound and wrapped and packed it off to Mary Anderson. Would she cable him, please, when she had read this play that had been written for her?

A fair sum remained of the money he had brought from America, and in view of the thousands that would soon be due from Hamilton Griffin there was no reason why it should not be spent on celebration. Oscar bought new clothes and began to take his meals at the Café de Paris, where he was soon securely lodged in the headwaiter's heart as a gentleman who understood to perfection the art of ordering food and wine and tipping those who served him. It was pleasant to exchange smiles with the habitués of the establishment—fashionable painters, actors, actresses, and poets—and invite to his table for a glass of wine and a cigarette those whose appearance seemed interesting.

One was M. le Comte de Montesquiou-Fezensac, who carried with him and placed on the table, where it slept or slowly walked among the plates and glasses, a living jewel, a tortoise with gilded shell, which Oscar pronounced to be aesthetically far finer as a pet

49

than the live lobster that had been favored by Gérard de Nerval; others were Maurice Rollinat and Edmond de Goncourt and Henri de Régnier and Jean Richepin; and then there was Robert Sherard, a young Englishman in whose veins poet's blood surely could be said to run, for he was a great-grandson of Wordsworth. Could one not hear, in young Sherard's voice, an echo of that other, immortal, voice? They dined frequently together, at Oscar's expense, since the Wordsworth blood was not tainted with gold. Robert swung between radiant faith in his own poetic gifts and utter despondency.

One mist-cloaked night he spoke of suicide. "It's the weather," Oscar said; "every passerby is like a specter, every cab a hearse. Tomorrow you will rise rejoicing and write a sonnet that will cause your distinguished ancestor to blush with pride in heaven, unless you have reason to doubt that that is where he is? Come, Robert, if there is a deadly family secret concerning him, you may confide in me with the complete assurance that I shall breathe it to no one who is an absolute stranger."

Sherard refused to smile. "My poetry is ridiculous," he declared. "I am sick of it; I am sick of myself."

"If this unfortunate tendency persists," Oscar said, "I shall be impelled to do away with you myself, because you are beginning to sound like some disgusting critic. Suicide, my dear Robert? Good heavens, it is the greatest compliment one can pay to society. Now, if you were a Verlaine, yes, perhaps, since it would save your friends the odious duty of paying their respects to the man you used to be by tidying up after you every night; but you aren't gross and sodden, you are young and handsome and somewhere in the future a honey-haired maiden is waiting to hear from your lips the poetry your passion for her will conceive."

Although Oscar had meant to devote himself to pure idleness in this interval before considering the suggestions for a change here and there in *The Duchess of Padua* that no doubt would be proposed by Mary Anderson and Hamilton Griffin, the memory of his absinthe-haunted wanderings after leaving the Café François Premier that strange night would not let him rest and at length began to take the shape of a poem. He was pleased with the poem when it was done, although it was unlike anything he had written before. Really, the poem was *very* good, too good to be kept any longer to himself, and he determined to give it a public unveiling at a party. The sooner the better—why not tonight?

Robert Sherard helped him to round up some appropriate guests. After the champagne glasses had been filled many times and the lights put out except for the candles on his writing desk, and after the laughter and whispering had died, Oscar looked up from the manuscript and explained that he would read his poem in English and then in French. "Its title," he said, "is 'The Harlot's House':

"We caught the tread of dancing feet,
    We loitered down the moonlit street,
    And stopped beneath the harlot's house.

"Inside, above the din and fray,
    We heard the loud musicians play
    The *Treues Liebes Herz* of Strauss.

"Like strange mechanical grotesques,
    Making fantastic arabesques,
    The shadows raced across the blind.

"We watched the ghostly dancers spin
    To sound of horn and violin,
    Like black leaves whirling in the wind.

"Like wire-pulled automatons,
    Slim silhouetted skeletons
    Went sidling through the slow quadrille.

"They took each other by the hand,
    And danced a stately saraband;
    Their laughter echoed thin and shrill.

"Sometimes a clockwork puppet pressed
    A phantom lover to her breast,
    Sometimes they seemed to try to sing.

"Sometimes a horrible marionette
    Came out and smoked its cigarette
    Upon the steps like a live thing.

"Then, turning to my love, I said,
    'The dead are dancing with the dead,
    The dust is whirling with the dust.'

"But she—she heard the violin,
    And left my side, and entered in;
    Love passed into the house of lust.

"Then suddenly the tune went false,
    The dancers wearied of the waltz,
    The shadows ceased to wheel and whirl.

"And down the long and silent street,
    The dawn, with silver-sandaled feet,
    Crept like a frightened girl."

His voice, fallen to a whisper with the last words, ceased, and he heard someone sigh. It was Sherard. "Oscar, Oscar," he murmured, "that is heartbreaking."

"Thank you, Robert. I now impose on you my French. I do not think it will bow your spirits too cruelly, for it is a very weak, a very faltering thing—indeed I may say that it too, like the dawn, creeps like a frightened girl."

The reception was overwhelming. It did not matter that this was due to the champagne and the kindly tolerance it inspired among those of his guests who understood only French; he was satisfied with that moment of utter silence after the last line in English and Robert Sherard's sigh—these were not counterfeit. It was gratifying, nevertheless, to be so enthusiastically applauded. The French did this sort of thing extremely well.

So many came up to shake his hand and throw their arms around him that Oscar was not really surprised to find the manager of the hotel shaking his hand too. How like the French, and how endearing. In England, would one's hotel manager interrupt his private affairs to salute you on your artistic accomplishments, however distinguished? He would regard you, a poet, as a dubious character who would try to slip away without paying the bill.

Then Oscar became aware that Monsieur Marchant had come not so much to shake his hand as to give him an envelope. He opened it and took out a slip of paper and read Mary Anderson's name and knew that it was the long-awaited cable. She was deeply sorry but she feared *The Duchess of Padua* would never attract a popular audience and she must therefore decline the play.

Young Sherard, who had been watching, asked if anything was wrong. "This is very tedious, Robert," Oscar said with a smile, handing him the cable. "I am so glad you liked my 'Harlot's House.'"

Tedious, indeed, since it soon appeared that no one else cared for the *Duchess*, and Hamilton Griffin's thousand dollars was gone with the rest of the American cash and there was even some question about paying Monsieur Marchant; but Willie, like the good chap he was, advanced the money and said nothing about the dismal accuracy of his prediction. The dollars and francs hadn't been wasted; Oscar had enjoyed spending every one of them, all the more because he hadn't noticed where they'd gone, and he would spend more in the same delightful heedless way when he had more to spend.

There was the rub: *when*. Dollars, francs, pounds—how could they be made? His *Poems*, published last year, just before the American trip, had sold well for poetry, and even so had made only a few pounds over the cost of the paper and printing and binding. He could not afford the time to write another play. For quick money, there seemed to be nothing to do but return to the lecture platform. He could lecture about America. The Yankee papers had had their games with Oscar, the prize ass-thete; turnabout was only fair play.

"Knowledge of art is severely limited in the States, I regret to say. One of the most distinguished citizens of Kansas City—yes, there is a place called Kansas City, but it is not in Kansas, it is in Missouri, I cannot tell you why—the eminent art patron Osiris C. Chitterling, whose wealth is measured not in tens of thousands but in millions of dollars, ordered for his palatial home a replica of the Venus de Milo after learning that the original was not for sale. Mr. Chitterling had not seen the Venus de Milo, but he had heard about her, and it was a great day in the Chitterling mansion on Catfish Avenue, with its beautiful view over Howling Wolf Gulch, when the crate arrived by railroad from Paris—not Paris, Illinois, or Paris, Georgia, nor yet Paris, Ohio, but Paris, *France*. The proud Chitterling and his charming wife, Prairie Chicken Chitterling, had invited the cream of society to witness the unveiling, and the atmosphere was tense as the lovely Prairie Chicken, blushing and tremulous, stepped up to remove the last covering. She did so. A gasp, a shout, a shriek. Dismay on every face. *The statue's arms had been broken off*. Broken off clean as a whistle. And what was almost as bad, the arms were nowhere to be found, and so they couldn't be stuck back on; someone had stolen them. The railroad company was responsible, of course, and Mr. Chitterling promised the tearful Prairie Chicken and their indignant guests that it would pay for the outrage or his name was not Osiris C. Chitterling. He would sue—sue for damages, heavy damages. And he did. And won."

4 LECTURING WAS A DREARY BUSINESS, WHEREAS IN AMERICA
it had never weighed heavily on him and often had been enjoyable. Oscar blamed himself for not having foreseen that Gulliver
would be bored at home. Anyone doomed by his desperate need
for money to lecture in English country towns would understand
why. Every High Street was the same: the town hall, the meeting
rooms, the hotel, the draper, the chemist, the ironmonger, the fish-
monger, the butcher, the greengrocer, the provisions merchant, the
wine-and-spirits merchant, the tobacconist, the public conveniences,
the people—gray, soggy, stupid. Dull.

October 16, his birthday; twenty-nine years old. *Twenty-nine
years old*, within a step of thirty, that dreadful age, that tombstone
on the grave of youth; and what profited it to chip off a year or
two when asked his age? A silly trick that should be beneath him;
he must get over it. And where was he? He was lecturing in Liverpool, and it had rained all day, for the sun had lost its temper with
Liverpool years ago and left the damnable city forever, and the air
was clammy and smelled of old boiled cabbage, and only thirty-
six lunatic Liverpudlians had come forth to hear him lecture. He
would never sink below this—making a display of himself in front
of thirty-six creatures whose grim faces testified that they thought
him a fool and despised him.

Tomorrow he was to return to his native land. The lecture bureau had booked a dozen or more appearances for him in Ireland,
including two in Dublin at the Gaiety Theatre. It could hardly
be said that he would be coming back in triumph. The fact that
he was lecturing at the Gaiety would mean to everyone in Dublin
that he was in fact no more than a traveling performer who appeared on a stage and bowed and smiled and spoke his little piece
for money and then went on to the next engagement and did it
all over again. He would not be Oscar Wilde the poet, Oscar
Wilde the playwright, Oscar Wilde with laurel wreaths on his
brow.

The page boy brought a note to his room at the Shelbourne
Hotel in Dublin. It was from a Constance Lloyd and said that
she and her grandmother Mrs. Atkinson would be happy if he

could find the time to call and renew the London acquaintance-ship they remembered so pleasantly.

The address was a good one, he noticed. Who was Constance Lloyd, who was Mrs. Atkinson? Nothing stirred in his memory. He could have met them at a tea or reception and got along famously as he got along with almost everyone and they would remember him because he had been so nice and was, after all, well known, whereas he could never hope to remember them among the hundreds of young ladies and middle-aged ladies and their mamas and grandmamas whom he met at teas and receptions, and was pleasant to even if they were frumps and wallflowers. (He always singled out frumps and wallflowers for special attention, if only a minute or two.)

But wait. Constance Lloyd. Wasn't there a Miss Lloyd who had given him a terrible half hour listening to her theatrical ambi-tions, a strong maiden with a remorseless grip? His arm smarted again where her fingers had dug in. Good heavens, yes; she was Miss Lloyd. *She* had remembered, all right, oh yes. And *he* had almost forgotten. That was a narrow shave for you. He would send her and Mrs. Atkinson, a powerful woman too, no doubt, a note of regret: "Dear Miss Lloyd, I am so sorry, but I find that I have a subsequent engagement," which should take care of them for good, if they weren't too stupid to miss the point.

Oscar sat down to write it. Suddenly a garden came into his mind, so vividly that he sat bemused. He knew the delicious scent of its flowers; he had been there. With this Miss Lloyd? Why otherwise should he think of her as he wrote her name? But then she couldn't be the terrible talker, for his garden memory was al-together sweet. On the other hand, perhaps he had managed to escape from her by rushing into the garden and hiding. He wav-ered back and forth. At last he examined himself in the mirror, made some necessary adjustments (hair, cravat, boutonniere), and went to see.

A handsome house. And the bell was answered by a very well-turned-out parlormaid. "Good afternoon," Oscar said. "Is Miss Lloyd at home? I am Mr. Oscar Wilde."

"Will you wait, please, sir?"

He waited. A hum of voices from somewhere, and laughter; rather attractive. The voices stopped. That would be the parlor-maid announcing his name. Here she was back again.

"Will you come this way, please, sir?"

"Thank you."

Now he would know. He felt agreeably excited.

"Oh, I am so glad you came."

There she was. He was lost, lost in her violet eyes. This was Constance Lloyd. And he had nearly not come. He was sure he was trembling, to think of it. How could he have forgotten her, how possibly have confused her with some stalwart, babbling female? She, Constance, was so slim, her voice was so soft, and her wrists and fingers were so marvelously fine. There was no other girl in the world like this—the violet eyes, the serene brow, the sweet lips.

"I was afraid you would have forgotten."

That was her voice again. He still said nothing.

Her hair was chestnut brown. But now he did not care for the word chestnut. There was nothing about this peasant word to suggest the color, the lovely, princess quality of Constance's hair.

". . . Because it was only for a minute or two, in the garden behind the house, and then that Miss Whatever Her Name Was pounced out and began to talk about the theater and you seemed so interested I thought I had better leave."

The garden behind whose house? It did not matter. It mattered that she had changed or he had changed in the two or three years since then, or however long it had been; must have changed or he could never have forgotten her. Two or three years, two or three years—good heavens, what could happen in two or three years. He had asked the maid if Miss Lloyd was at home; he had taken it for granted that it *was* Miss Lloyd, but she had not said Miss in her note; she had simply signed the lovely name Constance Lloyd; there was no (Miss) behind it.

But her grandmother was Mrs. Atkinson. Which meant that if Mrs. Atkinson had had a son and the son had married and his wife had given birth to a daughter and the daughter was Constance, her name should be Constance Atkinson—unless she had married a man named Lloyd, not Atkinson. The whole question was, then, Was Mrs. Atkinson Constance's paternal or maternal grandmother?

Still he hadn't spoken. He became aware that several young men and women were looking at him, and an elderly lady, who would be Mrs. Atkinson. Constance took him around, and he bent over Mrs. Atkinson's hand with great respect, longing to murmur, "Mrs. Atkinson, are you Constance's paternal or maternal grandmother?" The names of the others he did not catch. They had looked at him politely before; now they were beginning to stare, and he fancied he heard a giggle or two. He understood only too well. He was Oscar Wilde, who was supposed to be brilliant and witty and clever, and he had yet to prove that he could string one coherent word after another.

But he hadn't been prepared for this; no one, nothing, could have prepared him. Once he had been really in love, or had thought he was, with Florence; he had had heart enough then, and to spare. He could not have imagined himself losing all heart. But he had walked into this room and looked into this slight girl's violet eyes and lost his heart. The poem was true. The poem was true.

> Yet care I not what ruin time will bring
> If in thy temple thou wilt let me kneel.

But he must speak. With an enormous effort he found his tongue and spoke.

Not very much later Miss Constance Mary Lloyd and Oscar Wilde were alone. Her father was dead, he'd learned; her mother had married again, and therefore Constance lived with her maternal (God bless the word "maternal") grandparents. Her grandfather was not well and kept to his bed a great deal.

"The afternoon you called," she said, "when you did say something, after waiting for so long—it did seem dreadfully long, and I was worrying so much why you didn't and wondering if you simply didn't like us at all and were blaming yourself for having come and trying to think of how you could leave quickly without being too rude—when you did speak, you sounded, you sounded — I must tell you the truth, mustn't I?"

"You must always tell me the truth."

"Very well, then; you sounded awfully affected. And I know why, because you've told me, although I'd never have believed it then. You were nervous."

"Because I was frightened. I had discovered what it was to be in love."

"I love hearing you say that. Please say it again."

"Because I was frightened. I had discovered what it was to be in love."

58

"It is the second part I like mostly."

"I had discovered what it was to be in love?"

"Yes."

"I see. Then that was the part you really wished to hear again?"

"Yes."

"Forgive me, I shall try to do better. I had discovered what it was to be in love."

She laughed. "Did you," she asked, "discover it—immediately?"

"Immediately."

"Please tell me more. Or does it seem rather silly to you to talk about it?"

"I am devoted to the subject."

"It's so hard to believe that it should really have happened. I had wished that it would—no, I can't truthfully say that. All I had hoped was that you would notice me a little more than you did the first time. At least, I thought, if he does come, there won't be anyone to interrupt as we were interrupted before. And then those other people called and I thought, oh dear, if he should come this afternoon we'll never have a moment together, because they'll be all over him."

"But of course they saw that it would be quite useless to be all over me, because I wouldn't notice it if they were, because I was hopelessly, hopelessly in love, in love at first sight, and shall be, forever and ever."

"You do *believe* in love at first sight?"

"I not only believe in it, I have demonstrated my belief. It may be said that I am a living manifestation of love at first sight."

"But it wasn't really, you know."

"I beg your pardon. Whose testimony on that point should be given greater credence, yours or mine?"

She pressed his hand. "No, I mean that when we met at the party in London you didn't——"

"That time doesn't count; I hardly had a chance to see you. Even so I brought away with me, so deep in my heart that I didn't know it was there, a memory that bloomed into a garden when I wrote your name. Constance, Constance, Constance—I love writing your name, I love writing about you; it is my only solace when we're not together. Would you like to know what I've written to my friends and family?"

59

"Yes."

"Her name is Constance. That is how I always start; it is essential, you see, to announce your theme at the very beginning; the best composers will tell you so. Her name is Constance (there is no harm in stating your theme two or three times if it is a beautiful one). Her name is Constance, and we are going to be married. I proposed to her by letter because in her presence I display a tendency, extraordinary for me, to lose the power of speech. I am desperately, desperately in love and I think she is a little in love with me. She is very young and there is something quite wonderful about her violet eyes and masses of heavy hair curled like a crown above her ivory brow. You will gather from this, quite rightly, that she is the most beautiful and most precious person who ever lived; and she thinks I am the greatest poet, so in literature she is all right too. Since we became engaged I have been lecturing violently all over the place in order to make as soon as possible the money we shall need to set us up as a young married couple, but of course my engagements require me to be away from her, which is horrid; however, I fly back from the ends of the earth, or so it seems, to be with her if ever so briefly and do the foolish things known only to wise lovers, and when the ends of the earth a little too far for even a lover's winged feet, I send her telegrams at least twice a day and as a result the telegraph clerks have turned terribly romantic and sigh when I come in, but I give them my messages with a steely businesslike look as if they were written in a code in which *love* means 'buy such and such a stock,' and *my darling I adore you* 'sell immediately.' Then Constance sends me telegrams and letters too, which I wear next to my heart——"

"Do you?" she asked. "Do you really?"

"Here they are," he said, and he took out a sheaf of letters. "But I keep them even more securely *in* my heart, and as an additional precaution against loss by misadventure, I have caused them to be engraved on jeweled tablets in my mind. Shall I read to you from these tablets? Yes, I think I shall. But it is necessary first to hold you very close.

"Here is a letter that begins, *My darling Love*. That is a good beginning. What does it say next? *I love you most passionately, my darling Oscar, with all my heart, with all my mind, and I am yours to do with as you wish. I know that you must leave me now, but when you are my husband you will never leave me again because I shall bind you to me with chains fashioned from my love and my devotion and they shall never lose their strength but grow stronger from year to year.* It is a most beautiful letter. Can you wonder that I whisper it to myself as I would a sonnet? And this: *When you leave me, why must you take all my sleep away with you? But I know that you will bring it back to me and that I will find it again in your arms.* I wish I had written those words, they are so lovely. But I could not, they are my love's. And so I have written some others." He gave her a little book. "They are my poems," he explained. "They were all written for you, except that I did not realize it then. But the poem on the first page was written there last night, after I woke from a dream of you, and so it is especially yours."

Constance read:

> "I can write no stately poem
>   As a prelude to my lay;
> From a poet to a poem
>   I would dare to say.
>
> "For if of these fallen petals
>   One to you seem fair,
> Love will waft it till it settles
>   On your hair.
>
> "And when wind and winter harden
>   All the loveless land,
> It will whisper of the garden,
>   You will understand."

As he left her a grim thought struck him. What if the damned obscene thing should still be there? No, impossible; it had been banished years ago, and there was no sign of its return. But it was secret and cunning and perhaps there was a sign that he could not recognize. Perhaps when it came a second time it was even more insidious. Perhaps in these last months it had so deeply spread that he was beyond saving. He had held her in his arms and felt her trembling desire to be wholly his; how could he have forgotten, before tonight, to think of it? Her parting kiss was sweet on his lips. He couldn't sleep.

His train the next morning was to leave at ten. At nine he was in a doctor's office. The doctor looked like a man with no non-sense about him.

"Some years ago," Oscar said, "when I was at Oxford, I was given the mercury treatment for what was suspected to be syphilis. It left a dark line on my teeth, which I dare say you have noticed. Fortunately only medical men are aware of its possible signifi-cance or I suppose I shouldn't be welcomed in polite society. I was assured that the disease, if indeed it had been there, was cured. There has been no reason to think it has come back. But I am to be married soon and must be sure. There is something else. In spite of the Oxford incident, or perhaps I should say because of it, I am not a licentious person; but recently while living in Paris and working with great concentration for an extended period, I felt in need of—a change. I was sufficiently careless or sufficiently hard-pressed, put it as you will, to find it in a brothel. I didn't think any more about it afterward; there seemed to be no reason to. Now it is imperative to know if any harm was done. But I fear I am re-peating myself; forgive me."

"Were there several university incidents or one?"

"Several."

"With men or women?"

"Surely that is a rather astonishing question."

"There is a good deal of homosexual behavior in boys' schools and colleges that is purely transient."

"I am aware of that," Oscar said. "What bearing can it have on my case?"

"There would be less chance of true syphilis if the incidents were with young men of your own class."

"Indeed? Why?"

"I take it they wouldn't be male prostitutes. Syphilis is a pros-titutes' disease."

"I see," Oscar said. "The Oxford incidents were with young women. That is to say, they were reasonably young; I suspect one at least had reached an eminence of years I have yet to attain. A gentle soul. But a harlot, alas."

"Quite so. Now, you said there has been no reason to think the disease has returned or that you contracted it in the Paris episode. In other words, you have noticed no local symptoms?"

"None."

"Any minor complaints that bother you and that stubbornly persist?"

"No."

"Nothing at all?"

"Nothing at all. Although," Oscar added, "I am bothered by my appetite, which is large and expensive. It stubbornly persists."

"That can only be encouraged."

"No, doctor, no; above all things it should not be encouraged; it does splendidly by itself."

"I shall examine you now, sir, if you will be good enough to remove your clothes."

The examination took some time.

"Well, doctor?"

"I can give you a clean bill of health. May I offer my congratulations on your approaching marriage—and some advice?"

Oscar could have hugged him. "Thank you, thank you! Please do."

"In future you will be responsible not only for the welfare of your own body but for that of a young and, I am sure, beautiful and trusting person. To risk your health is foolish; to risk hers, wicked."

"I agree, my dear doctor, and am more than ever grateful. If ever again I am found in the company of— No," Oscar interrupted himself. "I was going to say that if ever again I am found in the company of the poor daughters of joy, it will be solely for the charm of their conversation; but you would think me less than in earnest, and I am most deeply and solemnly in earnest when I say that nothing shall ever stain that beautiful and trusting person—yours were good, true words, doctor—through fault of mine."

5 HE SNAPPED UP EVERY POSSIBLE LECTURE ENGAGEMENT AS long as it paid a few pounds above train fare and hotel bill. It was all tucked away against the wedding and honeymoon of Mr. and Mrs. Oscar Wilde and provision of a London residence for the young couple. They put their heads together about these things —that was a delightful exercise, putting heads together. The wedding would take place at St. James's Church, Paddington, in London. "It will be the most beautiful ever seen," Oscar said. "It has to be, to do justice to the bride." The press would be bound to turn out in great force, eyes peeled for superaesthetical folly. They would come to mock; they would stay to admire. For they would find no idiot Bunthorne with the type of maiden he might be expected to choose, but a conservatively dressed young gentleman and a beautiful girl exquisitely gowned. "Between us, my darling, we shall see to that. You have provided the beauty; I shall provide the gown."

Constance fondly smiled. "You will, dearest? It will be a precious memory, that I was married in a gown given to me by my love."

"And designed by me, darling, if you will let me."

"You, dear?" She was slightly taken aback.

"Yes. I would like to show the world how beautiful a beautiful girl can be when she is released from the hideous bondage of today's fashion. But forgive me, my own; I perceive that I am beginning to lecture."

"I love to hear you lecture."

"We have trivial things to do that are infinitely more important. I shall tell you, though, that in the new lecture I've been sketching out I denounce the corset. It will never be the same again, will tremble to raise its head."

"Oh, poor corset."

"Mind you, I am scrupulously fair to it. I admit that it is quite true that so long as the lower garments are suspended from the hips, a corset is an absolute necessity. The mistake lies in not suspending all apparel from the shoulders. Then a corset becomes useless, the body is left free and unconfined for respiration and motion, and in consequence is healthier. In fact, the root of all evil in fashion can be found in the same error of not realizing that it is from the shoulders, only from the shoulders, that garments should be hung. When they are, the principles of Greek dress may be realized, relying for beauty of effect on the exquisite play of light and line that one gets from rich and rippling folds."

Constance traced the outline of his lips with a fingertip. "But, dearest, we aren't living in Greek times."

"The laws of beautiful dress, as of human beauty, remain the same."

"Isn't it rather colder in the British Isles than in Greece?"

"Alas, yes. But the warmth of your clothes doesn't really depend on the number you wear but on the material they're made of. Over a layer of pure wool some modification of Greek costume is perfectly applicable to our climate, our country, and our century."

"Oscar, darling, am I to be married wearing a layer of pure wool underneath a Greek lady's toga, or whatever it was called? Oh, goodness. I shall try to like it, but I'm afraid I shan't, very much, even if my body is left free and unconfined for respiration and motion!"

"Let me tell you what I have in mind. A satin gown, in color I think pale cowslip—" He stopped and caught her hands in his and looked at her closely. "Tell me the truth, my love—remember, you must always tell me the truth. In your heart of hearts are you wishing that I would have nothing to do with this?"

"In my heart of hearts I wish only for your happiness. I feel that I never lived before the day we met. Then I am your creation, aren't I? You must do with your creation as you please, for only your pleasure can please her. But—but I cannot help hoping that I shan't look *too* Greek, Oscar darling."

"You shall be a vision of delight."

Oscar made a dozen and more starts at designing the dress. He threw away none because each had in it so much thought of Constance, and all these sketches accompanied him during his last weeks of lectures before the wedding. They were arranged on the shabby covers of the forlorn beds in the dismal bedrooms of the awful country hotels he stayed in, so as to greet him as he returned from the night's lecture and lift his spirits and set him to sketching again.

In the end he was satisfied. Here was pure beauty. He had known since childhood that he must spend his life in its pursuit. A hundred years from now, when the girl who had worn the wedding dress was dust mingled with the dust that had been his lover's arms and lips, a picture of the dress would still testify that someone had known the meaning of beauty.

The dress was a pale yellow. The high collar was cut away to leave exposed the full column of the bride's throat. The bodice was cut low in front so that the line of the throat would continue without interruption into the beginning rise of the breasts. The skirt was gathered into deep, rippling folds by a silver girdle; light and shadow would flow over the delectable satin as the bride moved toward the altar. Constance's veil would be of saffron silk strewn with tiny pearls, and there would be myrtle leaves and orange blossoms in her hair. Her bouquet would repeat the same contrasting deep green and velvet white.

The bridesmaids, Oscar decided, would wear pale-blue bodices and red-silk skirts. Amber beads twined around the stems of yellow roses would fall from their necks, and they would carry lilies and wear high-crowned hats on which cream-colored feathers and red ribbons would tremble and sway.

Finally, there would be two miniature ladies in large Gainsborough hats and translucent gooseberry-green silk gowns—the flower girls, their small arms filled with masses of roses. They would be very pretty and very solemn. It would spoil everything if they were to laugh. He would make a point of impressing upon them the grand nature of their roles and that God would be anxiously watching for signs of a giggle from His secret hiding place behind the altar.

If only God could be brought into play to ensure the seemly behavior of another lady! If only, Oscar thought, he could design *her* clothes for the wedding! (Perfectly simple to design them; to get her to wear them would be the trick.) Of course his mother would hardly err, as the little flower girls might be tempted to, by giggling; the trouble would lie quite in the other direction. She could, and very probably would, damage the atmosphere by being too majestical.

Oscar was proud of his mother, but it could not be denied that since Sir William's death Lady Wilde had become increasingly conscious of the honorable and artistic history of her side of the family and inclined to demonstrate its importance by dominating any social occasion. Her figure was queenly; her face, with the huge dark eyes and strong mouth, lent itself to commanding expressions; and she carried herself as though permanently gazing down on worshiping multitudes. This imperious mien, which required no emphasis, was emphasized by her clothes. Even in thinking of them Oscar would not permit himself a word stronger than "unfortunate," and he would not breathe a hint of criticism, but occasionally, when some new and even more elaborate means of ornamentation had struck his mother's fertile mind, his self-control was tested to the limit. It was extraordinary what she could do with a scarf, particularly if it had tassels, and two bracelets on her arm seemed to jangle with the power of twenty.

But she was a dear, fine woman, and she had a lion heart. And she was his mother.

"I wonder, Mother," he ventured, "if you have thought much about the wedding?"

"A great deal, dear."

"It does please you?"

"On the whole, yes. Constance is a lovely girl, and a very fortunate one. As she knows, which is to her credit."

"It is I who am fortunate, Mother."

"Of course I should expect you to say so."

"I am constantly amazed by my good fortune. Surely you must agree with me. Or is there anything in which the marriage doesn't live up to your best hopes?"

"My dear," Lady Wilde said in a sonorous voice, "you are not, of course, aware of it, as a gentleman shouldn't be, but you were a great catch, a very great catch, the catch of this or any season."

"Aren't you exaggerating, Mother," Oscar said, smiling, "—a trifle?"

"Certainly not. I have reason to know how many young ladies with handsome dowries set their caps at you. But Constance's pretty face caught your eye——"

"She isn't precisely dowerless, Mother."

"Two thousand pounds or so. But there, it may be for the best, in that she very well understands how fortunate she is."

"I can assure you she understands how fortunate she is in her mother-in-law to be."

"She is a sweet girl."

"I dare say you'd like to know something about the dresses Constance and the bridesmaids are to wear. There is a color motif, one might say——"

"Ah, yes? No, don't tell me; I should prefer to discover it for myself—it will come as a delightful surprise. My own dress," Lady Wilde continued, "will, I know, please you."

"Do let me see it."

"Shall I?" She hesitated, and Oscar looked at her expectantly; then she shook her head with a smile that might almost be called arch. "No, I think not. It will be my surprise for *you*, at the wedding."

The dress exceeded his darkest forebodings. Lady Wilde seemed to have become involved with one of the red-plush armchairs in the public room of an Atlantic liner; her dress had the same bulging, opulent look and was as intensely red as only red plush can be. After somehow managing to drape the armchair around her, and before walking away in it, she had noticed the shade on the massive floor lamp beside the chair. The shade had a design of heavy crimson roses and on Lady Wilde's head it towered over her tallest neighbor. It was impossible not to see her, and seeing her, difficult not to think of the Cunard Steam Ship Company. But after the first shock, Oscar did not care.

For Constance was next to him, and the minister was saying: "Wilt thou, Oscar, have this woman to thy wedded wife, to live together after God's ordinance in the holy estate of matrimony? Wilt thou love her, comfort her, honor and keep her in sickness and in health, and forsaking all others, keep thee only unto her, so long as ye both shall live?"

Oscar said, "I will."

The minister said: "Wilt thou, Constance, have this man to thy wedded husband, to live together after God's ordinance in the holy estate of matrimony? Wilt thou obey him and serve him, love, honor, and keep him in sickness and in health, and forsaking all others, keep thee only unto him, so long as ye both shall live?"

"I will," Constance said.

6

SHE LEANED ACROSS HIS NAKED BODY AND LOOKED AT THE clock on the bedside table. "It's almost three," she murmured.

"Remarkable," Oscar said.

"Remarkable, dearest?"

"I have always been led to believe that at this hour of the morning, if not before, the bride and groom fell asleep in each other's arms, having feasted at love's table until they could feast no more. Yet though I have feasted so greedily, I could not dream of sleeping for fear of falling into a dream, when no dream could bring this sweet reality, the touch of your breasts as you lean over me. I think you are blushing. Are you? Yes, you are. Why?"

"It's so strange to hear you say that word."

"What word?"

She whispered, " 'Breasts.' "

"To save your modesty, would you prefer to have me kiss them?"

"Yes."

"Delicious modesty. Such beautiful flowers, twin roses blooming on your—there, I almost said breasts again, didn't I? But caught myself in time, thank heavens, for if I'd said the forbidden word I shouldn't feel free to kiss these roses again, and again, and again. Now you are smiling. Why?"

"No, no."

"You are, and it's very discouraging. I tell you beautiful things, and you smile. And not a Mona Lisa smile. I could forgive a Mona Lisa smile. This is an almost-bursting-with-laughter smile, an I-find-you-terribly-funny smile. Isn't it? Isn't it?"

"Oscar, don't."

"I propose to tickle you until you tell me the truth. I propose to tickle you here—and here—and here—and *here*. Ah, that seems to be rather effective. Again?"

Constance shrieked, "Stop!"

"Then why were you smiling?"

"Oh!" she gasped. "It was—it was—it was your mother's hat— the hat she wore at the wedding. Oh, oh!"

"Why on earth should you think of my mother's hat when I am kissing your lovely breasts? Have they anything in common?"

"Yes."

"They have not. Then what is it?"

"Roses," Constance cried, shaking with laughter.

"Ah," Oscar said. Presently he laughed too. "Then I must find somewhere else to kiss you. Let me see." He propped himself on an elbow and looked at her face and her body. "To think how demure you were, how maidenly, how chaste, when I met you. And now you are not. You have grown wanton. You have grown bold enough to say that roses bloom on your breasts; and do you blush as a proper young lady should as she utters that Jezebel word? No longer. You laugh instead. Oh, Constance, Constance; oh, shameful Constance. How beautiful you are. Your feet are like little white doves and your legs are like the slim stalks of daffodils and your hips curve like a couch made artfully to receive and hold me while I rest my head in the garden of your breasts and taste the flowers growing there. Are you blushing again?"

"No."

"No. You have grown wanton, haven't you?"

"Yes."

"Yes. But it is I who have taught you." And he bent his head to her breasts.

"Oscar," she whispered, "who were they?"

"Who were who, my beautiful, my passionate love?"

"Those other women, the women you knew before you knew me."

"You are very sure, aren't you, that there were other women."

"Yes," she said. "Very sure."

"Why?"

"Because you are you. Because I can't think of a woman who would not feel drawn to you, as I was when we met. Why, I read about many of them."

"Come, come," Oscar said, laughing. "Many?"

"Lillie Langtry, for one."

"The reports of our love affair were enormously exaggerated. I know, because I exaggerated them. Lillie wished to make a splash and I wished to make a splash, so we made one together. There was no more to it than that. Never, never would Lillie have permitted herself to be found with me in the position that you now find yourself in. She reserved such intimacies for much, much wealthier men. Excuse me, I should not have said 'much, much'; I meant, of course, 'much, much, much, much, much.'"

"There were others."

"It would astonish you, my darling, to know how few."

"I wish there had been none. I wish I had met you when we were children. I would have known then that you were to be my life's love. I would have kept you within my arms and protected you from all others until it was time for us to meet as lovers, as man and wife, and lose our innocence together and learn from each other rather than there being one to teach and one to learn."

"You are the poet tonight," Oscar said. "With your body and your lips and now your words."

"But since the past can't be mine," she said, "the future shall be. There will never be another woman in your arms, because there will never be room; they will be filled with my love."

By and by he slept; his last memory was of Constance's flushed, damp face beneath his and her panting breath. He turned slowly and felt something as light as a clinging tendril of sleep trail across his eyes. He opened them wider. It was her hair. He had fallen asleep with his face buried in her hair. He longed to wake her and say, "I fell alseep, as I shall wish to die, instantly, pierced and transfigured, and your soft hair warmed me as I slept."

A great tenderness filled him. She had suffered, in the beginning of the night, for she had been innocent in body and in mind, and both had to be lost in pain. He had warned her and tried to ease the pain she must bear, but still the fire between her loins had made her gasp and seize her underlip between her teeth so sharply that they left a tiny wound bleeding even as the deeper wound bled, and he had despised himself for not being able to hold his pleasure in leash. Later the wounds gave only joy.

Cautiously he began to move from the tangled bed. Her right leg, outflung, was an obstacle in his path. How could he overcome it? He could not nudge the leg even ever so gently aside for fear of purloining her precious sleep, and to lift himself over it would surely destroy the delicate balance in which she lay.

Ah, here was an answer. It was only necessary to consider oneself not bound by convention and an answer would always appear. Conventionally one left a bed from the side. Then let us defy convention and strike out on a bold new course and get out of this bed *from the end.* Oscar did so. Constance slept on.

He found dressing gown and slippers and successfully avoided all furniture in the dim light on his way to the bathroom. Opening the door, he was dazzled by the blaze of light reflected by the mirrors and the white walls. White, the color of virtue; white, the color of the modern bathroom. There would be a modern bathroom in his and Constance's home; indeed there would, a magnificent, luxurious room, but without all this white that made one feel that one should occupy the sacred chamber with the downcast eyes of a vestal virgin. This should be a room to rejoice in, to flaunt one's nakedness in, to fondle the pliant, excellent flesh in.

He lay in a hot tub looking at the long pink island of his body and its various peninsulas. Except for sword and helmet and bright shield, the Gorgon-conquering hero stands naked in the sunlight, and the smallest of the vipers that rear from Medusa's severed head dwarfs the small symbol of his manhood. What an unpleasant connection; how had he come to think of it? Oscar thought of Constance.

But good heavens, it must be well on into the morning. Robert Sherard was coming to breakfast with Mr. and Mrs. Oscar Wilde on this, the first full day of their honeymoon in Paris.

Afterward Oscar walked back with Sherard toward his *pension.* "She is enchanting," the young man said. "I do hope she liked me. Do you think she did?"

Oscar had turned aside to a flower stall and stood plucking out mounds of color. "It isn't enough, it isn't nearly enough, but it will have to serve until we reach the next one. Will you wrap them, please?" he asked the flower vendor. "Very, very gently, for if one is so much as bruised they will not be worthy of their destination —Apartment thirty-seven, Hotel Wagram, rue de Rivoli." He wrote on a card: "These were pining to be near your loveliness," and showed it to Sherard.

"But there won't be room for more flowers, Oscar. I've never seen so many in one room in my life."

"Ah, didn't I show you the other room, then? There are three, you know. It is a suite deluxe."

"You didn't."

"Nor the bedroom?"

"No."

"There really *are* flowers in the bedroom. Robert, Robert, I must tell you—that is why I came out with you—I must tell someone, and I am delighted that it is to be you, because Constance was enchanted with you, I could see, as of course you were with her. Robert, I am in love."

"Really, Oscar. Do you consider that you are treating me to a great confidence?"

"I am bursting with love, saturated, double-, triple-dyed in love, at every pore I ooze love—no, that is a vulgar expression, I withdraw it. I was in love before last night, Robert, let me make that quite clear. I was in love with Florence Balcombe and I was in love with Lillie, or in love with the *idea* of Lillie, for Lillie was beauty and Lillie was fame, and I was hungry for both, as I still am, Robert—for fame, I mean. I am as hungry for fame as Eve was for the apple. And then I fell in love with Constance. I could think of nothing but Constance; I worshiped the ground she walked on. How glorious these trite old words become when dipped in the rainbow, love, how they flash and soar, like eagles' wings, how they pierce one to the heart and take one's breath away. But observe, Robert, observe——"

Sherard pulled him back from passing cartwheels. "For God's sake watch your step."

"Pray observe—what shall I have you observe? Ah, here, another flower stall; good. Pray observe these rosebuds, Robert. Pretty little things, aren't they? Quite perfect. Yes, they are, and I shall have two dozen of them, please, which you"—Oscar spoke to the flower vendor—"will send to this address with this card. Thank you. Is this enough money? It is? More than enough? I am delighted. Here is some more, so that it will be more than more than enough and so that you will remember me and this day for as long as you live, because it is as I am today that I wish to be remembered; on my tombstone these words will be carved: *Do not weep for the poor husk that lies here, for on*—what is the date, Robert?—*for on May 31, 1884, it strode the earth like a god.* Now, Robert, you have observed the rosebuds? They represent my love for Constance before last night. Tender, oh, so tender, and in its way quite perfect. But compare the rosebuds with my love for Constance this morning, which is this." And he picked up a huge, fully blossomed rose and crushed it to his lips.

"Thank you," the young man said, "for describing your love so beautifully."

"I have barely begun. Last night, Robert, was sublime. She lay

73

like a flower on the bed and I kissed her lips, her throat, her breasts, and felt her tremble and part beneath me as a rose parts its petals to receive the——"

"Oscar, Oscar," Sherard interrupted. "After all."

"After all?"

"I have just met your wife. It seems to me hardly proper that you should—should——"

"Are you *embarrassed?*"

"I am."

"Good heavens," Oscar murmured. "How curious. Forgive me, my dear boy. I perceive that you are blushing. Do you know that *she* blushed at the moment when—but there, I am becoming improper again, aren't I? Very well then, you must simply take my word for it that last night I reached the peaks from the valleys of—goodness me, I seem to be incorrigible. We must talk about something else. Perhaps you will be kind enough to suggest a subject."

"Tell me about the wedding."

"It went off splendidly. I believe there has never been such a turnout of the press. The cuttings should reach me tomorrow; I instructed Romeike's, the excellent press-cutting bureau, to send them on here."

"But you're not in Paris for good, Oscar?"

"Alas, no; two weeks only. We can't afford more. Our marriage, you see, was made in heaven, not in a countinghouse; that is to say, we married for love, not money, and thus for the first time in my life I have succeeded in doing something that is at once wholly wise and wholly delightful. I dare say nothing of the kind will ever happen again. How I thank God now that I didn't fall victim to the charms of Miss Lulu Sassafras, daughter of the Chicago pork king, nor yet to those of Hermione Croup, the headache-powder heiress. But lacking their golden embrace, I am obliged to return to the salt mines—the lecture halls, Robert. Never mind, it will not be for long; with Constance's dear lips to nourish me, I cannot fail to thrive. In the meantime there is all Paris to show to her. This afternoon we shall look in at the salon, and perhaps the Meissonnier exhibition; tonight we are to see Bernhardt in *Macbeth*; tomorrow Jimmy Whistler's friend Henrietta Reubell has asked us to breakfast; she is, of course, fascinatingly ugly and fascinatingly rich, and it would be quite touching, would it not, if she were to be so moved by Constance's youth and beauty as to appoint herself our fairy godmother and make it unnecessary for me ever to waste another thought on the terrible importance of earning a living? Or at least provide a house for us? So simple for fairy godmothers. Only one touch of the wand is required to produce a sugarplum castle.

"And yet—perhaps it would be dangerous to accept. Fairy godmothers' gifts have a habit of vanishing as the clock strikes twelve, leaving the recipients to a life of tears and poverty. None of that for us. Constance and I are going to live happily forever after." Oscar paused for a moment. "Are you thinking, Robert," he asked with a smile, "that living happily forever after sounds too boring for words?"

The young man said, "No, of course I'm not." He seemed shocked.

7

NUMBER 16, TITE STREET, WAS REALIZED WITH CONSTANCE'S dowry for which, they were agreed, there could be no better investment. The house was one of a row, built twenty years before, of red brick, rather narrow and not deep, but four stories tall and with two rooms on each floor. A surveyor said the property was sound, and the section of London in which it stood, Chelsea, with its pleasantly artistic atmosphere, couldn't fail to increase in value.

Tite Street's only disadvantage was the bordering slum called Paradise Walk; on the other hand, without it the leasehold of Number 16 would have commanded a far higher price. Thanks to Paradise Walk a fair amount remained to redecorate and furnish the house.

Several friends offered to help; Jimmy Whistler said he would do the whole job. Oscar was hard put to it to think of an irreproachable excuse: Jimmy was fearfully sensitive and had a gunpowder temper. In his hands Number 16 could become a thing of such blazing beauty that no one would be able to bear to live in it. Even millionaires blanched at the cost of the materials on which Jimmy doted.

Jimmy's friendship had meant much to Oscar and he did not wish to lose it, much less find himself challenged to a duel if, after six months' work on the house and the end nowhere in sight, Jimmy were to sniff in the air a hint of anxiety to get him out. Oscar said Constance was in tears and he desperately annoyed with himself for having given a contract and a substantial preliminary payment to Green & Co., Architects and Decorators, but that when Green & Co. were done he hoped he might feel free to call on Jimmy to rectify and gild with his exquisite taste the work of their gross hands. Only Jimmy's promise that they could rely on him would serve to dry Constance's tears.

"He was quite satisfied," Oscar reported to her. "Suspected nothing. It was mention of your tears that did it—that and the word 'gild.' He said he kissed your hand, and invited us to breakfast."

"Whatever shall we tell him when the house is finished?"

"Oh, he'll have forgotten by then."

"In a few weeks?"

"Well, we'll give a glorious party, and Jimmy will be too busy occupying the center of the stage to think of anything else."

Oscar explained and sketched his ideas in careful detail for Green's guidance and departed on the weary round of lecture engagements. He wrote every night to Constance and sent telegrams in between; the air was full of the music of her voice, he said, and he seemed to feel her fingers in his hair and their lips meeting. But a shadow lay over her answering letters.

At the first possible opportunity he rushed home. It appeared that Green had ideas of his own and that in Oscar's absence nothing Constance said could sway him; moreover, expenses were mounting horribly while work stumbled and faltered when it proceeded at all—Green's imbecile workmen seemed perfectly capable of destroying everything they touched. Oscar spoke sharply to Green; Green flared up; Oscar forbade him the premises and Green refused to budge. It could only be that Green was not going to have it said that he was incapable of measuring up to Oscar Wilde's standards of taste. It could not be denied that this was a sign of progress; two or three years ago someone like Green would have regarded as a wicked libel any suggestion that his work suited Oscar Wilde's taste; but on the other hand, if the house kept on the way it was going, Oscar Wilde's taste as demonstrated in his home would constitute a mystery, since no one except those hardy enough to clamber over pots of paint and piles of building materials would have the chance to examine it.

"Who would believe it?" Oscar said hotly to his friend Edward Godwin. "It is like a dream, a ridiculous dream. Do you know how long Green has been muddling about already? Almost two months. Am I fated to go through life with this revolting architect around my neck? Will we still be arguing over the shambles when my grandchildren are lisping their first words?"

"Your grandchildren, Oscar?"

"Perhaps I exaggerate. My children, then."

Quiet, sympathetic, always comforting Godwin, who indeed rather looked like an uncle, with his goatee and shaggy gray moustache, said, "My dear fellow, does this mean that Mrs. Wilde——"

"Yes. The happy event is of course some months in the future, but what are months in the life of a Green—mere wisps of time, fleeting shadows beside the great granite determination of Green to muddle on, and *on*, and ON, like the poem about Columbus by Longfellow, I think it was. What matters it to Green that there will be no nursery for the child's cradle, or rather that the space intended for the nursery will be so jammed with wreckage left by Green's laborers that it will require a Japanese acrobat to get into it?"

"Oscar, you must take legal action."

"There is, unfortunately, a contract."

"Refuse to honor it."

"Green threatens something called distraint."

"Then threaten counterdistraint."

"You see that this can go on forever, to nobody's satisfaction but the lawyers'. Meantime Green sits fast."

Godwin stroked his goatee. "I have it," he said, sitting up and snapping his fingers. "Put Jimmy in. Undoubtedly Green has never seen anything like Jimmy. Jimmy will *frighten* him away. And then Jimmy and I will finish the job. Never fear, I shall keep him under strict control. I can do it, you know, for I exercise a terrible power over Jimmy—he is secretly in love with my wife."

Though Jimmy was in fact a rather short, slight person, the newcomer to him would unhesitatingly describe him (unless he had happened to be in a rare, sweet mood) as immensely tall. It was a Mephistophelian quality of his to be able to loom at will. He looked a bit like Mephistopheles, at that. His face was dark and sardonic, his curly hair coal black except for the one white lock bristling out like a cockatoo's comb, and he possessed a terrifying laugh, *hargh, hargh.* If Jimmy weren't a great painter, he could be a successful Apache. So far as Oscar knew, only once had Jimmy's stupendous gall been thrown back in his face. Jimmy's pet poodle had had a sore throat, and Jimmy had sent for a doctor—not a vet, a doctor. And not *a* doctor but, when it came to sore throats, *the* doctor, the greatest sore-throat man in the United Kingdom, Sir Morell Mackenzie, who had looked into royal sore throats by the dozen and thought nothing of it. Sir Morell had never looked into a dog's throat, at least not in earnest, but when he arrived at Jimmy's and asked to see the patient and Jimmy brought forth the poodle and explained, "He has a *very* sore throat and is a *most exceptional* poodle—I am deeply attached to him, hargh!" Sir Morell coolly looked into the poodle's throat and wrote out a prescription. The next day Jimmy received a telegram: would he please come at once on an urgent matter to Sir Morell Mackenzie's residence? Sir Morell himself came to the door. "Ah," he said, "Mr. Whistler. I do hope you brought your brushes? This door, a most exceptional door—I am deeply attached to it—could do with a coat of paint."

"This may very well be the answer," Oscar said. "I know that if I were happily muddling along making some poor gentleman's home uninhabitable and Jimmy were to descend on me like the Demon King, I should take to my heels. Dear Godwin, I am so grateful. But as I do not have to tell you——"

"Tell me, in any event."

"—Jimmy's weak point is peacock feathers. Unless restrained he will smother Sixteen Tite Street in them."

"I shall limit him to two."

"I fear the effect of even two. Peacock feathers are to Jimmy as the bottle is to the drunkard."

"Very well then," Godwin said. "None."

Green withdrew, though not without a rear-guard action of legal documents. Godwin and Jimmy started to work; Oscar resumed lecturing. He had faith in Godwin, but occasionally a vision of Jimmy run amuck would drive him to the telegraph office, and a series of anxious inquiries peppered 16 Tite Street: "Dear Godwin, Is all well? The universe pauses for an answer." "Dear Godwin, Besieged in dreams last night by flock of irascible peacocks. You alone can comfort me." "Dear Godwin, Gold leaf also dangerous to our mutual friend. Stand fast." "Dear Godwin, Will be back at Tite Street this coming Thursday at four. Pray advise if I should prepare for disagreeable shock."

At four on Thursday, Oscar inspected his new home. The walls and woodwork in the study had been a heavy mahogany; now the woodwork was deep rose, the walls pale yellow. A small figure of Hermes stood poised on a column in one corner, and there were three pictures on the walls: children playing, Eros and a group of disciples, an Italian landscape. Constance had arranged Oscar's most cherished books; his school and college prizes, his Shakespeare, his Greek and Latin classics, and copies of their work inscribed to him by brother poets.

The jewel of the study was Oscar's writing desk; once it had been Thomas Carlyle's.

The dining room, not long ago a gastronomical graveyard

haunted by the shades of boiled mutton and boiled pudding and painted in the hue of overdone roast beef, had been made to bloom in buttercup yellow and daisy white. The chairs were white, the carpet was white; the people who gathered here would look out through a bow window to a garden of ferns and roses, where antique spirits new to England, fauns, dryads, would come, lured by youth and laughter.

In the drawing room, on the second floor, Jimmy had settled for two Japanese feathers, beautiful flame-colored things like small comet-tails swooping across the light-blue ceiling. A strip of dark gold against the white-yellow walls was the background for more Jimmy, half a dozen of his Venice etchings. The chairs were black and white, and the small grand piano was exquisitely lacquered in white.

There was a full-length portrait of Oscar by an American on the wall facing the fireplace. It wasn't much good, but Constance had insisted; the portrait was the only one they had.

Just across the landing from the drawing room, the smoking room was conveniently at hand for the gentlemen after dinner; although of course Oscar would cheerfully break convention by smoking at the dinner table and for that matter even in the drawing room, he knew that to do so would offend Constance's regard for the proprieties. And not for the world would he hurt this gentle creature, who would conceal any hurt, he was well aware, for fear of disturbing him, if ever so slightly. The smoking room was a decidedly interesting place to retire to—quite another, a Moorish, world: glass-bead curtains at the door and over the windows; ottomans, divans, and lots of pillows rather than chairs and sofa; colored-glass lanterns; dark red-and-gold wallpaper. At first inspection this room was the least pleasing to Oscar; it occurred to him that these self-consciously exotic trappings were, after all, the expected thing, whereas in no other respect were the first two floors of the brilliantly new 16 Tite Street self-conscious or expected. But Constance liked the smoking room, made a little joke about it, supposed this was the last time she'd be permitted to see it—and pressed his arm; and so Oscar too liked the smoking room.

One room the previous tenants would have recognized—the bedroom. It was frankly old-fashioned; it had to be to accommodate the needlework chair covers that were Constance's pride. They, rather than her dowry, she considered her prime gift to her home, for they were the product of her own fingers' great care and her great love. Could anyone, could Oscar, could Godwin, could Jimmy, tell her that there was no place for needlework chaircovers in such a modern scheme of decoration? Jimmy went into ecstasies over them, and was promised a set. He and Godwin had thought it best to retire and leave the bedroom and the small connecting room, which could serve as a spare bedroom or dressing room, to Constance. She put lace curtains and flowered draperies at the windows, a comfortable thick Axminster rug on the floor, and Chippendale bookcases against the walls and scattered flower-filled vases and knickknacks around the room; and in this setting the huge, high, old double bed looked precisely right.

The bathroom, on the top floor of the house, was not the bathroom of Oscar's dreams. To have turned it into that palatial chamber would have meant sacrificing one of the two small rooms on either side, and since these were to be the playroom, or day nursery, and the baby's bedroom, or night nursery, he wouldn't think of it. Anyway it was a pleasant sea green flecked with gold. Oscar was enchanted with his new home.

But here Constance's dowry ran out, and every penny he had managed to put aside from lecturing was gone too. Of course there was credit; you took credit for granted, you could jog along quite decently for six months, even a year, on credit, when you had a handsomely decorated house to impress tradesmen and you entertained well and often and your name was pretty constantly in the papers as Oscar made sure his was. In these circumstances credit would be delighted to supply your guests with wines and spirits and caviar and cigarettes and your breakfast table with bacon and your fireplaces with coal, down to the trivial expenses of your wife's hairpins and your morning newspaper; but at the end of the six months or a year there would come a day of reckoning.

And it couldn't be denied, Oscar saw after two or three months in the house, that his income did not give promise of being nearly robust enough to deal with the day of reckoning, despite all his industry and Constance's ingenious and gallant efforts to cut every possible corner, beginning with her wardrobe. He simply had to find something else to do. Considering that his reputation was so decidedly changed for the better, his presence so eagerly sought by hostesses anxious to add the luster of Oscar Wilde's wit to their salons, it would seem that he needed only pick and choose among manifold opportunities; but he had to scramble for lecture engagements, to drive himself late at night to turn an extra few shillings in book reviewing, to snatch at hackwork to which he could not afford to sign his name.

Contemplating the remorseless bills, angry to think that he could not clothe Constance in all the lovely gowns he wished to design for her, he was caught by an announcement in the *Times*. The announcement was of an appointment to fill a vacancy in the list of Her Majesty's inspectors of schools; more significant (for of course such sinecures were quarreled over like bones), the awarding of this boring, bill-paying, lifesaving job was in the hands of the Rt. Hon. Edward Stanhope, Vice-President of the Council on Education; and the Rt. Hon. Edward Stanhope was an Oxford contemporary of Oscar's. True, Oscar could not remember any occasion when he and the Rt. Hon. Edward Stanhope had quaffed from the same flowing bowl or listened together to the chimes at midnight, but on the other hand he had never fallen afoul of the Rt. Hon. Edward. The latter, however, it had to be admitted, might still be tainted in his rt. hon. judgment by the stories and cartoons of the Bunthorne days.

But there was a way around *that*. Oscar wrote to George Curzon, who had been a friend at Oxford, who was a coming man in the Conservative Party, and who knew Stanhope. Would Curzon please put in a good word—say that Oscar was a man of not absolutely negligible brains, wasn't the idler the uninformed might fancy him to be?

George Curzon answered most charmingly: yes, of course he would. And since few people, at any rate few political people, could resist Curzon, who no doubt would rise in due course to be Prime Minister or something very grand, the die would appear to be cast, the issue settled; Oscar Wilde was to become one of Her Majesty's inspectors of schools.

Very well; he vowed that he would not disappoint Curzon or Stanhope or Her Majesty; he would be a devoted, an outstanding, Inspector of Schools. At length he would come to Her Majesty's notice. "Ah, Mr. Wilde. You are, We believe, Our inspector who has been inspecting Our schools, We are informed by the poet laureate, as Shakespeare, Keats, and Shelley would have inspected, had they had the honor to be appointed to inspectorships. Also you are the author of the moving *Elegy Written in a Country Schoolyard* and the exquisitely lyrical *Sonnet On First Looking Into Blackpool Boys' Grammar School?*" "I am, Your Majesty. Your Majesty is most gracious." "Stay to tea, Mr. Wilde. There are cucumber sandwiches."

Such, alas, are the uncertainties of politics that Stanhope was moved on to another post and succeeded as Vice-President of the Council on Education by Sir Henry Holland, a much older man, a Tory of Tories, in whose mind Oscar Wilde would forever be Bunthorne, no matter what anyone said. And so the inspectorship went glimmering.

Let it go. Let it go. And good riddance. He would not accept an inspectorship now if they came to him on bended knee and begged him to accept, for at quarter to eleven Friday morning, June 5, the radiant fifth of June of this remarkable year, 1885, a date that would go down in history, his son was born.

8   THE BABY WAS A WONDERFUL BABY, AND THIS WAS NOT
merely Oscar's and Constance's opinion; it was the nurse's. Who
could be less prone to extravagant enthusiasms than a professional
nurse? But the nurse said frankly, "Mr. Wilde, you have a wonderful baby." She said it again and again. And then she whispered,
"The baby has a bridge to its nose." She looked frightened.

"All noses are bridged," Oscar said in a sharp voice to hide his
alarm.

"Yes," the nurse whispered again. "But not this early."

Oscar stared at her plain, large face. "What does it mean?" he
whispered, feeling frightened too. "It means," the nurse said slowly,
"that the baby is a genius."

The baby had a magnificent Wagnerian voice; its dramatic notes
were powerfully sustained. He sang most freely at first.

For the first few weeks the look in the baby's eyes had been
carefully noncommittal at best, at worst a look of distaste if not
indignation when Oscar came near. But then one morning Constance was occupied with something or other, the nurse was out of
the room, and the baby was asleep, and so nobody took him from
Oscar when he held him. After half an hour or perhaps even more,
the baby woke up and looked directly at Oscar. It was a penetrating
gaze—the gaze, after all, of a genius. The baby frowned. Oscar's
arms trembled slightly. He was afraid that the baby was going to
let out a Wagnerian protest at having been left unprotected for so
long in this man's arms. But instead the frown disappeared and the
baby smiled; that was when the new look came into his light-blue
eyes. "Hullo," he was saying. "You are my father." After that the
baby confined himself to two or three arias a day. Oscar knew, although of course he dared not say, that this was because the baby
now understood that Oscar was not a stranger but a close relation.

They named the baby Cyril.

Did he look like Constance or like Oscar or like both of them?
He had Constance's hair but otherwise looked only like himself,
a young genius. Life with him was extremely pleasant. Indeed, it
was delightful to have a genius in the house. To see a genius all
pink and plumply glowing, stripped naked for his bath, was a sight
for the gods.

And as the mother of the genius Constance was adorable; Oscar loved her more than ever. He urged marriage and families on all his unmarried friends. Only two things were required to make him utterly happy—a sister for Cyril and a larger income.

The sister would soon be provided; several months after Cyril's birth Constance was pregnant again. Of course the new baby would be a girl, because Oscar so profoundly wished it. She would be the enchanting girl who had died so many years ago, come back to life; the girl of the bright golden hair, the lilylike, white-as-snow girl, the girl of the poem, his little sister, and she would bear her name. Constance agreed: it was a lovely name—Isola.

A larger income was more difficult to achieve.

Oscar managed to squeak past the day of reckoning with tradesmen (not really a single day of reckoning, but several; when you had survived one, another was looming on the horizon) by dint of sundry desperate expedients. Two of these he felt to be particularly ignoble—cutting his lecture price from a minimum of ten pounds to five in an effort to bring in more engagements, and questioning tradesmen's accounts.

With adroit manipulation the latter tactic could stave off a crisis by as much as six weeks, although it was true that its efficacy deteriorated in strict proportion to the number of times it was brought into play. The cleverest move was not to question the cost of any single thing but *the thing itself*. You wrote in the margin of the statement of account, alongside the shrewdly selected thing (its proportions neither too large nor too small, and placed well back in time), "WHAT IS THIS?" The thing might be, for example, *5 lbs. best wht. sug.*, or *2 qts. mlt. vin.*, and say so plainly, but the tradesman's clerk would think that you had been unable to decipher his abbreviations, and after some days would return the statement with the *5 lbs. best wht. sug.* or *2 qts. mlt. vin.* duly and apologetically spelt out; thus, *five pounds best white sugar* or *two quarts malt vinegar;—very sorry, madam* (it would be taken for granted that Mrs. Wilde was doing the questioning).

You allowed five or six days to pass and then struck again, writing in the margin underneath the spelling out: *No; I understood what it was but I do not understand its being shown here since we have no record of its purchase and cook agrees with me in believing that it was wrongly charged to us.* (The longer this explanation and new challenge, the better; and it helped if the writing was not altogether but fairly illegible.) Faced with the damnable task of digging out from a busy shop's records proof of the purchase months ago of five pounds of sugar or two quarts of malt vinegar, the tradesman's clerk would not unnaturally push the beastly thing to one side, where it would rest in peace and quiet for another few weeks—perhaps even until the crisis had passed.

The new baby was another boy. A disappointment, but not for long; he was such a darling that no one could fail to love him, even though, on the basis of the nose-bridge test, he wasn't a genius. But it would be uncomfortable to have too many geniuses in the family. There was one problem—his name. It had been difficult enough to choose Cyril's; in his brother's case, Oscar seemed unable to get beyond Charles, John, Harold, Richard, and so on, which was absurd; you couldn't have a Cyril and a John or a Cyril and a Fred or a Cyril and a Sam; if you were a poet, if you were Oscar Wilde, you must have a Cyril and a—and a—well, and a something to equal Cyril or even surpass it, something beautiful, something rare. Cyril and—

Vyvyan.

Cyril and Vyvyan.

Four months after Vyvyan's birth, Oscar was working in his study one morning when Constance looked around the door. "Darling, a man is here from the greengrocer's with the cabbage and potatoes and other things for dinner."

"Cabbage?" Oscar said humorously; he was pleased with his work. "Not *cabbage*, my dear? The word is seldom mentioned in decent society. Royalty avoids it altogether."

"Cook has a way of preparing it so that it doesn't taste like cabbage. The man wants half a crown."

"Surely we have an account with the greengrocer?"

She looked apologetic. "He says he is sorry—he is a very *nice* man, Oscar—but he has been instructed not to leave the things unless he is paid."

"In that case he can take them back to the shop. He can also tell his employer that we are closing our account with him."

"Yes, dear, but I'm afraid we need the cabbage and the other things."

"We shall buy them at another greengrocer's."

"It's a very nice cabbage, and it seems a pity not to keep it since it's here. Also I don't know if another greengrocer will be open. They close early on Wednesdays."

"Is it Wednesday?"

She smiled. "Of course it is. Whatever have you been doing?"

"I have been— You shall hear what I have been doing. Listen." He read from his manuscript. " 'One afternoon I was sitting outside the Café de la Paix, watching the splendor and shabbiness of Parisian life and wondering over my vermouth at the strange panorama of pride and poverty that was passing before me, when I heard someone call my name. I looked around and saw Lord Murchison. We had not met since we had been at college together, nearly ten years before, so I was delighted to come across him again, and we shook hands warmly. At Oxford we had been great friends. I had liked him immensely——' "

But here Constance put her hand on his. "Darling, will you finish reading it to me in just a few minutes? I don't want to keep the greengrocer's man waiting, and if you agree that we should pay him the half crown—"

"Oh, very well then, pay him. But I shall write to them closing our account because of their impudence."

"Yes, dear," Constance said. There was a pause. He looked at her inquiringly.

"Aren't you going to pay him, then?"

"Could you give me the half crown, dear? There's nothing in my change purse and I don't have any banknotes."

"Yes, certainly." Oscar felt in his pockets and produced a sixpenny piece. His pocketbook was empty. Glancing through the desk drawers, he found two pennies and then a halfpenny. "Hold on a moment," he said, "there's some change in my other clothes in the dressing room," and he went upstairs and looked, at first sketchily; he distinctly remembered jamming a whole handful of silver into one of his pockets just the other day.

After a second and even a third thorough search, he was bound to admit that the handful of silver was no longer there; and not only had it gone, it seemed to have taken with it all the copper coins that ordinarily are such a nuisance in one's pockets.

There *must* be a banknote stuck away somewhere. With a zeal that would have done credit to the most conscientious of Her Majesty's inspectors of schools, Oscar now looked through the drawers of the bureau in the dressing room. Next he examined the drawers of Constance's small writing desk in the bedroom. Suddenly doubting the sincerity of his earlier efforts, he returned to the dressing room and conducted a fourth search through his clothes pockets. He recalled once, as a boy, having found a two-shilling piece in the tip of a boot, and so now he shook out all his shoes.

Feeling a little warm from his activities, he sat down for a few minutes; then he started up, remembering that the greengrocer's man was still waiting with his damn cabbages.

As was Constance. Her voice floated up the stairs. "Are you all right, dear?"

"Yes, of course." He now looked under the dressing-room bureau, the bedroom writing desk, and the bed itself. He went upstairs and looked under the bath. He thought, with a flash of real hope, of the cloakroom on the ground floor and hurried downstairs, past Constance's puzzled face. Here, surely would be his vanished handful of silver.

"Oscar?" Constance called.

"One moment."

He stood thinking. The smoking room. Swiftly and quietly, since he did not want Constance to inquire why he was going upstairs again, he climbed the flight of stairs to the smoking room and conducted an extraordinarily close hunt through divans and ottomans, under pillows, in ashtrays, humidors and cigarette boxes, and under the corners of the Persian rug.

He would write the greengrocer's man a check for half a crown (PAY TO THE ORDER OF Bloody greengrocer THE SUM OF Two shillings and sixpence. SIGNED Oscar Wilde). Oh, no, he would not, because he was overdrawn a hundred and fifty or a hundred and seventy-five, or was it two hundred pounds, at his bank and the manager had said not one more check, whatever the amount.

"Oscar?" Constance's voice came again. "Where are you?"

He left the smoking room, which appeared to have been struck by a sudden small hurricane, and joined her. "It's very odd, but I don't seem to be able to put my hands on a half crown, or two shillings for that matter—we have the sixpence, of course. Perhaps cook—"

"No," Constance said. "Cook has sixpence in her purse, or so she says, and she is an honorable woman. Never mind, I shall go next door."

He stared at her. "What?"

"I shall borrow the half crown from the lady next door; I only hope she's in. She's a lovely, gracious person, but the people on the other side——"

"Constance. How do you know?"

"Darling, this isn't the first time this has happened."

"Do you mean to say you've been in the habit of borrowing from the neighbors?"

"I wouldn't say 'in the habit,' dear, but more than once."

"I find this intolerable, Constance."

"Oh, good heavens, all neighbors do it. You mustn't think I mind. But that poor greengrocer's man—he has been waiting and waiting. Did I tell cook to give him a cup of tea, I wonder? I must ask her before going next door."

He caught her by the arm. "No. I refuse to have my wife borrowing."

"But, dear," she said reasonably, "if I don't have my housekeeping money and the bills aren't paid and there isn't a penny in the house, I'm afraid I must. Now, I shan't be more than a minute or two, and then you'll read the rest of your story to me, won't you?"

Fortunately the next morning brought a letter from Thomas Wemyss Reid.

Mr. Reid was the editor in chief of the great firm of Cassell's, publishers. The previous November, Mr. Reid wrote, Cassell's had put out the first issue of *Lady's World*, a monthly publication, price one shilling, for which he and Cassell's had entertained high hopes. These had not been realized quite so fully as might be wished. Mr. Reid wondered if Mr. Wilde, several of whose talks on subjects of interest to women he had heard, would care to examine the numbers of *Lady's World* so far published and give his opinion of them with a view toward reconstructing the magazine and then helping to edit it?

He would be glad, Oscar replied, to examine, most carefully, the copies of *Lady's World* and would then consider Mr. Reid's kind suggestion.

The copies of the magazine arrived; Oscar plunged into them. He sat down at Thomas Carlyle's desk to convey his thoughts to

Mr. Reid. First, he would like to say that after having read every page of the five numbers of *Lady's World* and devoted to them many hours of earnest thought, he would be happy to associate himself with Mr. Reid in the job of reconstructing and editing the magazine. Reconstruction was called for, certainly. As it was now, far too much space was given to illustrations, and in particular to illustrations of women's dress. He was very much aware, Oscar continued, of the importance of dress; he had written about it, he had lectured on it, as Mr. Reid knew; but in the field of women's publications, was not this more purely *feminine* and less *womanly* subject—dress styles, millinery, trimmings—quite adequately covered by the *Queen* and the *Lady's Pictorial,* and should not, therefore, *Lady's World* set itself apart from them by considering a wider range and dealing not primarily with woman's outer garments but with her inner self, how and what she *thinks* and *feels?*

Let *Lady's World* set for itself this high goal: to become the recognized mouthpiece for women's opinions on modern life and the arts. Let it set out to number among its contributors the most illustrious names and the most respected authorities.

Permit him to say, in closing, that it would be a pleasure and a privilege to edit *Lady's World.*

Mr. Reid thought Oscar's ideas were sound. April was now pretty well finished; no doubt Mr. Wilde would have various matters to clear up during May; would he care, then, to begin work for Cassell's, on a salary basis, on June first?

Oscar replied that he would prefer his salary to start from May first. He had spent many hours thinking about the magazine and proposed to devote all his time during May to writing and speaking to prominent and important people on its behalf. He was extremely enthusiastic and to put off full-scale operations until June would be an error; he felt certain Messrs. Cassell would not wish him to sustain any financial loss.

Very well; salary as of May first.

"I am to be the editor of a women's magazine," Oscar told Constance, "and I suppose there are people who would say that of all things it is the thing I am fittest for. But the greengrocer will be paid. No longer shall we spend our time searching upstairs and down for threepenny bits, we shall spend it writing charming letters to Lady Redingstoke and Lady Lotheringshire and Lady Glamishurst and the Hon. Gwendolyn Baldpate asking them to contribute to *Lady's World*, and then rewriting their articles in an effort to make them readable, for they will all accept, have no fear —all women love to be asked to write. And the greengrocer will be paid."

9

La Belle Sauvage
Ludgate Hill
London
14 July 1886

My dear Sarah Bernhardt,

I am now the editor (for my sins or my virtues?) of a monthly magazine published by Messrs. Cassell, called when it came to my attention *Lady's World*, a title which, suggesting as it did a chambermaid's journal (the frowsiest female is certain to call herself lady, whereas Lady Vere de Vere would faint to hear herself so described), I have had changed to *Woman's World*. And I have made other changes. When you so graciously received Constance and me in your dressing room after that forever memorable performance as Lady Macbeth (Constance is still in raptures over it), I can assure you that the farthest thing from my mind was that I should find myself involved in producing month after month a magazine for women; had I then known my fate, of course you would have been told, not only because I have always sensed in you since our very first meeting a kindly interest in my affairs, but because as an editor my clear duty would have been to carry away with me an agreement signed by you to write articles for the magazine. You would have signed it, my dear divinity, because you are the most generous, the most helpful, the most amiable of women, quite apart from being the most beautiful, *and because* I would have told you, as I am telling you now, that it would not in fact be necessary for you to write the articles at all—I would attend to that—you would merely sign them and receive payment for them at the rate of one guinea a page. Think how much bother this system saves!—does away with the tedious business of having to translate the articles from French into English, which is never really satisfactory in any event (unless your translator is a Baudelaire or an Oscar Wilde. I am writing this letter in English, which I shall then put into French).

And so we need merely select our subjects. My subscribers would be charmed, I know, to read "The History of My Loveliest Frock," by Sarah Bernhardt, and I should be charmed to write it—I think I can go so far as to say that you yourself will read it with lively interest and will learn much about your loveliest frock that you never knew before. Or would you prefer, to begin with, "How I Discovered America"? I really could do justice to that; I spoke in many of the cities in which you appeared on your American tour and should love to pay my respects to them in an enchanting French accent. Also to observe that Americans who say they come to France to finish their education are admitting that they are so unreasonable as to attempt to finish in a foreign land what they never had the courage to begin in their own. Pray do tell me that you think well of my proposal and give me permission to proceed.

Oscar

La Belle Sauvage
Ludgate Hill
London
4 March 1887

Dear Robert,

The address above is that of Messrs. Cassell and Co., surely one of the most charming addresses in London, and therefore quite misleading: it is not charming at all. Can any business office be charming? This one is quite horrid, if only because of such company rules as Thou Must Not Smoke and Thou Must Come To Work On Time. I am sure I should not know how to obey the second; in my opinion I have done very well indeed to arrive by eleven, considering that I am still unable to afford cabs and must come by underground railway from the Sloane Square station to Charing Cross and then walk to Fleet Street and Ludgate Hill; but the first rule seemed so ridiculous and impossible that I determined to try, telling myself that one makes up one's mind that one cannot, and one does not. Having proved this to my own satisfaction for a whole day, I then sensibly forgot it.

Even so I don't know how much longer I shall be able to continue with this nonsense, for it is nonsense, of course, as I knew when I agreed to "reconstruct" Messrs. Cassell's disgusting magazine *Lady's World* and edit the "reconstruction"; but various tradesmen had had the impudence to suggest that their bills were rendered not to provide scraps of paper for Cyril and Vyvyan to play with but to be paid, and I had no choice. The days of my first triumphs—persuading eminent people to write for the magazine, changing its title from *Lady's World* to *Woman's World* (a poor triumph, you say? not at all! I had to invent the most colossal lies to get it done: the Princess So and So, I said, had gone into a steady decline since learning that her name had been linked with *Lady's World*)—now seem ages ago, and everything is sheer drudgery. What would I not sacrifice for a new experience, even though I tell myself that there is nothing new under the sun—no "new experience," certainly. Have you found, as I have, that what are called *romantic experiences* simply don't exist? What do exist are romantic memories and a yearning for romance; no more. The most shattering, the most ecstatic, moment is only a shadow cast by an experience for which we long: a shadow, that is, that comes before the event rather than follows in its wake, as well-behaved shadows (your and my shadows on the pavement) do.

But that experience will never come. Nothing new under the sun, nothing new under the sun; *plus ça change, plus c'est la même chose*. Oh, I would die, surrender myself to the torture chamber, the rack, the wheel, for a new sensation! (And trust that to the last gasp of my breath I would remain the skeptic I believe myself to be.) Perhaps far away from that sun which is doomed never to shine on anything new there is a land of flowers that glisten like burnished coral and perfumes so rare and strange that to breathe them is to fall into a dream: a land where everything is perfect and deadly—where new sensations wait for us in the python coils of velvet shadows.

You may be led to think that I have been brooding over the death of Little Nell, to talk in this desperate way, but I have not —I have merely been editing the effusions of gifted women writers and thinking of graceful ways to return those manuscripts that are beyond saving, for to decline a story or poem without a charming lie is to lose a reader. The other day a perfectly tremendous (in point of size) poem arrived with the author's request for my candid opinion, and I am afraid that in replying I did not strictly observe this rule. I myself have always felt (I said) that there is much to be learned from the candid opinions of others, provided of course that they are complimentary, but in the case of your poem, herewith enclosed, I think it is unnecessary to go beyond saying that it was very naughty of you to rhyme "dawn" with "gone."

Did I ever thank you properly, Robert, for dedicating *your* poems to me? I am very proud of the dedication, and in my study the book always lies open at that page: To Oscar Wilde, Poet and Friend, Affectionately and Admiringly Dedicated; and as my eye falls on it I think of you and remember our moonlit wanderings and wish that you were here with me, my very dear friend whom I love—no, not here in this office: your bright hair would become tarnished and your smile would wither in an atmosphere so brutally commercial—but strolling with me in this gray city and transmuting its mists to showers of gold in the mirror of your friendship. A mirror fashioned so perfectly can never be dulled. True friendship is the ideal; it will survive, above treachery, above disloyalty, above everything mean and petty and base, when the little gods worshiped by little men are gone forever.

Oscar

PART 3

THE SLIM GILT SOUL

1

HE IMAGINED PUTTING IT TO CONSTANCE.

"I have been engaging in what are known as familiarities, with a young man, my dear, and I find that anything else bores me. The young man is our friend Tommy Milton. He is charming and sweet and thoughtful, as you know, and as you also know he adores me. I can have my way with Tommy, I can do with him as I please, he will grant me any favor I care to ask. But none of this was necessary, for it was not I who fell in love with Tommy, it was Tommy who fell in love with me.

"Tommy was the seducer, Tommy was Eve with the apple. I can't say I was very hungry, but I was bored, I was bored to death with my job, and I am afraid I had become only too well accustomed to you, dearest Constance. And I was curious. It can be said, I suppose, though it seems odd to think so now, that I fell into Tommy's net through boredom, curiosity, and conversation. Tommy is the most marvelous audience—of course you know that —but he isn't passive; he talks too, just enough to lead you on, if he wishes to lead you. I found myself talking, with Tommy, about the nature of love, the strange complexions love could wear, the different guises in which it had manifested itself in times past. 'And times present,' said Tommy. 'Greece lives today, in the hearts of the young and the beautiful and the strong and the un-afraid.' Frankly, between you and me, my dear Constance, very ordinary stuff; Tommy is not a poet. But it served its purpose, for when Tommy looked at me out of that sweet, that adorably child-ish, face of his and said he loved me and wished to be mine, and I must not refuse him or I would break his heart—well, really, could I, who had talked so much and so beautifully about love, and had protested my perfect willingness to undergo the most damnable torments if they were the price of a new sensation—could I, so brave, so willing, now stammer some sort of apology and run away? And besides—good heavens, I didn't *want* to break Tommy's heart."

He had been married for five years. The fact that to Constance (and to the millions like her) the scenes suggested by such an ac-count would seem evil and monstrous and mad was not the least of their attractions. At first, indeed, the knowledge that these embraces, these kisses, would be considered terribly wicked was for Oscar their only saving grace, for, physically speaking, they had struck him as ridiculous. But the sight of a rather large man of thirty-two and a youth of nineteen or twenty fumbling and grappling on a couch would so horrify a respectable British subject that he would turn pale and bolt from the room, and his lady, who provided him with short and murky ecstasies, and perhaps even at great intervals shared them, would faint clean away and never be quite herself again the rest of her life. This was a far, far cry from the vision of laughing boys and proud, passionate men on the golden sands of Greece; this was sniffling, clammy, stiff-collared, tight-trousered, horse-droppings-on-the-pavements London; but it *was* wicked, it *would* cause the whole of Messrs. Cassell's to go up in blue smoke, and what a pleasure it was to think of that.

Oscar had at first resolved to avoid further episodes, for the physical reward had seemed to him highly dubious, feebler even than that granted after five years by the marriage bed, and won at the pain of seeming to oneself downright grotesque. But then Tommy had called at Tite Street (Tommy's social credentials were the very best; his mother was a baronet's daughter, his father an Oxford don, and he himself had just gone up to Oxford, where in fact Oscar had met him through a mutual friend).

He had won Constance immediately. Oscar, at first irritated, even alarmed—for it would never have occurred to him, after the turn their friendship had taken, to ask Tommy to his home—was soon won over too. Tommy's behavior was irreproachable. He was an enormous hit with the children. Indeed Tommy was altogether to be admired. And there was the delightful sense of a secret shared with Tommy, an excitement simply in looking at him, as he so charmingly drank his tea. He must come again.

The second time the whole thing had seemed not quite so absurd to Oscar. Tommy was sweet. It was pleasant afterward to walk down Piccadilly with him (he had rooms in town overlooking Green Park) and think of the crass and ignorant world hurrying by. Another episode took place. It seemed pretty clear now that it was an acquired taste. Oscar discussed the point with Tommy. For some people, Tommy said. For himself, he had never known any other, had never lost the love he had first felt as a boy for boy sweethearts. He really could not think of having *intimacies* (the word made him shudder, and he pulled a delightfully droll face) with women, though he loved them, in a way—loved Constance, adored her, loved to touch her hand, she had such beautiful skin, and such wonderful eyes—he did hope she liked him, a little? Oscar assured him that she did, she did indeed, oh immensely, and Tommy gave a chuckle and clapped his hands together, for all the world like a little boy. On his next visit Oscar brought him a gift, a silver cigarette case, with "Tommy from Oscar" engraved inside.

The office clock pointed to four. "Ah," Oscar murmured. "Is there anything else today, my dear Arthur? That is, anything that absolutely refuses to be put off until tomorrow?"

Arthur Fish, the assistant editor, said he did not think so. "You will be in tomorrow, then, Mr. Wilde?"

"Good heavens, no, how foolish of me! I should have said, 'Anything that can't be put off until the day after tomorrow?'"

"You might glance at this proof."

"Certainly." Oscar glanced at it. "There. Dear me, I am quite exhausted. Don't you find the ceaseless whirl and struggle of the editorial life very wearing, Arthur?"

"It has been much less wearing, Mr. Wilde, if I may say so, since I've been working with you."

"How charming of you to tell me that. For my part, I can tell you in return that your cheerful face and extraordinary good humor, unruffled by the most savage female poet, will always cause me to remember this curious episode in my life, which otherwise I should have forgotten as soon as possible. Good afternoon." Oscar put on his hat, adjusted the flower in his buttonhole, and left the office.

In the adjoining corridor he ran into Mr. Gow, an important, heavy officer of the firm. "Oh, Wilde, I was on the point of coming in for a word with you. Can you spare a few minutes?"

"Alas, no."

"No?"

"Quite impossible. I am on my way to see Madame Carpathia Escuriol, who is, as of course you know, lady-in-waiting to Her Majesty the Queen of Romania. If I play my cards properly, as I am prepared to do if Madame Escuriol does not regard a friendly chat and cup of tea as only the prelude to more intimate dealings, which, frankly, are out of the question—Madame Escuriol has a moustache—I think I can promise you an article for *Woman's World* signed by Her Majesty. But above all things I mustn't be late, and my appointment is for half past four, sharp. Good afternoon."

Someone hailed him on the street.

"Hullo, Oscar. I say, how well you're looking."

"It is beyond my comprehension if I am, my dear fellow; the hours of this job are shocking—into the office anywhere from three to half past and quite unable to break away until four. And three afternoons a week! It used to be five, mind you, but the pace was more than human flesh could bear, and the year before last I knocked off one of the afternoons and last year another. Had to; I was wearing away to a shadow. You are about to say that I seem to you to have put on weight? Pure illusion. But I must be off; Madame Chelazion, confidential secretary to His Serene Majesty the Shah of Persia, is waiting to have tea with me at the Café Royal—if I am fortunate enough I shall succeed in persuading her to write an article for us giving the secret of His Majesty's hair dye, which is the envy of all the crowned heads of Europe. Good afternoon."

And he got into a cab. "The Café Royal, please, in Regent Street." Of course he could not afford the cab, but it made such a dashing exit. For that matter he could equally not afford the Café Royal; but perhaps Madame Chelazion *was* waiting somewhere or other in that splendid place, if there were a Madame Chelazion, and it would be a shame to miss her.

Three or four friends were waiting for him; one was Sherard, who had moved to London, and an hour passed quickly. "Someone over there keeps looking at you, Oscar," the young man remarked. "Do you know him?"

Oscar peered, and felt a mild shock. "Ah yes, of course; it is Ronald Leeward, the novelist. A great pity about him—he has been dead for some years."

"I don't think I know his work," Sherard murmured. "Dead artistically speaking, you mean?"

"Nothing of the sort; I mean physically."

"He's getting up," Sherard said. "Oscar, I believe he's coming over here."

"Extremely limber for a corpse; one has to grant him that."

It was Mr. Gow. "Well, Mr. Wilde! Which of these gentlemen is Madame Escuriol? You said she had a moustache, to be sure. Will you stop by my office in the morning?"

"Do sit down, Mr. Gow," Oscar said cordially. "Do you know that I would never have given you credit for being able to make a humorous remark? I refer, of course, to your asking me to come to your office in the morning."

"I was not endeavoring to be humorous, sir."

"I know; that is your charm—it is all done without effort, quite naturally, whereas I have to plan my effects with the aid of an attribute called intelligence. You see, Mr. Gow, tomorrow is Thursday, and one rule I scrupulously observe, despite the feeling of unease it gives me to observe any rule, is never to come to Messrs. Cassell's offices on Thursdays. Mondays, Wednesdays, and Fridays are my days; hours, half past three to four. Of course if you insist on the morning you could write to me; the letter should reach me well before lunch. The only difficulty is that some time ago I gave up reading letters from Messrs. Cassell. I dare say you won't believe me, but I have known charming young men who have come to London with the most glowing prospects and in a few weeks have been reduced to a state of mumbling idiocy all through the insidious habit of reading and answering business letters."

Mr. Gow had gone.

"A tiresome man," Oscar murmured. "I am delighted to think I shan't be seeing him again."

"You'll have to eventually, won't you?" Sherard asked.

"No. Not at any rate at Cassell's. I decided a few minutes ago that I have had quite enough of it. I have been working there far, far too long—for years, think of it—and work, after all, is the curse of the drinking class. Now I suppose I should really hurry home to bring this happy news to Constance."

It was only fitting for the new ex-editor of *Woman's World* to celebrate his release from the harsh bonds of office discipline by taking a cab home, but first he stopped at a toy shop. A small, elderly man came forward. He looked friendly and encouraging.

"Is it true," Oscar asked, "that the dolls and other toys talk among themselves at night when the toy shops are closed?"

"I can answer, of course, sir," the man said cautiously, "solely for our shop; the case may very well be different with others. No, I have never heard our dolls talking, though I have often stayed on late at night—the atmosphere is so pleasant. They merely *whisper*."

"I see. But your whispering dolls would no longer whisper, I dare say, if transported to a strange playroom?"

"Hard to say, sir, hard to say. Dolls are difficult creatures, rather like opera singers in temperament. Toy soldiers far more dependable—there is little imagination in the military mind and therefore they are not so sensitive to a change of surroundings."

Oscar nodded. "Quite so. May I taste a few?"

"But of course, sir. Coldstream Guards, Welsh Fusiliers, Heavy Dragoons?"

"Have you Light Dragoons? I must confess my taste for Heavy Dragoons was irremediably tainted by the song about them in *Patience*."

"Light Dragoons, certainly." The other produced a box of brightly painted cavalrymen mounted on handsome black chargers and politely extended it to Oscar, who selected one and tasted it with the tip of his tongue.

"They are for my older boy," he explained, "and although he would scorn to put a Light Dragoon in his mouth, his brother has not yet reached the age of discretion and is bound to sample these the first moment he can get at them. Yes, they will do nicely. Will you wrap them, please? Oh, one moment, I forgot to taste the colonel. This is he, I assume?"

"That is the major, sir. Here is the colonel."

"Of course; his expression is unmistakably vacuous." Oscar tasted the colonel. "Rather tart; a touch of liver, no doubt. I must instruct Vyvyan to avoid him. Now I should like a golliwog and a teddy bear."

"For the younger boy, sir? May I suggest this hippopotamus? He has just come in."

"An excellent suggestion," Oscar said warmly. "He bears a pronounced resemblance to somebody or other I know—yes, I have it. Not so much from the front as from the rear aspect. I shall have two of them, please, one to take with me, the other to be sent prettily wrapped with my compliments to Mr. Gow, Messrs. Cassell, La Belle Sauvage, Ludgate Hill." After paying and thanking the man, Oscar went outside to hail a cab, which of course the soldiers and hippopotamus had made a necessity.

Cyril and Vyvyan were waiting for him in the day nursery. The question was, what sort of entrance to make. Oscar decided to enter with simple dignity, upright, rather than on hands and knees or backwards; but first he sang a duet between a cow and a rooster outside the door as a concession to Vyvyan, who preferred elaborate comings-in.

Vyvyan was just over three and Cyril four and a half. As is frequently true of affluent relatives, they got along fairly well except when a question came up concerning their joint holdings. There had been no trouble here in Vyvyan's younger days, when he hadn't had a penny to his name and was happily unconscious of his poverty; but his wealth quickly increased with his gathering years and he was now almost as comfortably situated as his brother, with whom he shared the control of certain large investments.

One was a bull's-eye lantern. The bull's-eye lantern could be made to throw forth a powerful red light or white light or green light. Vyvyan had expressed an interest in the lantern at the first moment of seeing it and after strongly repeating this had been given joint control, over Cyril's protests. What annoyed Vyvyan was that joint control narrowed down to his being allowed to have the bull's-eye lantern flashed on him when he was the steam engine of the train of which Cyril was the conductor, who also operated the signal lights; but when Cyril became the engine and Vyvyan the conductor, the lantern was fastened on the front of the engine and the conductor had to signal in shouts.

Another annoying fact of life was that Cyril could eat licorice without getting sick and Vyvyan could not. The cash controlled by the brothers was usually put into licorice because Cyril was the purchasing agent. It was not true, Oscar had explained, that Cyril's curly hair had anything to do with his being able to safely eat licorice; Cyril's hair simply happened to be curly and Vyvyan's didn't. Curly hair had no special advantage over straight hair; it was not stronger and did not affect one's insides. Oscar also had made clear that for himself straight hair was quite as admirable as curly—he had no preference. Just as he had no preference, he had said in a slow, important voice, between the owners of the straight and curly hair. He loved them both very much, equally, so that it was impossible for him to think of Cyril or Vyvyan but only of Cyril-Vyvyan, or just as often, Vyvyan-Cyril.

But Oscar did have a favorite and the favorite was Cyril, and he strove constantly to hide the fact from Vyvyan's alert and fiercely vulnerable eyes. Oscar could not help himself; Cyril was such a handsome child, with his wavy hair and beautiful strong body. And his quickness, his grace. Vyvyan was attractive enough, but he would always be in his brother's shadow. Also, it was Cyril who, simply because he came first, had first given Oscar the delight of watching a baby discover its fingers, its toes, its feet, its entire important self, and learn how to roll and wriggle and crawl and finally stand up like an amiable drunk holding on to the handiest fence (the latticework gate at the top of the stairs) and trying to eat it at the same time; when Vyvyan maneuvered himself through the same enchanting stages, they were familiar, the keenest edge of their delight was gone.

Finally, Vyvyan was a boy, disappointing Oscar's hopes. Would there ever be a sister, another Isola? He did not think so. He did not think so.

But he did love Vyvyan; he did. Vyvyan no less than Cyril would be cherished and guarded, would want for nothing, just as so far in their lives both boys had known no want—look at all their beautiful toys. Oscar would provide. No more importunate greengrocers, no balky butchers. He had left his job, the regular income would stop, but this had been no heedless act. Never in his life had he felt more confidence in himself. Not all the excellent hours he had not spent in the Cassell office (any hour not spent in an office is excellent) had been given to delightful company; many—well, a *good* many—had been spent in silence and hard work at Thomas Carlyle's desk; and more ideas, lovely audacious ideas, were only waiting to be released. The money would be there for the boys' future.

In the nursery the two boys swarmed at his knees. Presently the temptation was too great and Oscar got down on the floor and was ridden. Everyone carefully pretended not to notice the presents because it was good manners. Finally Cyril said, "What is this?" frowning at the packages as if they had suddenly and rather rudely appeared. Vyvyan got off Oscar's neck and frowned at them too, suspiciously. And he *was* suspicious, Oscar knew, that the larger present would be for Cyril, or if it weren't, that somehow Cyril's would be better; and Oscar was pierced with doubts about the hippopotamus. He had been carried away by its aft resemblance to the ponderous Gow, but this could mean nothing to Vyvyan; would the hippo not seem a poor thing compared to the Light Dragoons?

"I must ask you to excuse me for these packages," he said swiftly. "I brought them in by mistake. You see, there is another to go with them, but it will not be ready until tomorrow. Would you mind waiting until then to open these?" He would bring home more dragoons, for Vyvyan, and the hippo could be declared a sort of general present for the nursery.

Cyril said he would not mind. Vyvyan said so too, more loudly.

"You are so polite," Oscar said, "I feel obliged to respond. I did not *intend*, and promised *not*, to tell you the story of an acquaintance of mine, a rather remarkable rocket, until you were older, because it is a very affecting story and has been known to reduce powerful men to tears, but I shall, in the hope that it may be of interest, if you wish me to."

"What is a rocket?" Cyril asked.

"What is a rocket?" Vyvyan asked.

"It is a round thing with a point, painted red, and tied to a stick. I mean the whole rocket is painted red, not just the point. When a match is applied to it the rocket makes a fizzing noise and rushes into the sky. Of course you haven't had occasion to learn 'The Star Spangled Banner,' which is the 'God Save the Queen' of the United States of America, but rockets appear in it. 'And the rockets' red glare,' the song says, 'and bombs bursting in air.' I dare say they were ancestors of the rocket I knew. Do you wish to hear about him?"

Cyril and Vyvyan would.

"It may take a little time. You aren't sleepy?"

They were not.

"Very well. The story of the remarkable rocket begins, as all good stories should begin, with a handsome Prince and a beautiful Princess who fell in love and were going to be married so that they could live happily ever after. Great celebrations were planned for the night of the marriage—a Court ball, where the Prince and the Princess would dance the rose dance together and the Prince's father, the King, would play the flute, which he played very badly, but no one had ever dared to tell him so, and then a wonderful display of fireworks. The fireworks were in the Royal Gardens waiting to be let off and of course were passing the time in intelligent conversation, for some of them were highly intelligent—a Roman Candle and a Catherine Wheel and a Fire Balloon and several Firecrackers.

"The Roman Candle had just made a very deep remark, which unfortunately I can't remember, when they heard someone cough. Everyone looked around and saw a tall red Rocket, with a sharp nose and a very haughty, superior sort of manner. He coughed again and cleared his throat. 'Ahem! How fortunate it is for the Prince,' he observed, 'that he is to be married on the very day on which I am to be let off. Really, if it had been arranged beforehand it could not have turned out better for him. But Princes are always lucky.'

" 'Sir, you are mistaken,' said the Roman Candle. 'It is quite the other way around.'

" 'Oh, how I hate rudeness and bad manners,' the Rocket cried, "such as have been displayed just now. I am an extremely sensitive person. No one in the whole world is so sensitive, I am sure.'

" 'What is an extremely sensitive person?' whispered the smallest Firecracker to the Roman Candle.

" 'Someone who, because he has corns on his toes, always steps on other people's toes,' the Roman Candle answered, and the little Firecracker almost exploded with laughter, which annoyed the Rocket. 'Why are you laughing?' he demanded. 'I am not laughing. It is obvious that you are a very selfish individual, for you must be thinking of something else when you should be thinking of me. I am always thinking about myself and I expect everybody to do the same. That is what is called sympathy. It is a beautiful virtue and I possess it in a high degree. Suppose, for instance, an accident happened to me tonight, what a misfortune that would be for everyone. The Prince and Princess could never live happily ever after. Really, when I reflect on the importance of my position, I am almost moved to tears.'

" 'If you want to give pleasure to others,' the Roman Candle advised him, 'you had better not weep. You had better keep yourself dry, or you won't go off when they light you."

" 'I shall weep if I choose,' snapped the Rocket, and he made a tremendous effort and screwed up his eyes and actually burst into real tears, which flowed down his stick like raindrops and nearly drowned two little beetles who were thinking of setting up house together and looking for a nice dry spot to live in.

"Ten o'clock struck and then eleven and then twelve, and at the last stroke of midnight the fireworks were set off by the Royal Fireworks Lighter. Whizz, whizz! went the Catherine Wheel, and

Boom, boom! went the Roman Candle, and Bang, bang, bang! went the Firecrackers, and the Fire Balloon soared up toward the stars, and in short everyone was a great success except the Remarkable Rocket. His tears had soaked him through and through. He was so wet that he would not go off at all. 'Ah, hah!' he said to himself as the Royal Fireworks Lighter marched away. 'I see! They are reserving me for some occasion even grander than the marriage of the Prince!'

"The next day the groundskeeper came with his men to make everything tidy. 'Ah, hah!' the Rocket said to himself. 'This is evidently a special delegation. I will receive them with the proper dignity,' and he put his nose in the air higher than ever. But this did not impress the groundskeeper, who simply said, 'Here's a bad rocket,' and threw him over the wall into the ditch.

" 'Bad rocket? Bad rocket?' said the Remarkable Rocket as he whirled through the air. 'Impossible! That man really said *grand* rocket, because they sound very much the same and indeed often are the same,' and he fell into the mud in the ditch. 'Evidently a fashionable watering place,' he observed, 'where I have been sent to repair my health.'

"A little frog with bright jeweled eyes and a mottled coat swam up to him. 'A new arrival, I see,' said the frog. 'Well, there is nothing like mud. It makes the world go round, they say. Do you think we will have a nice wet afternoon, sir?'

" 'Ahem, ahem,' said the Rocket, and he began to cough. 'What a beautiful croak you have, sir!' the little frog cried. 'Perhaps you would like to join our glee club? You will hear us this evening. Well, good-bye, I have enjoyed our conversation,' and he swam away. 'A very stupid person,' the Rocket said to himself. 'How I despise people who only talk about themselves when they should be listening to me talk about me.'

"Then a large white duck swam up and examined him. 'What a curious shape you have!' she said. 'May I ask if you were born like that or is it the result of an accident?' The Remarkable Rocket was made so indignant by this that he couldn't reply. 'You poor thing!' said the kindly duck. 'Deaf and dumb too, eh? Never mind, later on I shall bring you a few delicious worms with a garnish of tender water-lily roots,' and she swam off.

" 'I am glad she has gone,' the Rocket said to himself. 'Hopelessly ignorant,' and he sank deeper into the mud and began to think about his glorious position in life when two little boys came running down the bank with a kettle and some scraps of wood.

" 'Oh, look here,' cried one of the boys. 'Look at this old stick,' and he picked the Rocket out of the ditch.

" 'OLD STICK!' the Rocket said to himself. 'Impossible! GOLD STICK, that is what he said. Gold Stick is very complimentary. He mistakes me for one of the Court dignitaries. But who knows? That in fact is what I may be.'

" 'Let us put it into the fire,' said the other boy. 'It will help to boil the kettle.' And so they piled the scraps of wood together and put the Rocket on top and lit the fire.

" 'This is magnificent!' cried the Rocket. 'They are going to let me off in broad daylight, so that everyone can see me.'

"The boys went away to look for more wood but became interested in other things, as boys sometimes do, and forgot about their fire and their kettle. The fire burned on and the Rocket waited impatiently to feel himself go off; but he was very damp and took a long time to burn. At last, however, the fire caught hold of him. 'Now I am going off!' he cried. 'I shall go much higher than the moon, much higher than the stars, much higher than the sun itself. In fact, I shall go so high that——'

"Fizz, fizz, fizz!—and he went straight up into the air.

" 'Delightful,' he cried. 'I shall go on like this forever. Oh, what a success I am!'

"But nobody saw him. Nobody, nobody at all.

"Then he began to feel a curious tingling sensation. 'Now I am going to explode,' he cried. 'There is no doubt about it. I feel it in my bones. I shall make such a noise that nobody will talk about anything else until the end of the world!'

"And then he certainly did explode. BANG! Oh, it was a grand noise. But nobody heard. Nobody, nobody at all.

"All that was left of the Remarkable Rocket was the stick. The stick came tumbling down out of the sky and fell on the back of a goose who was taking a walk by the side of the ditch.

" 'Good heavens,' cried the goose. 'Apparently it is going to rain sticks,' and she rushed into the water. And the stick floated off her back and went drifting away to goodness knows where, and that was the very end of the Remarkable Rocket."

Cyril was still awake. "I liked the kindly duck best," he said. Vyvyan had fallen asleep but became half awake or perhaps a little more when the rocket went off with the bang, and hearing Cyril's remark about the kindly duck, said he did not remember that part, and so Oscar told it again.

"I shall have to go downstairs now," he said regretfully. "I believe some people are coming to dinner and I must get ready."

"Are they your friends or Mama's?" Cyril asked.

"Both our friends. Why?"

"I like your friends better than hers." Vyvyan did too, before he fell firmly asleep. Oscar carried him to bed and then came back to Cyril.

"I didn't know there was any difference between Mama's friends and mine. No, that is not what I meant to say. Mama's friends and my friends are the same. They are our friends *together*. Anyone who comes to call on us is her friend and my friend *too*."

"No, Papa," Cyril said, "because your friends don't call when Mama's friends are here and her friends don't when yours are."

"Yes, I suppose that is true, but it isn't true of all our friends. Mama and I know very well that some of our friends would not get along well together because they have different tastes. Some of Mama's relations, not the closest relations but the kind of relations you call relations by marriage, are Scotch and very strict. I don't mean that all Scotch people are very strict, because they aren't, but these relations by marriage are and they would be deeply hurt and offended if they were here at the same time in the same room with people who drank a glass of wine and smoked a cigarette. And so we keep them apart. It is really quite simple, you see."

"There are your friends and Mama's friends and they aren't the same. I like yours better because they are nicer."

"They are just as much Mama's friends as they are mine. Everything that Mama and I have is ours together, you and Vyvyan, and this house, and our friends—everything. You will always remember that, won't you?"

Cyril said, "Yes, I always will," and Oscar started to leave. He turned. "How are my friends nicer?"

"They are jollier and they laugh more."

"Oh?"

"Oh, yes. The one I like the very most is the one who is like—" Cyril thought for a moment. "He is like a lady," he said, smiling.

"Really?" Oscar said. "Which one is that?"

"*You* know, Papa."

"I'm afraid I don't," Oscar lied. Did *she* know?

"He is as nice as a lady," Cyril explained.

"Oh, he isn't *like* a lady, he is as *nice as* a lady?"

"As nice as a pretty lady, because the old ugly ladies aren't nice at all, and their mouths smell when they kiss me." Cyril suddenly said, "I suppose you dream, don't you, Papa?"

"Of course. I should not consider myself to be a gentleman if I didn't. Gentlemen are always polite, gentlemen are always kind and helpful, gentlemen are always careful that their clothes are tidy and their hair is well brushed, and gentlemen always dream. It is one of their most sacred duties."

"Well, then, what sort of dreams do you have?"

"Oh, magnificent dreams," Oscar said enthusiastically. "I dream of flower-starred hills in April, and cloudy galleons sailing in the blue sky, and dragons with eyes as big as plates and tails like golden pitchforks, and violet-gleaming butterflies, and the blue mist creeping around the enchanted hills of Avalon, and gardens where nightingales always sing and the new moon floats above the blossoms of the orange trees so close that I can cool my hands upon its silver sides, and—lots and lots of things like that. Do you dream too?"

"Yes," Cyril said. "About pigs, mostly. Don't you ever dream about them?"

"It is possible that I once dreamt of a flying pig."

"Mine aren't like that. They are just ordinary pigs." Cyril yawned. "I'm not sleepy," he quickly said.

"We have had a nice long chat and I really think it is time you went to bed. Besides, I have to go down and dress."

"Oh, very well." Cyril got up and put his arms around Oscar's neck. "Good night, Papa."

"Good night," Oscar said, kissing him tenderly, "my dearest boy."

Constance was arranging her hair as he came into the bedroom, her white arms curved as gracefully as a sleeping child's. It seemed to Oscar that she had changed hardly at all since the night in the flower-filled bedroom in Paris when he had first seen her beautiful naked body and kissed the roses on her breasts.

"I forgot to mention this when I came home," he remarked,

"but then, it is a matter of the smallest possible importance—"

"That means, I know," she said, smiling, "that it is of the very greatest importance."

"When I tell you, you will admit that you are quite wrong. Of the very greatest importance is who is dining with us tonight. The conversation I was having with Cyril has driven their names out of my mind. That of course is only to be expected of conversations that are very, very serious."

"What were you talking about?" she asked quickly. "There is nothing wrong? If there is anything wrong you must not keep it from me out of kindness."

"We were discussing pigs. Cyril dreams of pigs; I do not. Is this significant? I admit I don't know. Can you throw any light on it, my dear? Do you dream of pigs? It is a long time since you told me about your dreams."

Her hands resumed their delicate work, and she smiled again. "It is a long time since you last asked me. My dreams are usually of a garden. We are having four for dinner. There is Miss Chert——"

"A young woman whose profile was decided by unfortunate circumstances over which she had no control. That isn't mine, it is George Eliot's, in *Daniel Deronda*, but it deserves to be mine."

"You must admit she has beautiful eyes, Oscar."

"Do you know that that is the most damning thing one woman can say of another? It means there is absolutely nothing else worth mentioning, which is why she can afford to say it."

"Oh dear, does it? I must be careful never to say it again. Then, the Fosters are coming——"

Oscar had begun to change his clothes. He stopped and demanded, "Why?"

"You needn't pretend you don't know. They are coming because we agreed they had to come. They were very kind to us and we've put off and put off having them."

"Miss Chert and the Fosters," he said. "We shall perish."

"No, we shan't," Constance said, "because Tommy Milton is the fourth."

Oscar started to dress again. "Thank heavens for that."

"You really had forgotten Tommy was coming?"

"Completely."

"Then you *must* be pleasantly surprised."

He glanced at her. Her face was as innocent as her tone.

"He's such fun," she went on. "I'm so glad you met him and made friends; I really don't know what I'd do without Tommy on a night like tonight. There has to be somebody to take Miss Chert in to dinner and listen to her."

"Poor Tommy."

"He doesn't seem to mind, that's the most wonderful thing about him. I don't think he *does* mind, Oscar, he has such a sweet nature. And then of course he worships you."

"Oh, go on."

"Yes, he does, I can tell. A woman is conscious of these things, when a man may be blind to them." She finished her hair. "What was the matter of the very smallest possible importance you were going to tell me about?"

"I'm resigning my position at Cassell's."

"*Oscar.*"

"You must not look sad. If you knew everything, you would be delighted. I suffered so much from the boredom, the intellectual vacuum, that at times I felt I—let me see—that I was condemned to an eternity of Fosters and Miss Cherts and must do something desperate or expire." He went to her and put his hands on her bare shoulders. "My dearest, I'm not proposing to resume our miserable maneuvers with the tradesmen, to have you ask the lady next door for another half crown—I shall never forget that half crown. The fact is that I know I can afford to leave Cassell's."

"I must go up to the children."

"Do you think I could ever do anything that would mean they were to suffer?"

"No," Constance said. She looked up at him over her shoulder, and then she smiled, slowly and uncertainly. There was a glint of tears in her eyes.

"My darling," he said. He bent his head to hers. "Do you think I could ever hurt you?" She moved her head a little and he felt her lips against his cheek. He said softly,

"And when wind and winter harden, All the loveless land, It will whisper of the garden, You will understand."

His eyes were damp. "Your eyebrows are like larks' wings," he murmured, and kissed her lips. "My darling, I love you."

"Do you still, Oscar?"

"Have you had reason to doubt it?"

She nodded.

He drew his head back and looked at her wet eyes. "What reason?" he asked.

She looked away.

"Can't you tell me?"

"No."

"If you can't tell me, what am I to think? Must I think that it is something you find unmentionable?"

"Oh, dear," she whispered. "Oh, dear, oh, dear." Her damp skin was pink.

"Is it because I haven't been with you for so long, my darling?"

She could neither speak nor nod.

"I love to see you blush. You are again my chaste Constance who again must be made wanton. Do you think I haven't been with you because I ceased to love you? No, no. The work I was doing, the intellectual humiliations I was suffering, made me like a stranger to myself. Now that is over. I told you you would be delighted if you knew! Am I immodest, my darling? Of course I am. Because you love me. Because we shall be with each other tonight."

A most becoming, pale tinge remained in Constance's skin throughout the evening. She smiled at him often. He was anxious for their guests to be gone. Even Tommy, most of all Tommy. And at last they left, Tommy with a final backward glance that only Oscar could read: "You are very strange tonight."

Upstairs he opened the bedroom door and she cried out in amazement at the flowers and clutched his arm.

"Ah, ha," he said. "Shall I tell you the secret of this magic? Just before dinner I left with great stealth by the back way, aided by cook, and hurried to Sloane Square and ransacked the vendors' stalls and returned groaning under the delicious weight of masses and masses of flowers and smuggled them upstairs and hid them in my dressing room; and later, when you were safely downstairs, I crept up again and arranged them as you see, because I wished to whisper to you through their fragrance all night long of the garden that will always be ours, and of Paris. We are as we were then, my darling. Everything is as it was then."

He succeeded, almost, in persuading himself. But the flesh soon grew weary and in the end it was a performance. When he was sure she was asleep, he sighed.

Ideas for new work now came tumbling over one another, ideas so audacious, so challenging, that they refused to be set aside in favor of immediate pleasures but called Oscar to Thomas Carlyle's desk and kept him there for hour after hour. He owed these stories and essays to Tommy (Oscar thought of himself as deeply attached to but certainly not in love with Tommy). In grateful tribute Oscar drew an idealized picture of him in a story called "The Portrait of Mr. W. H.":

"It was a full-length portrait of a young man in late-sixteenth-century costume, standing by a table, with his right hand resting on an open book. He seemed about seventeen years of age and was of quite extraordinary personal beauty, though evidently somewhat effeminate. Indeed, had it not been for the dress and the closely cropped hair, one would have said that the face, with its dreamy, wistful eyes and its delicate scarlet lips, was the face of a girl."

In this new atmosphere Oscar began to look again at incidents that he had merely used as anecdotes. One afternoon, six years before, Basil Ward had been painting a most handsome young man; he was like a young god, so proudly, beautifully young. Looking at the finished canvas, Oscar had been moved to remark on how tragic it was that such a magnificent creature should ever grow old. Basil had said, "It *is* a tragedy, isn't it? How wonderful it would be if he could stay as he is now, while my portrait of him grew raddled and bent and hideous in his stead."

Here was the beginning of *The Picture of Dorian Gray*, which was meant to be a short story but soon developed into a novel. It introduced a character in the person of Lord Henry Wotton (named after a place in Gloucestershire, in honor of a friend, More Adey), with whom Oscar was frankly charmed; he had always had a soft spot for a title. Lord Henry once said to Dorian, "You, you yourself, with your rose-red youth and your rose-white boyhood, you have had passions that have made you afraid, thoughts that have filled you with terror, whose mere memory might stain your cheek with shame— Ah, but the only way to get rid of a temptation is to yield to it. Resist it, and your soul grows sick with longing. Live! Live the wonderful life that is in you! Let nothing be lost upon you. Be always searching for new sensations. Be afraid of nothing!"

It was with regret that Oscar finished *Dorian*. There were a hundred uses for the money it would bring, but the novel's completion would mean farewell to Lord Henry.

Lord Henry, however, refused to be left behind—took to going out with Oscar, in a manner of speaking, and to using Oscar to give voice to his observations and maxims. "I choose my friends for their good looks," said Lord Henry (or Oscar), "my acquaintances for their good characters, and my enemies for their good intellects. A man cannot be too careful in the choice of his enemies. I have not got one who is a fool. They are all men of some intellectual power, and consequently they all appreciate me. Is that very vain of me? I think it is rather vain."

2

SEVERAL ENGLISH EDITORS, WHILE PRAISING ITS BRILLIANCE, found *Dorian Gray* not suited to magazine publication. But *Lippincott's Magazine* did not hesitate; their editor spoke of the novel with tremendous enthusiasm and proposed to give the major part of his July issue to it. Occasionally one had to take off one's hat to the Americans. Although the magazine's major circulation was of course in the States, it was obtainable in England through the publishing firm of Ward, Lock & Co., who soon after receiving advance proofs of *The Picture of Dorian Gray* made an offer for the book rights.

Oscar was pleased to accept. The critics' attention would be called soon enough to the July number of *Lippincott's*. He could say without vanity, although far be it from him to run vanity down, that of all literary men in England he was the one whose activities the daily press most rejoiced in advertising. He enjoyed this, for the only thing worse than being talked about invidiously is not being talked about at all; but it couldn't be denied that the chance of a fair critical appraisal of *The Picture of Dorian Gray* would be improved if the author were unknown.

The July number of *Lippincott's* appeared on June 20. Oscar kept an anxious watch on the papers and instructed the Romeike press bureau to be on the alert. A few days later the clippings began to come in. The volume steadily increased.

The *Daily Chronicle* said:

> Dullness and dirt are the chief features of *Lippincott's* this month. The element in it that is unclean is furnished by Mr. Oscar Wilde's story. It is a tale spawned from the leprous literature of the French *Decadents*—a poisonous book, the atmosphere of which is heavy with the mephitic odours of moral and spiritual putrefaction.

The *St. James's Gazette* thought the only question was whether a government agency or the Vigilance Society would find it worthwhile to prosecute the author of *The Picture of Dorian Gray* and his publishers.

Punch said:

118

The portrait represents the soul of the beautiful Ganymede-like Dorian Gray, whose youth and beauty last to the end, while his soul, like John Brown's, goes marching on into the Wilderness of Sin. It becomes at last a deviled soul. And then Dorian sticks a knife into it, as any ordinary mortal might do, and a fork also. This is our Oscar's Wildest and Oscarest work.

The *Scots Observer*'s editor, W. E. Henley, was a poet whose work Oscar had praised; Oscar took it for granted that Henley had written the unsigned review:

Why go grubbing in muck heaps? The world is fair, and the proportion of healthy-minded men and honest women to those that are foul, fallen, or unnatural is great. Mr. Oscar Wilde has again been writing stuff that were better unwritten; and while *The Picture of Dorian Gray*, which he contributes to *Lippincott's*, is ingenious, interesting, full of cleverness, and plainly the work of a man of letters, it is false art—for its interest is medico-legal; it is false to human nature—for its hero is a devil; it is false to morality—for it is not made sufficiently clear that the writer does not prefer a course of unnatural iniquity to a life of cleanliness, health, and sanity. The story—which deals with matters only fitted for the Criminal Investigation Department or a hearing *in camera*—is discreditable alike to author and editor. Mr. Wilde has brains, and art, and style; but if he can write for none but outlawed noblemen and perverted telegraph-boys, the sooner he takes to tailoring (or some other decent trade) the better for his reputation and the public morals.

Of the clippings Oscar remarked, "Enough for a bonfire, and a better use for them could be devised only with difficulty, not to say discomfort."

Oscar's new friend Bobbie Ross was most comforting and amusing about the *Scots Observer* review. Bobbie was nineteen or twenty, a Canadian; he had been removed from Canada to England, though, at the age of two, before any damage could be done. Bobbie's family was rather distinguished, for Canadians; his grandfather had been a Prime Minister or something of the sort of one of those vast stretches of Canada that go on indefinitely on the map.

Bobbie refreshingly showed no signs of political leanings; as a Prime Minister's grandson he seemed hopelessly out of character

—one could see him, as Puck, in the enchanted wood near Athens, laughing at dunderheads. He laughed often, which was quite natural in one whose nose was almost alarmingly *retroussé*. Oscar had never seen such a nose—adorable. There was rather more to be said for Bobbie than for Tommy Milton; Bobbie was quite as charming, Constance and the children doted on him, and he had a poet's taste for words, which Tommy had not.

Oscar, Tommy, and Bobbie frequently lunched together, and there wasn't a hint of wounded feelings; they enjoyed one another. How different from similar situations with women, of which Oscar knew first-hand accounts and sensational stories in the *Evening News* (under Frank Harris' scandal-mongering editorship), with the disgusting jealousies and screechings and hair-pullings that could result.

Constance herself had made a bit of a scene when some gossip, utterly without foundation, about Oscar and the actress Bernie Beere came to her ears. This had not amused Oscar—he could not be amused by anything that hurt Constance—but it had touched him; her suspicions were so hopelessly wide of the mark. Bernie Beere was a dear old friend and too busy with her career and marriage and love affairs to have any time for *him,* even if he had sought such tender attentions. He managed to persuade Constance on the truth of that matter.

He had not been with her as a lover ever since the night when he had filled the bedroom with flowers. On certain nights she would exert a slight, oh so very slight, pressure of her arm or leg when they were in bed. He would not close his eyes to the humiliation, the bewilderment of this dear, sensitive creature.

He racked his mind. She was clear-sighted enough to see through the first answer that occurred to him: the toll exacted by creative work, which left him spent, quite empty.

"Constance, my dearest, it is very difficult for me to say this, but I have to."

The look in her eyes.

"There, there, my darling, it is nothing that will hurt you. It is because you have been hurt that I must say it—have been hurt, when you deserved none. Before I met you and fell so madly in love, long before, when I was still up at Oxford, I was very foolish and careless, as young men are, not necessarily because they enjoy doing foolish things but because it seems to be expected of all young fellows at college, who to begin with are very conscious of their new estate as *men* and deadly afraid of seeming in their friends' eyes in any respect less than men."

Constance began to turn away.

"No, you must listen. In consequence of my stupidity I fell ill. The cure was a lengthy and objectionable business, but it was done. Before we were married, my darling, indeed before I proposed to you, I made quite sure that the old illness had not returned, for it *can* return without—I can't think quite how to put it—without provocation, let us say. That is, I suppose, the nastiest of all its thoroughly nasty aspects. Another moment, darling, only another moment. Two or three weeks ago I had reason to believe that that youthful transgression— But the rest is evident from what I have said. It is very hard to bear. Until the doctors are finished with me—"

He was silent. In this moment of brutal shock to her (inwardly she was shuddering, for such things were never talked of, even the breath of such things never touched one's home), Oscar felt for the first time the delicious little stirrings and promptings of desire.

But she recovered. She was soon quite happy with his inspired and absolutely groundless revelation.

Oscar remarked, soon after the appearance of *The Picture of Dorian Gray*, "The English public takes no interest in a work of art until it is informed that the work in question is immoral and disgusting." The demand for the July issue of *Lippincott's* was the keenest in the magazine's history. All available copies were snapped up; more were sent from the States; a splendidly profitable trade was done in under-the-counter copies selling for as much as four times the published price.

From such pecuniary benefits authors were, of course, automatically excluded, since the arrangement of a royalty on every copy sold did not obtain in the magazine-publishing business. "Never mind," Oscar said, "I want none of it; it is tainted gold"; but when Norman Forbes-Robertson, an old friend who had recently taken over the Globe Theatre, asked him for a play, Oscar refused to consider an outright sale, as proposed by Norman—the basis must be a hundred pounds on drawing up an acceptable scenario, another hundred on completion of the play, and a royalty on every performance.

Norman balked. But he was not the only one in the theater to be drawn by Lord Henry's flashing lines in *Dorian Gray;* there was George Alexander, the handsome young actor who had gone into producing as well. One day at the Café Royal he paused at Oscar's table, took out a slip of paper, put it in Oscar's hand, and said, "My dear chap, do me the favor of accepting this and saying no more about it, will you?"

Oscar looked at the paper. It was a check for fifty pounds.

"I shall be charmed, Alec, if you will allow me one question."

"One only, then."

"Why *fifty* pounds? Why not a hundred? Or a hundred and fifty?"

"The hundreds will come later," Alec said. "The fifty is merely a token."

"Ah, I see. And of course tokens should not be too substantial or they cease to be tokens. But now I can't resist another question. A token of what?"

"Oh," Alec said, "of my esteem. And my hope that you will write a play very soon—and let me see it first."

Later on, Alec suggested putting down some sort of agreement in writing. Oscar could tell him that an idea for a play was coming along most promisingly. Alec was delighted. In another week or two he inquired after the play: hoped it was living up to its promise? Indeed yes, Oscar replied. Perhaps, Alec hinted with the utmost diffidence, Oscar had actually put pen to paper? No, Oscar hadn't got quite that far, but it really didn't matter because the writing was a mere formality, the whole plot was in his head. Since that was so, Alec would love to hear Oscar tell it—wouldn't he please, now, over another glass of wine? Ah, he couldn't do that, Oscar said sorrowfully, because it would quite spoil Alec's pleasure when it came time to read the play itself.

The plot ran that Lady Margaret Somebody-or-other is young and beautiful and happily married to handsome, wealthy young Lord Arthur Somebody-or-other. Through a kind friend the terrible news reaches Lady Margaret that Lord Arthur is carrying on with the attractive, mysterious Mrs. Erlynne; Lord Arthur knows but cannot tell, because it would break Lady Margaret's heart, that

Mrs. Erlynne is in fact her mother, whose death was announced to Lady Margaret when she was only a child by her broken-hearted father, abandoned by his wife for a handsome scoundrel. Lord Arthur's fancied infidelity so shocks Lady Margaret that she determines, or almost determines, to run off with the handsome Lord Darlington, who worships her, and indeed she writes a letter to this effect to Lord Arthur and goes to Lord Darlington's rooms; but the letter is found and opened by Mrs. Erlynne, who has long bitterly repented the tragic folly of her past and who now saves her daughter's name at the cost of her own, though without divulging her true identity.

The plot was nothing; the dialogue would be everything, when written. Oscar had a few lines in mind:

LORD DARLINGTON: Do you think, then, Lady Margaret, that if a husband is faithless the wife should not console herself?

LADY MARGARET: Console herself?

LORD DARLINGTON: Yes, I think she should—I think she has the right.

LADY MARGARET: Because the husband is vile, should the wife be vile also?

LORD DARLINGTON: Vileness is a terrible word, Lady Margaret.

LADY MARGARET: It is a terrible thing.

LORD DARLINGTON: Do you know I am afraid that good people do a great deal of harm in the world. Certainly the greatest harm they do is that they make badness so extraordinarily important. It is absurd to divide people into good and bad. People are either charming or tedious. I take the side of the charming, and you, Lady Margaret, can't help being one of them.

There was a touch of Lord Henry in Darlington, Oscar perceived.

DUCHESS OF SOMETHING-OR-OTHER: Dear Margaret, I am so pleased to see you. You remember Agatha, don't you? And how do you do, Lord Darlington? No, I won't introduce you to my daughter, you are far too wicked.

LORD DARLINGTON: Don't say that, duchess. As a wicked man I am a complete failure. Why, there are lots of people who say I have never really done anything wrong in the whole course of my life. Mind you, they only say it behind my back.

DUCHESS: Dear Lord Darlington, how thoroughly depraved you are!

LADY MARGARET: Lord Darlington is trivial.

LORD DARLINGTON: Ah, don't say that.

LADY MARGARET: Why do you *talk* so trivially about life, then?

LORD DARLINGTON: Because I think that life is far too important a thing ever to talk seriously about it.

DUCHESS: What do you mean? As a concession to my poor wits, please explain to me what you really mean!

LORD DARLINGTON: I think I had better not, duchess. Nowadays to be intelligible is to be found out. (*Bows and exits.*)

DUCHESS: What a charming, wicked creature! I like him so much. I'm quite delighted he's gone!

There was a knock on the study door. Oscar looked up and said, "Yes?"

It was the maid (above all things Oscar longed for the day when they would be able to afford a butler). She wore an agitated expression; she had been warned by Constance that Mr. Wilde's hours of work were sacred. "Excuse me, sir," she said, "but I told the young gentlemen and told them you was not to be interfered with but they said I must come and tell you anyway or they would do something dreadful."

"What young gentlemen?"

"One is a Mr. Johnson, sir, and the other's name I don't know. I asked him but he said he could not be bothered. At least I understood him to say he could not be bothered, sir."

"Couldn't he indeed," Oscar said. "Lionel, is it really you?"

A young voice came back: "Yes, Oscar."

"Splendid. I shall be with you in a moment, dear boy. Agnes, show Mr. Johnson and his friend in here, please." Oscar hurried upstairs to his dressing room to brush his hair.

He had met Lionel Johnson a year ago at Oxford, when the university's dramatic society had put on Robert Browning's *Stafford* and asked Oscar for suggestions for improvement, which he had been happy to supply. He had looked in on Walter Pater, who couldn't have been kinder, positively forthcoming for such a shy man, who usually murmured a few words and retired into a book (he had said once at the end of a lecture, "I trust everyone heard me?" and Oscar, unable to resist, had said, "We overheard you"—

Pater had been cool for some time afterward). Pater had spoken in the kindest way of an essay of Oscar's in *The Fortnightly Review* and then had mumbled exquisitely on various other things and had mentioned an undergraduate, Johnson, he thought the name was, whose poetry he thought interesting, at least Oscar thought he said interesting—Pater might just as well have said infuriating without anyone's being the wiser—and Oscar had looked up Johnson and liked him, though he wasn't a particularly handsome young man.

That could not be said of Lionel's companion this afternoon. Good Lord, he was beautiful. His face had a classic purity; Grecian, no less. But he seemed to be bored, or tired, or both. He barely responded to Lionel's introduction: "Oscar, this is Alfred Douglas; Bosie, Oscar Wilde."

"I am charmed, Lord Alfred," Oscar said. The youth languidly smiled; he seemed to suggest that he found Oscar faintly, and unintentionally, amusing. He was a son of the ancient house of Queensberry; his father was a marquess (Oscar vaguely remembered having met him years ago). "Bosie" (it had a sweet, childish sound) Douglas was an undergraduate at Oscar's old college, Magdalen. He truly had a beautiful face; his skin was white; the deeply red, marvelously curved lips, with the underlip so full, gave the mouth a slightly sulky look. His hair was like amber, and his eyes, Oscar thought, were violet blue.

"We came down for the day," Lionel said, "and Bosie was rather tired, and we haven't really been enjoying ourselves. It was only by threatening that domestic dragon of yours, Oscar, that we got in. I thought you might give us a cup of tea. I knew you'd like to meet Bosie. He is a poet too, you know."

"I am charmed," Oscar said and cursed himself for repeating the phrase. "I dare say you have been bored because you have been behaving circumspectly—have been doing nothing beautiful and dangerous. The only things one never regrets, you know, are one's mistakes." He had never been more brilliant, more fantastic, more charming. Lionel sat enraptured; but Bosie Douglas' lovely eyes looked at Oscar, when they looked at all, with indifference.

Reluctantly, Oscar took them up to tea with Constance in the drawing room.

When they had gone, Constance said, "What a very handsome young man Lord Alfred Douglas is."

"Yes," Oscar said. "But dull."

"Did you really think so?"

"He hardly said a thing—I was glad to see the last of him. It is difficult to believe that he is a poet."

"Oh," she said, "but doesn't he *look* the part."

3   THE PLAY LAGGED. OSCAR TOLD GEORGE ALEXANDER THAT IT
was no use struggling on against the grain; he must get away, then
come back quite fresh. Would Alec like him to return the fifty
pounds? Of course not, said Alec. A good thing, too; Oscar couldn't
imagine where the fifty pounds would have come from. He had
never been more deeply in debt. It was extraordinary to be so well
known, so successful—never the slightest trouble in placing anything he wrote, and more requests from editors than he could possibly fill—and to have to scrape for every shilling.

Shortly now, though, a collection of his stories, called *A House
of Pomegranates*, was to be published, and Ward, Lock would
bring out their edition of *Dorian*, which should have a great sale.

He finished the play in the early autumn, while staying for a
much-needed change near Lake Windermere. Lady Margaret
would be Lady Margaret Windermere. He called the play *A Good
Woman*, but the title didn't please him; it was, after all, merely
one of those drawing-room plays with pink lamps, and *A Good
Woman* sounded stark and Scandinavian. He crossed out *A Good
Woman* and wrote above it *Lady Windermere's Fan*.

"Oscar, my dear fellow," said Alec, "it's been worth waiting for.
It will play beautifully. Lord Arthur Windermere is made to meas-
ure for me, if you don't mind my saying so."

"My dear Alec, it was your handsome and graceful self that I saw
when Lord Windermere first came into my head. You were a constant inspiration to me, and to tell the truth I had a struggle ever
to get you off stage. I thought at one time that if only I could write
the whole play about you, it would be a joy."

Alec glowed with pleasure. Alec was at his most dangerous when
he glowed with pleasure.

"I don't think it's stretching things to say that much of it might
have been written by Sheridan. I'll tell you what, Oscar, my dear
chap—I hadn't intended to go this far, and perhaps at the moment
the business side of me is rather too much under the influence of
the artistic side; on the other hand, heaven knows you deserve to
be rewarded for a stunning piece of work; I'll give you a thousand
pounds for the play outright."

"My dear Alec. What can I say? Only this. My faith in you is such a strong and beautiful thing that I wouldn't dream of insulting it by accepting your generous offer."

Alec blinked; perceptibly his glow dwindled. "But my dear Oscar, does that make very good sense?"

"Of course it does, my dear Alec, the very best sense in the world. If I had no confidence in your judgment I would snap up your offer with a greedy little cry of delight. But, you see, I know that if in your opinion *Lady Windermere's Fan* is worth risking a thousand pounds on, there can be little chance that it won't bring the thousand pounds back and a good many more too. Can I do less than pay your opinion the delicate compliment of declaring myself willing to share, by means of a royalty arrangement, in all the money the play is going to earn?"

The glow disappeared. "You're quite certain? It *is* a gamble."

"Quite certain. Of course you will deduct from the first check you make out to me after the opening night your original fifty pounds and another hundred I think I must ask for now as an advance against royalties. I am tired, Alec, terribly tired; the creative energy I poured into fashioning the powerful plot of *Lady Windermere's Fan* has exhausted me, and I feel that I must refresh brain and soul in the pastoral simplicity of Paris. I shall need the hundred pounds to pay for my goat's milk and cheese and the rude hut that will shelter me. No, I beg your pardon, I shan't need a hundred pounds, I shall need a hundred and twenty-five. Goat's milk, I understand, has become frightfully dear."

When Oscar stopped in at Mathews and Lane's, the publishers, in connection with a new, limited edition of his poems, a young man came up to him. He couldn't be more than seventeen, eighteen at the outside; he approached timidly, really in quite a trembling state, a tinge of color, a blush, no less, on his pale, thin face—charming—and said (while the other clerks snickered), "I hope, Mr. Wilde, that you won't mind if I take the very great liberty of introducing myself, because I terribly admire your poems, which are an inspiration to me." Oscar said, "I would mind only if an admirer of my poems didn't introduce himself, but so far you haven't; what is your name?"

The boy said, "Edward Shelley."

"With that glorious name," Oscar remarked, "you are bound some day to write glorious poems. Or perhaps you have written some already? I should be proud to read them. We must have a talk over a cup of tea when you can spare the time."

At this the boy seemed almost ready to faint, but he managed to stammer, "How wonderful that would be." The other clerks, miserable creatures, snickered louder than ever.

Oscar felt quite drawn to the boy and always paused for a few words whenever he went to Mathews and Lane's office in Vigo Street, and later (since somehow the occasion for the cup of tea never seemed to present itself) he sent him an inscribed copy of *The House of Pomegranates* and a ticket to the premiere of his play—an excellent seat, too, next to Pierre Louÿs, the young French poet.

Disagreements sprang up between Oscar and George Alexander during the rehearsals of *Lady Windermere's Fan;* Oscar assured Alec that every suggestion he had made had been carefully considered, since Alec deserved no less, but surely he would grant that any work of art is constructed by its creator on the most precise and delicate lines, which can be altered even in the minutest detail only with great caution and at the risk even so of destroying the final effect so painstakingly planned for. In short, he would not change anything.

Alec persisted, with great reasonableness, although when he said "My dear Oscar" it was evidently something of a strain. Finally Oscar gave in, not, however, on the important change proposed by Alec, that Mrs. Erlynne's secret should be disclosed to the audience in the second act rather than the last, but on a minor detail.

Alec breathed heavily for a moment or two. "My dear Oscar, that is most gracious of you. I can't imagine how those poor chaps who put on Shakespeare's plays ever managed to tolerate him. As you know, he could be quite definitely unpleasant for as much as five minutes when called on at the last moment to rewrite half the play."

"My dear Alec, that is the penalty, willingly accepted by people so exquisitely thoughtful as you, for dealing with genius."

On the night of the premiere, Oscar watched his play come to life:

LORD DARLINGTON: I must say I think you are very hard on modern life, Lady Windermere. Of course there is much against it, I admit. Most women, for instance, nowadays, are rather mercenary.

LADY WINDERMERE: Don't talk about such people.

LORD DARLINGTON: Well, then, setting mercenary people aside, who, of course, are dreadful, do you think seriously that women who have committed what the world calls a fault should never be forgiven?

LADY WINDERMERE: I think they should never be forgiven.

LORD DARLINGTON: And men? Do you think that there should be the same laws for men as there are for women?

LADY WINDERMERE: Certainly!

LORD DARLINGTON: I think life too complex a thing to be settled by these hard and fast rules.

LADY WINDERMERE: If we had "these hard and fast rules," we should find life much more simple.

LORD DARLINGTON: You allow of no exceptions?

LADY WINDERMERE: None!

LORD DARLINGTON: Ah, what a fascinating Puritan you are, Lady Windermere!

LADY WINDERMERE: The adjective was unnecessary, Lord Darlington.

LORD DARLINGTON: I couldn't help it. I can resist everything except temptation.

The audience laughed like children at a Christmas pantomime. At the end of the first act, Alec and the cast were in towering spirits; they had a success, a wildfire success, a galloping, raging success.

MRS. ERLYNNE: Oh, yes! He's to call tomorrow at twelve o'clock. He wanted to propose tonight. In fact he did. He kept on proposing. Poor Augustus; you know how he repeats himself. Such a bad habit! But I told him I wouldn't give him an answer till tomorrow. Of course I am going to take him. And I dare say I'll make him an admirable wife, as wives go. And there is a great deal of good in Augustus. Fortunately it is all on the surface. Just where good qualities should be.

Laughter rippled throughout the theater.

Between the second and third acts Oscar was in the theater bar. He hardly touched the whisky and soda in his hand; the sweet song of compliments was better than drink. Tommy was there, and Bobbie, and Graham, and John Gray, the young poet with the enchanting profile, and Pierre Louÿs, and Edward Shelley, the slim and attractive and quite madly hero-worshiping boy from his publishers' office.

After innumerable curtain calls, the entire packed house was shouting "Author, author, author!"

Alec, cool-headed Alec, was beside himself. "Listen to them. Come on, Oscar, come on!"

"My dear fellow, I fully intend to, but I can't seem to find a match for my cigarette."

"You can't go on smoking a cigarette—it isn't done."

"That is why I am going to do it."

"Those people out there are giving you the biggest success anyone's had since God knows when and you are going to *annoy* them."

"They like to be annoyed. And oh, Alec, there is something I've been meaning to mention to you for some time, and now that we have a moment to spare I shall not put it off any longer, except that for the life of me I can't remember what it is. Don't keep fidgeting, Alec; you are almost jumping up and down. I can't possibly remember, and it's *most* important, if you insist on behaving like a hysterical woman."

"For God's sake, here is your match!" Alec roared. "Now go on, or they'll tear the bloody house down."

Oscar sauntered onto the stage. A few faces stood out from the great blur in front of him: Constance's; Bobbie's; the critic William Archer's; and another critic's, the fellow from the *Daily Telegraph*, what was his name—it didn't matter. *He* looked sour, the cigarette must really have annoyed him, but certainly it hadn't stopped anyone else; they were laughing and shouting and clapping their hands off.

When they stopped at last, worn out, Oscar favored them with an indulgent smile. "Ladies and gentlemen, I have had a perfectly wonderful evening—I could not have enjoyed myself more. The actors, every one of them, have surpassed themselves in the delightful rendition they have given us of this superb play. For your part, I think your response has been very, very intelligent indeed. In fact, I have to congratulate all of you on your triumphantly successful performance, by which I am persuaded that you think *nearly* as much of *Lady Windermere's Fan* as I do myself."

A gasp, then laughter; and applause, lovely, lovely applause followed. But the *Daily Telegraph* critic looked more sour than ever. Oscar tapped the ash from his cigarette, bowed, and left the stage.

"The critics," Alec predicted, "will be all over you for what I'm sure they'll call your damned effrontery. I don't mind. The play will run forever."

"The critics, ah, the critics," Oscar said. "What was it someone was saying of them the other day—that they could all be bought? And perhaps they can. Judging from their appearance, most of them can't be at all expensive. Alec, quite seriously, now, do you think there are wittier people anywhere than the author of *Lady Windermere's Fan?*"

"I doubt it, Oscar. At any rate, I've never met one."

"My dear Alec, I never have either. And I should be fearfully hurt if I ever did."

4   WITH THE EXCEPTION OF ARCHER AND ONE OTHER, THE critics came down heavily on Oscar for what they called his insolent behavior. One of the many letters he received from tremendously enthusiastic correspondents previously unknown to him said that if insolent behavior went hand in hand with the charm of *Lady Windermere's Fan*, Mr. Wilde would be forever remembered as a benefactor of the suffering British playgoer if he would give lessons in insolence to all other British playwrights.

Another correspondent wrote:

Sunday evening,
21st February, 1892

Dear Mr. Oscar Wilde,
    I must again thank you for the *House of Pomegranates* and the theater ticket. It was very good of you to send them to me and I shall never forget your kindness. What a triumph was yours last night! The play is the best I have seen on the stage, with such beauty of form and wit that it adds a new phase of pleasure to existence. Could Lady Blessington live anew the conversations would make her jealous. George Meredith might have signed it. How miserably poor everything else seems beside it! Except, of course, your books—but then your books are part of yourself.
    Please believe me, truly yours,

Edward Shelley

The poor boy must have been proud of this letter, must have toiled over it, to demonstrate that he was far more than a clerk— was on familiar terms, through his reading, with the witty Countess of Blessington and her *salon* at Gore House a half century and more ago. (But to say that George Meredith might have signed *Lady Windermere's Fan* was of course pathetically wrong; good heavens.)

Oscar could not help feeling even more strongly drawn to young Shelley after this. They must have their cup of tea and a good talk. Or perhaps rather more than that. Luncheon? No, the boy would be worrying about the time, having to get back to the office on the second of the minute; John Lane, of Mathews and Lane, seemed to be something of a martinet—Oscar had not taken to him at all. Dinner, then. In fact, why not give the boy an evening that he would remember for the rest of his life? Dinner at a fashionable hotel, roses and red wine on the table, candlelight, violins—

Dinner, with a seventeen-year-old clerk? Ah, but he wasn't your *ordinary* office clerk, far from it; he spoke well, dressed with taste, and his idol was not some dreadful music-hall or sporting person but—a poet. And he had blushed so charmingly. It would be delightful to dine with him. Perhaps the evening would not have to end with dinner. Afterward they might retire to—where? One of the other public rooms of the hotel? No; they must continue the intimacy of the dinner table with its candles and roses and wine.

A private sitting room, that would be the thing, and a bottle of champagne. But it would seem rather odd to the hotel management, wouldn't it, if he took only a sitting room? How could he explain it? Much better to take a suite of rooms for the night.

Tommy and Bobbie had approached *him; they* had made the advances; and in this case, it would be he who for the first time would be the active agent. He had gathered charming young men around him at the Café Royal and all the other excellent places here and in Paris but had never been alone with one of them as the pursuer, in a hotel bedroom.

How gradually, in almost imperceptible stages, he had come to this decision. Or had he known from the beginning that he would come to it, and was it that secret knowledge that excited him? Was it the actuality of being alone with young Shelley as his lover, the physical fact, lips to lips, slim white trembling youth and urgent, seeking, powerful man—this that was exciting—or was it simply the *idea*, the daring, beautiful idea at which the gross gray world frowned, which that savage ancient god, old scowling Jahveh, had thought he would burn from the face of the earth? But the golden sand and sunlight of Greece and the blue flame of sea and sky and youths and virile men could never be killed.

Oscar chose the Albemarle Hotel. He should keep rooms here, or at some equally good address, as a more or less permanent thing; it would be comfortable to have a place to entertain in occasionally away from home. And to work in, for that matter. At the moment

Cyril and Vyvyan were in a military phase, dragoons and hussars and fusiliers and guards all over the place, and there were two great forts, Cyril's on the left side of the nursery, Vyvyan's on the right, bristling with cannon that fired off volleys of building blocks, pebbles, cricket balls, and dried peas. The noise was not conducive to literary composition, and frequently Oscar had to interfere. If he worked somewhere else, the boys could fight their wars in peace.

And he could afford a *pied à terre*. The golden sovereigns were rolling in from *Lady Windermere's Fan*. If the critics' denunciation of Mr. Wilde's "insufferable effrontery" and "galling display of atrocious manners" and "childish exhibition" had had any result, it had only been to increase the public's anxiety to see his play. Glorious money, it made so many things possible—a butler at last, another maid. A really superior cook. New clothes for Constance and for himself. No more walking, no more depressing journeys on the underground—hansom cabs, always. No more vulgar crises with tradesmen, no desperate, artful parrying of long overdue bills. To think that not so long ago he had searched the house from top to bottom, and even his boots, for half a crown.

Oscar's hansom stopped outside the Mathews and Lane office in Vigo Street. "Wait for me," he told the driver. He was quite in the habit now of saying this. The other day a hansom had waited for four solid hours outside the Café Royal. Wouldn't it be a sensible idea to have a *permanent* hansom, always waiting for him—outside Tite Street or the Albermarle first thing in the morning, and so on right through the day?

The scribbling of the other clerks' pens stopped as Oscar entered the office and approached young Shelley.

"Edward, thank you for your charming note. It was exquisitely phrased; you are a born writer."

A delicate tinge of color rose in the boy's cheeks.

"We have never had our talk, have we?" Oscar continued. "We must make up for all this lost time. Rather than having a cup of tea together, will you dine with me at the Albemarle on Saturday?"

"Oh, Mr. Wilde! Are you *sure*?"

"I am quite sure. And if you don't accept I shall be thoroughly out of temper with you."

"Oh, Mr. Wilde."

135

The room seemed to echo with *"Oh, Mr. Wilde!"* The echo turned into a spiteful, giggling whisper from one of the other clerks.

"Well then, Edward?"

"Oh, yes. I shall be so—so proud, and so honored."

"So—so proud and so—so honored! Oh dear me yes." The whisperer, unable to resist the brilliance and daring of his performance, trying to smother a laugh, let out a gurgling snort.

"Shall we say eight o'clock at the Albermarle?"

"Oh, yes, Mr. Wilde. And thank you."

"Oh, yes, Mr. Wilde. And thank you."

Now there was a deep blush on the boy's face. Oscar felt his own skin burning. It would be kinder not to speak to Edward at the office again.

On Saturday afternoon at the hotel, after returning from the hairdresser's, Oscar prepared for the evening with extravagant care. After his bath, he hesitated between Canterbury Wood Violet and *Eau de Lubin. Eau de Lubin,* he decided—a scent with a touch of the masculine. His clothes had been laid out on the double bed. As he dressed, he inspected the room. The decor was well done, in soft grays and blues. Oscar had ordered the flowers himself—jonquils, tulips, and daffodils, and one huge cluster of red roses. And two small bunches of Parma violets, one for his buttonhole, the other for Edward's.

Oscar finished dressing and looked at himself in the full-length mirror. A tall man in beautifully tailored clothes. Thank God for his height. When you are six feet you can afford a few extra pounds. He turned to see himself in profile.

Hmm. Astonishing. He drew in his stomach. Better, but uncomfortable. The profile view was not important; one did not walk or sit *sideways* to one's companion. Oscar faced the mirror again. His cheeks were getting a little full. But he had always had a full face; it would simply not suit his face to be thin; it would look out of proportion under the superb head of hair—softly waved, delicately scented, and with not a single strand of gray, thanks to a wonderful liquid called Koko Marikopas, cheap at twelve and six the bottle. The name alone was worth the money. How many men of his age could show such a head of hair? "Men of his age"—stupid; made him sound old. He was, after all, still a young man. Wasn't thirty-five young?

But then the image in the mirror seemed to smile and wink and say, "We are quite by ourselves here, my dear fellow. We know very well, don't we, that we aren't thirty-five, we are thirty-seven."

Oscar turned away from the mirror, walked into the other room, where there were bottles and glasses and a siphon, poured some whisky, and drank it neat. And *that* was a foolish thing to do. He should have rung for champagne. Strong spirits on an empty stomach merely deepen a fit of melancholy.

When Cyril and Vyvyan asked Constance where Papa was tonight she would answer, "Papa will not be here tonight because he is finishing some very important work and he does not want to disturb us by coming home very late." Oh, his innocent beautiful sons. His Cyril, his Cyril, and his Vyvyan. His darling boys; he was a wicked man, he was not worthy of them.

Suddenly Oscar said, in a loud voice, "Nonsense!" Positively maudlin. In the same class as the death of Little Nell. He should be ashamed of himself. It wasn't his fault; it was the Scotch.

At five minutes to eight he glanced at himself in the mirror, from the front, and went downstairs with the two bunches of violets in his hand.

Young Shelley was waiting. "My dear Edward," Oscar said, "how charming you look. This is for you, a boutonniere. I saw the violets and thought of you. No, on second thought, I shall not give you yours, I shall give you mine so that you may put them into my buttonhole, and I shall put in yours. Is not that a better idea?"

The boy blushed. "Yes, Mr. Wilde."

"Would you mind very much, Edward, calling me Oscar? I like those of whom I am very fond to call me Oscar. And it doesn't make me feel so old."

"But you aren't old."

"Thank you, Edward. Yes, the violets are becoming to you; I knew they would be. Now put in mine."

The boy had to reach up, and his face came close; Oscar could see the fine childlike golden hairs on his upper lip and could hear his rapid breathing. The scent of the violets seemed to be his breath. His lips were parted. The tip of his tongue rested red against the pure white teeth.

He said, blushing, "There, I think that is all right."

"It is quite perfect," Oscar said. "Let us go in, shall we?"

He had reserved a corner table. "I have chosen our dinner, Edward, things that I felt sure would please you. But I was not certain about the champagne. Brut or sec?"

"I've never had champagne."

"Then this is a night that will live forever green and young and beautiful in your memory even though the world grow sere and old."

"Like Dorian," the boy said.

"Ah, you've read *Dorian?*"

"Oh, yes, Mr. Wilde! I've read all your books."

"Oscar, please. I must send you a copy of *Dorian,* which I shall inscribe 'To Edward, whom I—' No, I shan't tell you the rest of it, you shall discover it for yourself. Brut, I think we had better have. Edward, how delighted I am that you are to drink your first glass of champagne with me—the first of many, the first of very many. Have you been to Paris?"

"I've never been out of England."

"We shall remedy that. But then, perhaps your parents would object? You do live with them, I believe? Are they very strict?"

"I am the master of my own movements."

"Oh, that is very well said."

The boy blushed. "No, it sounded silly. I meant to say—I only meant to say that I am almost eighteen and I make my own living and I am—I am—"

"You are the master of your own movements. I don't think it sounded silly in the least. That is to say, you come in and leave and so on quite as you wish? I see. And now you must tell me about your writing. First, though, I must tell *you* how deeply moved I was by your saying that *Lady Windermere's Fan* could have been signed by Meredith. Very few people would be capable of making that observation, Edward; it shows an exquisite awareness of style. Do you know, I received a quite extraordinary number of letters about my play, and not a few were from persons made much of by the world, but of them all yours is the most precious to me. Isn't it deplorable, how persistently I talk about myself?"

"Oh, no, Mr. Wilde."

"Oscar. It is deplorable, it is, it is. I am always cropping up in my conversation, and I don't really know why, because I infinitely prefer to talk about youth and beauty. To *listen* to youth, wise, beautiful youth. As I now insist on listening to you, Edward. Tell me about your poems, for you must have written poems, you have a poet's eyes, a poet's lips—"

The boy blushed again. "There aren't any that are worth talking about."

"They are worth talking about because *you* wrote them. Tell me, Edward."

It was hopelessly common stuff, expressed with a painful, limping earnestness; but then, fortunately, the champagne was poured, and Oscar gave a toast, "To our friendship, Edward," and they touched glasses and drank, and the boy wrinkled his nose (a charming little nose) and looked at Oscar with a wondering smile—and drank some more.

And some more. He drank eagerly, copiously—was visibly relieved when the first, quickly emptied bottle of champagne was replaced, had his glass ready and waiting as the cork popped. The limping earnestness of his speech disappeared; he talked as he drank, abundantly. His talk covered a range of subjects absolutely withering in their lack of interest: where he had gone to school, his defeats and triumphs at school, his friends at school and his enemies, teachers who were sympathetic, teachers who were unsympathetic. He described his life at home, his family, his life at the office, his contempt for his fellow clerks, his consciousness of being meant for higher things and his moods of despondency when it seemed that he was never to attain them.

In vain Oscar endeavored to dam this stream. He refused to compete by raising his voice, but a cigarette might do the trick. The boy accepted the cigarette, permitted Oscar to light it, but then simply let it dribble out its life in an ashtray while he talked on. There was the subject of Mr. John Lane, of Mathews and Lane. Oscar not only considered Mr. Lane to be a bore, he came as close to actively disliking him as he could dislike anyone. It seemed that young Shelley remembered every word of every conversation he had ever had with Mr. Lane. He finished another glass of champagne. "*Then* do you know what he said?"

"I cannot im——"

"He said, 'Edward'—he calls me Edward—Edward, I trust this will be a lesson to you. Waste not,' he said, 'want not.' "

"He is quite mistaken. I have consis——"

"But I couldn't allow that to pass. 'Mr. Lane,' I said, very calmly

139

and quietly but looking him straight in the eye, 'I must point out, sir, that—' "

Oscar filled his glass and signaled to the wine-steward. Then he noticed that the boy was rubbing his nose.

"Is something the matter with your nose?"

"It's funny, but there isn't any feeling in it. It's as if it had fallen asleep."

"Ah," Oscar said, "that is proof that we have been sitting for too long in one spot. My nose does the same thing, particularly at dinner parties that I have no wish to attend but cannot escape. Do you know Lord Sunningdale? No, I don't suppose you do. He is an extremely tiresome person, almost as tiresome as Mr. Lane. At his last dinner party I was seated next to him and my nose fell sound asleep in the middle of his conversation. Of course he wouldn't have noticed because I have trained my mouth to smile through even the deadliest talk, but unfortunately my nose had fallen so fast asleep that it emitted a snore and there was nothing to do but ask Sunningdale to forgive it, which he did with exceedingly poor grace. I'll tell you what, Edward, we'll finish this bottle upstairs."

"Can we do that?"

"Of course we can, we can do anything we wish. Some people maintain that noses fall asleep through excess of drink, but they are wrong, it is the same thing as one's foot falling asleep and can be relieved simply by moving around. Ah, there is Frank Harris." Oscar nodded, then took the boy's arm. "We must hurry, or he will be after us; Frank can never resist dropping a few offensive words at the top of his voice in the middle of a crowded room, and his voice is the envy of Her Majesty's Lighthouse Service—he is the foghorn that walks like a man. It is a wicked piece of scandalous gossip without a grain of truth in it that Frank was flung out of the United States as an unspeakably undesirable alien because he debauched the daughters *and* the wives of all seven, or is it nine, justices of the U. S. Supreme Court while the rest of the sightseeing party of which he was a member was pausing for afternoon tea. But he would not thank me for saying so—Frank deeply resents all such slurs against his inability in the presence of the opposite sex to behave like a gentleman."

The sitting room of the suite was charming.

"Would you like a Scotch and soda now, Edward, rather than wait for the champagne?"

"Where is this?"

"This? Oh, these are the rooms I keep here. Rather comfortable, don't you think? I chose the flowers myself. Do you like them?"

"Why did we come here?"

"I thought it would be pleasant to be by ourselves. Here is your whisky."

"I don't want it. And I don't want to stay here."

"Edward, really, you are much too pretty to sulk."

"How dare you call me pretty!" the boy cried.

"How dare I? Because you are. I mean no harm by saying it; dear me, I should think you would be pleased. Consider all the boys in London of whom it cannot be said. Now, do drink your Scotch. *I* want one, and I refuse to drink alone. Your manners have always been charming, Edward; you won't disappoint me now?" And Oscar held up his glass and smiled and said he would give the same toast as he had given earlier, because if a toast is a beautiful toast, why not?

"Our friendship, Edward."

"Our friendship," the boy said rather sullenly; still, he said it. And he drank, and Oscar drank.

They were two very large Scotches; they had had a great deal of champagne; Oscar had known nothing like this intoxication since the strange night in Paris, years ago; again there was the feeling of not being in control of events or of oneself. And of not caring. He poured himself another Scotch and drank it down. The boy had another too. He was reciting poetry now, no doubt of his own composition; it was execrable. "Sublime, sublime!" Oscar cried, pouring another glass of Scotch and immediately plunging his cigar into it. Then the champagne arrived, and they sat down on the sofa together to finish it. It left a certain dryness in the mouth that Oscar thought might be relieved by brandy and soda. The boy declaimed a few more yards of doggerel and Oscar put his arms around him and kissed him, chiefly to stop the noise.

The boy shouted, "You have lured me into the bedroom!"

Oscar said, "How could I have lured you into the bedroom when we aren't in the bedroom in the first place?"

"We *are* in the bedroom."

141

"This is preposterous, Edward."

"We are, we *are*. You asked me to come in!"

Oscar looked around and perceived that they were in the bedroom.

"Well, then, why did you?"

"Because I trusted you. And you have insulted and degraded me!"

"Edward, Edward, please don't shout. Oh dear, you are weeping too. Don't weep, Edward, I can't bear to see you weep. If I say I am terribly, terribly sorry and beg you to forgive me, will you stop weeping?"

"You are not an English gentleman," the boy choked.

"No, I am not," Oscar agreed, "I am an Irish gentleman. Here, Edward, use my handkerchief, it has a lovely scent—*Eau de Lubin*; I put it on specially because I thought you would like it. Everything tonight was done for your sake, and now I have spoilt it all by drinking too much. I am so sorry. Do let us part as friends."

The boy was sniffling. "But I can't go home like this."

"Why, what is the matter?"

"They would know something dreadful had happened. They would smell the spirits and the champagne. And they would see how I look."

"You are perfectly free to spend the night here with me, Edward. It is a subject of great delicacy, but I shall add, for fear of being misunderstood—purely as friends. You can have a bath in the morning and I shall have your clothes valeted and your parents will be delighted to see you in such a fresh and blooming state."

"It is very kind of you, Mr. Wilde."

"Oscar," Oscar said.

In the morning, the boy asked, "That is lovely soap in the bathroom, Oscar—what is it?"

"*Peau d'Espagne*. I think I have another cake or two here, and you may have them to take home with you."

"Oh, thank you!"

He looked so charming, so fresh and rosy after his bath, that Oscar kissed him.

Thereafter, some rather childish, rather morbid, letters pursued Oscar for a while.

5   "LADY WINDERMERE'S" SUCCESS CONTINUED. "IT IS NOW TO
receive the supreme compliment," Oscar told Bobbie Ross. "A
travesty of it is to appear, a *musical* travesty—which is a ghastly
thought, isn't it?—called *The Poet and the Puppets*; and as if labor-
ing under the absurd delusion that the dullest critic could mistake whom they mean by the poet, the authors have put me into it
by name."

"You can't permit that, Oscar."

"Well, no, I can't, but they were so dejected when I told them I
couldn't that I felt sorry for them and said I was really opposed
only to hearing their preposterous figure of the poet referred to as
Oscar on the stage. I said I wouldn't mind if they used one of my
other names, of which there is an abundant supply, Oscar Fingal
O'Flahertie Wills Wilde. They chose O'Flahertie."

"Dear Oscar, you are the kindest and most forgiving of men.
Who are the authors?"

"Charles Brookfield and James Glover. Dear me, Bobbie, you
look thoughtful, and I wish you wouldn't, because it means you are
troubled by something or other. Are you?"

"Brookfield is a spiteful person. He doesn't like you."

"Brookfield? My dear Bobbie. Why in the world shouldn't he?"

"Did you ever do anything to offend him? He is awfully vain,
you know."

"I believe I once told him that a heliotrope necktie did nothing
for his complexion, or did I say that his complexion did nothing
for a heliotrope necktie? Poor Brookfield. It is his fate never to
rise quite high enough to be mediocre. As an author, that is. As
an actor he is not at all bad. I must be sure to say something
sweet the next time I see him, to make amends, although it is
perfectly true that his complexion and a heliotrope necktie are
disastrous together. But that is quite enough about him. There are
infinitely more interesting people to talk about—you and me, and
Bosie Douglas."

Bobbie smiled his Puck smile. "Bosie Douglas?"

"I have a fascinating story to tell. I met that beautiful young
man a year and a half ago, or perhaps it was more, when Lionel
Johnson brought him to Tite Street for tea, and it was not a suc-

cessful occasion; if my common sense didn't tell me that it is impossible for anyone to be bored when I set out to entertain him, I should say that he was bored."

"But you have no common sense, Oscar dear."

"You are quite right, Bobbie; nothing about me is common. I concluded that Lord Alfred Douglas was merely dull and thought no more about him—a preposterous statement, utterly false. I *intended* to think no more about him. But I was adding some chapters to *Dorian* for its publication as a book and had to reread much of it, and it struck me at once that I must have been thinking of Bosie Douglas when I wrote the description of Dorian—except that at that time I had never seen him. And yet the two are one and the same. Strange, don't you think?"

"Come, now, Oscar; the description of Dorian could be the description of any handsome young man, so long as he has honey-colored hair."

"Ah, but that is not all. Among my additions I wrote this sentence: 'It is the feet of clay that make the gold of the image precious.' Now, Bobbie, you may or may not believe me, but as I put down the words the thought of Bosie came into my mind, although the preceding sentence was 'She lacks the indefinable charm of weakness'—*she*, mind you. Was it not very strange, then, that I should think of him?"

"Not if he has 'the indefinable charm of weakness.' "

"That is precisely it," Oscar said triumphantly. "Bosie *has*. But I had no knowledge of it when I wrote my beautiful sentences; nevertheless, I thought of him. *Now* you cannot deny that this is very, very strange—delightfully sinister and interesting."

"Sinister, Oscar?"

"Sinister, my dear Bobbie, in the sense of ill-omened. Remember poor Dorian's fate. Since Bosie Douglas is so strangely linked to Dorian, might it not mean that I, as another Lord Henry, am to lead him to his downfall? For it was Lord Henry, remember, who told Dorian that the only way to get rid of a temptation is to yield to it—resist, and one's soul grows sick with longing. But in fact Bosie required no Lord Henry to advise him to yield to temptation; he was perfectly capable of yielding by himself. That is his weakness, his charming weakness, the feet of clay that make the gold of the image precious. And I am not to lead him to his downfall, I am to do exactly the opposite—save him from it.

"A few days ago I received a letter from Bosie. A charming letter, an exquisite letter, a letter only a young, beautiful poet could write. It had not been unexpected; I had sent him an inscribed copy of *The Picture of Dorian Gray*—surely I could do no less, considering that Bosie might have posed as the model for Dorian. But the letter was not one of thanks; it was an appeal for help, oh, most desperate, most moving."

"Isn't that rather astonishing, Oscar?" Bobbie inquired. "As I understand it, Lord Alfred is hardly a friend of yours; indeed, hardly an acquaintance. How can he justify making a desperate appeal for help to you?"

"Because he senses a kindred spirit in the author of *The Picture of Dorian Gray*. Dear Bobbie, Bosie Douglas is one of us. He is a gracious Greek boy who thinks only of love and beauty, and he has been betrayed by one to whom he gave his love—betrayed into the sordid hands of a blackmailer. Unless this brute is bought off or frightened off, he threatens to ruin Bosie's young and beautiful life—denounce him to his father, who I believe is something of a martinet. The poor boy—he is at his wits' end. That is to say, he *was*. I wrote immediately to reply to his appeal, to say that I was sure I could take care of the blackmailer. And I am sure I can."

"Dear Oscar," Bobbie said, "how? Blackmailers, you know, go on and on. There is always another copy of the letter or the photograph or whatever it happens to be. Or do you propose to frighten him off?" And Bobbie smiled at the thought. "Darling Oscar, you couldn't frighten anyone—your essential sweetness would come breaking through."

Oscar stroked his hand. "You are a very dear boy, and there is no one else to whom I can talk or wish to talk as I talk to you. No, I don't propose to soil my hands with this scoundrel; I propose, instead, to consult the excellent, the forever blessed, Edwin Levy."

"Who is the excellent, the forever blessed, Edwin Levy?"

"The excellent, the forever blessed, Edwin Levy is one of the earliest and certainly the unlikeliest of my disciples. He is a dear little businessman with great sad eyes and a bald head and a tremendous moustache, but when I say that he is a dear little businessman it is as if I said that Sarah is a dear little actress or that the sun is a dear little star—I call him a businessman only because that is how he chooses to refer to himself. A businessman can be anything, after all; it is such a vague, comfortable,

145

anonymous term; he can own all the diamond mines in South Africa, or be the secret power behind the Peacock Throne, or instruct the Maharaja of Mysore how much he can afford to waste in Monte Carlo next winter, and all this while he sits in a grubby office at which the shahs and sultans and maharajas of the world would turn up their gorgeous noses. That is the effect Edwin Levy has on me. I am persuaded that he knows all the secrets of the City of London, and of the fashionable world too. I am in awe of him."

"But you called him your disciple," Bobby said. "In awe of your disciple, Oscar?"

"Of course, dear Bobbie; all my disciples awe me, and you most of all, because you are the sweetest and gentlest. In fact, I don't know that I'm really entitled any longer to call Edwin Levy a disciple; I have the feeling that in his opinion I have rather slipped off since he first knew me. That was how long ago?—ten years, at any rate. Edwin Levy bought my first slim volume of poems, for he is not blind to beauty—his eyes are sad because he worships beauty but knows he can never create it. That is not my observation; it is his.

"The first knowledge I had of Edwin Levy's existence was a letter he wrote to me after reading my poems. It was not given to him, he said, to write poetry, but although he had been made sad by the discovery as a youth that he lacked the power to create beauty, perhaps it was just as well, for if that divine gift were granted to everyone, there would be no Prince of Poetry to stand supreme among us—which was the position he accorded me. I hardly have to tell you, Bobbie, that I was deeply touched by this superb compliment, fully warranted though I knew it to be. He went on to say that he would regard as a privilege the opportunity to serve me in any way he could. Certainly it was not in my heart to deny so modest a favor. I called on Edwin Levy and we got on famously together, as I had felt sure we would. I arranged with him to act as a steward of my interests while I was in America, and he insisted on my accepting an advance against my earnings there, with which I purchased, among other things, my magnificent fur coat—that same coat, Bobbie, that was to become the envy of every American who beheld it. I must add that the advance, seventy pounds, was repaid.

"Oh, Edwin Levy has been a tower of strength to me, bless him, bless him a thousand times. His only fault, and of course it isn't really, is that fairly often in the past he has been away on one of his mysterious journeys settling various crises—in the affairs of Patagonia and the life of the Dowager Empress of China, and so on —just when I have badly needed his advice and help. But he isn't away at present; I have an appointment with him; and mark my words, Bobbie, between us, Edwin Levy and I will make this black-mailer rue the day he was born."

"Is Lord Alfred to go with you to see Mr. Levy?" Bobbie asked.

"No, that isn't necessary; Bosie's letter to me gives all the details. Besides, it would be bound to embarrass him, and I wish to spare him all the embarrassment I can."

"Edwin Levy?"

Oscar smiled. "Dear Bobbie. Bosie, of course."

Edwin Levy put down Lord Alfred Douglas's letter. "A nasty business," he said. "A gutter business."

"I am profoundly sorry for this unfortunate young man," Oscar said. "He is a charming, gracious person, a beautiful person, who bears, moreover, a proud and ancient name, and his flowerlike life is in peril of being smeared with, as you say, the slime of the gutter. Of course I pity him and wish to help him."

"Are you good friends?"

"No, I can't say so. Acquaintances merely."

"Why should he approach you in this matter?"

"He may have nowhere else to turn."

"He has many friends."

"A few months ago, Mr. Levy, I am sure he wouldn't have approached me. We had met only once, seen each other in passing two or three times. But then, very recently, he read my book *The Picture of Dorian Gray*, and through it I think he saw me as he had not seen me before, saw me as one who would not turn from a kindred spirit in distress."

"I shall tell you why I think he approached you," Edwin Levy said. "I don't think it was because he read *The Picture of Dorian Gray*. Despite all the attention that book received, it was not a commercial success, was it? No. But *Lady Windermere's Fan* is a success, a huge commercial success, and an artistic success, and you are more famous than you have ever been, and have more money than you have ever had, and that is why, Mr. Wilde, I think Lord Alfred Douglas has approached you."

Oscar was shocked. "This is very harsh, surely."

"No, it is not. Let me tell you a little about that young man, that unfortunate young man, you called him, that charming, gracious person who bears a proud and ancient name and whose flowerlike life is in peril of being soiled. Lord Alfred Douglas is unfortunate, I agree. He is unfortunate in being the son of his father. You would never take him to be the son of the Marquess of Queensberry. The Marquess of Queensberry is an ugly little man, and as you know, Lord Alfred is—I shan't say beautiful, because I don't like to hear that word applied to a man, but handsome. If a son does not inherit his father's face and figure, what else can he inherit? The Marquess of Queensberry is a brave man, if bravery consists in riding to hounds and fighting in the amateur ring, but also he is unscrupulous, unprincipled, and foolishly, wickedly headstrong and determined to take pleasure for himself wherever he can and at whatever cost to others—*all this* his son inherits. And adds to it a fascination for the gutter."

"None of it is evident when one sees Lord Alfred," Oscar said. "Can it really be true?"

"I have my sources of information, Mr. Wilde. And I'm not in the habit of offering false information to my friends."

"Dear Mr. Levy, forgive me. But what am I to do? He has appealed to me. I can't ignore his appeal; as a gentleman I cannot. I could never bear to think of his pathetic letter without shame. It would weigh on me for the rest of my life."

Edwin Levy sat back and patted his bald head with a handkerchief; the late spring day was warm. "Help him, then," he said at last.

"How can I?"

"Give the blackmailer his own poison. In any blackmailer's life there are secrets that he will move heaven and earth to keep from the light. To learn what they are is an expensive, tiresome, nasty business, but it can be done. And if I agree to lend you a hand, Mr. Wilde," Edwin Levy said earnestly, "will you accept my word that Lord Alfred Douglas would be the very worst friend in the world for you, and after we get him out of this vile little mess, have no more to do with him?"

Oscar was silent.

"The chance of making a friend of him tempts you, does it? And you, Mr. Wilde, are you like your Lord Darlington, who can resist everything except temptation? Dear me," Edwin Levy continued in a friendlier tone of voice, "how I laughed at that, and at all the other clever things, and how proud my wife was to think that I knew their author. And I was proud too—not so proud, though, as I was of knowing the author of those beautiful poems."

"He is still the same person, Mr. Levy."

"Is he? Well, I should like to think so. But I wonder, would that young poet have been tempted to become the friend of someone who could write a letter like this? Someone in the position of having to write a letter like this?"

"Bosie Douglas is a young poet," Oscar said. "If a young poet is to know life to the full, as his poet's blood commands him to, he must know what it is to lie in the gutter. But his eyes will be on the stars."

Edwin Levy smiled. "That is beautifully said, and although in Alfred Douglas' case I don't for a moment believe it, I shall yield to it and agree to help you help him. But remember, Mr. Wilde, you were warned."

The lovely, white, naked body lay on the sand in an attitude indescribably graceful. Oscar bent over the golden head and the lips parted like rose petals. He tasted them: ah. Suddenly he was cruelly awake, even as he told himself that this was not a dream. He heard Constance whisper his name and knew that it was her lips he had tasted in his sleep, not Bosie Douglas'. "My darling, I am sorry," he said. "We must not sleep in the same bed again until my trouble is over; it is too much to risk."

Her hand rested lovingly on his cheek. She said softly, "Dear Oscar."

6

WHEN HE RECEIVED A NOTE FROM OSCAR TO SAY THAT THE matter was settled, Bosie came down from Oxford. Oscar had taken a private sitting room in the Royal Palace Hotel, in Kensington, for their tea and sandwiches; later they were to join Bobbie. Bosie looked so white and cold, so fragile, like a narcissus. He said, "Dear Oscar, how can I ever thank you?"

"How can you thank me? Ah," Oscar said musingly, "I wonder, I wonder. I think I have it. But I don't know—you may find it too great a request to grant."

"I shan't."

"Then you can tell me how you came to be called Bosie. I have had a passion to know ever since I first heard that adorable name."

"You mustn't be so modest, Oscar; are you always so modest in your requests? Oh dear, I do hope not. Very well, I shall tell you, but only if it is agreed between us that this is the first tiny seed pearl of the treasure of pearls that I am determined my thanks shall become. When I was little my mother's name for me was Boysie, which I made into Bosie, and I have never been able to get rid of it. I don't know now that I should want to get rid of it, really, but I must, I suppose—certainly I must before I am old."

"You will never be old, Bosie. You are Dorian come to life, but Dorian without his wicked heart."

The sandwiches arrived. Bosie sat on the sofa. "What are they?" he asked.

"Cucumber sandwiches, very, very thin. If it is not very, very thin a cucumber sandwich is the grossest insult known to the sensitive palate. It is perfect only if the slices of cucumber can be seen through." Oscar opened a sandwich and held one of the cucumber slices up to the window. "Yes, I can see through this admirably. It will be like eating a green shadow. I must positively not forget on some idle weekend to write a play about cucumber sandwiches. Dear Bosie, thank you, thank you for telling me the charming secret of your name. Now I am afraid you are going to learn how greedy I am—no, not greedy for cucumber sandwiches, I shan't have more than one, or perhaps two—greedy for information. Why did you write to me?"

Bosie ate a cucumber sandwich, and another, and licked the tip of one slim white finger. "They are excellent," he said. "I wrote to you begging you to help me because I knew you were kind."

"Ah, that is delightful to hear. But hadn't *The Picture of Dorian Gray* something to do with it?"

Bosie considered. "I don't think so. I hardly see how it could."

"I thought the book might have indicated to you that in spirit, in temperament, in tastes, we were not unlike each other. So at least I hoped—and hope, dear Bosie."

"But of course I knew we were from the moment we met, dearest Oscar. I have never had better cucumber sandwiches; I shall finish the whole plate unless you stop me, and if you dare to I shall be furious with you. How terribly I needed a kind, loving friend. But I despaired of finding him, for I knew how beastly, how horrid and false, people are, how ugly and coarse and cruel. I have learned that again and again. I learned it when I was still quite small, oh, quite small and innocent, and if ever I was in danger of forgetting it I was taught the same lesson again by the same teacher. Do you know who he was?"

"You mustn't frown, Bosie. You must never frown when you are with me. On your forehead a frown is sacrilege."

"My father. He is an inspired teacher. I am sure all that is vile was never taught by a teacher greater than he, always ready to instruct his children and his wife in some new beastliness. And his ardor hasn't lessened with the years, it has increased; his brutish little mind occupies itself constantly in an anxious search for new excuses to make us miserable. He would have been in ecstasies to hear from that monster."

"What monster?"

"The swine who tried to rent me. My father would have sent off letters about it to my mother and my brothers and sister—disgusting, poisonous, filthy letters. And how he would have grinned all over his hideous ape's face and what a shout of joy he would have uttered as he cut me off. But you saved me, Oscar. Dearest, dearest Oscar, you saved me. You are a saint."

"Bosie, it is very wicked of you to say such dreadful things about me. But who was the swine who tried to—rent you, I think you said?"

Bosie looked puzzled. "But you know, Oscar, of course you know. The filthy swine I told you about in my letter. You must have had to deal with him to get rid of him. Or aren't you familiar with that expression? You wouldn't be, of course you wouldn't be—you don't make a practice of dealing with black-mailers. That is all it means, really. You won't have this last sand-wich? Are you sure? Half of it then—I insist. Let us imagine that we are naked and I am in your arms and you are kissing me. Some-body knocks on the door and then gives a tremendous push and it flies open. That monster is there with a little assistant monster as witness and he threatens to go to the police or to my father or your wife unless we give him what he wants. That would be what is called renting us. Oh, I should love to see his face when he opens my letter. I sat down and wrote to him the moment I received your blessed note. How long ago that seems—quite another world. It will be a long time before he forgets what I had to say to him, even his thick hide will sting." And Bosie laughed.

It was a delicious sound. Oscar could not help himself; he had been excited by the casual, courtesan words, *Let us imagine that we are naked and I am in your arms and you are kissing me*; and the dream flamed in his mind, the white body turning seduc-tively on the golden sand; and he stared at the laughing boy, the beautiful boy, and got up—not gracefully, alas no, all too clumsily, as he knew, and hated his big, clumsy body but was excited even more by thought of its contrast with the beautiful slim body on the sofa. He almost stumbled. He sat down next to Bosie. "You beautiful boy," he said.

The scarlet lips parted just as they had in the dream. "Must we go on to see your friend Bobbie?" Bosie murmured. "I am sure he is very nice, but he must not expect not to share you with others. Why don't you send him a note? Then we can stay here together comfortably for the afternoon. Shall we? *I* should like to."

Bosie's love sustained him for a month. Then an antique official known as the Lord Chamberlain loomed up; this tottering ruin possessed the power of a censor to ban plays from the stage by refusing them a license. It appeared that the task of reading all plays intended for production was too much for him, and therefore he had appointed Edward F. Smyth Pigott to be his official ex-aminer of plays. Pigott (of course he would not call himself Pigott, he would be content with nothing less than *Smyth* Pigott) read and passed for production the vulgar burlesque *The Poet and the Puppets*, but when Oscar's new play, *Salomé*, came before him

—for Sarah Bernhardt had decided, and Oscar had been happy to agree, that its premiere should take place in London—Pigott rummaged deep in the dusty files of the Lord Chamberlain's office and emerged triumphant with a law forbidding the production of any play in which biblical characters appeared.

Oscar crumpled Pigott's announcement furiously into a ball. "Damn this Philistine England!"

There was only one way to hit back that would be dramatic enough. He would become a Frenchman.

"My resolution is deliberately taken," he told the London representatives of *Le Gaulois* and *Echo de Paris*. "Since it is impossible to have a work of art performed in England, I shall transfer myself to another fatherland, of which I have long been enamored."

The London papers got hold of this announcement. Oscar appeared in *Punch* in a revolting assortment of cartoons, grotesquely exaggerating his *embonpoint;* and in the *Spectator* the deplorable William Watson (a minor poet in whose poetry there was not enough fire to boil a steam kettle) delivered himself of these lines:

> And wilt thou, Oscar, from us flee,
>   And must we, henceforth, wholly sever?
> Shall thy laborious *jeux-d'esprit*
>   Sadden our lives no more forever?

Watson should be crowned Poet Nauseate. Oscar really did feel sick, though. The doctor said gravely, "Mr. Wilde, I shall be perfectly frank and tell you that you have been eating too much and drinking too much and smoking too much. We must put you under a strict regime for several weeks—no wines, no spirits, no cigarettes, and only the simplest foods."

"What are the simplest foods, doctor?"

"Porridge, dry toast, boiled eggs. A lean lamb chop, a boiled potato. Weak tea and blancmange. That is the sort of thing. Steamed rice is valuable too."

"How splendid. May I ask," Oscar inquired, "if you have seen *Lady Windermere's Fan?*"

"I have indeed," the doctor said, smiling.

"Did you enjoy it?"

"Heartily. I don't think I ever laughed so much in my life."

"Do you look forward to seeing another play by the same author?"

"Very much indeed."

"There will never be another. After my first full day of porridge, dry toast, boiled eggs, a lean lamb chop, a boiled potato, weak tea, blancmange, and a heaping plate of valuable steamed rice, I shall cut my throat."

"Then," the doctor said, "there is only one answer: you must go to a spa and take the cure. There is no steamed rice, no blancmange in this cure. No; massage, drinking the waters, and a somewhat restricted diet will do the trick. I suggest Bad Homburg, in Germany. Stay there for a month at least, Mr. Wilde. We must preserve you for more *Lady Windermeres*. Otherwise my wife would cut *my* throat."

If only Bosie could come. But of course then there could be no cure. Bosie's rose-leaf lips were for kissing and for laughter, not for the gloomy quaffing of medicinal waters; in his company one's table must always be furnished with the rarest wines, the richest foods; when he was near, one didn't go to bed at ten or rise at half past seven—with him the nights were long. Although Bosie could not be there in his young, sweet self, in a sense he would be; the remembered sound of his voice and the touch of his lips would fortify Oscar for the most damnable rigors of the cure. And wasn't the cure really *for* Bosie? Must not he be a friend, a lover, whom Bosie could love for more than his mind?

The first few days at Bad Homburg were excruciating (the German language alone, Oscar thought, was a kind of medicinal waters), but then the quaking in his stomach and the heaviness in his head departed, and he found himself actually anxious to work.

George Alexander had been after him for a successor to *Lady Windermere* ever since the play's first night. So had half a dozen others; for example, Herbert Beerbohm Tree, dear little Max Beerbohm's half brother. Herbert was an actor manager as was Alec, and quite as successful, but in his presence one was not conscious as one always was with Alec of a steely, businesslike mind steadily ticking away. Herbert made a beautiful audience; in fact, he had a wit of his own, and he would never refuse the extra glass of champagne that is the best glass of the whole evening.

Oscar would give Herbert first refusal of his new play. He had the first act in mind already; it would appeal to England's only intelligent critics, William Archer and A. B. Walkley; the rest were barbarians, to rank with the Huns and the Goths (the vulgar mass of critics had thrown their petticoats over their heads and keened and sobbed at the shocking pass the English theater had come to with *Lady Windermere's Fan*).

After a month at Bad Homburg Oscar felt years younger and was eight pounds lighter. The masseur, a powerful, talkative man, said he had never been more pleased with his work, although of course one had to grant that Mr. Wilde's diet and the water had played their part. The last he doubted, Oscar replied; he rather thought that the only effect of the thousands of gallons he had drunk was to permit him to share the intimate sensations of a Roman aqueduct.

On the cross-channel steamer, returning to England, he strode the deck like a lion. Constance and the children marveled over his appearance. Oscar carried both the boys on his back for a canter around the room.

His first call in London was to the doctor, to thank him.

"I am delighted, Mr. Wilde. Now we must keep you healthy with some form of regular exercise."

"I've no objection to massage, provided the masseur has difficulty in expressing himself, or, better still, cannot speak at all, only grunt. Yes, he may grunt."

"Massage is all to the good, but also I should like to see you go in for something more active—one of our sound old country sports."

"Forgive me, doctor, but I'm afraid I deplore the popular idea of our sound old country sports. The English country gentleman galloping after a fox—the unspeakable furiously chasing the uneatable."

"What would you say to golf?"

"It is odd that you should mention it; I was thinking of the very same thing. The clothes are attractive, if one has a good leg. And I believe there is a links—or does one call it a link?—fairly close to the country place I am taking for the rest of the summer."

This was Grove Farm, near Cromer, in Norfolk; some friends who lived in the neighborhood had recommended it to Constance as quiet and attractive. Oscar felt that he had the new play at his fingertips, but he doubted that he could write it in London in the dying weeks of summer. It was to be in four acts. Grove Farm was so pleasant, and the absence of the Café Royal and similar temptations so helpful, that by the first week of September he was able to tell Beerbohm Tree that two acts were done and the third almost finished. Oscar was delighted with them; he longed for an audience.

"I thought we might ask Lord Alfred to join us for a few days," he said to Constance. "Would you mind?"

"Mind? Goodness me, no. Have you changed your opinion of him, then?"

"I've forgotten what it was."

"Don't you remember when he came to tea that day? You found him dull."

"Ah, yes; and so he was. I dare say the poor boy's troubles were weighing on him. He could hardly be blamed for seeming apathetic."

"Oh, dear," Constance said. "What is the matter? What troubles?"

"Most unfortunate family life. I understand that his mother, Lady Queensberry, couldn't be more charming, but the marquess is an extremely difficult man. I met him once, I can't remember where, years ago. He has a monkeyish little face and bristling red hair. A great fox hunter. Also an amateur boxing champion. He is the author of the Queensberry Rules, you know."

"I didn't know," Constance admitted with a smile. "What are they?"

"Rules for fair play in the prize ring. Out of the prize ring, it would appear that fair play is the last thing the marquess thinks of. His behavior to his wife and children was outrageous and disgusting, Bosie has told me, and at length the marchioness had no choice but to divorce him. You may be sure there were ample grounds. Bosie's life as a child must have been agony."

"How wicked, how very, very wicked to make a little boy suffer —it is unforgivable. The poor young man. We must be very kind to him."

"You are a dear," Oscar said.

A flurry of telegrams arrived from Bosie; had missed train connections, would be delayed; had not missed train connections, would not be delayed; a thousand apologies, had missed train connections after all—sorry for being such a fearful nuisance—could they ever forgive him.

Constance laughed over the telegrams. "He *is* polite. It says a great deal for his mother's care and guidance. They must be very close."

"Yes, he is devoted to her, and she to him. Apparently he takes after her in everything; certainly he doesn't after his father—never in a hundred years would one guess that there was any relationship between them, this handsome, sweet boy and the ugly, spiteful little man."

Oscar had been leading a simple life at Grove Farm, up early and in bed early and drinking hardly anything, but he shuddered to think that Bosie, the beautiful son of a noble house, should have any cause, however trifling, to rank the Wildes as middle class in tastes or habits or manners. So Oscar devoted a good deal of nervous thought to the menu, the wine, and the domestics' service.

Bosie, stepping down from the station cab in the early-afternoon sunshine, looked hardly a day over seventeen, though in fact he was twenty-two. "I was delayed in London by family friends," he explained, "and then, of all the stupid things to do, I actually managed to miss my station; I went on to heaven knows where before I discovered my mistake, and in the confusion of scrambling out of the carriage before being carried off again, I left behind the flowers I brought for Mrs. Wilde and the box of your favorite cigarettes, Oscar."

"Never mind," Oscar said. "We have flowers in profusion and thousands and thousands of cigarettes, and the very best present you can bring is yourself."

Constance said, "We are delighted you are here, Lord Alfred. And it will be quite useless for you to try to leave us too soon, for I shall arrange to have you miss all your train connections."

Bosie's young laugh rang out.

Later he praised the dinner and wines to the skies. Constance, it was plain to see, was enchanted.

After dinner, Oscar said, "Bosie, I have taken a great liberty with you, have made you a character in my new play. Do you mind?"

"I am flattered and delighted, Oscar; at last I shall be famous. Please tell me the clever things I say."

"There isn't very much of you, because if there were you would steal the whole thing and demolish the plot, but what there is I like very much. In order to confuse everyone hopelessly, I have called you Lord Alfred, a lesson taught by the magnificent and doomed Edgar Allan Poe in his story *The Purloined Letter*—the very best disguise is none at all."

"Yes, of course, and do I smoke gold-tipped cigarettes?"

"Most certainly you smoke gold-tipped cigarettes. Lady Stutfield says to you, 'How very, very charming those gold-tipped cigarettes of yours are, Lord Alfred,' and you reply, 'They are awfully expensive. I can only afford them when I'm in debt.' "

Bosie burst into laughter. "Oh, glorious."

"Then Lady Stutfield says, 'It must be terribly, terribly distressing to be in debt,' but you correct her. 'One must have some occupation nowadays,' you point out. 'If I hadn't my debts I shouldn't have anything to think about. All the chaps I know are in debt.' 'But,' she asks, 'don't the people to whom you owe money give you a great, great deal of annoyance?' 'Oh, good heavens, no,' you say. '*They* write; I don't.' "

"Oscar, you are really too wickedly perceptive," Bosie declared. "How ever did you know I am always in debt?"

"Ah, that is a virtue of my own nature and my own race, and it sings out to me in you. You have nothing more to say in *A Woman of No Importance*, and in fact in the last act you won't appear at all, but that is all right—you simply wouldn't belong there. The play is about a saint, Mrs. Arbuthnot, and a sinner, Lord Illingworth. Lord Illingworth has never married. Lady Hunstanton, at whose country home the play takes place, says of him, 'He may marry any day. I was in hopes he would have married Lady Kelso. But I believe he said her family was too large. Or was it her feet?' "

At this Constance and Bosie went off into shrieks; when he was able to speak again Bosie cried, "Oh, more, more! More Lady Hunstanton. Oscar, you cannot, you absolutely cannot refuse to us more Lady Hunstanton. Mrs. Wilde, please insist."

"I insist, Oscar!"

"Very well, then; let me see. Ah yes, Lady Hunstanton is assuring another of her guests, Mrs. Allonby—*not* Mrs. Arbuthnot, please note; Mrs. Arbuthnot is the saint—that life in the country need not be in the least unsophisticated or unsophisticating. 'Why,' she says, 'it was from Melthorpe, which is only two miles from here, that Lady Belton ran away with Lord Fethersdale. I remember the occurrence perfectly. Poor Lord Belton died three days afterwards of joy, or gout. I forget which. We had a large party staying here at the time, so we were all very much interested in the whole affair.'"

Bosie said, "I would be happy to spend the rest of my life with Lady Hunstanton. Do give us more of her."

"No," Oscar said; "I would prefer you to hear Mrs. Allonby's definition of the Ideal Man. I confidently count on its being so savagely attacked by the critics that it will become famous. They will take care to associate me with Mrs. Allonby, who is not a saint, but never with Mrs. Arbuthnot, who is. I make this remark merely to demonstrate their bias. Here is Mrs. Allonby—but I can't remember it all, I shall have to get her speech from my manuscript."

When he returned, he read: "'The Ideal Man. Oh, the Ideal Man should talk to us as if we were goddesses, and treat us as if we were children. He should refuse all our serious requests, and gratify every one of our whims. He should encourage us to have caprices, and forbid us to have missions. He should always say much more than he means, and always mean much more than he says. He should never run down other pretty women. That would show he had no taste, or make one suspect that he had too much. No; he should be nice about them all, but say that somehow they don't attract him. If we ask him a question about anything, he should give us an answer all about ourselves. He should invariably praise us for whatever qualities he knows we haven't got. But he should be pitiless, quite pitiless, in reproaching us for the virtues that we have never dreamed of possessing. He should never believe that we know the use of useful things. That would be unforgivable. But he should shower on us everything we don't want. He should persistently compromise us in public, and treat us with absolute respect when we are alone. And yet he should be always ready to have a perfectly terrible scene whenever we want one, and to become miserable, absolutely miserable, at a moment's notice.'"

He paused. "You aren't the Ideal Man, then, dear," Constance said, smiling. "Or are you, I wonder? Is that the side of you I don't know?"

"Most emphatically I am not the Ideal Man according to Mrs. Allonby's definition; if I were, I should find myself unbearable. Now, Mrs. Arbuthnot, the saint, although the world would hardly call her that, is the mother of Gerald Arbuthnot, to whom Lord Illingworth has offered the chance of a brilliant career. Mrs. Arbuthnot knows that Lord Illingworth is Gerald's father; the young man and Lord Illingworth do not know. The dramatic question is—when the truth comes out, which way will Gerald turn? Toward the marvelous job and the man who refused his name to the betrayed girl and their infant son? Or will Gerald turn away from that glittering prospect in order to remain with her, his mother? I haven't decided. You must advise me."

"To his mother, of course," Constance said; and Bosie cried, "Of course, of course."

"Ah, but I haven't presented the case fairly. You don't know Lord Illingworth, the father. You would be drawn to him at once if he came into the room. His appearance is most distinguished. His smile seems meant for you alone, and you feel that you could listen to him for hours and hours, his manner is so charming, his voice so delightful. This is the kind of thing he says, in talking with Gerald, after the boy has confessed that he is ignorant of the world and feels afraid of it: "You mustn't be afraid, Gerald. Remember that you've got on your side the most wonderful thing in the world —youth. There is nothing like youth. The middle-aged are mortgaged to life. The old are in life's lumber room. But youth is the Lord of Life. Youth has a kingdom waiting for it. Everyone is born a king, and most people die in exile, like most kings. To win back my youth, there is nothing I wouldn't do—except take exercise, get up early, or be a useful member of the community.'"

Bosie laughed. "He sounds like you, Oscar."

"My dear boy, how absurd. *I* take exercise, *I* get up early, do I not? And listen to Lord Illingworth on marriage—can you conceive me talking like this? 'Twenty years of romance make a woman look like a ruin,' he remarks, 'but twenty years of marriage make her something like a public building. Men marry because they are tired, women because they are curious. Both are disappointed. When one is in love one begins by deceiving oneself and ends by deceiving others, which is what the world calls a romance. But a really *grande passion* is rare nowadays; among most people there is simply not the capacity for one, they are too trivial, too shallow. How sad for them. For in life nothing is really serious except passion.'"

"Oscar, if after things like that you have the young man go with his father," Constance said, "you *will* be set on by the critics. And you won't be able to blame them, for they will think you are absolutely in earnest—they don't know that you write these things with your tongue in your cheek; they've never seen you with your family, playing with the boys on the nursery floor."

Oscar could not sleep. Was Bosie, too, lying awake? Had there been a special meaning in his glance as they had parted for the night? Constance had been with them the whole evening. It could very well be that he was waiting for him, was expecting him, was hurt perhaps (he was so terribly sensitive) that Oscar had not come to his room. Constance and Oscar had their own bedrooms at Grove Farm, and Bosie's, at the end of the corridor, was separated from them by a smaller empty room. The house was solid; it would not creak and pop suspiciously as he passed from one bedroom to another.

Then it was settled, was it? He *was* going? Oscar felt the pleasant tickle of tightening flesh, a small quick dance of invisible fingertips over his skin. He lay still for another few moments. Then he got up, in one swift, determined movement. There was a full moon; its light filled the room. But he would need a light in the hallway. Oscar found a match and put the flame to the lamp wick. The little leaping circle of blue fire settled into a pale even glow. He opened the bedroom door. Might he see, floating toward him down the hall, another pale globe, another lamp, held by Bosie, unable to wait longer, coming to him? The hallway was empty and silent.

He must make sure that Constance was asleep. He crossed to her door and opened it. He recognized the gentle rhythm of her breath.

Oscar entered the room a little way, raised the lamp, and looked down on her closed eyes and dreaming face. Her dream was pleasant; a soft smile curved the sweet lips. He looked at her now, the graceful lines of her neck and breasts, without the slightest stirring of desire. This new love was the rarest, the most precious, most gracious love, this love that was more than love because it was friendship too and therefore a love that no woman could give.

"Oscar."

Thinking of Bosie, he had seen without seeing a flicker of her eyelids. Her eyes were open now and looking into his. She said again quietly, "Oscar."

"Yes," he said.

"Why are you smiling?"

"Because you were," Oscar said. "I came in because I thought I heard a cry from you. And found you smiling. I wonder what your dream was? It must have been very happy."

"I am still so close to it that I can tell you. I was dreaming of our garden. We were in it together."

"Some day we shall be again. Good night, my darling."

"Good night, Oscar dear."

He closed the door and returned to his room. The moonlight had grown cold.

But they could be alone on the golf links. Before Bosie's arrival, Oscar had played a few holes every day.

"I did not *play* it, really, I *teased* it," he explained. "It is not quite *all* nonsense; the grass is refreshing to walk on, and there is something to be said for anything that requires one to wear special clothes—I exclude deep-sea diving. But this tremendous lashing about with clubs, this digging and gouging, these paralytic crouchings on the putting green—when the whole thing could be got through so much more easily and simply by not hitting and cutting and chopping and tapping the ball but by taking it in your hand and *throwing* it. However, my doctor would be beside himself with admiration—I haven't missed a day in the last week. That is due to you, my dearest boy. So many things are due to you. Do you know that I am grateful to the scoundrel who tried to rent you? Would we have ever really known each other without him?"

Bosie played golf superbly. Poised to drive, he was like a slim white birch, curving, then released in a sweeping flow.

"Of course we would have, Oscar. Eventually I would have got over my shyness with you."

"Bosie, were you really? The first time we met? Were you *shy?*"

"I was dreadfully shy; I didn't know what to do. Couldn't think of a thing to say. I'd never felt such a fool, and I'd never less wanted to. I was sure you must have thought me the stupidest person you'd ever met. I suppose I *should* be grateful to that monster, though. He did bring us together. I've forgotten to tell you, Oscar—he was absolutely, wonderfully furious with my letter. It almost threw him into convulsions; he positively *foamed*. And there was nothing, nothing, nothing he could do, because you'd been so clever. Oh, wouldn't he *love* to have me again, wouldn't he though."

"Bosie, you don't mean the brute who tried to rent you?"

"Of course I do."

"Then did he have you once? That hideous little man?"

"But you knew, Oscar."

"I didn't know. I thought there was someone else, who was his accomplice. I thought the ugly little man was only the blackmailer, not your lover. I was sure that was what you said in your letter to me."

Bosie put his arm around Oscar's shoulders. "Darling Oscar, he wasn't my lover. It was purely a matter of one evening, and all the fault of the champagne. Can't you see that *that* was why I was so desperate, so terrified? To have people think that he, that little brute, that monster, had meant anything to me. Who would have believed that it was only a foolish mistake?"

"It was a very foolish mistake," Oscar said.

"It was, it was."

"You must never permit yourself——"

"Never, never. I loathe ugliness in everything. You will see, Oscar, you will meet my friends—sweet, charming people, not like that little brute. When you return to London I shall give you the names of two or three I am sure you would like to meet. I was with them before I came here; it was that, really, that delayed me."

"Yes, I think I had better meet your friends, if only to protect you."

Bosie laughed. "You don't know how silly that is. Protect me from Maurice and Alfred!"

"My dearest boy," Oscar said, "in many respects you are still a child, and I am altogether in earnest when I say that I intend to look after you. Your life is too precious to risk soiling at the hands of these beastly blackmailers."

"They are not like that, Oscar. You will see."

7

OSCAR WENT TO SEE MAURICE SCHWABE FIRST, AT HIS ROOMS in Margaret Street, off Regent Street. Schwabe was a gentleman, an attractive chap in his early twenties. Within a short time they were Oscar and Maurice to each other. Maurice would be charmed if Oscar could come to a small dinner he was giving the next evening; he apologized for its being such short notice, but then he hadn't been in a position before today to ask Oscar anywhere—he had longed to meet him but somehow had never been able to manage it. "Of course," he added, "I suppose I could have asked a relative of mine for an introduction, because I believe you know him—Frank Lockwood?"

"I *have* met Sir Frank," Oscar said, "but I can't possibly remember where."

"He married my Auntie Julia, poor thing—Julia, I mean. He is so much the barrister I am sure my poor aunt can never feel certain while Frank is making love to her whether he isn't under the impression that he has risen to address a learned judge. I should hate to have met you under his auspices; this is so much nicer—under Bosie's. Or are you angry with him at the moment? So many of his friends so often are. It is very stupid of them. Bosie isn't like anyone else, the ordinary standards don't apply. He is himself, beautiful and unique."

"Ah, I do so agree. I can't imagine being angry with Bosie; it would be as wicked and pointless as losing one's temper with a flower. I was a little concerned about him, though. It will amuse you to hear, Maurice, that I thought I should protect him against such evil companions as you and Alfred Taylor."

"That is almost the funniest thing I have ever heard. It is *quite* perfect. Oh, you must tell Alfred. Shall we go to see him now, you and I? Why shouldn't we? I think it is a charming idea. Please say yes, Oscar, and I shall grow even fonder of you."

"Dear Maurice, that is irresistible."

Alfred Taylor's rooms were in Little College Street, not far from the Houses of Parliament; but Oscar would not hold that against him. He had been expecting Oscar. "Bosie sent me a note last week to say you would be looking in, and yesterday I had another. He will be here later on, unless there is a telegram from him at the last minute announcing that he has been unavoidably detained. I hardly think that will happen, though, because he told me to make arrangements for a small dinner party tonight. If you hadn't called, Mr. Wilde, I would have got in touch with you to inform you of this royal command."

"I like that—royal command!" Oscar exclaimed. "And have you made arrangements, Alfred? Please observe that your name to me is Alfred, as mine to you must be Oscar."

"Thank you, Oscar. Yes, I have booked a private room at Kettner's."

Maurice promptly declared that it would be his dinner. "In that way, you can't leave me out. Only the four of us, Alfred?"

"I've asked a nice new boy to come too," Alfred said with a smile. "His name is Sidney Mavor. He is quite excited to think that he is going to meet Mr. Oscar Wilde."

Alfred's rooms were lit by candlelight; the air was perfumed; dark drapes covered the windows. A divan stood almost in the middle of the floor, with mounds of cushions. Beneath one's feet the rugs seemed soft as fern. Oscar had been in an atmosphere like this on the rue Blondel, where presently from behind an Oriental screen a laughing girl, half naked, would appear, and there would be iced champagne and warm, perfumed water and dainty little towels.

Alfred suggested a cup of tea. Alfred was as comfortable as an old shoe; possibly no gentleman in London seemed less likely to *wear* an old shoe. Alfred wore patent-leather slippers, black-silk socks, exquisite dove-gray trousers, a velvet smoking jacket, a white shirt crisp as a dairymaid's bonnet, and an Old Marlburian tie. But his face was not a fop's, though it was elegantly shaved and powdered; a silly, superior stare could never glaze those friendly eyes. Alfred's face was loose, crinkly, a kind if rather *puppyish* face. Pouring the tea, he chatted on cozily.

There was a freedom here, a consciousness of being a member of a select group infinitely superior to that world in the crass sunshine outside. Dear, sweet, generous Bosie, who could have kept these good companions, this private world, for himself, but who (with a smile, knowing so much more than Oscar at that time knew) had freely offered them to Oscar.

Suddenly he saw himself and Bosie as they truly were to each other: the youth, the man, in the noblest of all relationships, offering all to each other without meanness, without jealousy, each content that his lover should sip as he willed from other lips, knowing that his lips would always be the dearest.

"Dear Alfred," Oscar said, "I cannot tell you how happy I am that we are friends."

"Dear Mr. Wilde," Lady Queensberry said, at her country place near Bracknell, where Bosie and Oscar were spending the weekend, "I am so very pleased that you and Bosie have become friends. Yours is an influence he desperately needs, that of an older man who will be to him everything his father was not and could never have been. But, Mr. Wilde"—and here she put her hand on Oscar's and let it rest there—"it would not be fair to you, and I could not bear to think, that you should so generously enter into this friendship with my son knowing only one side of his nature, the side you have seen today, the side you have always seen, I have no doubt—an affectionate, thoughtful, tender nature. For there is another side."

Her leisurely steps had found the way, seemingly by chance, to a path through the yellowing October woods. In the muted, arboreal light Lady Queensberry's slim figure and cameo profile looked youthful enough to pass for those of Bosie's sister: here was the source of his beauty. How *could* this lovely lady have given her hand to that ugly, that really monkeylike, little man, the marquess?

"Shall we sit down?" she asked, indicating a fallen tree trunk. "This is a favorite place of mine. The unpleasant things in my life seem very far away."

"I am distressed that there should be any," Oscar said.

"It is the other side of his character," she continued somberly, "to which I owe the unpleasant things. I don't mean that he is responsible for all of them, or even, I suppose, in the last analysis, for any. They come from his father—the dreadful Douglas temperament. My other sons don't have it, thank God, thank God, nor has my daughter. But Bosie's chief faults would not be so disturbing in her; people almost expect to find them in a pretty young girl. You see, Mr. Wilde, he is vain, and he is *all wrong* about money."

Oscar laughed, for from the sinister sound of "the dreadful Douglas temperament" he had expected some quite shocking revelation. Vanity, extravagance—good heavens, the one was a graceful flower for a beautiful youth to wear, the other an aristocratic trait that ran strongly in Oscar's own blood.

He apologized for his laughter. "Forgive me, dear Lady Queensberry; I seem to make light of what you have told me, and anything any mother says of her children should never be made light of. I am grateful to you, and I shall not forget."

"I had to warn you, even if it should lose Bosie your friendship. I pray that these faults—they are very real, Mr. Wilde—will not."

"His friendship, and his mother's, if I may now claim it, are far too dear to me ever to be lost."

"Thank you. And you won't tell him?"

"Tell him?"

"Of my warning. Please do not. He has a temper, you see—this too I am bound to warn you of."

Bosie had a temper. Could a rose frown? A hyacinth shout and stamp? Even if they could, it would be adorable. But Lady Queensberry was watching him anxiously, and Oscar put on a serious face. "I promise that Bosie will never hear a word from me about the nature of our talk."

Later Bosie asked, "Did mother ask you to go on that nice walk in order to tell you horrid things about me?"

"How absurd, Bosie. Lady Queensberry would never say horrid things about you. She is devoted to you. She worships you."

"Of course she does. And I am devoted to her, and there is the trouble. Mother can't bear to think that anyone else should have any part of my affection and love. She wishes to have it all for herself. This leads to her undermining me, in the sweetest and gentlest way possible, to my friends."

"My dearest boy," Oscar protested, "your mother told me how delighted she is that we are friends—does that sound like undermining?"

"Ah," Bosie said. "Then you *did* talk about me. I understood you to say you didn't."

"I said nothing of the sort. I said——"

"Darling Oscar, don't, don't ever try to hide things from me, I beg of you, for I could not bear to think that there is anything in which you aren't as completely open and frank and candid with me as I am with you, as I wish always to be, because of our love."

"I am not hiding anything from you."

"You were trying to, Oscar, and of course it was quite useless.

167

I could tell when you came back from your walk that Mother had been up to something because of the way you looked, as though you were afraid that if you looked at me openly and frankly you would give the show away——"

"Bosie, Bosie, this is preposterous——"

"—and I would know that Mother had warned you about me and made you promise you wouldn't say a word."

"Bosie, you are making all this up."

"She *didn't* warn you about me?"

"She did not."

"Not a single thing?"

"Not a single thing."

"Nothing, *nothing*?"

"Nothing."

"You talked only about the birds and the flowers and the lovely autumn woods and nice safe things like that?"

"Yes!"

"Why are you faltering, then? Oh, Oscar, Oscar! Not telling me the truth, not daring to tell me the truth—trying to hide it. For you *are* hiding it, aren't you? You were warned about me, weren't you? You were, you were!"

"For God's sake, Bosie!" Oscar cried, almost desperately. "Then I *was*."

"Ah. Bless you, Oscar, bless you for telling the truth. You have saved our love."

"But not by your mother. Your mother said not a word against you, she would be incapable of it. Do you think it could make the slightest difference to me if she *had*? I don't concern myself with other people's opinions—good heavens, I hope I am above that— not even those of so beautiful and gracious a lady as your mother, not even the opinions of a man who knows more of what is going on in the world than all your city people and politicians and diplomatists and newspaper writers put together. If I had taken *his* warnings to heart, we would never have become friends."

"Who was this?" Bosie asked.

"My friend Edwin Levy. I told you that a good friend helped me to help you in your trouble. He knew a great deal about your family; he knows a great deal about everything; it is his business to keep well informed. He told me that your father is a wicked, unscrupulous person and that you, Bosie, as regards character, that is, are cast in his image."

Bosie gave a shout of laughter. "Oh, that is really too precious! Think of his telling you that, the dirty little Jew."

"That is not very kind to someone who was very kind to me, and who helped you."

"I am sure I beg his pardon," Bosie said graciously. "He is a clean little Jew. I am cast in my father's image, am I? Oh dear, how he would love to hear it—how he would *dote* on the thought. This is a very, very clever chap, this Edwin Levy of yours, I can see that—his shrewd Semitic eye pierces at once to the heart of things. We must communicate this darling bit of information to the marquess. Dear Sir, The eminent Edwin Levy, who knows everything, says that Bosie owes all his unfortunate tastes to you. It follows, then, that when you criticize him, you are in fact criticizing yourself. In future, you had better seize every opportunity to boast of how perfectly wonderful the dear boy is, how brave, how handsome, how kind, how courteous, how *generous*—above all, how very, very generous." Bosie was seized by another fit of laughter.

The weekend at Lady Queensberry's was followed by a weekend at Oxford; Bosie had a handsome set of rooms on the High Street that he shared with young Viscount Encombe, who could not have been more charming. They were looked after by an agreeable but plain youth called Walter Grainger. Oscar thoroughly enjoyed himself.

It was difficult to settle down into the humdrum routine of work after all that wine and laughter. The last act of the new play, A *Woman of No Importance*, dragged.

Whenever he felt really down in the dumps there was the infallible tonic of a visit to Alfred Taylor's. He was the most hospitable fellow in the world and usually had an attractive friend staying with him. Young Sidney Mavor, for instance, had beautiful manners, and behaved quite like a little lord. Oscar saw Sidney two or three times at Alfred's and then at the Albermarle Hotel, for the night. There was none of Edward Shelley's hysterical nonsense, and Oscar sent him a silver cigarette case inscribed *Sidney from O.W. October 1892.*

Oscar took it for granted that there was a certain amount of risk in coming to the heavily curtained rooms on Little College Street.

"That is one of the most charming things about being here," he told Alfred. "It adds a taste, a spice, a very rare spice. I do hope I'm not mistaken—there *is* a risk, isn't there?"

"Would you forsake me, Oscar, if it were as safe as your Aunt Nelly's?" Alfred asked, his blue eyes twinkling.

"My dear fellow, it is charming of you to give me an Aunt Nelly; I have always regretted not having one. Of course I wouldn't forsake you, but the quite safe soon tends to become the quite dull, don't you think?"

"Yes, I do."

"You are such an agreeable old chap," Oscar said affectionately. "You didn't mean that, you only said it because you can't bear to think of hurting anyone's feelings. You would really like a perfectly safe life, wouldn't you?"

"Well, yes," Alfred said, "I would, because I don't like trouble; and since I am what I am, and English laws are what they are, there is always the chance of it. I must tell you honestly, though, Oscar, that I don't think it's a very big chance. We are awfully circumspect here, there aren't any frightful drunken parties with brutal women, and I make it a point to be on the very best of terms with the policemen on the beat. And you know how well behaved our boys are; they are perfect little gentlemen, all of them. There is much, much less chance of trouble with them than with—well, than with—" Alfred's amiable, puppyish face assumed an uncomfortable look.

"You mustn't stop now, dear Alfred, or I shall never forgive you. Less chance of trouble with our little lads than with——?"

"Oscar, I had no intention of getting into this, but since I have I'm glad of it. Because you are a decent, kind person, and you were quite right when you said I couldn't bear to think of hurting your feelings. If I *do* hurt them now, and lose your friendship, I shall be miserable, but I am going to tell you nevertheless. It isn't our little lads, as you call them, who are most likely to cause you trouble. It is Bosie."

"Bosie?" Oscar said. "But I thought you liked him."

"I do, of course. Who could resist Bosie? But liking someone doesn't mean that he can't harm you. Bosie can do you harm in spite of himself, in spite of his love for you, Oscar, which I am sure can't be doubted. There is a terrible thing in his life, his feud with his father. It is a shocking thing to say, but I have found my-self thinking that Bosie and his father are like lovers who have come to hate each other because each has discovered in the other things he despises in himself."

"Dear me," Oscar murmured. "Surely this is very profound, Al-fred, and therefore quite false?"

"Neither will leave the other alone," Alfred went on. "They are always exchanging horrible letters and thinking of new insults and jeers and jibes. One would think it was really a waste of time on Bosie's part. Everyone knows the marquess is a beast, not fit to be in society, and *Bosie* knows everyone knows it. There is nothing he can possibly prove about his father beyond what the marquess has proved again and again and again by his own behavior. But Bosie won't stop and the marquess won't either until they have destroyed each other; and if because of your love for Bosie you should become involved in their feud—that, Oscar, is how I think you can be very badly hurt."

As Alfred sat back on the sofa and sipped his tea with a troubled face, Oscar said, "You are a dear old nanny with a heart of gold, and I promise to remember every word."

From his honey-colored hair to his little white dovelike feet, Bosie was perfection. Bosie was his dawn, and his fiery noon, and his cool, hushed evening sweetness. There had never been such a love as his and Bosie's. It was far more than a sexual love, though a madness of kisses could never be quite dismissed when Bosie was near. Bosie's love was the gift of gifts. Give it up? Never.

If there was this evil in Bosie's life, could not he, Oscar, with the power of his love, discover the root bed from which the poisonous plant had grown, and by digging it up and stamping it out with laughter, kill the plant, kill the feud, bring father and son together?

Oscar said one day, "Bosie, do you know why you dislike your father?"

"I thought that was quite clear, darling Oscar; I don't dislike him, I abominate him."

"Ah, yes. Do you know why?"

"Does it matter?"

"I rather think it does," Oscar said gently. "It distresses me to think that there should be anything ugly, anything painful, in your beautiful life. I should like to exorcise it if I can."

"Oscar, you *are* a love, but you can exorcise and exorcise and my frightful father will not disappear. If I thought such things would do the trick, I would be sticking red-hot needles into a waxen image of the foul little monster all day long."

"What has he done to you, Bosie? Tell me some of the things you remember."

"It is not what he has done to me but what he has done to all of us. When we looked to him for love we got a curse and a blow. He would fill our house with his whores and his drunken friends. He demanded of my mother that she live on equal terms with his mistresses. He only thinks of his disgusting appetites, his loathsome sensuality. I believe with all my heart, and I have for years, and I always shall, that his physical self, his leering hideous apish face and his squat little hairy body and his narrow squinting eyes and his coarse revolting skin and his smell, his smell of dung and urine, of steaming cesspits—I believe that all this is the expression of his soul."

Oscar allowed a minute to go by. "But, Bosie, dearest boy, there must be some good in him—long buried, perhaps, and so deeply that he does not know himself that it is there."

"Why *must* there be?"

"You are the proof of it. You are your father, in part. He can't be wholly evil or you would not be what you are."

"Dear Oscar, one would hardly expect to hear this kind of nonsensical logic from you. Let us face facts, disgusting though they are. If you are determined to bring about a reconciliation between my atrocious father and me, you will first of all advise me to pay some respect to the voice of parental authority, won't you, for at present I pay none, less than none. I am delighted to flout it, to do the opposite of what he tells me, not only because I hate him but because I love *you*. Must I stop loving you, Oscar? Must this be our last meeting?"

Oscar laughed. "Of course not."

"But Oscar, darling, if I am to obey my father, I have no choice, for he has ordered me never to see you again."

"When did he do that?"

"In his latest letters. He fires them off at me regularly, you know. He said he was filled with alarm and indignation—he is chronically filled with alarm and permanently indignant—to learn from friends that I have taken up with you and have been seen with you in many places on what would seem to be terms of the greatest intimacy; I think he said the greatest and most disgusting intimacy. Your reputation, he said, is odious. No, I beg your pardon, he said your reputation is a stench in the nostrils of all decent men. He said one had only to read your books and so-called witticisms—he heavily underlined 'so-called'—to know that you are corrupt, decadent, and filthy. As a parting shot he said that if he saw you on the street he would be tempted to give you a good thrashing, to which I immediately replied that I hoped with all my heart he would try, since you were a large, strong man and any such attempt would end with his having his teeth knocked out, a consummation that would suffuse me with pious filial joy. But now I see that I shall have to write again to him and say I am sorry and I didn't mean a word of it and of course I shall give you up at once." Bosie looked at Oscar with a mischievous smile.

"Why didn't you tell me this before, Bosie?"

"Dear Oscar, my father's letters are not worth talking about. But I beg your and his pardon—I forgot. They *are* worth talking about, they *are* worth listening to, you and he agree."

The marquess was a former amateur lightweight champion of Great Britain. Very well, Oscar silently addressed him, let us box a few rounds—the Marquess of Queensberry vs. Oscar Wilde. In weight we are woefully unmatched, true, but experience is all on your side; your life has been one long battle, and from what I understand you always set out to annihilate the other man (or woman, or child; there is no chivalry in you, my lord), whereas I am content with—well, you shall see. Ah, we face each other, you with a scowl, I a smile. A flurry of gloves, my bold black marquess; swish, swish, swish, swish—those are your huge swinging blows designed to crush me but which I duck with graceful ease; and now my turn—flick, flick, flick—a little tickling tap *here*, and *there*, and *there* again, and again and again and again, so swiftly, so subtly that you can't resist; your scowl vanishes, you smile, you chuckle, you laugh, and down you go, roaring with laughter; and as you lie there, quite beside yourself, you are convinced that Oscar Wilde is a prince of good fellows.

"Has the marquess any soft spots, any favorite subjects, aside from boxing and hunting?" Oscar asked Alfred Taylor.

"Yes, he has one great soft spot, certainly: he is an atheist. As an atheist he has in him the stuff of which martyrs are made; in other times he would have died at the stake with a last defiant squawk of belief in his unbelief; such is the passionate quality of his atheism that he has sacrificed his privileges as a Scots peer in the House of Lords rather than take the House's Christian oath. And he caused a famous scene one night at the theater by inter- rupting the most affecting and pious passage of Tennyson's play *The Promise of May* with a denunciation of the author for having written such superstitious twaddle and the actors for being such dupes as to appear in it."

A few days later Oscar was lunching with Bosie at the Café Royal when he saw a shadow pass over the fair young face.

"Is anything wrong?"

"My father has just come into the room."

"Really? Where?"

"You can't see him; behind you. No, don't turn around, it's too obvious, and one never knows what he might do. Oh, the little beast. Now he's sitting down. Now he sees us. I think he's going to come here, Oscar."

"Splendid."

"No, he isn't. He's pretending he hasn't seen us. But that won't last long. He will begin to glance over here and work up a good head of steam and then do something violent and ludicrous."

"Bosie, go and ask him to come to our table."

Bosie stared. "Are you mad?"

"No, my dear boy, I am quite sane. If you will do as I say, and do it very nicely, like the sweet gracious boy you are, we shall draw your little beast's fangs. Trust me, we shall."

"You don't know what you're up against, Oscar."

"I do."

"Very well, but don't blame me for what happens."

Oscar told the waiter to set a third place at their table, had a sip of wine, and finished his cigarette. Bosie had been gone for a long time. He did not turn around; he nodded to someone across the room who probably was Reggie Turner, because there couldn't be two noses like Reggie's in London.

Then he felt a prickling on the back of his neck.

"Here is my father," Bosie's voice said coldly.

Oscar got up, turned, and faced father and son.

The marquess was uglier than even the most biased report would have him. Oscar felt sorry for the absurd squat little thing. He dressed like a jockey trying to look the gent. He did not smell, but his skin was coarse. He had big yellowish teeth, and tufts of ginger hair stuck out of his nostrils. It seemed that some was sticking out of his ears too.

Beside him stood the golden, beautiful youth whose skin was soft as roses.

"Lord Queensberry, it is very kind of you to join us," Oscar said.

"I haven't joined you," the marquess said aggressively in a testy, shrill voice. "I came to look at you, and now that I have looked at you, I shall leave."

"Ah, that would be a pity," Oscar said. "Whatever shall I tell my Aunt Jane?"

"I don't give a damn for your Aunt Jane, sir. What does your Aunt Jane have to do with me?"

"It was my Aunt Jane who asked me to meet you, so that I could give her my impressions of you. I have been after your son for weeks to arrange it, but for some reason he has been very shy about bringing us together. My Aunt Jane is an extraordinary woman," Oscar said seriously. "I can never begin to repay her for all the things she did for me. She taught me to shoot, on her great estate in County Tipperary; as a markswoman she was unrivaled, and even today, old and failing though she is, she can bring down a brace of ducks with as pretty an action as you would care to see. Whatever skill I have as a horseman I owe to Aunt Jane, and it was she who blooded me."

Bosie became concerned with his handkerchief, and the marquess, without appearing to notice that he was doing so, sat down with them.

"She has a remarkable sense of humor, and when touched to the quick her power of invective is something Swift would have envied. I shall never forget her retort to the Bishop of Gallybagh when that eminent windbag asked her why she never went to church." Oscar smiled reminiscently; Bosie now seemed to have his features under control. "She would go to church, my Aunt Jane told the bishop, when the Holy Ghost personally demonstrated to her why it was that—but I cannot repeat her language, for fear of shocking your son. Lord Alfred, perhaps you will leave the table?"

"I shall not," Bosie said.

"Is your Aunt Jane in the way of being an agnostic, then?" the marquess inquired.

"Agnostic? Agnosticism is feeble stuff to Aunt Jane." Oscar

chuckled. "She is a full-blooded atheist. 'Lemon squash for Christians, claret for agnostics, and brandy for atheists,' I have often heard her say. Aunt Jane's one failing is a tendency to be absent-minded; she has often been known to wind up the cat and put out the clock—it was for this reason that my last birthday presents to her were a windable cat and a clock that can be put out in any weather. We still have a good laugh remembering the ball she gave half a dozen years ago. Oh, a gorgeous affair. Aunt Jane spared no expense. The only thing she forgot was to send out the invitations, and in consequence, on the great night nobody arrived. This was bad enough, but the next time was perhaps worse, for then Aunt Jane sent out the invitations but forgot to give the ball."

A rasping sound escaped the marquess; it seemed to be a laugh. "I should like to meet your Aunt Jane and have a talk with her," he declared.

"And she would like nothing better than to have a talk with you," Oscar said heartily, "but since this would be difficult to arrange, in view of the fact that Aunt Jane only exists in my imagination, perhaps you will have a talk with me instead?"

Bosie got out his handkerchief again and the marquess peered at Oscar; finally he said, "I will be damned. You made up that whole story? There is no Aunt Jane?"

"Not so far as I am aware, although," Oscar added, "I dare say before long there will be one, for it is well known that nature imitates art, and Aunt Jane seems too good not to exist, don't you think, Lord Queensberry?"

"It is a great pity. I had been looking forward," the marquess said, "to hearing the rest of what Aunt Jane told the Bishop of Gallybagh about the Holy Ghost. Why did you do it?"

"Ah, I have explained that. I wanted to have a talk with you, about atheism, and the only way to do it seemed to be to persuade you that I am not altogether a bad fellow."

An hour later the marquess was still talking. Two days afterward Bosie handed Oscar a letter in which his father said he had been quite mistaken about Oscar Wilde, who was a capital chap, and he was glad to approve of their friendship.

8 A REPORT OF THIS TRIUMPH WAS GIVEN TO BOSIE'S MOTHER
at Salisbury, where she owned a beautiful old house called St. Ann's
Gate, in the shadow of the great gray Gothic cathedral. "It is clear,"
Lady Queensberry said, laughing, "that you are a magician, Mr.
Wilde. Oh, if only you would manage the marquess for me!
Though the divorce has brought my release from the miseries of
my married life, Queensberry does his utmost to remind me of
them in a stream of insulting letters and telegrams. One can tear
up letters unread, of course, but not telegrams. And then there is
the awful business of squeezing out of him the twice-annual pay-
ments on the divorce settlement; he consistently delays them until
the last possible second of the ultimatums my solicitors are obliged
to lay down. Such a nasty, mean little man. Won't you wave your
wand and transform him?"

Oscar wished he could; he wished also that he could wave a magic
wand over the last act of *A Woman of No Importance*. He was
forced to admit to himself that Bosie had something to do with
the last act's sluggishness. Bosie spent less and less time at Oxford
(as a student he was an adorable failure), more and more in London; and who could struggle with pen and paper when Bosie was
waiting to be entertained?

And there were such jolly afternoons at Alfred Taylor's, and
such dinners at Kettner's and the Solferino and the Florence and
the Savoy, and such suppers at Willis'. And Maurice Schwabe and
Alfred were always turning up with new boys; Maurice's latest was
a most attractive one with a charmingly vulgar name, Fred Atkins,
who had been a billiard marker or a bookmaker's clerk and who
tried so hard to overcome his low background by behaving in a
genteel manner that he said "Pardon" in a strangled voice every
time he cleared his throat. Fred's ambition was to be a music-hall
singer. Maurice spoke of taking him on a little trip to Paris as his
private secretary, which struck everyone as a delicious idea, it was
so grotesque; and Fred said he would like to visit the Moulin Rouge
but Oscar said he had better not because the Moulin Rouge
swarmed with women and women were the ruin of young fellows.

It began to seem that the only way to finish the last act would
be to go off somewhere. Constance suggested Babbacombe Cliff,

177

at Babbacombe, near Torquay in Devon. Babbacombe Cliff was an enchanting place, designed for its owner, Lady Mount-Temple, by Ruskin, and extremely comfortable even in bitter weather thanks to central heating (a Yankee idea, quite ugly, and worth its weight in gold).

Lady Mount-Temple, a distant relative of Constance's, was a large, kind, artistic person; her house owed many of its distinctive decorative touches to famous painters who had been entertained there, but Lady Mount-Temple had chosen the wallpaper. There was a different pattern of wallpaper in every bedroom and Lady Mount-Temple had named each one to suit the pattern: Sweet Pea, Daisy, Marigold, Primrose, Cowslip, Sweet William, Poppy, Snowdrop, Crocus, and Petunia. Oscar liked her and knew she liked him. She was going to be traveling and visiting friends for the next two or three months.

At Babbacombe Cliff his work picked up astonishingly. He had been having a miserable time with Lord Illingworth's closing moments in A *Woman of No Importance* (Gerald Arbuthnot, that nobleman's illegitimate son, was to spurn his offer and remain with Rachel Arbuthnot, the boy's mother, as Bosie had hoped he would); but now there was no trouble in writing his last lines.

> LORD ILLINGWORTH (*to Mrs. Arbuthnot*): How curious! At this moment you look exactly as you looked the night you left me twenty years ago. You have just the same expression. Upon my word, Rachel, no woman ever loved me as you did. Why, you gave yourself to me like a flower, to do anything I liked with. You were the prettiest of playthings, the most fascinating of small romances. (*Pulls out his watch.*) Quarter to two! Must be strolling back to Lady Hunstanton's. I don't suppose I shall see you there again. I'm sorry, I am, really. It's been an amusing experience to have met, amongst people of one's own rank, and treated quite seriously too, one's mistress and one's bastard.

As he reread the lines Oscar knew that the Lord Chamberlain and his faithful donkey Smyth Pigott would be thrown into the blind staggers by that final thunderbolt, and he simply couldn't afford to defy them. "Bastard" would have to go, but he would turn the amputation to good account:

178

It's been an amusing experience to have met, amongst people of one's own rank, and treated quite seriously too, one's mistress and one's ——

MRS. ARBUTHNOT *snatches up glove and strikes* LORD ILLING-WORTH *across the face with it. He gives a start. He is dazed by the insult of his punishment. Then he controls himself, sighs and leaves the room.*

MRS. ARBUTHNOT (*falls sobbing on the sofa*): He would have said it. He would have said it.

Later, GERALD *enters the room and sees* LORD ILLINGWORTH'S *glove lying on the floor. He picks it up.*

GERALD: Hallo, Mother, whose glove is this? You have had a visitor. Who was it?

MRS. ARBUTHNOT: Oh! No one. No one in particular. A man of no importance.

Bosie would like that.

Oscar could not deny that work made far better progress when Bosie wasn't about, but ah, he missed him, he missed him. Little remained to do on the play but odds and ends of rewriting here and there; surely Bosie's presence wouldn't interfere too much. There were, after all, many rooms in the house. Bosie would love to be in a bedroom called Petunia. (Oscar had installed himself in Lady Mount-Temple's boudoir; the decorations had been inspired by scenes from *Alice in Wonderland,* and so the room was called Wonderland.)

Everything seemed to turn Oscar's mind to Bosie. The name of the tutor specially engaged by Lady Queensberry to help him in his ailing studies was Campbell Dodgson, and Dodgson, Charles, was the real name of the author of *Alice.*

One splendid morning a letter came from Bosie, hardly a letter, more of a note, but that was all right, because he was most affectionate and asked Oscar's opinion of his latest sonnet, which he enclosed. It was called "In Praise of Shame" and told how the poet had dreamed that to his bed there came a pageant of all the passions. A voice cried, "I am Shame," and the poet, waking, thought that Shame was the loveliest thing of all.

Oscar read the sonnet a dozen times (he did not, honestly, think

179

much of it) because Bosie's touch was still on the paper, and he *must* have been thinking of Oscar while he wrote.

Oscar took pains with his reply. The sonnet, he told Bosie, was altogether lovely. He marveled that Bosie's red rose-leaf lips had been formed as sweetly for song as for a madness of kisses—a charming phrase, Oscar thought, and he seemed to see Bosie, so slim, so golden. His *soul* was slim and golden too, a slim gilt soul that walked between passion and poetry. There was a really sublime phrase; Oscar put it into the letter and added that he was sure that Hyacinthus, whom Apollo so passionately loved, was Bosie, in Grecian times.

That should be enough, but Bosie had said in his accompanying note that he was "all alone" in London, and it occurred to Oscar that this was quite naughty of him—Mr. Campbell Dodgson, the tutor, had been engaged to spend a month with him at his mother's in Salisbury. Gently, poetically, Bosie must be admonished; Oscar asked him why he was alone in London and when he intended to go to Salisbury, and he urged him to hurry to that gracious cathedral town and cool his hands in the gray twilight of Gothic things. Bosie must feel free to come to Babbacombe Cliff whenever he wished; it was a lovely place and only lacked him; but Bosie was to go to Salisbury first. He signed the letter

> Always, with undying love,
> Yours,
> Oscar

He had written Bosie many charming letters but never one so beautiful; Oscar wondered if Bosie would realize that it put his sonnet quite in the shade.

Beerbohm Tree was delighted with *A Woman of No Importance*. There were differences of opinion, though, over the casting; Tree would not yield, as he should, considering how enormously he was in Oscar's debt for permitting him to have the play. Oscar decided to see him in London and settle matters.

First he would stop at Salisbury. Bosie had just come up from Oxford. He didn't mention Oscar's letter; in fact, he seemed on edge. When they were alone the truth came out; he hadn't been "all alone" in London but instead had been having an affair with a youth named Alfred Wood, whom he had met at Taylor's rooms and who later had stayed with him at Oxford. And now Wood had sent Bosie a threatening letter.

"Think of his impudence," Bosie said indignantly. "When I was so sweet to him. I gave him one of my suits, and handkerchiefs, and heaven knows what else; and who paid for his food and the wine he drank, I should like to know? But of course the little beast says nothing about that."

Oscar sighed. "Where is the letter?"

"Oscar, dear, please don't put on that compassionate, superior look, it is too much to bear, and you really haven't the figure for a wayside shrine."

"I only asked for the letter, Bosie."

"I don't have it," Bosie said sulkily. "It made me so furious when I read it that I tore it up *and* put it down the w.c., if you insist on knowing, which is where young Master Nasty Wood belongs too. And I should like to tell him so."

"I dare say he would become far more amenable. Did you make him any promises?"

"No, of course not."

"Perhaps you misread the letter."

"I am not an idiot, my dear Oscar. Oh, I don't mean to be so rude and horrid, forgive me, forgive me. It's only that I wasn't made for these ugly things, they simply put me out of my mind, and I am not myself. Darling Oscar, will you see him for me? You know how wonderfully you managed the last time. Oh, I know—there was never to *be* another time. But this really wasn't my fault. It was all that wretched Taylor's fault. One trusts him to behave like a gentleman and not have beastly little blackmailers at his rooms."

"He wouldn't have people he knows to be blackmailers at his rooms."

"He should make it his business to know."

"You must be sure to reprimand him, Bosie. Very well, I shall see your Alfred Wood. How shall I arrange it? Or will you?"

"Darling Oscar. I shall, of course."

Oscar went on to London. Two days later a note came from Bosie saying that he had heard again from Alfred Wood and had telegraphed him to meet Oscar at half past eight the next night at the Café Royal.

Oscar was there at eight; he refused invitations from a score of friends to join them, sat down by himself, and ordered wine.

Presently a young man appeared who could only have been Alfred Wood: he was attractive in a rather common way, wore a distressing tie, was highly ill at ease and doing a very poor job of pretending not to be. Oscar called out, "Mr. Wood?" and the young man looked around with painful eagerness. "Do join me," Oscar said. Alfred Wood's approach to the table was performed with a care that would not have been excessive in a tightrope walker; but having successfully occupied the chair Oscar waved to and accepted and consumed a glass of wine, he became less cautious and even smiled.

Before long they were on the best of terms. Oscar suggested supper—not here; it was a little noisy, didn't Alfred think so? They went to the Florence in Rupert Street, where Oscar had arranged for a private room. Alfred reverted to his tightrope walking, but the champagne soon changed that.

"My dear Alfred," Oscar said, "I am so glad we've met and I hope we'll be friends for a long, long time. Shall we drink to it?"

"Thank you, Mr. Wilde. I'm sure I hope so too."

"Oscar, please, dear Alfred; I insist on first names with my friends. Yours is a charming one, and you share it with a very dear friend of mine, Lord Alfred Douglas. He was distressed by your letter, Alfred."

"I was only asking for what he promised me, Mr. Wilde—Oscar. It isn't right for a rich chap like him to make promises to a young fellow and then not live up to it, is it now?"

"Ah, but he did give you some things, I believe," Oscar pointed out. "A suit, and handkerchiefs, and so on?"

"He did that," Alfred Wood snickered. "Oh, yes." He snickered again; and then, dropping this mysteriously mirthful mood, he said, "There are those as would do certain things if they had the chance, but I am above it. I only want what I was promised. It isn't right," he repeated, "for a rich chap to have his bit of fun and then welsh on his promises."

"Lord Alfred isn't rich," Oscar said, "he's quite poor; but I do agree that he should live up to his promises. What did he promise?"

"I'm out of employment, Mr. Wilde, Oscar, and that's why I did what I done. The noble young gent promised me money, but then he welshed."

Oscar took some sovereigns from his pocket. "These are for you, dear boy, with my affection and Lord Alfred's apologies. No, you mustn't thank me: I am in your debt for the pleasure of your charming company."

Bosie was often seized by these sudden, and for one so delicate, coarse appetites. The facts might be that the letter hadn't been threatening at all, simply a demand for payment. Everything was provided for Bosie, and he had an allowance of several hundred a year besides. He simply hated to pay for anything. He hated it like fury. The important thing to Bosie had been not to be subjected to the embarrassment of having Oscar read the letter *in his presence*. And that was rather touching, wasn't it—rather preciously childlike.

Although the Lord Chamberlain and Smyth Pigott had kept *Salomé* from reaching the stage (in Paris as well as London, as it turned out: the play's troubles had daunted Sarah and other producers), it was to be published in both cities. And in a most beautiful edition—bound in Tyrian purple and antique silver. Oscar preferred his French publisher, M. Bailly of the Librairie de l'Art Independant, to his English, John Lane of Mathews and Lane; possibly his distaste for Lane had been increased by the unhappy experience with young Shelley and the hysterical letters the boy was always writing; in any event, when asked by Bailly to come to Paris to discuss one or two points, Oscar was glad to accept.

His companion was Fred Atkins, the youth who said "Pardon" in a strangled voice and who despite this affliction yearned to be made glorious on the stage. Taking Fred to Paris was simply a courtesy to Maurice, who had meant to go with them but had been delayed at the last minute. Maurice spent a good deal of time in Paris; of course it was more prudent if one pursued one's affairs with such unabashed vigor; the French did not take the grim English view: they granted that one's private business was one's private business, not a matter for the public prosecutor.

Fred was still plagued by a hot curiosity concerning the Moulin Rouge. He must put aside these lewd thoughts, Oscar sagely instructed him. "Always remember my warning, dear Fred; women are the ruin of young fellows. Dear me, how much anguish, how many tears would have been spared if these golden words had been solemnly impressed on every young chap setting out into the world, by his mother."

183

Fred said something in his obscure voice. It would be difficult to imagine anyone more deplorably equipped to burst into song for the pleasure of music-hall audiences; but he was young and passably good-looking and amusing as a companion if only because he would receive with every sign of labored thought the most preposterous observations one cared to make. His trip to Paris was obviously the greatest occasion in his life, and Oscar did him proud, as Maurice would have wished: took him to lunch at the Café Julien, then to the famous hairdresser Pascal, where Fred almost but not quite had his hair curled, and to dinner, with lots of wine.

After dinner, in an excess of good feeling, Oscar gave him a sovereign with which to satisfy his foolish heart's desire and go to the Moulin Rouge.

"By yourself, of course, Fred; I should shudder to enter that unholy den, and besides, I am going to the theater. Mind now, if you come back with a repulsive disease from having touched one of those filthy women, Maurice will never forgive me."

Fred promised to be a good boy. He leered slightly as he said so. Oscar considered the leer to be an accident; he did not think Fred had the ability to produce a leer at will.

Shortly after Oscar returned to Babbacombe Cliff, Constance left for an Italian trip with her aunt. He settled down to work. The rehearsals of *A Woman of No Importance*, beginning in a few weeks, would demand his presence in London, but before then he hoped to have a new play well advanced. With it he would demonstrate that the jeweled words of *Salomé* had not been lost or even dulled in great popular success. The play would be of about the length of *Salomé* and would be called *La Sainte Courtisane*.

La Sainte Courtisane began promisingly; then a telegram arrived:

I HAD MEANT LONG BEFORE TO THANK YOU FOR HAVING LOOKED AFTER THINGS SO WELL IN LONDON AND CAME TO LONDON TO THANK YOU BUT FOUND THAT YOU HAD GONE TO PARIS AND SO NOW I AM GOING TO COME TO BABBACOMBE CLIFF AS YOU SUGGESTED AND I AM SORRY I HAVEN'T LET YOU KNOW EARLIER THAT I AM COMING IN FACT I AM ON MY WAY AM SENDING THIS TELEGRAM FROM EXETER WHERE WE HAVE HAD TO

CHANGE TRAINS AND OH YES I AM BRINGING MY
TUTOR WITH ME AND WE WILL BE THERE VERY
SOON.

Bosie's telegrams were so delightful, so essentially Bosie, that
one never minded paying for them. No doubt the tutor had paid
for this one. Oscar was a trifle apprehensive: what would he be
like—a paralyzing bore with icy eyeglasses?

Campbell Dodgson was a charming fellow. Since meeting Bosie,
he informed Oscar, his life had been a whirl, confusing but
enjoyable for one accustomed to a stationary, cowlike existence.
Lionel Johnson told him Bosie desperately needed tutoring in
logic, Aristotle, Bacon, and history, and had written to Lady
Queensberry recommending him. He agreed to put in a month's
hard work with Bosie, but subsequently this ambitious schedule had
to be cut to a week because of Bosie's difficulties in getting from
one place to another. At last they managed to meet, and Bosie
slaved away like a dog for at least an hour and a quarter, when he
slapped his book closed with a bang and announced, Good heavens! They must rush if they were to catch the train for Torquay,
where Oscar was expecting them. "Oscar?" Campbell asked rather
feebly. "Did he mean Oscar Wilde?" "Of course," Bosie replied.
"Was there another Oscar in the world?" Campbell was put to
work cramming clothes into all kinds of trunks and bags and port-
manteaus. Halfway to the station Bosie discovered that he had forgotten his books. They turned back. Their next attempt brought
them a little closer, but Bosie had forgotten his cigarettes. The
third attempt was almost successful: they were actually in sight of
the station when Bosie found to his horror that he had left behind
the beautiful scarlet-morocco dispatch case Oscar had given him.
So they had to take a later train. They had reached Exeter when
Bosie remembered that he hadn't let Oscar know they were coming.

"This after he'd told me you were expecting us!" Campbell
finished apologetically. "I can only hope you don't mind."

"My dear chap, I am delighted. As a sign of my pleasure I am
going to put you in Sweet Pea."

"I say," Campbell murmured. "Sweet Pea?"

"Or Poppy or Marigold, if you prefer. Bosie is in Petunia. I
think it suits him wonderfully well, but he seems to fancy Sweet
William—he is so charmingly fickle, you know."

185

Oscar had ordered a magnificent dinner for his guests. "I apologize for the champagne; at such short notice I was unable to lay in your favorite, Bosie."

"Never mind." Bosie smiled. "This goes down very well."

Brandy followed, and then whisky and soda for the rest of the evening.

When Bosie came down to the breakfast table, no one would have known that he had drunk so much; his skin was fresh and clear, his eyes bright; and again Oscar marveled at his extraordinary beauty, beside which the small annoyances caused by his occasional lack of thought melted away to nothing—became gratitude for his radiant presence.

It was a lovely week. The evenings, of course, were useless for work; Campbell's tutoring had to be fitted in where best it could during the days, and Bosie liked the days to follow the same agreeable pattern of morning tea at nine, breakfast at ten, morning sherry at twelve, luncheon at half past one, afternoon tea at five, brandy and soda at six, dinner at half past seven.

La Sainte Courtisane came to a halt. Oscar told them the story of the play; Campbell said, "If only it could be written down in the words you have just used, nothing more would be necessary— it would be a masterpiece."

Bosie agreed. "A twin sister to *Salomé*; it is in the same mood."

"Ah, how sweet of you to mention *Salomé*, Bosie; otherwise I might have forgotten. She arrived today, in her royal Tyrian robes and delectable, rather tired silver—the very first copies from Paris." He wouldn't have forgotten; they were to be the grand event of the evening, of the week; ever since the package had come in the post he had had a struggle to resist bringing out the beautiful things.

"I think her raiment suits her," he remarked, giving a copy to Bosie and another to Campbell. "But I must warn you, Campbell: if you should be so gracious as to award her a place among your books, she may forget her surroundings and begin to dance. You would be well advised to put her between Gibbon and Hume. A glance from either of those gentlemen should make her behave."

Campbell laughed. "I'll remember. What a beautiful book."

"Quite hideous," Bosie said.

He had opened his copy. Now he banged it shut and pushed it away.

Oscar turned to him. "I beg your pardon?"

"Your ears must be full of wax, or whatever the revolting stuff is that gets into them. You should have them cleaned out," Bosie said. "I spoke distinctly enough for anyone to hear. You heard me, didn't you, Campbell? Never mind, I shall say it again. I said the book is quite hideous." He raised his voice. "I said the book is quite hideous." He raised his voice again; "I said it is quite hideous," he screamed. "It is quite hideous. It is quite hideous. It is quite hideous." His mouth was stretched open to the limit, pulling the lips thin and tight. "Can you hear me?" He got up and stalked from the room, slamming the door.

They said nothing.

Then Oscar picked up the book. "But it isn't hideous," he said in a wondering voice. "It is beautiful, isn't it, Campbell? You do think so, don't you?"

"I do think so," Campbell said.

Oscar got up. "He must be ill."

"I was told—I have heard—that is," Campbell said, "some people say he is inclined to be not altogether responsible at times."

"He must be ill. I must go and see to him. Excuse me, will you please, Campbell?"

"Of course," Campbell said. "But perhaps I can— Can I help?"

"No, no. Thank you, Campbell. You are a good chap."

Oscar knocked on Bosie's door. Presently it was pulled open, with such force that the displaced air made a small wind. With the doorknob still in his hand Bosie stood staring at him. His hand shook.

"Bosie, dearest boy, you are not well."

"Oh, you utter hypocrite," Bosie said. "Loathsome, crawling, filthy hypocrite. Oh, you revolting creature. Fat, disgusting creature. Oh, I can't bear hypocrisy; if there is anything I cannot bear it is hypocrisy. And you are the lord of hypocrites. You are the fat lord of all the hypocrites in the world."

"Bosie, Bosie." Oscar came into the room. He tried to close the door behind him, but Bosie held on to the doorknob. Then he released it and kicked the door closed. His shoe left a black mark on the flower-colored paint, and he kicked the door again, twice.

"Bosie, Bosie, you will hurt yourself."

Bosie marched to the shelf of books beside his bed, selected two of them, and in great handfuls tore the pages out. "Those are your poems and your pretty stories," he said. His face had become like someone else's; Oscar couldn't think whose. He hated to see Bosie's beautiful face twisted and ugly. Oscar held out his hands in a clumsy gesture; Bosie would know that he was reaching out toward him to help him.

"Bosie, I must help you. I love you and I must help you. Please tell me what is wrong. I can help you if you will tell me what is wrong."

"Oh, God, you fat disgusting hypocrite," Bosie cried.

"Dearest boy, don't, don't," Oscar said, near tears. "Was it the book that upset you? But it couldn't have been, because it isn't a hideous book, Bosie, it isn't, really. It is quite perfect and beautiful. Campbell thinks so and I think so and all the people in Paris think so. Everyone who has seen it thinks so."

"Everyone who has seen it thinks so." Bosie imitated Oscar's voice ludicrously, mincingly. "*I* don't think so." He screamed again, "It is a hideous, hideous book. Oh, thank God I have seen you for what you are, you loathsome, foul betrayer, you obscene hypocrite, you fat, fat, foul, foul betrayer! Oh you fat, disgusting thing. To think that I should have polluted myself by touching you, by letting your fat foul greasy fingers touch me. Oh God, no, I cannot bear it. *I cannot bear it.*"

The ugly mask Bosie's face had become was his father's. Afraid he would be sick, Oscar hurried from the room.

Early in the morning he heard wheels on the drive outside, and when he got up he learned that Bosie had gone.

At the breakfast table Campbell Dodgson carefully talked about the delightful weather. "I hate to leave. I have thoroughly enjoyed my week here."

"It was most unkind of Lord Alfred to subject us to such a scene," Oscar said. "There is something essentially common in a temperament that will permit such things."

Campbell looked unhappily at his plate.

"Something essentially common," Oscar repeated. "Must you really leave, Campbell? I have to go to London tomorrow, and I'd be most grateful for your company until then."

"Alas, I couldn't possibly put off my other arrangements." He left soon after; the copy of *Salomé* was under his arm. Bosie's copy lay where Oscar had left it. He picked up the book and looked at it sadly. At that moment someone came to the front door and knocked. It was a telegram. He opened it and read:

DARLING OSCAR I BEG YOU TO FORGIVE ME I WAS INSANE WITH JEALOUSY IF YOU WILL LOOK AT THE FIRST PAGE OF THE BOOK YOU WILL SEE WHY IT IS NOT A HIDEOUS BOOK IT IS QUITE PERFECT AND BEAUTIFUL AS YOU SAID IF IT WERE NOT SO BEAUTIFUL IT WOULD NOT HAVE HURT ME SO MUCH AND IF YOU HAD NOT WRITTEN IT I WOULD NOT HAVE BEEN HURT AT ALL BUT YOU DID WRITE IT AND IT IS BEAUTIFUL AND IT IS YOU AND THEREFORE I WENT MAD WITH RAGE AND HATE AND JEALOUSY OH I BEG YOU TO FORGIVE ME AND JOIN ME HERE I CANNOT COME TO JOIN YOU THERE BECAUSE IT WOULD BE TOO PAINFUL IT WOULD REMIND OF THE HORROR OF LAST NIGHT I AM WRITING BUT PERHAPS YOU WILL BE HERE BEFORE THE LETTER REACHES YOU OH I PRAY YOU WILL BE I AM AT THE PALACE HOTEL BRISTOL WITH ALL MY LOVE

BOSIE

In that first moment of receiving the book, Bosie had turned to the dedication page and there had read, in the fine italic typeface: A mon ami Pierre Louÿs.

No one among all his friends, Oscar had considered, more deserved the honor than Pierre. Pierre had been one of the very first to hear the story of the play, had praised it to the skies, and later, falling in with Oscar's conceit to write the play in French, had helped him with the difficult bits. One of the first bound copies had gone to Pierre; it would come to him, Oscar had thought with delight, absolutely out of the blue; he would be overwhelmed.

Pierre had responded to that gorgeous compliment with a trivial jest, in a telegram. Indeed, Oscar had not been altogether sure that the telegram was a jest; perhaps it was worse, an insult, an obscene insult; the French was obscure and Oscar was too proud to ask some expert in Parisian blague for a translation. Terribly hurt, he had written an angry (but beautifully phrased) note to Pierre and enclosed the telegram.

Oscar sat down to reply to Bosie's telegram: DEAREST BOY

AM COMING AT ONCE. But then he paused. He would not send the telegram. He would not respond to Lord Alfred Douglas ever again.

In the morning a letter came from Bosie with tear marks on it. Oscar rushed to Bristol.

9

THEY MET AND EMBRACED AT THE PALACE IN BRISTOL. BOSIE was just like a little child; he wept and then smiled and then was content to sit quietly with his hand in Oscar's.

Oscar said, "We must never, never have such a scene again—never again must there be a misunderstanding—Bosie, you must tell me everything, any fancied reason for jealousy, for real reason there could be none; oh, there will be other loves, but they will be as they have been in the past, purely transient—our love is different, immortal, secure; but no more scenes!"

Bosie wept again and said yes, yes, and smiled. Oscar wiped away his tears, and they kissed each other, simply and sweetly. "Oscar, don't leave me. Please, can't we go to the Savoy for a little while at least? I was staying at the Savoy when I sent the sonnet to you, and I feel the same deep, hushed happiness now that I felt then. It would be so poetically right to be there together."

Oscar agreed. He preferred the Savoy among all London's hotels; it was the center of the world. He had never been happier than during their first few days at the Savoy—quite by themselves; long lazy hours of talk and sweet silences. If only this idyll could go on forever. But there were bills to be paid; the present bill for their connecting rooms, and Bosie's bill for his earlier stay at the hotel (and the bill at the Palace in Bristol, and some other bills he had forgotten to mention); and Oscar had to face the horrid practical world again (he had never been so far in debt) and make the necessary arrangements with his bank manager, Mr. Lowe.

Not unnaturally, that courteous person asked, "How is your new play progressing?"

"Splendidly," Oscar said. "Herbert Beerbohm Tree has the highest hopes, foresees a success even greater than that of *Lady Windermere*. There will be tickets for you and Mrs. Lowe for the first night; I'll mention it to Mr. Tree this evening; as it happens, I'm dining with the Trees."

As a matter of fact, he was, though he disliked to leave Bosie, who hadn't been invited. (After all, the Trees couldn't be expected to know that Bosie was with Oscar at the Savoy.) Bosie smiled. "Never mind, it can't be helped; I'll spend the time reading, perhaps work on a new sonnet, and the hours will soon be gone."

"We'll have a late supper when I get back," Oscar said.

He could easily have stayed longer at the Trees', because of the excellent company, Max Beerbohm and Reggie Turner and Stella Campbell—and Herbert was his most charming self, extremely complimentary and agreeable—but Oscar left before eleven.

A pretty little page boy, smart as a pouter pigeon in his beige tunic and tight trousers, was on duty behind the hotel doors; Oscar remembered his face and smiled at him. "Hullo, you're up late, aren't you?"

"Oh, no, sir. Quite early yet, sir."

Oscar found a two-shilling piece. "Do you know that I've forgotten your name?"

"Herbert, sir."

"Now that's very odd, because I was dining with a Herbert tonight. I don't suppose you're another Herbert *Tree*, are you?"

"No, sir; me name's Tankard, sir."

"Herbert Tankard, Herbert Tankard—much better than Tree; he will be jealous when I tell him. Here, Herbert Tankard, and good night, Herbert Tankard," and Oscar gave him the coin and walked to the waiting lift. To be thrust all innocent and glowing into the world as a Tankard, he thought, as a Herbert Tankard; good heavens. And some day pretty little Herbert Tankard will be old and rheumy Herbert Tankard and by then may the gracious Greek gods grant that he will have the memory of many kisses to take down with him into the grave, above which will stand the gray stone reading FAREWELL, HERBERT TANKARD. Except that it will not read FAREWELL, HERBERT TANKARD, it will read HERE LIES HERBERT TANKARD—JESUS CALLED AND HE WENT.

Ah, the pleasure of walking along a hotel corridor late at night —the soft warm air, the sleepy silence, the velvet-crush feeling of the carpet. A harem softness and silence. Then, from behind one of the closed, proud, mysterious doors, a little laugh, a sigh.

Oscar walked on, smiling, and came to 361 and raised his hand to tap. He paused, because he heard another sound.

It was a giggle.

Oscar looked at the door. 361. THREE-SIX-ONE.

But perhaps the sound had come from another door.

No; it had come from behind this door, Bosie's room, because there it was again. Giggle. What an expressive word; it *is* the sound. A silly, no, a nasty sound, a filthy little oh-what-a-secret-we've-got sound. Oscar walked away, to the end of the corridor, back again; once more. And once more.

Now there was silence. Quietly he unlocked the door. The room was dark, but the stealthy corridor light showed him two heads, one with honey-colored hair, the other black, on the pillows in Bosie's bed.

Oscar quickly closed the door and walked through to his room.

He sat down on his immaculate bed. Presently he sighed; a small sigh. He undressed, put on his pajamas, and got into bed. For a while he tried to read, but it was no use; he could only listen. He got up and crept on bare feet to the connecting door and put his ear to the keyhole. No mistaking it. The daintiest little sound; a snore.

Bosie did not snore except when he had had a great deal to drink, and then he produced a surprisingly deep snore. His black-haired love was snoring so lightly, not he. And that meant that Bosie had gone about the pursuit of love quite deliberately—hadn't been drinking to excess—had known every moment what he was doing.

Oscar returned to his bed. Sometime during the night there was more giggling, but he pressed his hands tightly to his ears and shut out the sound in the racing beat of the pulse in his blood.

Someone was shaking his shoulder. He opened his eyes and looked up into Bosie's beautiful face. "Oscar, dear, do you have a few pounds?"

"Yes, I suppose so. Why?"

"Must you ask why?"

"Forgive me. There on the chest of drawers."

"Thank you."

Bosie's hair was rather tousled, but otherwise he looked fresh and neat. He was wearing a lilac-silk dressing gown Oscar had given him. He took the money from the chest of drawers and left the room.

Oscar found his watch: ten o'clock. He couldn't have slept much. The rollicking sound of young laughter came from the next room. Oscar longed for a cup of tea, but if he rang, the waiter or maid would have to come to his room through Bosie's room.

In half or three quarters of an hour Oscar judged from various sounds that the boy had gone. He rose and put on his dressing gown and slippers and gave the connecting door a tap.

"Do come in," Bosie said.

He was sipping a cup of tea by the snug coal fire; there was no fire in Oscar's room.

"Ah, you have your tea; when did it come?"

"The maid brought it just now," Bosie said. "I rang for her earlier to make up the fire and told her to bring tea later; they so often forget. Would you like a cup? Oh, there doesn't seem to be another; what a bother. Will you ring?"

He was still in his dressing gown. His bare legs were crossed; the lilac silk was slanted over the white skin dappled with golden hair. He wore curved Turkish slippers.

"Bosie, don't you think you are being perhaps a little careless?"

"What on earth do you mean?"

"Was your boy here when the maid made up the fire?"

"Yes, of course. And very sweet he looked, peeping shyly out of bed."

"I am sure the maid must have thought so."

"It's a matter of the most complete indifference to me what she thought," Bosie said idly, "if indeed she is capable of thought, which seems doubtful. Makes quite a decent fire, though."

The bed had the appearance of a large soft animal that had been savagely attacked, spilling its entrails on the floor. Only the bottom sheet was still in place; there were glistening smudges on it.

"The bed must have looked charming to her too."

"Well, that would depend. If she liked the look of Johnny, yes."

"I don't mean when he was in it, I mean later, when he was gone and she brought your tea. I mean how the bed looks now. That was how she saw it."

"Quite true," Bosie drawled. "So she did."

"She could hardly have failed to notice the stains."

"Could hardly have. I wonder," Bosie mused, "if she thinks we shed a pearly dew in the night? Do be a dear and give me a cigarette, Oscar; I am afraid Johnny and I finished mine."

Oscar fetched a cigarette. "Where did you meet Johnny?"

"He was wandering up Piccadilly like a sweet little lost fawn.

Oh, he is a darling. Not a bit of nonsense. We were in bed before you could say Jack Robinson."

"It is no use, Bosie," Oscar said; "you will simply have to give up this sort of behavior. It is too promiscuous."

"You filthy swine," Bosie said, "how dare you speak to me like that?"

And there was the look, the black beast look, the look of his father.

"How dare you, how dare you, how dare you. You great fat filthy whore, do you think that writing your odious cheapjack plays makes you someone who can criticize me? *Me?*" In one swift motion Bosie smeared his cigarette in a long dirty smoldering line against the arm of his chair. He leaped from the chair, half fell, and scrambled to his feet like an animal.

Oscar fled into his room, slammed the door, fumbled vainly for the key, and leaned against the door to keep Bosie from following. The door shook; Bosie screamed the dreadful gutter words at him.

At last silence fell. Oscar knelt with difficulty to listen at the keyhole. He could hear nothing.

"Bosie?"

There was no answer.

Oscar opened the door, trembling.

"Bosie, where are you?"

The room was still warmly alive; the smell of Bosie's favorite cologne was in the air. The wardrobe was empty; the drawers had been pulled out and emptied and now hung tilted disconsolately toward the floor. A beautiful expensive silk shirt Oscar had given Bosie was draped over the lamp on the table. Oscar picked up the shirt and saw that it was torn almost in two. A half-empty jar of vaseline stood on the floor beside the bed. The chamberpot beneath the bed was filled to the brim. Oscar drew back in disgust.

He trembled again. He was perspiring, suddenly, as he looked at a sketch on a sheet of Savoy notepaper of a figure with gross belly, huge pendulous behind, and fat-cheeked face. A long, limp worm dangled between the legs. Bosie wouldn't have left it lying here beside the chamberpot, would he? Bosie couldn't sketch like this; it must have been done by the boy. But if the black-haired boy had drawn the obscene thing, he could only have done so from Bosie's description. It must have been done last night or early this morning, done before Bosie had fallen into his rage, because by then the black-haired boy had gone.

Someone was knocking at the door. Oscar crumpled the sketch into a ball and pushed it into his pocket. The knock sounded again. It *could* be the marquess standing there, his face distorted by the same black rage that seized Bosie—*Sir, you are corrupting my son.* How ludicrous that was. Whoever it was knocked once more. Oscar got up and opened the door. Alfred Taylor's friendly blue eyes met his.

"Dear Alfred, this is a wonderful surprise. Do come in. Come through to the other room; this one is not very orderly, I fear."

"I heard from somebody or other that you were staying at the Savoy," Alfred said, "and came to ask why we haven't seen you for so long. But my dear chap, aren't you feeling well?"

"I am perfectly all right now," Oscar declared. "The sight of you has quite done away with the little upset I had. Do sit down; I shall ring for tea."

"I thought you might care to drink a glass of wine with me this afternoon," Alfred said. He smiled. "It is, as a matter of fact, my birthday."

"Your birthday. My dear fellow. We must have a party. Ah, Alfred, this is precisely what I need—the very jolliest kind of party, with some charming young guests. Shall we say at Kettner's, tonight at eight?"

"Unfortunately I'm engaged this evening," Alfred replied. "Perhaps you wouldn't mind postponing the party for a few days. That would give me the chance to arrange for the sort of guests I know you would like."

"It is to be your party, Alfred; please choose the night that will suit you best. Some new young guests, I hope?"

"Quite new," Alfred said, smiling again. "I venture to think you won't be disappointed. What pleasant rooms you have here."

"I find them to be rather depressing," Oscar said.

Later in the morning, after Alfred had left, Oscar stopped at the desk downstairs to see if his rooms could be changed. They could, but, alas, the hotel wanted cash now. His wily dodging and scheming must begin again.

Just before eight, on the night chosen by Alfred Taylor, Oscar entered the private dining room he had engaged at Kettner's. It was not so magnificent as some restaurants, but Kettner's at its best was very good indeed, and they had taken pains with the room, as Oscar had requested—a crackling fire, red lampshades on the candles, fresh flowers, a beautiful array of glasses, champagne ready in the ice buckets on their gleaming stands.

The two young men got up as Oscar came in. They looked nervous, which added to their charm. In his comfortable, friendly way Alfred said, "Oscar, Charles and William Parker."

"Ah, you are brothers, then?"

"Yes, Mr. Wilde," Charles Parker, the more attractive of the two, said.

"Do please call me Oscar, won't you? I like people whom I like to call me by my Christian name. And may I call you Charles, or Charley?"

"That's all right, Mr. Wilde."

"Oscar."

"Oscar."

The dinner started splendidly; Oscar's stories kept the boys laughing. "Well, Charley," he said, "an attractive young chap like you—what is your ambition in life?"

Charley said, "I've often thought I'd like to go on the stage."

"You are pretty enough for it, certainly. I am sure many of the young ladies of the theater would be jealous of your eyes and lips and complexion."

Charley blushed at the compliment, and Oscar said, "Your blush is charming. It does you great credit; a blush is the banner of modesty, but you have every right to be vain." Charley finished another glass of champagne and the waiter filled the glass.

The only slightly unfortunate effect produced by the champagne was the boys' tendency to talk about a mysterious individual in the hitherto uncelebrated town of Datchet, whose greatest boast was that this individual wrought mighty deeds of commerce there and otherwise illuminated the streets. Who was this titan? Oscar inquired at last, "Is he one of the Barings, or perhaps a Rothschild? I am beginning to feel jealous of him, Charley. Come, confess his name."

"Why, Mr. Wilde, Oscar, he's our father."

"Ah. A man of considerable fortune, I take it. A banker?"

It appeared that he had something to do with horses.

"Let us drink to him," Oscar said warmly. "Datchet Senior, I salute you. Excuse me, I meant to say Parker Senior, I salute you. And how old are you, Charley?"

"Nineteen," Charley said.

"A delicious age. Look at this tender bit of Noisette de Veau simply begging to be popped between your rose-leaf lips. Do you know I had a young friend who thought Noisette de Veau was the name of a French ballet dancer? Isn't that absurd? William, does it upset you that I should be feeding Charley while Alfred leaves you to shift for yourself? I think that is very cruel of you, Alfred."

William said, "It doesn't upset me."

"Ah, what is this?" Oscar asked, inspecting a new dish. "Preserved cherries? Of course they are. Charley, do have one."

Charlie said, "I will, with pleasure."

"But I think we can give them a better flavor," Oscar said. "Take the next one from me," and he placed a cherry between his lips.

Charley tittered and with his fingers took the cherry from Oscar's lips.

"No, dearest boy—with *your* lips from mine." And Oscar put another cherry between his lips and Charley leaned forward and put his mouth to Oscar's and ate the cherry. "Ah," Oscar cried, "this is the boy for me!"

Later, after paying the bill, he asked Charley if he would like to go to the Savoy with him. Alfred bowed good night and William grinned as they left.

"My cab, please," Oscar said to the doorman. The hansom came clopping up. "Here we are, Charley—in with you, my dear."

"Is it *your* cab, Oscar?"

"I adore the way you pronounce my name. Yes, of course it is my cab. Oh, not *mine*; I don't own it; I merely keep it, don't you know. It is a very nice cab and I was distressed to think that others would be sitting in it, horrid financiers and ruffianly women of the streets, and therefore I proposed to the driver, who is a respectable gentleman named Barkis—a descendant, my dear Charley, of the original, famous Barkis, although not, I regret to say, legitimate; it is not generally known, but the original Barkis, Barkis of *David Copperfield*, had an affair in the back of his cart with a daughter of King Prognathous the Third of Bohemia, who was traveling incognito at the time, and my Barkis, the Barkis who is driving us, was the fruit of that passionate union; seen in profile he is the image of his royal grandfather—I proposed that he should wait on me in the mornings with his cab and remain in attendance throughout the day. The only difficulty was, when would the horse sleep, since I am generally up rather late—of course Barkis, being a cabby of long experience, sleeps while he drives—but this was settled by letting the horse sleep when I do, that is, in the mornings. He and I rise at noon. It is an admirable arrangement."

Charley left the Savoy in an hour or so. Oscar slept heavily.

In the morning he felt wretched; he had had too much to drink last night. Two letters arrived. One was a charming apology from Pierre Louÿs; the second was from Bosie.

Dearest darlingest Oscar,
  When you left me the other night, that dreadful night, to go to the Trees', I was miserable and could think of nothing but finding solace. The little beast I found was perfectly horrid, there was a demon of wickedness in him. He put me up to everything, and it was because I was hating and loathing myself that I flew out at you as I did. My own dear darling, you are my only love, you are the reason for my life, and everything is too terrible without you. I think of you constantly, so sweet, so noble, so tender, and I know that my life with you was a sonnet, as life without you is a dirge. Please be with me again, my own dear darling love, and write to me at Salisbury, where I am staying (quite penniless).
                              Always your own devoted boy,
                                                      Bosie

A third envelope contained the Savoy's bill for the past week, forty-nine pounds, and a request for immediate payment.

Oscar put his hands to his head. He had come to a dividing line, which was represented by Bosie's letter. He could answer it or ignore it.

He began to tear up the letter. Perhaps he would read it once again, though.

My own dear darling, you are my only love, you are the reason for my life . . . I think of you constantly, so sweet, so noble, so tender . . . my life with you was a sonnet, as life without you is a dirge . . . be with me again, my own dear darling love. . . .

Good heavens, what was Oscar, a frail reed to fear his love? It was Bosie who was frail. He was the boy, Oscar was the man. He, not Bosie, had the will power to command and control. Bosie stood desperately in need of his strength, of his love.

Oscar found pen and paper. There were tears in his eyes as he wrote Bosie that his letter had come as a thing of delight, as red and yellow wine; still, he was sad. The scenes that Bosie made killed Oscar's spirit; they blighted the beauty of life. To see Bosie, Greek and gracious, made ugly with unjust hatred, to see his curved lips distorted with bitter words—rather than this, Oscar wrote, he would choose to be blackmailed by all the renters in London. He wanted Bosie, wanted his grace and beauty; but how he was to manage it he did not know. His bill at the hotel was forty-nine pounds for one week. Why wasn't Bosie here, his dear, wonderful boy?

He signed himself "Your own Oscar."

PART *4*

THE LITTLE TENT OF BLUE

1 AFTER AN UNFORTUNATE EPISODE WITH THE MARQUESS, Bosie and Lady Queensberry's father began to receive furious, insulting letters about Oscar from Queensberry. The letters continued, off and on, for the next two years. There was, too, a ridiculous little attempt at blackmail.

One afternoon, following another fight, Bosie shrilly flung out of Oscar's hotel rooms (taking with him his latest conquest from the streets); and shortly thereafter, at his club, Oscar opened an envelope and found inside a card from the marquess reading, "To Oscar Wilde, posing as somdomite."

Constance was waiting for him at home that evening. "It is very good of you to be here," Oscar said. "I hope my note didn't upset your plans for the evening."

"No, but it wouldn't have mattered if it had. You said that this was important." She smiled. "And how very seldom I have the chance to do anything for you."

She was almost the girl of their honeymoon eleven years ago. The great changes were in him. Because of her blessed innocence, his task tonight was easier, but he hated it nonetheless.

"My dear, something dreadful has happened."

"Not the children?"

"The children are safely tucked in bed at their school. As I told you in my note, I telegraphed the headmaster not to have Cyril come up for the weekend; if anything were wrong, I would have heard in reply."

"Is it because of this something dreadful," Constance asked, "that you didn't want him here?"

"Yes; he would know I was disturbed. And besides, I don't know how much time I shall have to spend with the solicitors. Constance, I am going to prosecute Bosie Douglas' father for libel. He has assailed me most brutally and most hideously like the reptile that he is, and I feel that my life will be ruined unless I draw his fangs." Oscar took out his handkerchief and dabbed at his damp face. "Forgive me for using such terms, but they are all he deserves. I cannot of course proceed without your full knowledge and support. Thus my note asking you to be in tonight."

"Whatever has Lord Queensberry done?" she cried.

"It is difficult to say without shocking you."

"But I understood you to be friends."

"Never friends. He is a man to whom Christ's name is vile; could *he* be a friend of mine? Oh, I got along well enough with him once because I made it my business to do so, hoping to settle the horrible feud between him and Bosie; but since then the marquess has reverted to his disgusting savage self. Two years ago he married a girl of seventeen and abandoned her twenty-four hours later; and last year—I told you none of this at the time because I saw no need to distress you—he launched an attack upon me in letters to his son and Lady Queensberry's father. I warned him through my solicitors——"

"Attack you?" Constance exclaimed. "He should thank you for all you've done for Lord Alfred. How could he attack you?"

"His imagination is diseased. He conceives the world to be in a conspiracy against him."

"Then he should be ignored."

"I can't ignore his latest slander; it is too infamous and degrading. This afternoon I went to the Albermarle Club, for no reason that I can think of now; it means little enough to me, and I hadn't been there for weeks. The porter gave me an envelope. I opened it and found a card—Queensberry's card. He had handed it to the porter ten days ago, the eighteenth February; the porter had made a note of the date after putting the card in the envelope. Mind you, Constance, it was the porter who did that, not Queensberry. Queensberry had written hideous words on the card, addressed to me, and left the card in all its naked horror. Anyone who had cared to look could have seen it, if not for the porter's discretion—his kindness."

"What were the hideous words?" she asked in a low voice.

" 'To Oscar Wilde,' " Oscar said, " 'posing as—' No, I cannot say it. In effect it was, to Oscar Wilde, posing as a person of—as an unnatural person."

Her hands rose slowly, in the attitude of prayer, and covered her mouth. "He must be mad."

"He is mad."

"Then he can be put away in an asylum."

"The Marquess of Queensberry? I hardly think so. But he *can* be prosecuted for libel and his madness and vileness displayed in a courtroom dock so that the world will see him for what he is, and he will be convicted, and the ivory tower of my life and my art will be cleansed of his foul stain."

"Oh, Oscar," she said. "Oscar, Oscar. In a courtroom? But that will mean lawyers, and people rushing to hear, and a great sensation—Oscar Wilde prosecuting the Marquess of Queensberry. Oscar, the newspapers, the talk, the scandal."

"The only scandal is in his evil mind."

"We know that, my darling. And since we know, do we have to expose ourselves to this horrible, ghastly thing, a trial? No one else saw his wicked card. You told me it was in an envelope. No one will ever know unless you make it public in a courtroom."

"But if I don't seize him by the scruff of the neck and drag him into court," Oscar said, "don't you see, he will boast about what he has done. He won't rest until he's spread the story of his loathsome libel in every club in London."

"Who will believe him?"

"He'll say I was afraid to prosecute. He will delight in saying it. He has been itching to call me a coward ever since I turned him out of my house. He knew I could pick him up and shake him as a terrier would a rat, and he turned tail and fled, he and his paid bully. You were away then, Constance, and again I told you nothing of it for the same reason—why should I distress you with a sordid and meaningless story? And I can thrash him in court as I could have thrashed him then. Good God. Does he think *he* is any match for Oscar Wilde?"

"It wouldn't be the marquess, it would be his barristers."

"I should like to see the barrister who could get the better of me on the witness stand. I'd have the courtroom roaring with laughter at him. He would never be the same man again."

Constance looked down.

"Do you think me full of conceit?" he asked. "But isn't it the truth, that I could make mincemeat of any barrister alive? Do you think some little titled nobody would have dared to set his legal dogs on Sheridan? Not on your life. But *I* am the author of a play as brilliant as *The School for Scandal*; you know they've said that, Constance, and yet this little brute dares to challenge me. Perhaps that is the least bearable thing of all, his insolence. His insolence. Oh, his insolence—but I'm getting into a temper, which is quite ridiculous. My dear, the trial won't be pleasant, I agree, though I can promise you that some of it will be highly amusing, at least while I am on the stand, but it won't last long. Perhaps you would like to go away while it is on?"

"And take the children?" she asked.

"Of course, if you wish to, but why? Wouldn't it be a pity to take them out of school?"

"Do you still think of them as babies, Oscar?"

"Good heavens, no, I am very much aware of their age, it makes me so excessively aware of my own. That isn't the true reason, Constance; that was only designed to make you smile—I am aware of their age because I am aware of their intelligence and their sense of humor, which isn't at all childlike. Do you know what Vyvyan did when he was here last, during the Christmas holidays? He's always had a fond eye for my walking stick, the gold-headed one, and I told him I'd give it to him when he grew to be as tall, which led to a great deal of measuring and stretching himself out to the limit; but no matter how far he stretched he lacked a few inches. I don't know if he considered surreptitiously sawing off those inches from the bottom, I dare say not, because both Cyril and he have tremendous respect for beautiful things and wouldn't for their lives do anything to damage them, and that stick is beautiful; and so, when I came in one day, he took the stick from my hand and said 'Look, Papa, I am not only as tall as it is, I am *taller*.' And he was. He had tied some books to his feet. Wasn't that clever? And delightful? And I am inclined to think," Oscar added, "though mind you, I shan't swear to it, that the books were copies of the plays of some of my contemporaries, which would demonstrate Vyvyan's exquisite tact, to say nothing of his taste." He laughed.

Constance smiled briefly. "It would be better for them if they were still babies," she said, "if this trial is to take place. Better if they were of almost any other age. Then they wouldn't be in school and their lives wouldn't be made wretched and horrible with all the whispering and laughing and pointing at them as the sons of Oscar Wilde, whose name is in every newspaper because of the beastly trial. Oscar, your two boys are at the most sensitive of all ages, and I think I am afraid—oh, I *am* afraid—that the experience they will have to go through will mark them for the rest of their lives."

Oscar took out his cigarette case, looked at it, and put it away again.

"I could not be more ashamed," he said at last. "I never thought of my sons."

"You would have, my darling."

"I don't know. I suppose I have been blinded by this hateful man and his feud. Perhaps it was something the marquess did when his boy was my boy's age that began their feud. There won't be a trial, Constance; he may behave as he wishes and boast as he wishes, and may his ugly Godless soul rejoice in it."

She put her arms around him. "Thank you."

"Forgive me," he said. "That would be more fitting." He kissed her cheek. "I have to go."

"Can't you stay tonight?"

"No, I must return to the hotel. When I sent my note to you I also sent one to Bobbie Ross, asking him to meet me later on—I wanted to discuss with him what had happened. It was his solicitors who acted for me before, writing to the marquess to warn him, and I supposed I'd go to them again. But now all that is settled, as I shall tell Bobbie. He is a very good soul, you know. I think perhaps his is the very kindest soul in the world—after yours, my dear."

Bosie was waiting for him at the hotel. He now showed no sign of apologizing for or even acknowledging their crisis of a few hours ago. "I have put up at the Cadogan, in Sloane Street," he said calmly. "Would you like to drive there and see my rooms?" He peered at Oscar. "Are you all right? You look rather odd."

"I found this card at my club this afternoon."

He took the card from his pocket and gave it to Bosie.

"What on earth is this? 'To Oscar Wilde posing as—' As a *what?*"

"Sodomite," Oscar said.

"But it doesn't *say* sodomite. It says *som*domite. S-o-m-d-o-m-i-t-e!"

"It isn't always true that people with filthy minds can't spell. In this case it is."

"I've never noticed before that he couldn't spell."

"He has never had occasion before to try to spell that disgusting word."

"But it doesn't matter," Bosie said. "I say, I say—" His face broke into a smile. "Oh, Oscar darling, this is wonderful. It is absolutely, absolutely *wonderful.* We've got him. We've got the little beast at last."

There was a knock on the door; Oscar opened it on Bobbie Ross's small, neat figure and Puckish face. "Dear Bobbie," he said, "I am so glad you are here."

"Bobbie, *Bobbie,*" Bosie shouted. "I say, we're in the most wonderful luck. Look at this."

Bobbie read the card. "How indescribably vile."

"Of course," Oscar said. "It was written, after all, by the Marquess of Queensberry."

"This was what you meant, was it," Bobbie asked, "when you said in your note that there was now nothing left but a criminal prosecution?"

"I thought so then, but I have changed my mind. I'm not going to sue him."

"You are *what?*" Bosie said.

"I am not going to sue."

"Have you gone mad?"

"No. I haven't," Oscar said. "Quite the opposite."

"But, darling Oscar, don't you see the marvelous position we're in? And he, the stupid little brute, he has put us there. He *thinks* he is so shrewd, but he really isn't, and then of course at heart he is a coward, and his stupidity and his cowardly heart have put him in *his own trap.* Oh, wonderful, wonderful; oh, glorious—his own trap. He thought it would be a trap for you, but instead it turns out that he set it for *himself,* and it will be the *end* of him."

"I don't know that I follow you, Bosie," Bobbie said.

"It is perfectly clear. The little beast thinks he has protected himself by writing 'To Oscar Wilde, posing as a sodomite.' Not a *sodomite,* but *posing* as one. And on top of that, he has misspelled the word. Now, how can he possibly defend himself by proving to a jury that it isn't a libel but the truth? That Oscar is *posing* as a *somdomite?* What *is* a *somdomite?* How does one *pose* as one? Not that any of that matters, really."

"The misspelling isn't significant," Bobbie said. "The word 'posing' may be."

"But it doesn't matter, I tell you," Bosie cried. "The only thing that matters is *this.* We, our lawyers that is, will put *me* in the witness box and I shall describe to the judge and the jury and the whole crowded courtroom my father's true nature; I shall tell them everything about him; they will learn the hideous filthy things he has done, they will see him in his *true light*, they will know that he is a monster of wickedness and duplicity whose word can no more be trusted than—than—whose word, simply because it *is* his word, is false, and a lie, a monstrous lie, and of course the jury will convict him, and we shall have won. We shall have won. That is how he has been too clever for himself. He has given *me* the chance to denounce him before *the world*."

"You are not going to have that chance, Bosie," Oscar said. "There is not going to be a prosecution."

"You cannot mean that you're afraid of *losing?*"

"I'm not afraid of losing. Quite without any performance from you in the witness box, I would render your father and his lawyers ridiculous. I am afraid of the effect on my children of a sordid public trial."

"It will not be a sordid trial. It will be a glorious, glorious triumph, a wonderful, *triumphant* trial."

"Glorious or sordid, there won't be a trial. I have exposed myself to enough; I can't expose my children to the same sort of degradation."

"Oh, you coward!" Bosie shouted.

And there was the look on his face. He ran from the room.

In the morning he returned. He was calm and beautiful. "Surely you're not afraid, Oscar? I can't believe you are *afraid*. Afraid of my father? The little beast who has tormented us for so long? And now of all times, when we have the chance to get rid of him, to silence his poisonous tongue forever—*afraid?* Oscar Wilde, afraid of the Marquess of Queensberry? Of course people will always say so; when the test came, they will always say, the brave, brilliant Oscar turned coward, ran away. *We* will know why you refused the test, that it was not because you were afraid but in the kind but oh so foolish belief that in some way it would spare your children."

"It would spare them."

"But, Oscar, dear, sweet, kind Oscar, how? Do you think your refusing to meet him in court would stop my father's loathsome taunts? Oh, heavens, how foolish. He will crow about it, he will strut and crow and boast, the brave Oscar Wilde is a coward, he ran away from me. And what will that evil mind of his think of to do next? Something even more blatant, more savage, more horrible

—and what will your two boys think of their father? They will be bound to hear what everyone will be saying, their school friends will hear whispering and gossiping about you when they go home for the holidays, and like the cruel little beasts that most children are, they will bring the whispers and the lies back with them to school, and your boys will hear again and again, and again, Oscar Wilde is a coward, a coward, a coward. And false though it is, as you and I know, will your boys ever be able to forget it as long as they live? Oscar Wilde is a coward, a coward, a coward, afraid even to consult his lawyer about the effect on his family of the Marquess of Queensberry's wicked libel.'"

Bobbie Ross came in. "Isn't it true," Bosie demanded, "that Oscar owes it to his family to take legal advice?"

Bobbie said cautiously, "I don't think it could do any harm."

"There now," Bosie said. He grasped Oscar's hands and pulled him from the chair.

Charles Humphreys, senior partner of Humphreys, Son, & Kershaw, a bald, serious man, said after prolonged inspection of the marquess' card, "It would be difficult to ignore. But I must ask you, Mr. Wilde, is there any truth in Lord Queensberry's insult?"

"None whatsoever."

"Then, sir, if you institute criminal proceedings against him, you should succeed."

Bosie laughed. "Of course."

"But the cost," Oscar said. "The expense will be tremendous. I don't know that I can afford a trial. I shan't attempt to disguise from you, Mr. Humphreys, that although my two new plays are huge successes, I have always lived in advance of my income, and I am, at the moment, to be quite frank, in debt."

"But good heavens, Oscar," Bosie cried. "We shall take care of the cost, of course."

"We, Bosie?"

"My family. My mother has loads of rich relations, you know. For years and years they have been longing for the chance to pay my father back in his own coin—to make up for all the humiliation and grief he has caused us—they have even discussed the possibility of having him put out of the way in an asylum. Oscar, they wouldn't hear of your paying a penny of the legal costs. You'll be their champion, their knight in armor; they will bless you and thank you for coming forward—forever and ever you will be remembered as the family benefactor."

And Mr. Humphreys' grave eyes seemed to say, *Justice must be done, my dear sir.*

Oscar sat down to write to Constance; he could not quite face bringing his news to her himself.

Dear Constance,

This afternoon my solicitor applied in police court for a warrant for the arrest of the Marquess of Queensberry, the first step in proceeding against him for his atrocious libel. And so the die is cast, and I cannot retreat. But I would not if I could. I have acted on the soundest legal advice, of which we did not have the benefit when we had our talk the other night, and when you have heard me out you will, I know, feel as I do, that in all honor, and in all fairness to my family and to myself, I could not abide by my earlier decision. In the first place, a warrant was applied for, although the usual custom is to issue a simple summons, because we are convinced that Queensberry would pay no attention to the latter; but now he cannot escape and must endeavor to defend himself, a hopeless task. He will have to enter "a plea of justification" to prove that his libel was "published" —the legal term—"for the public benefit." No justification is possible. Queensberry's only faint hope, the only straw at which his counsel can grasp, is my work. There is nothing else. And of course any attempt to show that my beautiful poems and stories and *The Picture of Dorian Gray* are the product of an "unhealthy mind," that they prove their author to be "an unnatural person," is doomed to failure. Queensberry has no case. Squirm and lie as he may, he will suffer the most disastrous defeat. The trial will be very short, and although I told you that it would not be pleasant, I am now persuaded that it will be disagreeable solely for the defendant.

I also told you, I remember, that if I did not bring him to justice, Queensberry would boast of his fancied victory. He would do more—would go on to grosser and grosser acts against me, and would make my name, of which one day my sons will be as proud as I am, a laughingstock—would make it common and cheap. That is the shameful mark they would have to bear in their glorious youth and young manhood, indeed throughout their lives, if I did not perform my duty as their father and halt the vicious brute who threatens them.

I have another duty. Once I was appealed to in the most pathetic terms by Lady Queensberry to "wave my magic wand" and save her and her family from the almost daily persecution and humiliation heaped upon them by the marquess. Alas, I told her, I had no magic wand. But now something perhaps more powerful is in my hands, the weapon of the law. I would be most grievously failing this noble and long-suffering lady if I did not use it to strike down our common foe.

Oscar

He read the letter again. "Queensberry's only faint hope, the only straw at which his counsel can grasp, is my work. There is nothing else."

Good heavens, he was beginning to *believe* what he had written. It was a thundering lie. But Constance would never know, Queensberry's lawyers would never know. None of Oscar's loves would ever step forward against him, of course; they liked him too much.

It *would* have to be assumed, though, that a copy of the letter the blackmailers had tried to use, the letter that spoke of Bosie's slim gilt soul and rose-leaf lips, had fallen into Queensberry's hands, and that his counsel would point to it as proof that its writer at least *posed* as a sodomite. The defense must not be allowed to bring the letter forward first. The prosecution must, and thereby disarm them in advance. He must be sure to tell that bald, serious Charles Humphreys the whole history of the letter. ". . . red rose-leaf lips . . . madness of kisses . . . your slim gilt soul walks between passion and poetry." This was, of course, the lyrical effusion of a poet—Humphreys must think of it as a *poem in prose*, as a *sonnet*; indeed, it *had* been made into a sonnet, in French, by Pierre Louÿs. (After the blackmailers had produced the letter, he had *asked* Pierre to turn it into a sonnet.) There were no weak points in the case of Mr. Oscar Wilde vs. the Brute.

2

"WHILE YOU WERE AWAY, MR. WILDE," TRAVERS HUM-
phreys, Charles Humphreys' rather pleasant son, said, "Lord
Queensberry's solicitors, Messrs. Day, Russell and Co., asked Edward Carson, Q.C., to lead for them, and he has accepted the brief.
You will be cross-examined, of course, after your testimony, and
it is Mr. Carson who will do so."

"Ah," Oscar murmured. "I have no doubt he will perform his
task with all the added bitterness of an old friend."

"Mr. Carson is an old friend of yours?"

"I was a student at Trinity College, Dublin, before I went up to
Oxford, and Carson was there at the same time. I seem to remember a nickname he had—could it have been 'Rawbones'? I am
afraid it was. Dear me. 'Rawbones'! I suppose he will, inevitably, be
reminded of it when he sees me in court, since I am so abundantly
not a rawbones and he, I believe, still is. I beat him out in one
or two competitions, I seem to remember. But of course I did. I
won the Berkeley Gold Medal for Greek, on which Carson had set
his dour eye. I suppose the thought of that lost prize will be searing
him every moment. How fortunate I am, Sir Edward—considering
that we must do battle against lost prizes and remembered nick-
names—to have you on my side."

Sir Edward Clarke gravely inclined his head. It was more or less a
guarantee of purity to be associated with him. Queensberry's
lawyers must have been confounded to learn that he had accepted
the brief. That, no doubt, explained why they had gone after a
champion thought by many to be Sir Edward's equal, if not his
superior, at the bar—Carson. How amusing; they could not have
selected anyone whom Oscar would have preferred to meet. He
knew Carson, he knew that puritan nature. He had tied him into
knots long ago; he could do it again.

Bosie took Sir Edward's silence as his cue to start explaining in a
charming manner how the case should be run. Travers Humphreys
coughed; Bosie withdrew into a cloud of cigarette smoke.

"I have here a copy of Lord Queensberry's amended plea of
justification, Mr. Wilde," Charles Humphreys said. "I should like
you to read it."

Oscar and Bosie read.

213

Central Criminal Court. To wit: At the Sessions of Oyer and Terminer and General Jail Delivery holden for the Central Criminal Court District at Justice Hall Old Bailey in the Suburbs of the City of London on the twenty-fifth day of March in the year of our Lord One thousand eight hundred and ninety-five comes into Court the said John Sholto Douglas Marquess of Queensberry in his own proper person and having heard the said Indictment read says he is not guilty of the premises in the said Indictment above specified and charged upon him and of this the said John Sholto Douglas Marquess of Queensberry puts himself upon the Country.

Second Plea.

And for a further plea in his behalf to the Second Count of the said Indictment the said John Sholto Douglas Marquess of Queensberry says that Our Lady the Queen ought not further to prosecute the said Second Count of the said Indictment against him because he says that the said alleged libel according to the natural meaning of the words thereof is true in substance and in fact in that the said Oscar Fingal O'Flahertie Wills Wilde between the month of February in the year of Our Lord One thousand eight hundred and ninety-two and the month of May in the same year at the Albermarle Hotel in the County of London did solicit and incite one Edward Shelley to commit sodomy and other acts of gross indecency with him the said Oscar Fingal O'Flahertie Wills Wilde and that the said Oscar Fingal O'Flahertie Wills Wilde did then indecently assault and commit acts of gross indecency and immorality with the said Edward Shelley.

And that the said Oscar Fingal O'Flahertie Wills Wilde in the month of October in the year of our Lord One thousand eight hundred and ninety-two at the said Albermarle Hotel did solicit and incite one Sidney Mavor to commit sodomy and other acts of gross indecency and immorality and did then and there commit the said other acts of gross indecency and immorality with the said Sidney Mavor.

And that the said Oscar Fingal O'Flahertie Wills Wilde on the twentieth day of November in the year of our Lord One thousand eight hundred and ninety-two at a house situate at 29 Boulevard des Capucins in Paris in the Republic of France did solicit and incite one Frederick Atkins to commit sodomy and other acts of gross indecency and immorality with him the said Oscar Fingal O'Flahertie Wills Wilde and did then and there commit the said other acts of gross indecency and immorality with the said Frederick Atkins.

214

And that the said Oscar Fingal O'Flahertie Wills Wilde on the twenty-second day of November in the year of our Lord One thousand eight hundred and ninety-two at the said house in Paris did solicit and incite one Maurice Schwabe to commit sodomy and other acts of gross indecency with him the said Oscar Fingal O'Flahertie Wills Wilde.

And that the said Oscar Fingal O'Flahertie Wills Wilde in the month of January in the year of our Lord One thousand eight hundred and ninety-three at the house situate and being No. 16 Tite Street in the County of London did solicit and incite one Alfred Wood to commit sodomy and other acts of gross indecency and immorality with him the said Oscar Fingal O'Flahertie Wills Wilde and did then and there commit the said acts of gross indecency and immorality with the said Alfred Wood.

And that the said Oscar Fingal O'Flahertie Wills Wilde about the seventh day of March in the year of our Lord One thousand eight hundred and ninety-three at the Savoy Hotel in the County of London did solicit and incite a certain boy to the Defendant unknown to commit sodomy and other acts of gross indecency and immorality with him the said Oscar Fingal O'Flahertie Wills Wilde and did then and there commit the said other acts of gross indecency and immorality with the said boy unknown.

And that the said Oscar Fingal O'Flahertie Wills Wilde on or about the twentieth day of March in the year of our Lord One thousand eight hundred and ninety-three at the said Savoy Hotel did solicit and incite another boy to the Defendant unknown to commit sodomy and other acts of gross indecency with the said Oscar Fingal O'Flahertie Wills Wilde and did there commit the said other acts of gross indecency with the said last mentioned boy.

And that the said Oscar Fingal O'Flahertie Wills Wilde in the said month of March in the year of our Lord One thousand eight hundred and ninety-three at the said Savoy Hotel and again in or about the month of April in the year of our Lord One thousand eight hundred and ninety-three at a house situate at and being No. 50 Park Walk and again between the month of October in the year of our Lord One thousand eight hundred and ninety-three and the month of April in the year of our Lord One thousand eight hundred and ninety-four at a house situate and being No. 10 St. James's Place all the County of London did on each of the said occasions incite one Charles Parker to commit sodomy and other acts of gross indecency and immorality with him the said Oscar Fingal O'Flahertie Wills Wilde and did then and there commit the said other acts of gross indecency and immorality with the said Charles Parker.

And that the said Oscar Fingal O'Flahertie Wills Wilde between the month of October in the year of our Lord One thousand eight hundred and ninety-three and the month of April in the year of our Lord One thousand eight hundred and ninety-four at the said house No. 10 St. James Place did solicit and incite one Ernest Scarfe to commit sodomy and other acts of gross indecency and immorality with him the said Oscar Fingal O'Flahertie Wills Wilde and did then and there commit the said other acts of gross indecency and immorality with the said Ernest Scarfe.

And that the said Oscar Fingal O'Flahertie Wills Wilde on several occasions in the month of June in the year of our Lord One thousand eight hundred and ninety-three in the City of Oxford and also upon several occasions in the months of June July and August in the year of our Lord One thousand eight hundred and ninety-three at a house called "The Cottage" at Goring in the County of Oxford did solicit and incite one Walter Grainger to commit sodomy and other acts of gross indecency and immorality with him the said Oscar Fingal O'Flahertie Wills Wilde and did then and there commit the said other acts of gross indecency and immorality with the said Walter Grainger.

And that the said Oscar Fingal O'Flahertie Wills Wilde upon several occasions in the months of August and September in the year of our Lord One thousand eight hundred and ninety-four at Worthing in the County of Sussex and on or about the twenty-seventh day of September in the said year at the Albion Hotel Brighton in the same County did solicit and incite one Alphonse Harold Conway to commit sodomy and other acts of gross indecency and immorality with him the said Oscar Fingal O'Flahertie Wills Wilde.

And that the said Oscar Fingal O'Flahertie Wills Wilde did in fact at the said times and places commit the said other acts of gross indecency with the said Alphonse Harold Conway.

And that the said Oscar Fingal O'Flahertie Wills Wilde in the month of July in the year of our Lord One thousand eight hundred and ninety did write and publish and cause and procure to be printed and published with his name upon the title page thereof a certain immoral and obscene work in the form of a narrative entitled "The Picture of Dorian Gray" which said work was designed and intended by the said Oscar Fingal O'Flahertie

Wills Wilde and was understood by the readers thereof to describe the relations intimacies and passions of certain persons of sodomitical and unnatural habits tastes and practices.

And that in the month of December in the year of our Lord One thousand eight hundred and ninety-four was published a certain other immoral and obscene work in the form of a magazine entitled "The Chameleon" which said work contained diverse obscene matters and things relating to the practices and passions of persons of sodomitical and unnatural habits and tastes and that the said Oscar Fingal O'Flahertie Wills Wilde published his name on the contents sheet of the said magazine as its first and principal contributor and published in the said magazine certain immoral maxims as an introduction to the same under the title of "Phrases and Philosophies for the Use of the Young."

And the said John Sholto Douglas Marquess of Queensberry further says that at the time of the publishing of the said alleged libel in the second count charged and stated it was for the public benefit and that the matter contained therein should be published because before and at the time of the publishing of the said alleged libel the said Oscar Fingal O'Flahertie Wills Wilde was a name of letters and a dramatist of prominence and notoriety and a person who exercised considerable influence over young men, that the said Oscar Fingal O'Flahertie Wills Wilde claimed to be a fit and proper person to give advice and instruction to the young and had published the said maxims hereinbefore mentioned in the said magazine entitled "The Chameleon" for circulation amongst students of the University of Oxford, and that the said works entitled "The Chameleon" and "The Picture of Dorian Gray" were calculated to subvert morality and to encourage unnatural vice, and that the said Oscar Fingal O'Flahertie Wills Wilde had corrupted and debauched the morals of the said Charles Parker, Alphonse Harold Conway, Walter Grainger, Sidney Mavor, Frederick Atkins, Ernest Scarfe, and Edward Shelley as aforesaid, and that the said Oscar Fingal O'Flahertie Wills Wilde had committed the offenses aforementioned and the said sodomitical practices for a long time with impunity and without detection wherefore it was for the public benefit and interest that the matter contained in the said alleged libel should be published and that the true character and habits of the said Oscar Fingal O'Flahertie Wills Wilde should be known that the said Oscar Fingal O'Flahertie Wills Wilde might be prevented from further committing such offenses and further debauching the liege subjects of our said Lady the Queen and that such liege subjects being forewarned might avoid the corrupting influence of the said Oscar Fingal O'Flahertie Wills Wilde.

And that the said John Sholto Douglas Marquess of Queensberry is ready to verify wherefor he prays Judgment and that by the Court he may be discharged and dismissed from the said premises in the said indictment above specified.

Oscar kept his shock from his face. "I am frankly amazed, gentlemen," he observed, "to find that Lord Queensberry is capable of composing such a powerful and unique work of fiction."

"Of fiction, Mr. Wilde?" Humphreys said.

Bosie spluttered. "All lies."

"We were disturbed by these charges, Mr. Wilde," Sir Edward said, "and I feel that I must ask you to assure me on your honor as an English gentleman that there is no truth in them."

"You have my assurance, Sir Edward, on my honor. Forgive me if I seemed to dismiss the charges too lightly. But on second thought, they are *not* all fiction."

"No, sir?"

"No; it is perfectly true that I wrote *The Picture of Dorian Gray* and 'Phrases and Philosophies for the Use of the Young.' And when I have said that, as I am proud to say it, I have reached the limit of the facts in this document. I beg your pardon; not quite the limit. The people whose names are given here are real people; all the rest is disgusting and wicked nonsense. It is a tower of lies, built on an innocent foundation."

"That is well put, Mr. Wilde," Sir Edward remarked. "We must do all we can to learn precisely how the tower of lies was built. Let me explain why. If we had only the marquess' libelous card to deal with, that would be a relatively simple matter. We had assumed that he would attempt to justify the libel on purely literary grounds. Perhaps that was his original intention; perhaps his solicitors, perhaps Carson, suggested to him that that would not be good enough, as indeed it would not have been. In any event, this plea raises far more serious questions. It has been put together very cleverly. You will observe that it does not charge you with *having committed* sodomy; it merely says that you *solicited* these people to commit this gravest of all offenses with you—unsuccessfully. But it does say that you were guilty of indecent practices with them. Obviously the marquess' solicitors and Carson are satisfied that on this basis they will win, that the plea shows you, and amply shows you, to have been guilty of *posing* as a sodomite, and that therefore the libel was not a libel and was published for the public benefit. But they will have to demonstrate that these allegations are true. They will have to do so, if they can, with credible witnesses. The more thoroughly we are prepared for them, the better."

"I think it would be advisable to go through the plea point by point with Mr. Wilde," Charles Humphreys said.

Oscar nodded. "By all means."

"The first allegation is that you 'did solicit and incite one Edward Shelley to commit sodomy and other acts of gross indecency' and that you 'did then indecently assault and commit acts of gross indecency and immorality with the said Edward Shelley.' Who is he, Mr. Wilde?"

"He was a clerk in the offices of my publishers. Whenever I had occasion to go there, he would make a point of expressing his admiration for my work; it soon turned out that he had literary ambitions and had written some poetry—very poor poetry, I am sorry to say. I tried to help him; I invited him to my house and he dined with my wife and me; also, I had dinner with him once at the Albermarle. Apparently he had great difficulties at home, troubles with his parents, which must have affected his mind, because he began to write very morbid letters to me. I can only conclude that the balance of his mind has become increasingly disturbed, for him to have made this charge, or that he was bribed. Whatever the case, it seems a poor return for an act of kindness."

"I quite agree. The next name is that of Sidney Mavor, with whom similar acts are alleged."

"It is quite false. Indeed, there are powerful and wicked hands at work here, to turn these friends—for they were friends, good friends; I enjoyed their company, as they enjoyed mine, and I flatter myself that I contributed something to their appreciation of art and life—to turn them into shameless liars. Or are they quite shameless, I wonder? I cannot believe that Shelley and Mavor, whatever their present state, will actually appear in court to try to support these lies, for they would be shattered, they would weep tears of contrition, the moment they saw me."

"They would, they would," Bosie cried. "It is all my father's influence—he has corrupted them."

An hour later Sir Edward and Humphreys were satisfied; they thanked Oscar for his patience. He sighed with relief on reaching the street and sank back in the hansom. "Telling bald, serious lies to a bald, serious man in a bald light of a serious office is an exhausting business," he informed Bosie. "But Sir Edward is rather sweet, isn't he? And I like young Humphreys."

"They weren't *all* lies," Bosie pointed out.

"Quite so, they weren't. I never, never did indecently assault and commit acts of gross indecency and immorality with the said Edward Shelley; I only tried to. And I never committed the same with the said Frederick Atkins. As for soliciting poor dear *Maurice* to commit sodomy—good heavens, what are we coming to? And Alfred Wood. That rather hurt, to have *your* love affairs blamed on me. My dear boy, please don't take me seriously. I am only trying to be amusing after all that dull talk. But wouldn't it have stirred them up if I'd said, 'Gentlemen, the two boys to the defendant unknown with whom I am supposed to have romped in bed at the Savoy—Lord Alfred can tell you everything you could possibly care to know about them, can't you, Bosie?' As of course I didn't, and wouldn't."

"It is very noble of you, Oscar, I am sure."

"I am incorrigibly noble. But oh, Bosie, Walter Grainger— Walter Grainger. That I should indecently assault and et cetera *Walter Grainger*. Good God, to indecently assault Walter would be like indecently assaulting a newspaper kiosk."

"Oh, I don't know," Bosie said sulkily.

"You don't mean you ever did? Really, dear boy, that was very naughty of you; a gentleman should always leave his servants alone; I assure you I did, after you wished poor Walter on me. Now don't look annoyed; we shall soon be at the Café Royal, where Frank Harris and Bernard Shaw are waiting to have luncheon with us."

"If this news is intended to delight me," Bosie declared, "I am sorry, but it does not. I shall lunch by myself. Harris is objectionable enough but Shaw would put anyone off his food; he only eats carrots and nuts, I have heard. Why on earth did you ask them to luncheon?"

"I didn't ask them, Frank asked me. He is anxious to give me advice about the trial."

"He will try to discourage you."

"Dearest Bosie, nothing in the world could discourage me. I am going to have the time of my life with Carson. And you are quite wrong to dislike Shaw—I say this because I know he likes *me*. He sent me his plays to read, and I complimented him on them and did him the honor of associating his work with mine by calling *Lady Windermere* Opus One of the Wilde-Shaw Celtic School, his *Widowers' Houses* Opus Two, *A Woman of No Importance* Opus Three, his *The Philanderer* Opus Four——"

"Really, Oscar, I do see your point. Is it necessary to go on?"

"And furthermore, being the sort of chap he is, some time ago he got up a petition in the interest of the convicted Chicago anarchists and asked lots of eminent British literary figures to sign it, and I was the only one who did. There were stars in his eyes, my dear boy, when he told me so."

"None of this," Bosie said, "makes Shaw's peculiar clothes and sickly white skin and red hair any more agreeable. I shall lunch by myself."

Nevertheless he later came to the table where Oscar and the other two were in earnest discussion. Oscar's part appeared to be to try to convince Frank that unless he lowered his voice they would have the building down around their ears.

"*Listen* to me," the short, powerful Harris boomed impatiently. "Your case——"

"My dear Frank, how can one not listen to you? You are overwhelming."

"I mean to overwhelm you; you need overwhelming, to bring you to your senses. Oscar, face the facts; your case against Queensberry is hopeless."

"What utter nonsense," Bosie said indignantly.

"Do be quiet. This is of the utmost importance. You cannot win, Oscar. The literary part of the defense Queensberry's counsel will make is nothing; I could testify to the high moral qualities of *Dorian*, and so could Shaw and a thousand others, and it would be useless, not because *Dorian* is not a moral work, it is, but because judges and jury will be concerned with far different things. I am sure I know what Queensberry has been up to: he has had his private detectives digging into every muck heap in London to find witnesses against you. They will have been well paid and they will swear to anything, while Queensberry poses as the saintlike father who is only trying to save his son."

"Saintlike father," Bosie burst out. "Not when I have finished with him."

"Lord Alfred, in this you are an innocent; you don't know what you are talking about. When Sir Edward Clarke has heard a few of these witnesses, Oscar, he will throw in his hand, and you will be ruined." Harris cleared his throat. "Now, here is what you must do."

"I shan't listen to any more of this," Bosie said.

"Then leave." Bosie sat. "You must write a letter to the *Times*, Oscar, and say that you were insulted by the Marquess of Queensberry and sought redress in the court but soon learned that it was an error, since no jury would bring in a verdict against any father, even though that father was quite wrong. Then you must go to France or Italy for a holiday, and remain abroad until the newspapers have simmered down. And you must take Constance with you. It is *essential* to be seen everywhere together, the picture of a devoted husband and wife."

Bosie got up. "You are advising Oscar to run away. How can you pretend to be a friend of his?" He left.

"It *isn't* very friendly of you, Frank, now is it?" Oscar murmured.

"Oh, my God. Ask Shaw. Who is being Oscar's real friend? I, or that young idiot who keeps egging him on?"

"Harris' argument seems sound to me," Shaw said. "The marquess won't bring the Queensberry rules of fair play into court with him; he will strike you with every dirty blow he can think of. And if he should produce a string of witnesses, what will you say?"

"There you have it in a nutshell," Harris boomed. "What will you say?"

"That his witnesses are liars, and blackmailers, and thieves, and poor unbalanced creatures," Oscar replied, "and that I treated them with kindness, even so, and think of them still with kindness—and pity. Never fear, Frank, I shall defeat this scarlet marquess."

"Oscar, you are lost," Harris said.

From the doorway Bosie called, "Oscar, come on. *Come on*."

In the cab Oscar said, "Harris, though objectionable in many respects, is a well-meaning fellow. Of course his advice, to leave the country, is absurd. How can I leave the country? I have just returned to it. I cannot continually be leaving the country. I should feel like a missionary or a commercial traveler. Besides, it wouldn't be fair to Sir Edward, or Humphreys *père et fils*, or, for that matter, Ned Carson, because I shall make him famous, and he would never forgive me, would he, if at the last moment I decided not to and left him to drag out the rest of his miserable existence in its present state of undistinguished obscurity? No, he would not, and he would be quite right. But there was one bit of good sense in Frank's dulcet roarings, do you know, Bosie?"

"I cannot imagine."

"When he said that Constance and I should be seen everywhere together. That is *very* sound. But I shall add to it: we should be seen together in public places before the trial, *with you*, to demonstrate that you share in the spirit of domestic harmony reigning between us."

"What public places?"

"What better than the theater? And what better plays to see than *An Ideal Husband* and *The Importance of Being Earnest?* Or have you seen them often enough?"

"Dear Oscar," Bosie said with his enchanting smile, "to tire of them would be to tire of you, which is impossible."

3

ON APRIL FIRST, TWO NIGHTS BEFORE THE TRIAL WAS TO begin, Oscar, Constance and Bosie entered a box at the St. James's Theatre. Oscar could hear the whispers rising from the packed house: *Look, Oscar Wilde. And his wife. And Alfred Douglas. Oscar Wilde. Oscar Wilde. Oscar Wilde.*

The house was always packed for his plays: for *Lady Windermere's Fan*, for *A Woman of No Importance*, for *An Ideal Husband*, for *The Importance of Being Earnest*; it was gratifying to see that he could pack two houses at the same time—here, at the St. James's, *Earnest*, and *An Ideal Husband* at the Theatre Royal, where it had opened three months ago.

The Prince of Wales had attended that first night. After the performance, when Oscar had expressed the fear that the play was overlong and should be cut, the Prince had said, "You must not remove one word, Wilde."

An Ideal Husband had taken a fearfully long time to write because of the interruptions—the scenes, the crises—caused by Bosie. Never mind, it was all over with now, all in the past; and the black beast in Bosie was going to be defeated. How charming he looked, there at Constance's side, laughing at *Earnest* like a golden child, though he had seen it so often before.

Listen to the audience. Who could blame them? Lines like these would never pall. Even the critics hadn't been able to resist *Earnest* when the play had opened six weeks ago; *all* the critics, not only the perceptive Archer and the astute Walkley. Their reception had been ever so slightly shadowed by Shaw's remark: yes, *Earnest* had amused him, of course, but he thought a comedy should touch as well as amuse to be altogether successful.

But Shaw could be forgiven; poor fellow, his own plays suffered horribly at the hands of critics and public. On *Earnest*'s first night everyone in the audience, critics included, got up and cheered. George Alexander said he had never seen anything like it. The three earlier plays each had a serious vein, deliciously topped with comedy; but *Earnest* was all comedy, all beautiful nonsense.

A magic spell had seemed to touch the play from the moment the first preposterous notion had occurred to Oscar: two pretty

224

girls, unknown to each other, have a passion for the name of Ernest. It had required only three weeks to write—at Worthing, in Sussex. Anyone in the theater would have jumped at the play; George Alexander was the lucky man to get it, because Alec advanced Oscar a hundred and fifty pounds when he was desperate for money to pay the school bills. Alec had decided to take the part of Jack for himself, and as Jack he was magnificent—so perfectly serious, so perfectly absurd. Really, it was the performance of Alec's career, as it should be; this was the play of anyone's career.

After the second act, Oscar went backstage to Alec's dressing room.

"I thought I should come around to give you a comforting word or two, my dear fellow. You have no need to worry about your fading powers; the lines of my play improve with age and will conceal any gaps in your performance."

"I'm not worrying about my fading powers——"

"Ah. You admit they *are* fading, then?"

"They are not fading, and I wouldn't be worrying about them if they were. I am worrying about you. Oscar, do you know that you and your wife and Lord Alfred couldn't be more conspicuous than you are in that box, and that everyone in the theater is talking about you?"

"I don't know that they are, my dear Alec," Oscar said. "I merely assume it."

"They are talking about you because your coming here and showing yourself and Constance and Lord Alfred so publicly just before the trial is bound to be thought in the worst possible taste."

"It would be the worst possible taste if we went to someone else's play. We wished to be seen. After all, we are on the eve of a very great victory."

Alec sighed. "Are you so sure, Oscar?"

"Good heavens, yes. Mrs. Robinson, the palmist, has told us so. Bosie and I consulted her the other day, at Constance's request— Constance believes implicitly in Mrs. Robinson. And so you see, Alec, I cannot lose. Of course I knew that before going to Mrs. Robinson, but I wanted to please Constance and make her quite happy, which she now is."

"Despite Mrs. Robinson, I wish you would withdraw from the case and go abroad. How can you possibly believe in a palmist, how can Constance, when your whole career may be at stake?"

"If Mrs. Robinson had said I was not going to win, of course I wouldn't believe her, but since she has told the truth, I am obliged to. Alec, dear Alec, you must not worry your handsome head about me; I am going to give that nasty little man the thrashing he has been threatening for years to give Oscar Wilde, and on the night of my triumph you and I will drink a glass of champagne together between the acts, exactly where we are now."

Again Alec sighed. "I hope so, Oscar, God knows. With all my heart I hope so."

Oscar returned to his box. "Alec is in great spirits—congratulates us in advance and says we must drink a glass of champagne with him on the night of the victory. He is delighted that we came, since we are all looking so well—radiant. Particularly you, my dear, as he instructed me to tell you."

"That was kind of him," Constance said. "If he really said so." She had not wanted to come to the theater tonight and she was not happy.

Reggie Turner had urged the same mean course as Alec, and dear devoted More Adey, and a dozen others. Some friends, Maurice for one, had even set him the example and left for France. If he were Alfred Taylor, he would have followed Maurice; Alfred had been involved in a police raid—with Charley Parker—and would be hard put to defend himself.

But Oscar Wilde was not Alfred Taylor. Bring those poor corrupted boys into court, Atkins and Wood and Parker, and whose word would be believed—theirs or the word of the author of *The Importance of Being Earnest?*

Would it turn out that even Bosie's latest promise, made with such assurance in the solicitor's office—that his family would pay the legal costs—would not be kept? Oscar had had to ask Ernest Leverson, Ada's husband, to advance the money; and Ernest, perhaps with a nudge from Ada, had handsomely agreed. At least Ada had the fullest faith. With the exception of Constance, it was the women who had faith, not the men—Ada, Adela Schuster, Mrs. Robinson, and—Oscar smiled. One whose faith was as the faith of ten, his mother.

Curtain; applause.

"They will be applauding like that in the courtroom a few days from now," Bosie said. "Cheering too."

Turning with a smile to Constance, Oscar saw tears in her eyes.

4

OSCAR DROVE TO THE OLD BAILEY FROM HIS HAIRDRESSER'S.
He could not remember when he had last been up and about at
this hour, but of course on the first morning of the trial no con-
siderations of personal comfort could diminish the importance of
being early. It would be pleasant to make that remark as he entered
court, but he supposed he had better not.

He wore a new frock coat, new trousers, white shirt, high winged
collar, black tie, patent-leather shoes, and fawn gloves and carried
rather than wore his silk hat because he did not wish to disturb his
carefully waved and delicately tinted hair.

The courtroom was packed, of course; the air was close. Perhaps
that was why a vase of flowers had been placed in front of the
judge's chair. Oscar sniffed his scented handkerchief.

There was Queensberry. Oscar's gorge rose; he had never really
known the expression's meaning before. There was Bosie's angelic
face, his lips forming silent words Oscar could easily read: "Be
brave, my darling." There was Carson, little changed, it seemed—
long, thin, handsome, cold as stone. Oscar smiled and nodded.
Carson looked away. Poor Carson.

Oscar sat down and turned to his counsel, just behind him. "Did
you know, Sir Edward," he remarked, "that one of Ned Carson's
ancestors was a Roundhead general? I wonder if I may have a
glass of water? No, not now, when I go into the witness box."

The audience stirred; the audience rose. Mr. Justice Henn Collins
had entered. His wig and the ermine and scarlet robes could not
disguise the indisputable and comfortable fact that His Lordship
possessed an affable little greengrocer's-man sort of face.

A grand jury had considered Oscar's charge against Queensberry
and returned a "true bill," whatever that was; all to the good, at
any rate. If the jurors had thought there was nothing in the charge
and the evidence offered by the prosecution, young Humphreys
had told him, they would not have returned the bill, and all would
have been finished, with the marquess triumphant.

Queensberry, though, was grinning like a monkey at the judge.
The judge pushed aside his vase of flowers and nodded, but not
to him. Young Humphreys explained in a whisper, "The clerk of
arraigns will now read the indictment."

"Ah, I see," Oscar murmured, and sniffed his handkerchief. Bosie was smiling, enjoying himself. Here was the clerk of arraigns, a dumpy man with an unfortunate face. His voice was clear, although he read without troubling to punctuate.

" 'One. First Count. Central Criminal Court. To wit: The Jurors for Our Lady the Queen upon their oath present that John Sholto Douglas Marquess of Queensberry contriving and maliciously intending to injure one Oscar Fingal O'Flahertie Wills Wilde and to excite him to commit a breach of the peace and to bring him into public contempt scandal and disgrace on the eighteenth day of February in the year of our Lord One thousand eight hundred and ninety-five and within the jurisdiction of the said Court unlawfully wickedly and maliciously did write and publish and cause to be written and published of him the said Oscar Fingal O'Flahertie Wills Wilde a false scandalous malicious and defamatory libel in the form of a card directed to the said Oscar Fingal O'Flahertie Wills Wilde according to the tenor and effect following that is to say "To Oscar Wilde, posing as sodomite" meaning thereby that the said Oscar Fingal O'Flahertie Wills Wilde had committed and was in the habit of committing the abominable crime of buggery with mankind to the great scandal and disgrace of the said Oscar Fingal O'Flahertie Wills Wilde to the evil example of all others in the like case offending and against the peace of our said Lady the Queen her crown and dignity.

" 'Two. Second Count. And the Jurors aforesaid upon their oath aforesaid do further present that the said John Sholto Douglas Marquess of Queensberry contriving and maliciously intending to injure the said Oscar Fingal O'Flahertie Wills Wilde and to deprive him of his good name fame credit and reputation and to provoke him the said Oscar Fingal O'Flahertie Wills Wilde and to excite him to commit a breach of the peace and to bring him into public contempt scandal and disgrace on the said eighteenth day of February One thousand eight hundred and ninety-five and within the jurisdiction of the said Court unlawfully maliciously and wickedly did write and publish and cause to be written and published of him the said Oscar Fingal O'Flahertie Wills Wilde a false scandalous malicious and defamatory libel in the form of a card directed to the said Oscar Fingal O'Flahertie Wills Wilde containing divers false scandalous malicious and defamatory matters of and concerning the said Oscar Fingal O'Flahertie Wills Wilde according to the tenor and effect following that is to say "To Oscar Wilde, posing as somdomite" to the great damage scandal and disgrace of the said Oscar Fingal O'Flahertie Wills Wilde to the evil example of all others in the like case offending and against the peace of our said Lady the Queen her crown and dignity.' "

If the jurymen never knew Oscar's name before, they knew it now. Their faces were edifying—dull British respectability. One could hardly hope to fill a jury with Reggie Turners and Max Beerbohms, however. Never mind; dull British respectability came to see *The Importance of Being Earnest,* and were transformed, were made to laugh, were made young again. He would be in command, as surely as in the theater. They would laugh *with him.*

Queensberry was asked how he pleaded to the indictment.

Not guilty—also, that the libel was not a libel, that it was the truth, and that it was published for the public benefit.

The jury was sworn in, and Sir Edward rose to address them with the opening speech for the prosecution.

"May it please you, my lord, gentlemen of the jury. You have heard the charge against the defendant, which is that he published a false and malicious libel in regard to Mr. Oscar Wilde, in the form of a card left by Lord Queensberry at a club to which Mr. Wilde belongs. It was a visiting card of Lord Queensberry's, with his name printed upon it. On that card his lordship wrote 'To Oscar Wilde, posing as a sodomite.' The words of the libel are not directly an accusation of the gravest of all offenses; the suggestion is that there was no guilt of that offense, but that in some way or other Mr. Wilde did appear and pose to be a person guilty of or inclined to the commission of the gravest of all offenses."

Every syllable could be heard and understood; Sir Edward's manner was grave but not too grave; he was not *superior.* Oscar warmed to him.

"Now, gentlemen, one would gather from the plea of justification brought before this court by the defendant that Mr. Wilde has been unsuccessfully soliciting the persons named in the plea to commit with him the gravest of all offenses, and that although that offense is not alleged to have been committed, Mr. Wilde has been guilty of indecent practices. It is for those who have taken the responsibility of putting into the plea these serious allegations to satisfy you, gentlemen, if they can, by credible witnesses, or evidence that they think worthy of consideration, that the allegations are true.

"Mr. Oscar Wilde is a gentleman thirty-eight years of age—"

Oscar winced.

"—the son of Sir William Wilde, a very distinguished Irish surgeon and oculist. Sir William died some years ago; Lady Wilde is still living. Mr. Oscar Wilde went to Trinity College, Dublin, where he greatly distinguished himself for classical knowledge, winning some conspicuous prizes—"

Oscar smiled again at the unsmiling Carson.

"—and went on to Magdalen College, Oxford, where he had a brilliant career. In 1884 he had the good fortune to marry a daughter of the late Mr. Horace Lloyd, Q.C., and from that day to the present he has lived with his wife, who has borne him two children, at Tite Street, Chelsea. He is a member of the Albemarle Club."

Sir Edward's admirably enunciated account continued, introducing the name of Lord Alfred Douglas—a welcome guest of Mr. and Mrs. Wilde's at Tite Street and the country places where they had stayed. "Mr. Wilde met the defendant for the first time at the Café Royal in November, 1892. There had been strained feelings between Lord Alfred Douglas and his father owing to unhappy family circumstances, and Mr. Wilde endeavored to heal the breach between them. Mr. Wilde did not meet Lord Queensberry again between that time and the early part of 1894.

"Before that second meeting, Mr. Wilde became aware that statements were being made against his character. There was a man named Alfred Wood whom Mr. Wilde had met once but knew very little indeed about. Wood had been given some clothes by Lord Alfred Douglas, and he stated that in the pocket of a coat so given to him he had found four letters that had been written by Mr. Wilde to Lord Alfred. Whether he did find them in the pocket or whether he stole them—that is a matter, gentlemen, on which we can only speculate.

"In any event, Wood went to Mr. Wilde and wanted Mr. Wilde to give him something for the letters, representing that he was in great distress and trouble and wanted to go to America. Mr. Wilde gave him fifteen or twenty pounds wherewith to pay his passage. Wood then handed over three very ordinary letters that Mr. Wilde had written to Lord Alfred, but the fourth letter, which was

231

supposed by Wood and his associates to be of some importance, was retained. His associates were named Allen and Cliburn, and something has been found out about them.

"Shortly afterwards, Allen called on Mr. Wilde and said he had the fourth letter and asked Mr. Wilde to give him something for it. Mr. Wilde absolutely and peremptorily refused. He said: 'I have a copy of that letter and the original is of no use to me. I regard it as a work of art.' With that he dismissed Allen, but gave him ten shillings for himself. Soon afterwards Cliburn came to Mr. Wilde and said that Allen was so grateful for his kindness that he was returning the letter. Cliburn then handed over the letter and Mr. Wilde gave him half a sovereign for his troubles."

Sir Edward permitted himself a pause, a sip of water.

"Having once got the original letter into his possession, gentlemen, Mr. Wilde kept it. He said then, as he says now, that he looked upon the letter as a sort of prose sonnet. He told Allen that it would probably appear in print in sonnet form, and it did so. On the fourth of May, 1893, a literary and critical magazine called *The Spirit Lamp*, edited by Lord Alfred Douglas, was issued. On the first page was a sonnet in French described as *a letter written in prose poetry by Mr. Oscar Wilde to a friend and translated into rhymed poetry by a poet of no importance*—a most modest description, considering that the poet was M. Pierre Louÿs. And now, gentlemen, I shall read you the letter."

Oscar glanced at Queensberry. The ugly mouth, with its pendulous underlip, hung half open; he looked stupidly astonished.

In a solemn voice Sir Edward read the letter in which Oscar had written of Bosie's red rose-leaf lips, made as much for song as for a madness of kisses, and of his slim gilt soul walking between passion and poetry.

There were no sounds in the courtroom. Oscar looked at Bosie. Like his father's his lips were half open; but on his face there was an expression of delight.

"The words of that letter, gentlemen," Sir Edward observed—and now his voice was superbly cool and dry—"may appear extravagant to those in the habit of writing commercial correspondence——"

Good, sympathetic, wholesome laughter broke from the audience.

"——or writing those ordinary letters that the necessities of life force upon one every day; but Mr. Wilde is a poet, and the letter is considered by him as a prose sonnet, and one of which he is in no way ashamed and is prepared to produce anywhere as the expression of true poetic feeling, and with no relation whatever to the hateful and repulsive suggestions put to it in the plea in this case.

"In the early part of 1894, Lord Queensberry met Mr. Wilde and Lord Alfred Douglas again in the Café Royal. Shortly after that Mr. Wilde became aware that the defendant was writing letters that affected his character and contained suggestions injurious to him, against which his solicitors were instructed to protest. Then, on the twenty-eighth of February of this year, Mr. Wilde went to his club and received from the porter the card left by Lord Queensberry. Hitherto the accusations had been made in letters to members of Lord Queensberry's family, and thus Mr. Wilde could, if he had chosen, have taken action, but he did not wish to—and he will not now, further than can be avoided—did not wish to bring into prominence the relations of Lord Queensberry with his family. On the first of March a warrant was applied for and on the following day Lord Queensberry was arrested. Hence these criminal proceedings.

"Now, gentlemen, there are two counts at the end of the plea of justification that are extremely curious. It is said that in the month of July, 1890, Mr. Wilde published a certain immoral and indecent work with the title of *The Picture of Dorian Gray* and that this book was intended to be understood by its readers as describing the relations, intimacies, and passions of people guilty of unnatural practices. And secondly, that in December, 1894, there was published a certain immoral work in the form of *The Chameleon*, relating to the practices of persons of unnatural habits, and that Mr. Wilde had joined in procuring the publication of *The Chameleon* as the contributor of 'Phrases and Philosophies for the Use of the Young.'

"Mr. Wilde did contribute these 'Phrases and Philosophies'— epigrammatical statements such as those many of us have enjoyed when being entertained by such a play as *A Woman of No Importance*. They give brilliancy to dialogue and even supply wisdom in a witty form. Mr. Wilde is not responsible for the rest of the magazine. It was edited by an Oxford man who asked Mr. Wilde to contribute. Directly Mr. Wilde saw the magazine he noticed there was a story in it called 'The Priest and the Acolyte,' which is a disgrace to literature. When Mr. Wilde saw that disgraceful and abominable story he communicated with the editor and indignantly insisted that the copies of the magazine should be suppressed, and the magazine was withdrawn. It is strange indeed, then, to find that publication put upon the particulars as justifying the charges against Mr. Wilde.

"As for the volume called *The Picture of Dorian Gray*, gentlemen, it is one that can be bought at any bookstall in London. It has Mr. Wilde's name on the title page and has been published five years. The story of the book is that of a young man of good birth, great wealth, and great personal beauty whose friend paints a picture of him.

"Dorian Gray expresses the wish that he could remain as in the picture, while it aged with the years. His wish is granted; but upon the picture, and not upon his own face, the scars of bad conduct fall. In the end he stabs the picture and falls dead, and the picture is restored to its pristine beauty, while Dorian Gray's servants find on the floor of his room the body of a hideous old man." Pausing, Sir Edward directed a stern glance at Carson. "I shall be surprised if my learned friend can hit upon any passage in that book that does more than describe as novelists and dramatists may—nay, as they must—describe the passions and fashions of life.

"Witnesses will be called who will prove the publication of the libel, and my learned friend has the task of satisfying you that the excuses made in the plea of justification are true."

Sidney Wright was summoned to the witness box. He was, he told Sir Edward, the hall porter at the Albemarle Club. On the eighteenth of February Lord Queensberry had written some words on a card and told him to give it to Mr. Oscar Wilde. "I looked at the writing on the card," Mr. Wright admitted, "but didn't understand it." He put the card in an envelope, noted the date on the back, and ten days later handed the envelope to Mr. Wilde.

"Thank you, Mr. Wright," Sir Edward said, and glanced toward Carson.

There was no cross-examination.

"Mr. Oscar Wilde."

Oscar rose and walked to the witness box. He smiled his amusement and enjoyment of the unique occasion. The glass of water was put in front of him. "Thank you," he said. The judge's pleasant little face inspected him with interest. Oscar made him a small bow.

"Mr. Wilde," Sir Edward began, "pray tell the jury something about yourself."

"With great pleasure, sir. I am the prosecutor in this case. I am thirty-nine years of age."

Carson made a note.

"Since 1878, when I came down from Oxford, I have devoted myself to art and literature. In 1881 I published a book of poems and afterward lectured in England and America. In 1884 I married Miss Lloyd. I have two sons, the elder of whom will be ten in June and the second nine in November."

"In 1891 did you make the acquaintance of Lord Alfred Douglas?"

"Yes; he was brought to my home by a friend. Since then he has visited us often, and I have often been a guest in Lady Queensberry's home. I was aware that there had been some estrangement between Lord Alfred and Lord Queensberry, and I attempted, at the Café Royal in November, 1892, to put them on good terms with each other. I did not see the defendant again until March, 1894, but in 1893 I heard that some letters that I had addressed to Lord Alfred had come into the hands of certain persons."

Sir Edward nodded. "I see. Did one of these persons say that he had found letters of yours?"

"Yes, a man named Wood. He saw me at the rooms of Mr. Alfred Taylor and told me he had found some letters in a suit of clothes that Lord Alfred had been good enough to give him."

"Please tell us what happened, Mr. Wilde."

"When Wood entered Mr. Taylor's rooms he said, 'I suppose you will think very badly of me.' I replied, 'I hear that you have letters of mine to Lord Alfred Douglas, which you certainly ought to have given back.' He handed me three or four letters and said they had been stolen from him a day or two ago and he had had to employ a detective to get them back. I read the letters and said that I didn't think them of any importance. Wood said, 'I am afraid of staying in London, as this man and other men are threatening me. I want money to go to America.' I asked him what better openings as a clerk he could find in America, and he replied that he was anxious to get out of London in order to escape from the man who had taken the letters from him. He made a very strong appeal to me. I paid him fifteen pounds. The letters remained in my hand all the time."

"Did some man shortly afterward come with another letter?"

"Yes; a man called and told me that the letter was not in his possession. His name was Allen. I said, 'I suppose you have come about my beautiful letter to Lord Alfred Douglas.' He said, 'A very curious construction can be put on that letter.' I said in reply, 'Art is rarely intelligible to the criminal classes.' He said, 'A man offered me sixty pounds for it.' I said, 'If you take my advice you will go to that man and sell my letter to him for sixty pounds. I myself have never received so large a sum for any prose work of that length, but I am glad to find that there is someone in England who considers a letter of mine worth sixty pounds.' He was somewhat taken aback, by my manner perhaps, and said, 'The man is out of town.' I replied, 'He is sure to come back,' and advised him to get the sixty pounds. He then changed his manner a little, saying he hadn't a single penny and that he had on many occasions been trying to find me. I said that I couldn't guarantee his cab expenses but that I would gladly give him a half sovereign. He took the half sovereign and went away."

"Was anything said about a sonnet?" Sir Edward asked.

"Yes. I said, 'The letter, which is a prose poem, will shortly be published in sonnet form in a delightful magazine, and I will send you a copy of it.'"

"Did Allen then go away?"

"Yes, and in about five minutes Cliburn came to the house. I said, 'I cannot bother anymore about this matter.' He produced the letter, saying, 'Allen has asked me to give it to you.' I did not take it immediately but asked, 'Why does Allen give it back?' He said, 'Well, he says that you were kind to him and that there is no use trying to rent you, as you only laugh at us.' I took the letter and said, 'I will accept it, and you can thank Allen for me for all the anxiety he has shown about it.' Then I looked at the letter and saw that it was extremely soiled. I said to him, 'I think it is quite unpardonable that better care was not taken of this original manuscript of mine.'"

The judge smiled; the jurors laughed, and the laughter spread happily through the courtroom.

"Yes, Mr. Wilde?" Sir Edward prompted, smiling himself.

"Oh, he said he was very sorry, but the letter had been in so many hands. I gave him a half sovereign for his trouble and said, 'I am afraid you are leading a wonderfully wicked life.' He said, 'There is good and bad in every one of us.' I told him he was a born philosopher, and he then left."

People chuckled here and there. Queensberry looked furious. Carson was definitely glum. What else could one expect of a Puritan whose forefathers with fire and sword had ravaged laughing Ireland?

"To pass to 1894," Sir Edward resumed; "it was March of that year, I think you said, that you saw Lord Queensberry again?"

"Yes, again at the Café Royal."

"Shortly afterwards you became aware that he was making suggestions with regard to your character and behavior?"

"Yes, those suggestions were not contained in letters to me. At the end of June, 1894, there was an interview between Lord Queensberry and myself at my house. He called upon me, not by appointment, about four o'clock in the afternoon, accompanied by a gentleman with whom I was not acquainted but who may have been on not unfamiliar terms, to judge by his appearance, with what I believe is known as the prize ring.

"The interview took place in my library. Lord Queensberry was standing by the window, I was by the fireplace. He said to me, 'Sit down.' I said to him, 'I do not allow anyone to talk like that to me in my house or anywhere else. I suppose you have come to apologize for the statement you made about my wife and myself in letters you wrote to your son. I should have the right any day I choose to prosecute you for writing such a letter.' He said, 'The letter was privileged, as it was written to my son.' I said, 'How dare you say such things about your son and me?' He said, 'You were both kicked out of the Savoy Hotel at a moment's notice for your disgusting behavior.' I said, 'That is a lie.' He said, 'You have taken furnished rooms for him in Piccadilly.' I said, 'Somebody has been telling you an absurd set of lies about your son and me. I have not done anything of the kind.' He said, 'I hear you were thoroughly well blackmailed for a disgusting letter you wrote to my son.' I said, 'The letter was a beautiful letter, and I never write except for publication.' Then I asked, 'Lord Queensberry, do you seriously accuse your son and me of improper conduct?' He said, 'I do not say that you are it, but you look it.' "

Among the spectators, someone gave a great burst of laughter. Oscar tried to single out the cause of this obscene merriment but could not. Mr. Justice Collins said sharply that if he heard the slightest disturbance again he would have the court cleared. Oscar gave him a sparkling glance.

"Will you continue, please, Mr. Wilde?" Sir Edward requested. "You were saying—"

"Lord Queensberry said, 'But you look it, and you pose as it, which is just as bad. If I catch you and my son together again in any public restaurant, I will thrash you.' And I said, 'I do not know what the Queensberry rules are, but the Oscar Wilde rule is to shoot at sight.' I then told him to leave my house. He said he would not do so. I told him that I would have him put out by the police. He said, 'It is a disgusting scandal.' I said, 'If it be so, you are the author of the scandal, and no one else.' I then went into the hall and pointed him out to my servant. I said, 'This is the Marquess of Queensberry, the most infamous brute in London. You are never to allow him to enter my house again.' "

Oscar looked about for applause. There was none (of course this wasn't a theater, after all) but a murmur of approval rose throughout the courtroom. "It is a lie," he added, "that I was expelled from the Savoy Hotel at any time and that I took rooms in Piccadilly for Lord Queensberry's son."

Sir Edward asked, "When was it that you heard the first statement affecting your character?"

"I had seen letters from Lord Queensberry, not to his son, but to a third party—members of his own and of Lady Queensberry's family."

"It is suggested, Mr. Wilde, that you are responsible for the publication of the magazine *The Chameleon*, on the front page of which some aphorisms of yours appear. Beyond sending that one contribution to the magazine, had you anything to do with its editing or preparation or publication?"

"Nothing whatever."

"Until you saw this number of *The Chameleon*, did you know anything about the story 'The Priest and the Acolyte'?"

"Nothing at all."

"Upon seeing that story in print, did you communicate with the author and editor of the magazine?"

"He came to see me at the Café Royal to speak to me about it."

"Did you approve of the story?"

Oscar waited for a moment. Then, in a slow, grave voice, he replied, "I thought it bad and indecent and I strongly disapproved of it."

"Was this disapproval expressed to the editor?"

"Yes."

"I see. Now, Mr. Wilde, the other question relates to your book *Dorian Gray*. Was it first published in serial form?"

"It was first published in *Lippincott's Magazine*," Oscar said, "and afterwards in book form with some additional chapters. It was much reviewed."

"Your attention has been called to the statements that are made in the plea of justification referring to different persons and impugning your conduct with them?"

"Yes, sir."

"Mr. Wilde—is there any truth in any of these accusations?"

Again Oscar waited. Every eye was on him, every breath held; the judge himself was leaning forward, breathless.

"There is no truth whatever in any of them."

A great wave of sympathetic sighs swept over the room.

"Thank you, Mr. Wilde," Sir Edward said, and sat down.

Oscar touched the scented handkerchief to his nose and sipped from his glass. He awaited with serene confidence Ned Carson's cross-examination.

Carson rose; long, lean Carson, Rawbones Carson, of the dour eye, the black hair, the thin lips, and the sickle chin. The distinguished advocate, Carson; the Ulsterman, the "Castle blood-hound"—a favorite of the Queen's men who governed Ireland; he would be second-best when matched against Oscar Wilde.

His voice was scraped raw; it seemed to quiver at the edges.

"You stated that your age was thirty-nine. I think you are over forty. You were born on the sixteenth of October, 1854."

"I have no wish to *pose* as being young," Oscar said with a smile. "I am thirty-nine or forty."

"But being born in 1854 makes you more than forty?"

Oscar bowed. "Very well, Mr. Carson. As you wish."

"What age is Lord Alfred Douglas?"

"Oh, about twenty-four, I should say."

"You have stayed with him at many places?"

"Yes, to be sure. And he with my wife and me."

"You have stayed with him at Oxford?"

"Yes."

"And Cromer and Torquay?"

"Yes."

"And in various hotels in London?"

"Yes."

"You never took rooms for him?"

Oscar shook his head.

"Well, Mr. Wilde?"

"I thought I indicated my answer, Mr. Carson. No, I never took rooms for Lord Alfred Douglas."

"Did you ever take rooms for yourself in addition to your house in Tite Street?"

"Yes, at Ten St. James's Place. I kept them from the month of October, 1893, to the end of March, 1894."

Carson's stern glance fell; he said "Ummm" and paused. He was *very* thin; did he take pleasure in anything?

"You read 'The Priest and the Acolyte,' Mr. Wilde?"

"Yes, Mr. Carson."

"You have no doubt whatever that it is an improper story?"

"From the literary point of view it is highly improper. I must explain, Mr. Carson, that for a man of literature to judge it otherwise is impossible—by literature, I mean of course treatment, selection of subject, and the like. I thought the treatment rotten and the subject rotten."

"Aren't you of the opinion that there is no such thing as an immoral book?"

"I am," Oscar said firmly.

"Then may I take it that you think 'The Priest and the Acolyte' is not immoral?"

"It is worse." Carson's raven-wing brows came up. "It is badly written."

Little "ah" 's of appreciation sprang up here and there in the courtroom, and one lovely laugh.

Carson's voice became savage. "Is not 'The Priest and the Acolyte' the story of a priest of the Church of England who falls in love with the acolyte who serves him at the altar? Is not this boy discovered one night in the priest's room in circumstances that damn them both? Does not the priest then poison the boy rather than lose him, and then poison himself?"

"You show an admirable grasp of the story, Mr. Carson, so far as I can tell. I read it myself," Oscar added, "only once, last November. Nothing will induce me to read it again."

Carson looked stung. "Do you think the story blasphemous?"

"I think it violates every artistic canon of beauty."

"That is not an answer."

"It is the only one I can give, Mr. Carson."

"I shall ask you again. Did you and do you think the story blasphemous?"

"The story filled me with disgust."

"Answer the question, sir. Did you or did you not consider the story blasphemous?"

"I thought it disgusting," Oscar said calmly.

"Do you know that when the priest in the story administers poison to the boy he uses the words of the sacrament of the Church of England?"

"That I entirely forgot."

"Do you consider *that* blasphemous?"

"I think it is horrible. 'Blasphemous' is not a word of mine, Mr. Carson."

Carson reached to an associate for a paper; he said, "I shall read you the passage in question: 'Just before the consecration the priest took a tiny phial from the pocket of his cassock, blessed it, and poured the contents into the chalice. When the time came for him to receive from the chalice, he raised it to his lips, but did not taste of it. He administered the sacred wafer to the child, and then he took his hand; he turned towards him; but when he saw the light in the beautiful face he turned again to the crucifix with a low moan. For one instant his courage failed him; then he turned to the little fellow again, and held the chalice to his lips: "The blood of our Lord Jesus Christ, which was shed for you, preserve thy soul and body unto everlasting life." ' Do you approve of those words, Mr. Wilde?"

"Disgusting," Oscar said. "Absolute twaddle."

Carson sneezed furiously. Oscar maintained his own serenity of expression, but with some difficulty.

Carson gave a trumpet blast into his handkerchief and said, "I think you will admit that anyone who would approve of such a story would pose as guilty of improper practices?"

"I do *not* think so in the person of another contributor to the magazine. It would show," Oscar pointed out, "very bad literary taste. I strongly objected to the whole story. I took no steps to express disapproval of *The Chameleon* because I think it would have been beneath my dignity as a man of letters to associate myself with an Oxford undergraduate's production. I am aware that the magazine may have been circulated among the undergraduates of Oxford, but I do not believe that any book or work of art ever had any effect whatever on morality."

Carson said quickly, "Then am I right in saying that you do not consider the effect in creating morality or immorality?"

"Certainly, I do not."

"So far as your works are concerned, you pose as not being concerned about morality or immorality?"

"I don't know whether you use the word pose in any particular sense, Mr. Carson."

"Isn't it a favorite word of your own?"

Oscar took him up sharply. "Is it? I have no pose in this matter. In writing a play or a book, I am concerned entirely with literature, that is, with art. I aim not at doing good or evil, but in trying to make a thing that will have some quality of beauty."

"Listen, sir." Carson accepted another paper. "Here is one of the 'Phrases and Philosophies for the Use of the Young' that you contributed to this precious magazine: 'Wickedness is a myth invented by good people to account for the curious attractiveness of others.' You think that true?"

"Oh, dear me." Oscar laughed. "I rarely think that anything I write is true."

"Did you say rarely, sir?"

"I said *rarely*. I might have said never. I mean, not true in the actual sense of the word."

"Ummm." Carson inspected his paper and said, "Here is another. 'Religions die when they are proved to be true.' Is that true, Mr. Wilde?"

"Why, yes," Oscar said, "I hold that it is. It is a suggestion toward a philosophy of the absorption of religions by science—but it is too big a question to go into now."

"Do you think it was a safe axiom to put forward for the philosophy of the young?"

Oscar smiled. "Most stimulating."

"Another: 'If one tells the truth, one is sure, sooner or later, to be found out.' Well?"

"That is a pleasing paradox, but I don't set very high store on it as an axiom."

"Is it good for the young, Mr. Wilde?"

"Anything is good, Mr. Carson, that stimulates thought in whatever age."

"Whether moral or immoral?"

"There is no such thing as morality or immorality in thought. There *is* immoral emotion."

Carson scanned the paper again. " 'Pleasure is the only thing one should live for'; is that true?"

"I think that the realization of oneself is the prime aim of life, and to realize oneself through pleasure is finer than to do so through pain. On that point, Mr. Carson, I am entirely on the side of the ancients—the Greeks. It is a pagan idea."

" 'A truth ceases to be true when more than one person believes in it'?"

"Perfectly," Oscar said. He glanced at the judge; the dear chap was smiling. "Excuse me, Mr. Carson, where was I? Ah, yes. 'A truth ceases to be true when more than one person believes in it'— that would be my metaphysical definition of truth, something so personal that the same truth could never be appreciated by two minds."

" 'The condition of perfection is idleness: the aim of perfection is youth'?"

"Let us say half of it is true—the life of contemplation is the highest life, and so recognized by the philosopher."

Carson waited for a moment or so, cleared his throat, and looked at the jury. Doubtless he had up his sleeve the choicest, that is to say the most damning, quotation of the lot, in his opinion.

After another meaningful glance at the jurors, Carson read slowly, " 'There is something tragic about the enormous number of young men there are in England at the present moment who start life with perfect profiles and end by adopting some useful profession.' What have you to say about that, Mr. Wilde?"

"Oh, I should think that the young have enough sense of humor——"

"You think it is humorous?"

"I think it is an amusing paradox, an amusing play on words."

"What would anybody say would be the effect of 'Phrases and Philosophies' taken in connection with such a story as 'The Priest and the Acolyte'?"

"Ah, Mr. Carson, there you have a point," Oscar said graciously. "It was the ideas that might be formed that made me object so strongly to the story. I saw at once that maxims that were perfectly nonsensical, paradoxical, or anything you like, might be read in conjunction with it."

Carson, not pleased, exchanged "Phrases and Philosophies for the Use of the Young" for a book. "This is in your introduction to *Dorian Gray*, Mr. Wilde," he said: " 'There is no such thing as a moral or an immoral book. Books are well written or badly written.' That expresses your view?"

"My view on art, yes."

"Then I take it that no matter how immoral a book may be, if it is well written it is, in your opinion, a good book?"

"Yes—if it were well written so as to produce a sense of beauty, which is the highest sense of which a human being can be capable. If it were badly written, it would produce a sense of disgust."

"Then a well-written book putting forward perverted moral views may be a good book?"

Oscar shook his head. "No work of art ever *puts forward* views, Mr. Carson. Views belong to people who are not artists."

"Then I will suggest *Dorian Gray* as being open to the interpretation of being such a novel?"

"That could only be to brutes and illiterates. The views of Philistines on art, Mr. Carson, are incalculably stupid."

Carson was not put off. "An illiterate person reading *Dorian Gray* might consider it such a novel?"

"The views of illiterates on art are unaccountable; I am concerned only with my view of art. I don't care twopence what other people think of it."

"The majority of persons would come under your definition of Philistines and illiterates, Mr. Wilde?"

"I have found wonderful exceptions, Mr. Carson."

"Do you think the majority of people live up to the position you are giving us?"

"I am afraid they are not cultivated enough."

"They are not cultivated enough to draw the distinction between a good book and a bad one?"

"Certainly not."

"Don't you think, sir, that the affection and love of the artist of *Dorian Gray* might lead an ordinary individual to believe that it might have a certain—let us say a certain tendency?"

"I have no knowledge of the views of ordinary individuals," Oscar said with a winning smile.

"But you did not prevent the ordinary individual from buying your book?"

"Well, Mr. Carson, I've never discouraged him." Oscar gave a laugh; it was echoed in the courtroom. The judge seemed to be chuckling.

Carson found another place in the book. "I am going to read some passages to you, Mr. Wilde." Oscar courteously inclined his head. The raw voice began:

" 'I turned halfway round and saw Dorian Gray for the first time. When our eyes met I felt that I was growing pale. A curious instinct of terror came over me. I knew that I had come face to face with someone whose mere personality was so fascinating that, if I allowed it to do so, it would absorb my whole nature. . . . Something seemed to tell me that I was on the verge of a terrible crisis in my life. I had a strange feeling that Fate had in store for me exquisite joys and exquisite sorrows. I knew that if I spoke to Dorian I would become absolutely devoted to him. . . . He is all my art to me now. I couldn't be happy if I didn't see him every day; of course sometimes it is only for a few minutes. But a few minutes with somebody one worships mean a great deal. It is not merely that I paint from him, draw from him, model from him. Of course I have done all that. He has stood as Paris in dainty armor, and as Adonis with huntsman's cloak and polished boar-spear. Crowned with heavy lotus blossoms he has sat on the prow of Adrian's barge, looking into the green, turbid Nile. He has leaned over the still pool of some Greek woodland and seen in the water's silent silver the wonder of his own beauty. But he is much more to me than that. . . . Unconsciously he defines for me the lines of a fresh school, a school that is to have in itself all the passion of the romantic spirit, all the perfection of the spirit that is Greek. If you only knew what Dorian Gray is to me!' "

The reading ended in a nasty cough; poor Carson's throat. He drank a glass of water. "Now I ask you, Mr. Wilde, do you consider that the description of the feeling of one man toward a youth just grown up was a proper or an improper feeling?"

Oscar said seriously, "I think it is the most perfect description of what an artist would feel on meeting a beautiful personality that was in some way necessary to his art and life."

"You think that is a feeling a young man should have toward another?"

"Yes, as an artist."

Again Carson consulted the book. "Here is another passage; Basil Hallward is speaking to Dorian: 'It is quite true that I have worshiped you with far more romance of feeling than a man usually gives to a friend. Somehow, I have never loved a woman. I suppose I never had time. Perhaps, as Harry says, a really *grande passion* is the privilege of those who have nothing to do, and that is the use of the idle classes in a country. Well, from the moment I met you, your personality had the most extraordinary influence over me. I quite admit that I adored you madly, extravagantly, absurdly. I was jealous of everyone to whom you spoke. I wanted to have you all to myself. I was only happy when I was with you. . . . One day I determined to paint a wonderful portrait of you. It was to have been my masterpiece. It is my masterpiece. But, as I worked at it, every flake and film of color seemed to me to reveal my secret. I grew afraid that the world would know of my idolatry.'" Carson paused and looked up. "Do you mean to say, Mr. Wilde, that that passage describes the natural feeling of one man toward another?"

"It would be the influence produced by a beautiful personality," Oscar replied.

"A beautiful person?"

"I said a 'beautiful personality.' You can describe it as you like, Mr. Carson. Dorian Gray's was a most remarkable personality."

"May I take it that you, as an artist, have never known the feeling described here?"

"I have never allowed any personality to dominate my art."

"Then you have never known the feeling you described?"

"No," Oscar said a little impatiently. Then he added gently, "It is a work of fiction, you see."

Still Carson kept on. "So far as you are concerned you have no experience as to its being a natural feeling?"

"I think it is perfectly natural for any artist to admire intensely and love a young man. It is an incident in the life of almost every artist."

"But let us go over it phrase by phrase."

Oscar groaned inwardly.

"First, this phrase: 'I quite admit that I adored you madly.' What do you say to that, Mr. Wilde? Have you ever adored a young man madly?"

"No, not madly; I prefer love—it is a higher form."

"Never mind about that. Let us keep down to the level we are at now."

"I have never given adoration to anybody except myself," Oscar said serenely.

That brought a wonderful laugh. Carson was nettled. "I suppose you think that a very smart thing?" he snapped.

"Not at all."

"Then you have never had that feeling?"

"No, Mr. Carson, I haven't. The whole idea was borrowed from Shakespeare, I regret to say—yes, from Shakespeare's sonnets."

"I believe you have written an article to show that Shakespeare's sonnets were suggestive of unnatural vice?"

"On the contrary, I have written an article to show that they are not. I objected to such a perversion being put upon Shakespeare."

"Another phrase, Mr. Wilde: 'I have adored you extravagantly.' "

Oscar said with great innocence, "Do you mean financially?"

"Oh, yes, financially. Do you think we are talking about finance?"

"I don't know what you are talking about, Mr. Carson."

"Don't you? Well, I hope I shall make myself very plain before I have done. 'I was jealous of everyone to whom you spoke.' Have you ever been jealous of a young man?"

"Never in my life."

" 'I wanted to have you all to myself.' Did you ever have that feeling?"

"No," Oscar assured him sincerely. "I should consider it an intense nuisance."

" 'I grew afraid that the world would know of my idolatry.' Why should he grow afraid that the world should know of it?"

"Because, Mr. Carson, there are people in the world who cannot understand the intense devotion, affection, and admiration that an artist can feel for a wonderful and beautiful personality. These are the conditions under which we live. I regret them." It appeared that someone had clapped. The judge shook his head mildly.

"These unfortunate people," Carson said, his voice quivering, "these most unfortunate people, who have not the high understanding that *you* have, might put it down to something wrong?"

"Undoubtedly; to any point they chose. I am not concerned with the ignorance of others."

Carson returned to the book. "Pray give your attention to this passage; again, Basil Hallward is talking with Dorian: 'I think it right that you should know that the most dreadful things are being said about you in London—things that I could hardly repeat to you.' Dorian replies, 'I don't wish to know anything about them. I love scandals about other people, but scandals about myself don't interest me. They have not got the charm of novelty.' Hallward continues, 'They must interest you, Dorian. Every gentleman is interested in his good name. You don't want people to talk of you as something vile and degraded. Of course you have your position and your wealth, and all that kind of thing. But position and wealth are not everything. Mind you, I don't believe these rumors at all. At least, I can't believe them when I see you. Sin is a thing that writes itself across a man's face. It cannot be concealed. People talk of secret vices. There are no such things as secret vices. If a wretched man has a vice, it shows itself in the lines of his mouth, the droop of his eyelids, the molding of his hands even. But you, Dorian, with your pure, bright, innocent face and your marvelous untroubled youth—I can't believe anything against you. And yet I see you very seldom, and you never come down to my studio now, and when I am away from you and hear all these hideous things that people are whispering about you, I don't know what to say. Why is your friendship so fateful to young men? There was that wretched boy in the guards who committed suicide. You were his great friend. There was Sir Henry Ashton, who had to leave England with a tarnished name. You and he were inseparable. What about Adrian Singleton and his dreadful end? What about Lord Kent's only son, and his career? Dorian, Dorian, your reputation is infamous.' "

248

Carson closed the book. "Does not this passage suggest a charge of unnatural vice, Mr. Wilde?"

"It describes Dorian Gray as a man of very corrupt influence, though there is no statement as to the nature of the influence. But as a matter of fact," Oscar added with a confidential air, "I don't think that one person influences another, nor do I think there is any bad influence in the world."

Carson raised his handsome brows. "A man never corrupts a youth?"

"I think not."

"Nothing could corrupt him?"

"If you are talking of separate ages, Mr. Carson."

"No, sir, I am talking common sense."

"I don't think one person influences another."

"You don't think that flattering a young man, making love to him, in fact, would be likely to corrupt him?"

Oscar shook his head. "No."

"Ummm." Carson paused and took up the letter to Bosie. "Where was Lord Alfred Douglas staying, Mr. Wilde, when you wrote that letter to him?"

"At the Savoy. I was at Babbacombe, near Torquay."

"It was a letter in answer to something he had sent you?"

"Yes, a poem."

"Why should a man of your age address a boy nearly twenty years younger as 'My own boy'?"

"I was fond of him. I have always been fond of him."

"Do you adore him?"

"No, but I have always liked him. I think it is a beautiful letter. It is a poem. I wasn't writing an ordinary letter, you see, Mr. Carson. You might as well cross-examine me as to whether *King Lear* or a sonnet of Shakespeare was proper."

"Apart from art, Mr. Wilde?"

"I cannot answer apart from art."

"Suppose a man who was not an artist had written this letter, would you say it was a proper letter?"

"A man who was not an artist could not have written that letter."

"Why?"

"Because nobody but an artist could write it. He certainly could not write the language unless he were a man of letters."

"Really. I can suggest, for the sake of your reputation, that there is nothing very wonderful in this 'red rose-leaf lips' of yours?"

"A great deal depends," Oscar said with a gentle smile, "on the way it is read."

Everyone was laughing. Ned *was* upset. He said scornfully, " 'Your slim gilt soul walks between passion and poetry.' Is that a beautiful phrase?"

"Not as you read it, Mr. Carson. You read it very badly."

"I do not profess to be an artist, and when I hear you give evidence, I am glad I am not."

Sir Edward said in an august voice, "I don't think my friend should talk like that"; and then to Oscar, "Pray do not criticize my friend's reading again."

Oscar bowed his head. "I beg his pardon," he murmured.

"Was that the ordinary way in which you carried on your correspondence?" Carson asked.

"No, but I have often written to Lord Alfred Douglas, though I never wrote to another young man in the same way."

"Have you often written letters in the same style as this?"

In a kindly way, Oscar explained, "I don't repeat myself in style."

"Oh, you don't. Here," Carson said, reaching for a second piece of paper, "is another letter that I believe you also wrote to Lord Alfred Douglas. Will you read it?"

Another letter? What other letter could they have that they'd consider damaging enough to bring up here? Is this what Ned had been leading up to? Had it all been a trap, to spring his second letter, whatever it was, on Oscar?

"Will you read it, Mr. Wilde?" Carson said again.

"No, I decline. I don't see why I should."

"Then I will." And in a voice that became wonderfully soft, a lover's voice almost, Carson read the letter Oscar had written at the Savoy, the letter he thought of as the "red-and-yellow-wine letter" —the letter that had come as a cry from his heart, appealing to Bosie never to make such horrible, killing scenes again, never to distort his curved lips with hideous words.

Utter silence pervaded the courtroom. Carson wagged the letter almost playfully. He asked, "Is *that* an ordinary letter, Mr. Wilde?"

Above all, Oscar must show no trace of the shock Ned had given him. He would be indignant, even arrogant.

"Everything I write is extraordinary, Mr. Carson. I do not *pose* as being ordinary, great heavens. Ask me any questions you like about it."

"Is it the kind of letter a man writes to another?"

"It was a tender expression of my great admiration for Lord Alfred Douglas. It was not, like the other, a prose poem."

"Were you living at the Savoy?"

"Yes, I was there for about a month, and had also my house in Tite Street. Lord Alfred had been staying with me at the Savoy immediately before I wrote that letter."

Here there came a welcome pause. The judge adjourned court for lunch.

5

CHARLES AND TRAVERS HUMPHREYS WERE NOT HAPPY ABOUT the letter, and in Sir Edward's eyes Oscar saw a distinctly reproachful look. He could not say: "Gentlemen, you mustn't blame me, it it Lord Alfred's fault." What would that avail in any event? He had written the letter. At least, thank God, Queensberry's detectives hadn't found the letter from Bosie to which it was an answer!

Oscar said, "I am profoundly sorry; I had quite forgotten having written the letter Carson so unexpectedly produced; but after all, is it really of much importance, considering how magnificently everything else has gone so far?"

"Very true," Charles Humphreys admitted, "things have gone well; I must compliment you, Mr. Wilde, on your behavior, your aplomb in the witness box—you carried everyone with you, judge, jury, everyone; Carson will soundly regret trying to match swords in matters literary; let us only hope he will continue."

Sir Edward nodded and no longer seemed reproachful. "But I trust," he said, "that they have no more surprises to spring on us."

Carson's first question of the afternoon was not concerned with literary matters. "This young man Alfred Wood, Mr. Wilde—how long had you known him?"

Oscar considered. "I think I met him at the end of January, 1893. I met him at the Café Royal, where he was sent to find me by Lord Alfred Douglas, who wrote from Salisbury. Lord Alfred asked me to do what I could for him."

"Who was Wood?"

"So far as I could make out, he had no occupation but was looking for a situation. I dare say he was about twenty-three years of age."

"Do I understand that the first time you met him you took him to supper?"

"Yes, at the Florence restaurant—because I had been asked to be kind to him. Otherwise," Oscar said with a smile, "it was rather a bore."

"Was anybody else there?"

"No, no one else."

"Had you a private room at the Florence?"

"Yes. I went there so that I could get a check cashed, because the next day was Sunday."

"How much money did you give Wood then?"

"Oh, two pounds or so."

"Why?" Carson barked.

"Because Lord Alfred had asked me to be kind to him," Oscar replied gently. "I don't care about different social positions."

"I suggest, sir, that you first had immoral relations with him and them gave him money?"

Oscar's smile disappeared. "That is monstrously untrue."

"Ummm. Then you met Wood again?"

"Yes. I heard from Mr. Alfred Taylor that Wood wished to see me, and I met him in Mr. Taylor's rooms."

"Did you consider that he had come to levy blackmail?"

"I did," Oscar said, "and I determined to face it."

"And the way you faced it was by giving him fifteen pounds to go to America?"

"That is an inaccurate description. I saw that the letters were of no value and I gave him the money after he had told me the pitiful tale about himself—this was foolish, perhaps, but it was out of pure kindness."

"I suggest that you gave him thirty pounds, not fifteen." Carson's voice was positively painful to hear. He took some water, then continued, "Did you give him five pounds more the next day?"

"Yes," Oscar said. "He told me that after paying his passage to America he would be left almost penniless. I gave him five pounds."

"Had you a farewell lunch at the Florence?"

"Yes."

"It was after lunch that you gave him five pounds?"

"Yes."

"After he went to America did he ask you for money?"

"No."

"Did he call Taylor by his Christian name?"

"Yes, I believe so."

"And did Wood call you 'Oscar'?"

"Yes."

"What did you call *him*?"

"His name," Oscar pointed out, "is Alfred."

"Didn't you call him 'Alf'?"

Oscar made a little gesture of distaste. "No, I never use abbreviations."

"Did you not think it a curious thing," the raw voice asked, "that a man with whom you were on such intimate terms should try to blackmail you?"

"I thought it infamous," Oscar agreed, "but Wood convinced me that such had not been his intention, though it was the intention of other people. He assured me that he had recovered all the letters."

"And then this man Allen, I think you said his name was, came with a letter, possession of which you knew he had secured improperly?"

Oscar nodded. "Yes."

"What was Allen?"

"I am told he was a blackmailer."

"*Was* he a blackmailer?"

"I never heard of him except as one."

"And so then you began to explain to this blackmailer what a loss your beautiful manuscript was?"

"I described it as a beautiful work of art."

"May I ask why you gave this man, who you knew was a notorious blackmailer, ten shillings?"

"I gave it out of contempt."

"I see. The way you show your contempt, Mr. Wilde, is by paying ten shillings?"

"Yes, very often," Oscar said agreeably.

"I suppose he was pleased with your contempt?"

"Yes, he was apparently pleased at my kindness."

"And a few minutes afterwards Cliburn came to your door?"

"Yes. Allen had mentioned my kindness to him."

"And you began discussing with him what a beautiful manuscript and work of art the letter was?"

"Yes."

"Did you tell this blackmailer that the letter was to be published as a sonnet?"

"I told Allen, not Cliburn. I told him it was to be published in an Oxford magazine, *The Spirit Lamp*. That," Oscar explained, "was to show my indifference."

"Ah. But you had got back the letter?"

"Yes."

"Did you say to him, 'I'm afraid you are leading a wonderfully wicked life'?"

"Yes, I did. I meant generally in being mixed up in this attempt to blackmail me."

Carson waited for a bit. Slowly he asked, "Did you ever have any of your beautiful letters, except the one that was found out, turned into a sonnet?"

He had hit on something there. Oscar smiled to show that he was thinking nothing of the sort. "I require to read a great deal of modern poetry before I can say, Mr. Carson."

"Come, sir, answer the question."

"Well," Oscar admitted, "at the present moment I can't recollect another."

"Did you ever ask Lord Alfred Douglas to preserve that letter?"

"No."

"And therefore you never thought of turning it into a sonnet till it was discovered, did you?"

"But I never did turn it into a sonnet," Oscar said quickly. "When I saw it, I at once thought it would turn into a sonnet."

Carson's face became eloquent with disbelief; he glanced at the jury with a shrug. Oscar inspected the ceiling. There was another pause. Ned must be preparing to strike off in another direction.

"Were you staying at the Albemarle Hotel, Mr. Wilde, about the twenty-sixth of February, 1892?"

"Yes."

"At that time were Messrs. Elkin Mathews and John Lane, of Vigo Street, your publishers?"

"Yes."

"Did you," Carson asked, "become fond of their office boy?"

"I really do not think," Oscar said sternly, "that that is the proper form for the question to be addressed to me in. I deny that that was the position held by Mr. Edward Shelley, to whom you are referring. I object to your description."

Carson seemed pleased. "What age was Mr. Shelley?"

"I should think about twenty. I first met him in October when arranging for the publication of my books. I asked him to dine with me at the Albemarle Hotel."

"Was that for the purpose of having an intellectual treat?"

Ned's sarcasm was indeed heavy. "Well, for him," Oscar said blandly.

"On that occasion did you have a room leading into a bedroom?"

"Yes."

"Did you give him whiskies and sodas?"

"I suppose he had whatever he wanted. I don't remember, really."

"Do you remember that he stayed all night?"

"He did not."

"And that you embraced him and kissed him?"

"I did not."

"And committed acts of the grossest indecency with him?"

"I absolutely and with the utmost contempt deny it."

Carson said, "Ummm."

Another pause. Oscar permitted himself a survey of judge and jury. They seemed still to be with him; he was sure of it. Well, Ned, what next? Absurd little Alphonse Conway, perhaps?

This proved to be an extraordinarily accurate guess. "Did you become intimate with a young lad named Alphonse Conway at Worthing, Mr. Wilde?"

"He became a friend, yes."

"He sold newspapers at the kiosk on the pier?"

"No, I didn't know that. It is the first I have heard of his connection with literature."

Carson was not amused. "What was Conway?"

"Oh, he led a happy, idle life."

"He was a loafer, in fact?"

"He seemed to me to be just enjoying life, Mr. Carson." Oscar almost added, "It is possible, you know."

"How old was he?"

"A youth of about eighteen."

"How did you make his acquaintance?"

"When Lord Alfred Douglas and I were at Worthing, we were accustomed to go out in a boat. One day when the fishermen were launching a boat on the high beach, Conway with another lad assisted in getting the craft down to the water. I said to Lord Alfred, 'Shall we ask them to come out for a sail?' He assented, and we took them. After that Alphonse and I became great friends, and

I asked him to lunch with me. He also dined at my house and lunched with me at the Marine Hotel."

"Was his conversation literary?" Carson inquired.

"On the contrary, quite simple and easily understood." This brought several chuckles. "He had been to school, you see, where naturally he had not learned much." The room filled with lovely laughter; the judge smiled.

Carson cut in, "He was a simple country lad?"

"He was a nice, pleasant creature. His mother kept a lodging house, and his desire was to go to sea."

"Did you give him anything?"

"Oh, yes, but not money."

"Did you give him sums amounting to five pounds?"

"Never. I gave him a cigarette case in which I placed a paper inscribed 'Alphonse from his friend Oscar Wilde'; I called him Alphonse, but he did not call me Oscar. I also gave him my photograph, on which I wrote 'Oscar Wilde to Alphonse.' And I gave him a book called *The Wreck of the Grosvenor*."

Carson turned; one by one, a book, a cigarette case, a photograph, and a walking stick with a silver top were handed up to him. He waved them, more to the jury than to Oscar. "Are these the presents, Mr. Wilde?"

Faithless Alphonse had given his gifts to the enemy. "They appear to be," Oscar admitted. "I forgot the walking stick. Alphonse was very proud of it, I believe. It must be a very great inconvenience to him not to have it. I do trust it is to go back to him, Mr. Carson, when its inscrutable purposes have been served in this courtroom?"

The jury had been looking a little glum; this seemed to cheer them up. "Its purposes will be served, never fear," Carson snapped. "You were fond of this boy?"

"Naturally. He had been my companion for six weeks."

"Did you take him to Brighton?"

"Yes."

"And provided him with a suit of blue serge?"

"Yes."

"And a straw hat with a band of red and blue."

"That," Oscar said with a small deprecatory wave of his hands, "was his unfortunate selection."

257

Bosie laughed loudly. Apparently no others were entertained. The judge's air seemed to have grown less cordial.

Carson's black brows drew together. "You dressed this newsboy up to take him to Brighton, did you?"

"No," Oscar corrected him; "it was that I did not want Alphonse to be ashamed of his shabby clothes. He told me his father had been an electrical engineer and had died young."

"You provided him with new clothes in order that he might look more like an equal?"

"Oh, no. He could not look like that. No, I promised him that before I left I would take him somewhere, to some place to which he wished to go, as a reward for his being a pleasant companion to myself and my children. He chose Portsmouth, but I told him it was too far. So we went to Brighton. We dined at a restaurant and stayed the night at the Albion Hotel, where I took a sitting room and two bedrooms. We returned next day."

With this, court was adjourned. Oscar rose jauntily. He had enjoyed his hours in the witness box—most stimulating. On the way out he bowed to Carson with a friendly smile, but Carson ignored him. "Dear me, Ned," Oscar silently addressed that stern figure, "your manners have become atrocious."

Oscar dined with Bosie. They dined well, by way of a preliminary celebration. Bosie was his sweetest, most loving self and at his most handsome. His skin was really like a child's, and the dainty cheeks—after all the champagne and brandy, and the excitement—flushed adorably. "My dear, you were magnificent," he repeated. "Oh, glorious. I have never loved you so much as when you threw that insulting brute's words back into his teeth and made the whole courtroom laugh at him. What a vulgar, horrible, disgusting voice he has."

"Poor Ned, he has a nasty cold. Most unfortunate for him. When at his best, as I recall, he speaks with a charming soft brogue."

"I despise him," Bosie declared.

It was impossible to chide him for his carelessness with the letter. The marquess would be defeated, and with him the black beast in Bosie would be killed.

"Oh, I cannot wait to go into the witness box," he exclaimed.

"I do hope Sir Edward will put me in it tomorrow. Not, of course, my darling," he hastened to assure Oscar, "that I wish in the least to cut short your superb, superb performance. Oh, no, never."

Oh, the lovely light in his blue eyes.

Upon entering the witness box the next morning, Oscar bowed to Carson and again was ignored. After fiddling about with his papers, Carson asked, "You told me yesterday that you were intimate with Taylor?"

"I don't call him an *intimate* friend," Oscar explained. "He was simply a friend. It was he who arranged the meeting of myself with Wood about the letters at his residence, Taylor's residence, that is, Thirteen Little College Street."

"How long have you known him?"

"Oh, since the early part of October, 1892. He used to come to my house, to my chambers at Ten St. James's Place, and to the Savoy when I was staying there. I have been to his house—oh, seven or eight times, perhaps."

"You used to go to tea parties there?" Carson asked. "Afternoon tea parties?"

"Yes."

Carson's voice was less scratchy today. "How many rooms did he occupy?"

"Let me see. A bedroom, a sitting room, a bathroom, and a kitchen."

"Did he do his own cooking?"

"I don't know. I don't think he did anything wrong," Oscar added, cautiously peering at his antagonist.

Carson obligingly entered the trap. "I haven't suggested that he did."

"Well, you know, Mr. Carson, cooking is an art."

The first laugh of the morning rippled through the room, and Ned didn't like it one bit, Oscar could see.

"Another art?"

Oscar met his dark gaze with innocent, wondering eyes.

After a silence Carson said, "Did he always open the door to you?"

"Sometimes he did, sometimes his friends did."

"Did his rooms strike you as being peculiar?"

"No—except that he displayed more taste than usual."

"There was rather elaborate furniture in the rooms, wasn't there?"

"The rooms were furnished in good taste."

"Is it true that he never admitted daylight into them?"

Oscar looked puzzled. "Really, I don't know what you mean."

"Well, was there always candle or gas light there?"

"No."

"Did you ever see the rooms lighted otherwise than by gas or candles, whether by day or by night?"

"Yes, certainly."

"Did you ever see the curtains drawn back in the sitting room?"

Oscar explained, "When I went to see Taylor, it was generally in the winter about five o'clock, tea time, but I am under the impression of having seen him earlier in the day when it was daylight."

"Are you prepared to say that you ever saw the curtains otherwise than drawn across?"

"Yes, I think so."

"It would not be true, then, to say that he always had a double lot of curtains drawn across the windows, and the room, day or night, artificially lighted?"

"I don't think so."

"Can you declare specifically that any daylight was ever admitted into the room?"

"Well, I can't say as to that." Oscar permitted himself a tiny yawn.

"Who was there when you went in the daylight?" Carson demanded.

"I think Mr. Taylor only."

"Can you recall any specific time at which you saw daylight enter that room?"

"Oh, yes," Oscar responded with a glowing smile to show how pleased he was to be able to furnish precise information. "It was a Monday in March." This sounded ridiculous, which was how he wished it to sound—I saw daylight enter that room on a Monday in March—thereby making Carson's whole line of questioning absurd. "Yes, a Monday in March. Nobody else was there."

"Were the rooms strongly perfumed?"

"I have *known* him to burn perfumes. I wouldn't say the rooms were *always* perfumed."

"Did you ever meet Wood there?"

"Only on one occasion."

"Ummm." Carson paused. "Did you ever meet a man named Sidney Mavor there?"

"Yes."

"How old was he?"

"Oh, twenty-five or twenty-six."

"Did you know that Taylor had a lady's costume, a lady's fancy dress, in his rooms?"

"No," Oscar replied.

"Did you ever see him with one on?"

"No. I was never told that he had such dresses. Mr. Taylor is a man of great taste and intelligence," Oscar continued, "and I know he was brought up at a good English school."

"Is he a literary man?"

"I have never seen any created work of his."

"Did you ever discuss literature with him?"

"Oh, he used to *listen*," Oscar said with a smile. "He was a very artistic, pleasant fellow."

"Was he an artist?"

"Not in the sense of creating anything. He was extremely intellectual and clever, and I liked him very much."

"Are you in the habit of constantly communicating with him by telegraph?"

"No, but I have telegraphed to him. He was, after all, a friend of mine."

"Did you get him to arrange dinners at which you could meet young men?"

Oscar said sharply, "No!" with such conviction that he was almost persuaded it was true. He glanced at the jury. Apparently they had swallowed this whole; and yet he sensed a less friendly feeling in that prim black-clothed mass of British respectability.

"But you have dined with young men?" Carson pressed.

"Often. Ten or a dozen times perhaps, at Kettner's, the Solferino, and the Florence."

"Always in a private room?"

"Generally, not always; but I prefer a private room."

"Did you send this telegram to Taylor: 'OBLIGED TO SEE TREE AT FIVE O'CLOCK DON'T COME TO SAVOY LET ME KNOW AT ONCE ABOUT FRED'?"

261

"I don't recollect it."

"Who was Fred?"

"Oh, a young man to whom I was introduced by a friend. His other name was Atkins."

"What was it you wanted to know?"

"I really can't remember."

"Were you very familiar with him?"

"Oh, I liked him."

"Did he call you 'Oscar'?"

"Yes, and I called him 'Fred.' I always call by their Christian names people whom I like," Oscar explained. With his most gracious smile, he added, "People I dislike I call something else."

No one laughed. Carson's voice became as raw as it had been yesterday. "Did you know that Taylor was being watched by the police?"

"No, I never heard that."

"Did you know that he was notorious for introducing young men to older men?"

"I never heard that in my life," Oscar said with a show of astonishment.

"How many has he introduced to you?"

"Do you mean of those mentioned in this case?"

"No, young men with whom you afterwards became intimate."

Oscar considered. "I should say about five."

"They were young men whom you would call by their Christian names?"

"Yes."

"Were these young men all about twenty?"

"Well yes—twenty or twenty-two. You see," Oscar explained, smiling again, "I like the society of young men."

Now there was a laugh. Oscar did not care for the sound of it. He frowned slightly.

"What was the occupation of these young men?"

"I don't know if these particular young men had occupations."

"Have you given money to them?"

"Yes. I think to all five—money or presents."

"Did *they* give *you* anything?"

Oscar was genuinely shocked. "Me? *Me?* Good heavens, no."

"Among these five," Carson asked, "did Taylor introduce you to Charley Parker?"

"Yes."

"Did you become—friendly with him?"

Oscar replied in a matter-of-fact manner. "Yes, he was one with whom I became friendly."

"Did you know that Parker was a gentlemen's servant out of employment?"

"No."

"But if he were, you would still have become friendly with him?"

"Yes. I would become friendly with any human being I liked."

"How old was he?"

"Really." Oscar laughed. "I don't keep a census."

"Never mind about a census. Tell me how old he was?"

"I should say about twenty. He was young, and that was one of his attractions."

"Was he a literary character?"

"Oh, no."

"Was he an intellectual? Was he an educated man?"

"Culture was not his strong point—he wasn't an artist. Education," Oscar added, "depends on what one's standard is."

"Where is he now?"

"I haven't the slightest idea. I have lost sight of him."

"How much money did you give Parker?"

"During the time I have known him I should think four or five pounds."

"Why? For what reason?"

"Because he was poor," Oscar said, "and because I liked him. What better reason could I have?"

"Did you ask what his previous occupation was?"

"I never inquire about people's pasts."

"Nor about their future?"

"Oh, that is problematical."

Sir Edward interposed. "There is no point," he said, "in arguing about that." Oscar smiled and bowed his head. Sir Edward did not give an answering smile. It had been a tedious stretch, to be sure; the jurymen were looking thoroughly bored, or was it perhaps distaste? Oscar must introduce a little light and fun, must really get Ned properly annoyed and nasty so that he would give Oscar

263

some decent openings; he couldn't have him going on and on with this unpleasant business of establishing that yes, Alfred Taylor did introduce him to young men, and yes, he dined with them in private rooms, and yes, he gave them money and presents.

But still Carson persisted. "Where did you first meet Parker?"

"At Kettner's."

"And Taylor introduced you?"

"Yes."

"Did you become friendly with Parker's brother?"

"Yes. They were my guests, and as such I became friendly with them."

"On the very first occasion that you saw them?"

"Yes. It was Taylor's birthday, and I asked him to dinner, telling him to bring any of his friends."

"Did you know that one Parker was a gentleman's valet and the other a groom?"

"I didn't know it, but if I had I should not have cared. I didn't care twopence what they were. I liked them." Oscar paused and then said, smiling, "I have a passion to civilize the community."

That brought some smiles.

Carson asked harshly, "What enjoyment was it to you to entertain grooms and coachmen?"

"The pleasure to me was being with those who are young, bright, happy, careless, and free. I do not like the sensible, and I do not like the old."

Someone clapped. It was Bosie.

"Taylor accepted your invitation by bringing a valet and a groom to dine with you?"

"That is your account, Mr. Carson, not mine."

"Were they persons of that class?"

"I am surprised at your description of them. They didn't seem to have the manners of that class. They seemed to me pleasant and nice. They spoke of a father at—it was Datchet, I believe—spoke of him as a person of wealth—well, not of *wealth*, but of some fortune. Charley Parker told me that he was desirous to go on the stage."

"Did you call him 'Charley,' Mr. Wilde?"

"Yes."

"Ummm. And what did you have for dinner?"

"Well really, I forget the menu." Veal, though, Oscar thought;

264

something to do with veal, wasn't there? And a rather absurd joke of his? Dear me, it was a pity those things hadn't been written down. A rather absurd joke would come in quite usefully just now.

"Was it a good dinner?"

"Oh, yes. Kettner's is not so gorgeous as some restaurants, but it was Kettner at his best."

"With the best of Kettner's wines?"

"Yes, certainly."

"All for the valet and the groom?"

"No, Mr. Carson," Oscar said reprovingly; "for my friends. For Mr. Taylor, whose birthday it was."

Carson kept harping on the words "valet" and "groom," each time emphasizing them a bit more: "You did the honors to the valet and the groom?"

"I entertained Mr. Taylor and his two guests."

"In a private room, of course?"

"Yes, certainly."

"Did you give them an intellectual treat?"

"They seemed deeply impressed."

"During the dinner did you become more intimate with Charles than the other?"

"I liked him better," Oscar admitted.

"Did Charles Parker call you 'Oscar'?"

"Yes. I like to be called 'Oscar.'"

"You had wine?"

"Of course."

"Was there plenty of champagne?"

"Well, I didn't *press* wine upon them."

"You did not stint them?"

"What gentleman would stint his guests?" Oscar replied grandly.

"What gentleman would stint the *valet* and the *groom*?"

Oscar said vigorously, "I object to that remark."

Sir Edward seconded him.

Carson pressed on, "Now, after dinner, did you say, referring to Charles Parker, in the presence of Taylor and William Parker, the brother, 'This is the boy for me'?"

"Certainly not."

"And did you ask Charles, 'Will you come with me?'"

"I did not. After dinner I went back to the Savoy Hotel, but I did not take Charles Parker with me."

"Did you not drive him to the Savoy?"

How well Oscar remembered that drive—the young boy beside him and a ridiculous story made up about the driver. Had Charley laughed at it? He must have.

"No, he did not come to the Savoy at all."

"Did he and any of these other young men who visited you at the Savoy have whiskies and sodas and iced champagne?"

"I can't say what they had."

"Do you drink champagne yourself?"

"Oh, yes," Oscar said cheerfully. "Iced champagne is a favorite drink of mine—strongly against my doctor's orders."

"Never mind your doctor's orders, sir."

"I never do." This brought a good many laughs. "Later I had rooms at St. James's Place, and when Taylor wrote to me saying Charley Parker was in town, I asked him to come to tea. He came to tea five or six times there."

"What was he doing there?" Carson demanded.

"Why, visiting me. I liked his society. Sometimes he came with Taylor, sometimes alone. I gave him a Christmas present, a silver cigarette case."

"Did improprieties take place there?"

"None whatsoever."

"When he came to tea, what was he doing all the time?"

"What was he doing?" Oscar repeated. "Why, having his tea, smoking cigarettes, and, I hope, enjoying himself."

"What was there in common between this young man and yourself? What attraction had he for you?"

Very well; Ned, with his heavy emphases, his insinuating pauses, and his raw, pushing voice—Oscar would try to get this over with once and for all and give him an explanation he would be unable to twist into something else.

"What attraction, Mr. Carson? This: I delight in the society of people much younger than myself. I like those who may be called idle and careless. I recognize no social distinctions at all of any kind, and to me youth, the mere fact of youth, is so wonderful that I would sooner talk to a young man for half an hour than—" He smiled at Carson's dark, doubting face. "—well, than be cross-examined in court."

"Do I understand," Carson said more harshly, "that even a

266

young boy you might pick up in the streets would be a pleasing companion?"

"I would talk to a street arab, with pleasure."

"You would talk to a street arab?"

"If he would talk to me. Yes, with pleasure."

"And take him to your rooms?"

Oscar shrugged. "Be it so."

"Did you write Charles Parker any beautiful letters?"

"I don't think I have ever written letters to him."

"Have you any letters of his?"

"Only one."

"Do you remember this one?" Carson was handed a piece of paper; he read, " 'Am I to have the pleasure of dining with you this evening? If so, kindly reply by messenger or wire to the above address. I trust you can, and we can spend a pleasant evening.' The letter was signed 'Yours faithfully.' "

Sir Edward said, "I would like to see the handwriting."

"We will see all about that," Carson told him. "Parker himself will be here, which is better."

Were they really going to produce Charley? Despite Charley's and his tender friendship, their love, and all the wine and the laughter? Oscar was conscious of a stir in the courtroom, sly whispers and laughs.

"In March or April of last year, Mr. Wilde, did you go one night to visit Parker at Fifty Park Walk, about half past twelve at night?"

"No."

"Is Park Walk about ten minutes' walk from Tite Street?"

"I don't know," Oscar said, and added by way of kindly explanation, "I never walk."

"I suppose when you pay visits you always take a cab?"

"Always."

"And if you visited, you would leave the cab outside?"

"If it were a good cab." Perhaps Ned thought that this would damn Oscar in the eyes of the jury. Oscar was inclined to think that from the tedium of their pedestrian lives they would look up with awe to a man who *never* walked.

"When did you first meet Fred Atkins?"

"In October, 1892. I was introduced to him in the rooms of a gentleman in Margaret Street, off Regent Street."

267

"Did he seem to you an idle fellow?"

"Well, yes. But he was ambitious to go on the music-hall stage."

"Did you ask him to go to Paris with you?"

"I must explain," Oscar said, smiling. "One Sunday I saw him and the gentleman who has been mentioned lunching at the Café Royal. I was going to Paris on my own account in reference to the publication of a book. This other gentleman was also going to Paris, and it was suggested that we should all go together, as he had promised to take Atkins. It was arranged that we should go on a Monday, but subsequently the gentleman found that he couldn't go until Tuesday or Wednesday. Then, as Atkins seemed very much disappointed, the gentleman asked me if I would take him over. I said, 'With the greatest pleasure,' and I took him."

"How long had you known Atkins then?"

"Oh, about a fortnight. We went by the club train. I paid for his ticket, but the money was refunded to me afterwards by the gentleman. I took him to lunch at the Café Julien. He was practically my guest, as representing the gentleman I have mentioned."

Carson asked, "After lunch, did you suggest that Atkins have his hair curled?"

"He suggested it himself, and I said it would be very unbecoming. I told him it was a silly thing to do, an absurd thing. I should have been very angry if he had had his hair curled."

"Well, *did* he get his hair curled? At Pascal's the hairdresser, under the Grand Hotel?"

"No, I think not."

"You dined with him?"

"Yes."

"Gave him an excellent dinner?"

"I never had anything else." Oscar paused and added, with his most charming smile for the jury, "I do everything excellently."

The jury remained glum.

Carson persisted, "Did you give him plenty of wine?"

"As I have said before, anyone who dines at my table is not stinted in wine. But if you mean did I *ply* him with wine, Mr. Carson, I say 'No'—it's monstrous, and I won't have it."

Carson almost seemed taken aback. "I have not suggested it."

"But you have suggested it before."

There was a pause. For the first time during all his hours in the witness box, the long day yesterday and now this morning, Oscar felt tired and dull. He drank some water, sniffed at his perfumed handkerchief, and brightened again.

"After dinner," Carson resumed, "did you give Atkins a sovereign to go to the Moulin Rouge?"

"Yes. I went that night, I think, to a French theater, and when I got back to the hotel Atkins had gone to bed."

"Did gross indecencies then take place between you and him?"

"Anyone who said that, Mr. Carson, would be telling a most infamous, a most damnable, lie."

"Did the gentleman referred to arrive the next day?"

"He came on the Wednesday, and we all three returned together. I gave Fred a cigarette case. I found him a pleasant, good-humored companion, but I didn't see much of him after I got to Paris, as I had business to look after."

"Did you ask him to promise that he would say nothing about going to Paris?"

"No. I thought it was the great event of his life."

"How old was he?"

"About twenty."

"Did you give him money, Mr. Wilde?"

"Yes, five pound fifteen to buy his first song for the music-hall stage. He told me," Oscar added, "that the poets who wrote for the music hall never took less."

"Did you consider Atkins respectable?"

"Respectable? Yes, I thought him pleasant and young. He was good-natured. I heard him sing. He was—well, interesting."

"No improprieties ever took place between you and him?"

Oscar raised his eyes to the ceiling. "None whatever."

"Ummm." Carson fiddled with his papers and then asked, "You knew a man named Ernest Scarfe?"

"Oh, yes. He was introduced to me by Taylor. He is a young man of about twenty, of no occupation."

"Did you know he was a valet and is a valet still?"

"No. I have never met him in society, but he has been in *my* society, which is more important." Oscar looked hopefully toward the jury. There were no smiles.

"Did you ask him to dinner?"

"Yes, I asked him to dine with myself and Mr. Taylor at Kettner's."

"Why?"

"Why? Because I am so good-natured," Oscar explained gravely. "It is a good action to ask to dinner those beneath one in social station."

"Did you ever give Scarfe any money?"

"Never."

"Did you give him any presents?"

"Let me see. Yes, a cigarette case, which cost four pounds. It is my custom to present cigarette cases."

"Ummm." Carson paused at length; he seemed at a loss, Oscar thought. It *was* possible that he had run out of a supply of questions, that this interminable cross-examination had come to an end. It would be a shame to end so tamely. If only before he sat down, Ned would give him the one really good opening he had been waiting for!

"When did you first know Sidney Mavor?"

Oscar sighed. "In September, 1892."

"Who introduced you to him?"

"The same gentleman who introduced Atkins."

"Did you give Mavor money?"

"No. I don't think I even gave him a cigarette case—no, but wait," Oscar carefully amended; "it may be true that I ordered Thornhill's in Bond Street to send him one."

"When?"

"That would have been—let me see—in October, ninety-two."

"But you had known him only a month?"

"Quite long enough to get to feel an interest in him."

"Why did you give him a cigarette case when you had known him only a month?"

"I give presents to anybody I like."

"Did he stay with you at your rooms or a hotel?"

"Mr. Mavor stayed with me one night at a hotel in Albemarle Street. I asked him to stay with me for companionship, pleasure, amusement." Some nasty laughter erupted. Oscar was annoyed with himself for permitting this stupid laughter to affect him. "I like to have people staying with me," he said defensively. "I took two bedrooms, one for him, one for myself. He never stayed with me another night. On the occasion referred to, I was passing through London and I wanted his society, as he was a smart, pleasant young fellow."

"And did you find pleasure in his society that night, Mr. Wilde?" Carson asked dryly.

Some horrid laughter broke out. "Yes, in the evening and at breakfast." The laughter swelled. The jury and the judge were somber. "It amused and—pleased him—" Oscar groped a bit. "—pleased him, that I should ask him to be my guest at a very nice, charming hotel."

"Is this he?"

A photograph of a smiling, fair boy was handed up to Oscar. It was Sidney, but younger here, quite charmingly younger. "Ah," Oscar said, "taken at a period earlier than that at which I knew him."

Carson displayed a cigarette case. "Is this the one you gave Mavor?"

"No, really, I couldn't be sure. I have given so many, you see." Oscar wondered why he had said that. He was, possibly, beginning to stumble a bit. Why had Carson even bothered to ask the question, when he had merely to look inside the cigarette case to see engraved there "To Sidney from O.W."? Had Carson hoped that he would say it wasn't the case he had given Sidney in order then to confront him with the inscription for the benefit of the jury? Oscar must be careful; it was a trap, which he might very well have fallen into. But he didn't need to be careful with Ned—Ned, old Rawbones, who never, never could get the best of Oscar, no, not if he were to keep him in this wretched place for a thousand years. Oscar must remember his genius.

The photograph and cigarette case were restored to the cache from which they had come. Oscar wondered how many other presents, given with love, received with charming, boyish thanks—and kisses—were waiting there, with Alphonse's *Wreck of the Grosvenor* and proud silver-mounted walking stick.

"Do you know Walter Grainger?" Carson asked.

This was better, much better. They had left the dangerous ground—the Alphonses, the Charley Parkers, the Mavors, the Ernest Scarfes—and come to territory that was perfectly safe; there had been no nights in hotels with poor homely Walter.

"Yes," Oscar said cheerfully.

"How old is he?"

"Oh, I should say he was about sixteen when I knew him. He was

271

a servant at a certain house in the High Street, Oxford, where Lord Alfred Douglas had rooms. I have stayed there several times. Grainger waited at table. I never dined with him. If it is one's duty to serve, it is one's duty to serve; and if it is one's pleasure to dine, it is one's pleasure to dine." Oscar gave judge and jury a smile.

The judge and jury remained dour. For that matter, it *was* pretty feeble stuff. He looked at Carson hopefully.

"Did you ever kiss him?" Carson asked.

Now he would hear a chuckle or two, he would be bound. Oscar waited for a few moments, to get the maximum attention, and then said with a charming smile, "Oh, dear no. He was a peculiarly plain boy. He was, unfortunately, extremely ugly. I pitied him for it."

Carson's finger shot forward; his dark face was ablaze. He shouted, "*Was that the reason why you did not kiss him?*"

Oscar stared at the thin, triumphant face. "Oh, Mr. Carson," he stammered, "you are pertinently insolent."

"*Did you say that in support of your statement that you never kissed him?*"

"No, no. It is a childish question. It——"

"*Did you put that forward as a reason why you never kissed the boy?*"

"No. No, not at all. I——"

"*Why, sir, did you mention that this boy was extremely ugly?*"

"For this reason. For this reason." For what reason? God give him a reason. God give him a reason that will make all this seem absurd, for if he could not make it seem absurd, he was lost, as Ned was so sure he was—clever, prying, patient Ned. "For this reason. If I were asked why I did not kiss a doormat, I should say because I do not like to kiss doormats. I do not know why I mentioned that he was ugly, except that I was stung by the insolent question you put to me and the way you have insulted me throughout this hearing. Am I to be cross-examined because I do not like it?"

"*Why did you mention his ugliness?*"

"Oh, it is ridiculous—ridiculous to imagine that any such thing —that any such thing could have occurred under any circumstances——"

"*Then why did you mention his ugliness, I ask you?*"

"Perhaps you insulted me; you insulted me by an—an insulting question."

"*Was that a reason why you should say the boy was ugly?*"

"I did not mean—I was not—I had no intention—"

"*Why did you say he was ugly?*"

"It is foolish, it is ridiculous——"

"*Why?*"

"I will not—I cannot, cannot——"

"*Why?*"

"—cannot——"

"*Why, sir? Why? Why? Why? Why?*"

Oscar half turned in the witness box. There was no escape. But he did not wish to escape; he would not run from him.

"*Why? Why? Why?*"

Flushed, trembling, he said with great effort: "You sting me, and—insult me, and try to—to unnerve me, and at times one says things flippantly—flippantly, when one ought to speak more seriously. I admit it."

"You said it flippantly?"

"Yes, it was a flippant answer."

Ned could afford to smile and laugh and sneer. He had won, Oscar had lost.

But Carson's face was sad. That Oscar could bear least of all.

6

THAT NIGHT SIR EDWARD TOLD OSCAR THAT IN VIEW OF all the circumstances it would be almost impossible to persuade the jury to convict of a criminal offense a father who, at least in the jury's eyes, was trying to save his son from what he, the father, believed to be and widely denounced as being an evil and corrupting friendship. Therefore, Sir Edward had continued, it would be in his best interest to consent to the prosecution's being withdrawn and to permit him, Sir Edward, to announce in court that they agreed to a verdict of not guilty on the basis of the charge of "posing"—that the words "posing as a sodomite" on Lord Queensberry's card had not been a libel. Otherwise Mr. Wilde might very well be arrested *in court* on a charge of committing acts of gross indecency with various male persons, and tried, and, if found guilty, sentenced to jail for a period of up to two years under Section Eleven of the Criminal Law Amendment Act.

Very well; Oscar agreed, he would spare himself the possible arrest in court. He now had the opportunity to leave the country before the director of public prosecutions decided to act.

The next day, at the Cadogan Hotel, a smart little page boy brought up a bottle of hock, a seltzer siphon, and half a dozen glasses. Oscar thanked him and asked his name.

"Chester, sir."

"And a very nice name too. Here you are, Chester."

"Oh, thank *you*, sir."

Bosie said he wanted nothing to drink; he was going out to try to learn if a prosecution was already under way. Bobbie Ross and Reggie Turner weren't thirsty either. "I am," Oscar said. "I don't think I've ever been so thirsty. Good heavens, how thirsty I am." He mixed hock and seltzer, drank off the glassful without pause, and poured another. "Ah, that is very good. These are charming rooms, aren't they? Bosie is very comfortable here. Do refrain, Reggie, I beg you, from looking distraught, or annoyed, or impatient, or whatever it is you are looking—it couldn't be more unbecoming; your face is made only for laughter. Bobbie, that remark is addressed to you too. Will you have a cigarette?"

"No, thank you," Bobbie said. "Oscar, we *are* impatient, and very worried. It is an absolutely ridiculous chance to take, waiting here. We must get you over to France as soon as we possibly can."

Someone knocked on the door. "Oh, dear," Oscar sighed. "Will you see who it is, Bobbie, please? Needless to say, I do *not* wish to see any newspaper people." He went into the next room, Bosie's bedroom; in a few minutes Bobbie followed.

"It was a journalist, Oscar, someone from the *Star*. I sent him away. But he had news."

"How very odd. One expects to get only the latest scandal from journalists, never news."

"After Queensberry's acquittal, his solicitor sent all their witnesses' statements to the director of public prosecutions, who took them up with the Home Secretary, Mr. Asquith, and the Solicitor-General, Sir Frank Lockwood——"

"Maurice's uncle," Oscar murmured. "That is quite enough, dear Bobbie; I know the rest. I once offended Asquith at a luncheon and Sir Frank despises Maurice and all his friends, and therefore— therefore— Oh, never mind, it doesn't matter. Is there any more hock?" He returned to the sitting room.

"Oscar, it does matter," Bobbie said urgently. "They decided that a warrant for your arrest should be applied for, and this man from the *Star* says it has now been issued, which means that police officers must be looking for you now, Oscar, now."

"Now, now, this very now," Oscar murmured. "Will you send that nice little Chester for more hock, Bobbie?"

"Oscar," Reggie cried. "You must leave. Do you realize what what will happen otherwise?"

"Where is Chester?" Oscar asked. "Please send for Chester." He sat down. "I am tired, suddenly. Of course I know what will happen. I knew from the beginning what would happen. It was my fate, you see, always, to rise to the very topmost pinnacle, and then plunge to the depths. Am I drunk? I must be, to utter such wretched nonsense. Yet how can I be? On hock and seltzer? Where is Chester? *Have* you sent for Chester, Bobbie?"

"Oscar, *Oscar*," Bobbie pleaded.

Oscar did not move.

"For God's sake, Oscar," Bobbie cried. "Come now, or it will be too late."

There was another knock on the door. It was smart little Chester.

"Dear Chester, will you bring more hock, please?"

The pretty little chap scurried away.

If only dear Edwin Levy were still here; but he was dead, suddenly, just a month ago. He could have got Oscar out of this; anything was possible for that wonderful little man.

There was still time to leave for France, sane, healthy France. Oscar pursed his lips. Was the son of Sir William and Lady Wilde a man to run away? Would he wish his children to remember him as a man who had done so? Was he ready to admit, by running away, that the marquess had won?

"You must stay, you must fight, you must stand up like an Irish gentleman to this rabble of liars and blackmailers," his mother would have declared. "No son of mine could ever dream of running away."

If he should lose, he would be jailed; and his children would remember him not as a man who ran away, but as a prisoner. Which would he prefer? His sons must never remember him as a man who ran away.

What sentimental humbug. For the sake of it would he trust himself to the hands of a British jury?

He had been the master of that jury for all the time he was in the witness box—for all but the very last, when he was tired. They admired him, they wished him well, they would have found the marquess guilty and cheered his victory if not for that one stupid answer. He could never be so stupid again; the next time he would win.

He could not win. He had damned himself.

Oscar struggled up a little in the chair. He was extremely tired. He filled his glass with hock and seltzer and sank back again.

"Must we pull you from the room?" Bobbie said despairingly. "Oscar, dear Oscar, please, please come."

"It is too late, Bobbie, the train will have gone."

"Only let us get you out of the hotel, where the police must know you to be—there'll be other trains."

"Dear Bobbie, dear Reggie, how boring all this is, is it not? And how sweet you are to me. Do have some hock. It is very good hock. And isn't Chester a smart little lad?"

"Oscar," Bobbie groaned.

Someone else rapped on the door. "I wonder if I have inherited my Aunt Jane's memory," Oscar murmured, "and am giving a party but have forgotten that I am giving it? But of course I don't have an Aunt Jane, do I? Will you see who that is, please, Reggie? No kindly newspapermen, remember, but anyone else."

Two men stood there. "Is Mr. Wilde here?" one asked. Reggie nodded. "We are police officers, sir. May we come in?"

"Oh yes, please do," Oscar called.

"Thank you, sir." They entered the room. "You are Mr. Oscar Wilde?" the same man asked.

"I have every reason to believe so." Oscar smiled and shook his head. "Forgive me. I did not mean to be—flippant."

"We hold a warrant for your arrest on a charge of committing indecent acts, sir. I must ask you to come with us."

"Yes, of course. Where shall I be taken?"

"To Scotland Yard and then to Bow Street Station."

"I see. Can I have bail?"

"That I don't know, sir—it is something for the magistrate to decide."

Oscar got up and looked around. "My coat, Bobbie—where did I put it?" There were tears in Bobbie's eyes; his Puck's face was contorted with pain. Oscar squeezed his hand. "Oh, there it is; thank you, Reggie. Very well, gentlemen—you observe that I am giving you the least possible difficulty."

Smart little Chester was standing by the door. "You have very beautiful lips," Oscar whispered as he passed. "Always remember that Oscar Wilde told you so."

7

APRIL WAS LOVELY; IT WAS INTERMINABLE FOR OSCAR. HE had known as long ago as that moment of Carson's devastating question, "*Was that the reason why you did not kiss him?*" that there was no hope. But when a few compassionate men on the jury voted, in the trial of *Regina* v. Wilde, for his acquittal—even in the face of that damning string of witnesses—Oscar felt hope. And he thought he could feel sympathy from Mr. Justice Charles. The others on the jury, the necessary brutes and Philistines, weren't able to budge the compassionate ones, and the jury was discharged; the trial, in effect, was a draw.

May was perfection; Oscar remained in the courtroom. Alfred Taylor chivalrously refused, as a prisoner charged as Oscar was, to turn Queen's evidence and go free. However, Oscar's hope drained slowly and cruelly away in this trial. Mr. Justice Wills, a kindly person, was a fairly near neighbor in Tite Street; not that neighbors were necessarily friends, but at least he was aware of Constance and the children. At the very end, though, the judge's manner changed; he lashed the prisoners with his tongue.

"Oscar Wilde and Alfred Taylor, the crime of which you have been convicted is so bad that one has to put stern restraint upon oneself to prevent oneself from describing, in language which I would rather not use, the sentiments which must rise to the breast of every man of honor who has heard the details of these two terrible trials."

That crime was committing gross indecencies with members of the same sex. Indecencies, *not* sodomy. Had the charge in the indictment been sodomy, and had Oscar been convicted of it, the sentence would have been life imprisonment.

"That the jury have arrived at a correct verdict in this case I cannot persuade myself to entertain the shadow of a doubt; and I hope, at all events, that those who sometimes imagine that a judge is halfhearted in the cause of decency and morality because he takes care no prejudice shall enter into the case, may see that this is consistent at least with the utmost sense of indignation at the horrible charges brought home to both of you. It is no use for me to address you. People who can do these things must be dead to all sense of shame, and one cannot hope to produce any effect upon them. It is the worst case I have ever tried. That you, Taylor, kept a kind of male brothel it is impossible to doubt. And that you, Wilde, have been the center of a circle of extensive corruption of the most hideous kind among young men, it is equally impossible to doubt. I shall, under such circumstances, be expected to pass the severest sentence the law allows. In my judgment it is totally inadequate for such a case as this. The sentence of the court is that each of you be imprisoned and kept to hard labor for two years."

The harshness of this sentence astonished Oscar. Where, he wondered, had they sent poor Alfred? And what precisely was "hard labor"? Would Alfred's hard labor be the same as *his?* Alfred was younger and thinner; perhaps his hard labor would be harder. Oscar hoped not. Whatever Alfred must endure, he wished to endure; he wished that Alfred could know he *was* enduring it, wished they could endure it together—could do their hard labor side by side, picking whatever it was called or treading whatever *it* was called. Had the authorities deliberately separated the two archcriminals, Wilde and Taylor, because of fear that if kept together they would corrupt the most model prisoners?

After the conclusion of the second trial, Oscar spent the weekend in Newgate Gaol.

He was convinced, on the twenty-seventh of May, that whatever followed, nothing could surpass, nothing could *equal,* the torments of the recent spring. He sat in a police van, a large dark coffin on wheels, bound for prison in North London, a model prison, he was told. That was encouraging. What was a model prison? What was a model crime? A model execution? A model abscess? Was this a model police van? It was terribly uncomfortable, even though he had it all to himself.

Oscar wondered if anyone had ever ridden to prison dressed as he was, in frock coat and striped trousers and patent-leather shoes and winged collar and top hat? Would this splendor (rather damaged, to be sure, by the weekend in Newgate, where there were no valets and no hairdressers) favorably or unfavorably impress the officials waiting to receive him at Pentonville? No other clothes had been brought to him to wear for his entrance into the mysteries of a model prison; if they had been, he would not have worn them. He would enter prison grandly, as a gentlemen should, dressed as a gentleman; and as a gentleman he would conduct himself throughout the term of two years.

The police van gave a final great bump and halted. He heard the click of a padlock; the van door opened, and he blinked in the harsh reflection of daylight from whitewashed brick walls. A voice said, "Lively now." He tried to make an orderly exit from the van but his limbs were cramped and he got up awkwardly and knocked his hat against the roof.

A large man in uniform helped him out. "Thank you," Oscar said, smiling. "You are most kind." The other took his arm and steered him up some steps, through a doorway, and into a room with a strange sweet-sour smell, where a man sitting at a table asked Oscar his name, his age, his place of birth, his profession, his religion, was he single or married, had he any children; Oscar gave the answers courteously and told the truth about his age.

Then he was taken to an adjoining room and weighed. Fourteen stone—a hundred and ninety-six pounds. It was years since he had been so slim. He wondered what the food was like in a model prison. Plain, no doubt (no pâtés, no hothouse asparagus, no moules a la fécampoise), but hearty, considering that hard labor was part of one's sentence. Where did one dine in prison, in some kind of crude restaurant, with one's fellows, or in one's room—that is, one's cell?

Oscar's height was measured as six feet, and weight and height were written down. He was told to surrender his personal effects. "May I keep my watch, please?" he asked; Constance had given it to him. "The truth is, I have a sentimental attachment to it." No, he could not keep the watch; his belongings would be returned to him at the end of his term. "Ah," he said, "I see. Thank you." He passed over the watch, his silver and gold coins, and his wallet and pocket notebook.

A new man appeared and led Oscar down a corridor deeper into the building; the sour-sweet smell was always in the air; but now the air, which had been dry and warm, grew clammy. His guide pointed to an open cell. "Take off your clothes and wait there."

"Forgive me," Oscar said, "but—all my clothes?"

"Do you want to have your bath with any of your clothes on?"

Oscar smiled politely. He took off his frock coat and looked in vain for a peg on which to hang it. Puzzled, he stood holding the coat. His guide had disappeared.

Nearby a hoarse voice said "*Gerrout.*" Oscar could not see the speaker. He studied his coat. He had better continue undressing, as instructed. There was nothing to do but put his coat on the damp floor. He unbuttoned his waistcoat, put it on top of the coat, slipped his braces over his shoulders, let his trousers fall, and stepped out of them.

Another uniformed figure passed by with a glance at Oscar. He took off his tie and collar and shirt and put them on top of the trousers. Surely he need not go beyond this stage for the time being? But his guide had unhumorously stressed *all* his clothes. Oscar took off his underclothes. He had lost weight but his white flesh was still pendulous. Oh, God, he prayed, shivering in the cool air, do not let any more men come by while I am here, do not let them see my terrible nakedness. Holding his arms alternately around himself for warmth and turned away from the deadly corridor so that at least the passersby could not see *all* of him, he took off his socks and shoes. The floor was dreadfully cold. Breathing rapidly, he stepped on top of the pile of clothes and stood, somewhat huddled over, arms crossed in front, listening with wild fear for the sound of strangers approaching.

The hoarse voice he had heard before said, " 'Ere, you." A man with an inflamed, pimply face beckoned him to follow. He was led to a door marked "Baths." There was only one bath inside; it was half filled with grayish water on which a thin scum floated. There was no soap or towel, and the floor was slippery with muck.

"That's your bath. *Get in*, will you? Others is waiting."

"But may not I have clean water and a towel?"

"Do you think this is the bleedin' Savoy, fat-arse?"

"No," Oscar said gently, "I did not think it was the Savoy." He got into the obscene bath.

After his bath, he was handed a scrap of damp brown towel. Then, still damp, he had his medical examination. It was brief; the doctor was an ugly, unsmiling man who said nothing. Oscar was led away and given a coarse, drab set of clothes stamped with the flaring arrows that marked the British prisoner.

The walls and ceiling of his cell were of the same whitewashed stone; the stone floor was gray. There was a plank bed at one side with a thin, neatly folded blanket. Oscar lay on the bed, hid his face, and wept. Later he heard a key turning in the lock of the heavy, metal-faced door. The door opened and something was pushed into the cell; the door was closed and locked again. A pleasant smell pervaded the air. Oscar could *sense* the rich bubbling heat of food. Merciful *God*, he was hungry.

He sat up, rubbed his sleeve across his wet eyes, and stared at the floor. A tray, with a tin cup and tin dish and spoon on it, lay there. He picked up the tray and put it on the wooden table that stood against the other wall of the cell. The smell was *delicious*. There was a dark heavy liquid in the cup. Oscar sniffed at it. Cocoa. Was cocoa the regular drink in a model prison, or perhaps only the evening drink? He would leave the cocoa until the last. Now for the dish. A stew? Never mind. He stirred it with the spoon and then raised the dripping spoon to his mouth. He doubled over, retching. They had waited, the beasts who ruled this wicked place, until the smell of hot food would come to you as an ecstasy, and then they put before you this hideous grease, these shreds of fat. He groped for the cocoa, drank half the cup, and retched again; it was greasy too.

He slept. He stood on a sunny hillside, above the flashing sea. A smiling youth came up the hill to join him. He peered eagerly but could not quite make out the face above the beautiful body; in another moment he would know.

The sun and sea faded; the beautiful youth was gone. Oscar opened his eyes and stared at the cold walls of his cell. From the abyss his love reached out to Bosie. Sweetest golden-haired child, you are more than my beloved, you are my teacher, though you are so young, for your wisdom is infinite and older than the ages, it is the secret of all creation, it is the everlasting and all-saving power of love: *that* you have taught me—that your love can fall like a shower of gold over this wretch in the deepest darks of the pit and make him pure and radiant as he was when you lay in his arms and pressed against his mouth your rose-leaf lips and breathed your honey breath into his lungs. Oh, Bosie, Bosie, Bosie, I love you.

8

THE CELL MEASURED SLIGHTLY MORE THAN FIVE PACES IN
length and three in width. The ceiling was three feet above Oscar's head, the single window a foot above. Light came through
this narrow rectangle of opaque glass as through a gray cloud. No
direct light entered the cell; a slit above the door captured a thin
backwash from the jets of illuminating gas that burned along the
galleries of the cellbock. In the door itself a peephole could be
opened from the outside. There were gratings in the end, or window, wall for ventilation, but a gummy filth impossible to root out
clogged half of them.

The prison food consisted of a kind of coarse porridge for breakfast and slight variations of bacon and beans, grease-soaked stew,
suet pudding, greasy soup, black bread, cocoa, and water for
lunch, which seemed to come from the source of the pervading
sour-sweet smell. Porridge usually appeared again at night. These
meals could not be decently dealt with by organs accustomed to
quite different foods.

For reading Oscar was provided with a Bible, a hymnbook, and
a prayer book. No books could be taken from the prison library
until three months of one's term had been served; at that time too,
paper and pen to write a letter would be supplied, and one would
be permitted to receive a single letter and a single visitor. Two
visitors would be allowed every three months thereafter, but they
must come at the same time.

In the mornings he got up at six, if he had been lying on the
plank bed, to the sound of the prison whistle; but usually he was
walking up and down the cell. The cell door was unlocked and the
stinking night air rushed out. Then he scrubbed the cell's floor
with brush and soap and water that had the same sweet-sour smell
—disinfectant. He placed his tin dish and bowl in front on the
table, his cup behind, and his brush behind that. He folded his
blanket and put it at the end of the bed, then waited for morning
inspection. The warder entered the cell and examined its arrangements while Oscar stood at attention. Afterward he ate what he
could of the morning meal, emptied the remains into his latrine
bucket, and cleaned the bowl in the other bucket, with the soapy
water and disinfectant.

The cell door was then unlocked again and Oscar joined the line of other prisoners who lived in his block. Under the warders' eyes they next walked in step to the exercise yard and trudged in a circle for three quarters of an hour. The yard was squeezed in by the prison buildings, and all one could see of the sky was a little tent of blue. Of course it was not always blue. No talk was permitted in the cellblock or in the exercise yard. There was no common place where the prisoners' hard labor was done. In effect, Oscar had been sentenced to solitary cellular confinement. There *was* talk in the exercise yard, though; there was a movement of lips shrouded by bent heads, a kind of gray ghostly whispering between one man and the next, but without practice it could be understood even less than the chirruping of the sparrows perched on the cellblock roof.

The hard labor was brought to Oscar. In his absence a pile of tarry rope would be placed in the cell. The rope had to be picked apart into fine shreds. In shredded form it was called oakum. Oakum was the word he hadn't been able to name when wondering precisely what hard labor could mean. One *picked oakum.* "Picking" was a genteel word for the brute fact. It was a matter of digging one's fingernails into the hard tarry rope and ripping strand from strand. Soon his nails were cracked and the tender flesh was torn. After several days Oscar wept to see his bleeding, tar-smeared fingers. He was weeping a good deal now.

Half an hour was allowed for the midday meal; then oakum-picking continued until five. At seven, after the evening meal, they turned off the gas jets burning in the gallery outside. Punishment for not picking one's quota of oakum, or for speaking when not addressed by an official, or for not keeping one's cell clean and in the proper order was imprisonment in a dark cell on a diet of bread and water; for graver or repeated infractions of prison discipline, one was flogged. Occasionally you could hear a flogging— the crack of leather on flesh, the shrieks and long, shuddering groans.

Oscar prayed for strength to endure.

The key turned in the lock; Oscar stood to attention. A man in black wearing a clergyman's collar entered the cell. He looked healthy, his skin had an excellent tone, and his rather large blue eyes were clear and bright. "I am the prison chaplain," he said.

Oscar bowed his head. Since he had not been asked a question, it was not his place to speak. For that matter, what could he say? The chaplain had not said "Good morning"; he had said "I am the prison chaplain." Certainly one should not say in return, "I am a prisoner."

The chaplain hadn't closed the door behind him. He could not be blamed; the cell stank. Oscar stank, too—he was permitted a single, filthy bath a week. His hair was clipped short in ragged tufts; there was no Koko Marikopas in prison, and the tufts were sprinkled with dirty gray. His cheeks were haggard, his eyes were bleary, his hands were smeared with tar, and some of the finger-nails were badly torn.

"Do you read your Bible?" the chaplain asked.

"Yes, sir," Oscar said.

"That is well," the chaplain said.

Oscar hoped the chaplain would leave now, because he was afraid that the excitement of the interview would overcome him. These were the first words he had exchanged with an educated man since entering Pentonville.

"Did you have morning prayers in your home?" the chaplain asked.

"I fear we did not," Oscar said apologetically. "I am sorry."

"Ah," the chaplain said. His face changed. "You see where you are now." He nodded and left the cell.

Oscar thought he had offended him. Then he realized that the change in the chaplain's expression had been a kind of smile. The chaplain had not been offended; he had been pleased. The chaplain was a stupid, coarse man. The sorriest prisoner who with bowed shoulders trudged the dusty exercise yard was gentler and wiser than he. Pentonville was unfortunate in its chaplain. In this, as in everything, Pentonville was unfortunate.

Oscar returned to the oakum.

As he picked, he remembered a story about the little son of a famous man. The famous man was Charles Darwin. For years, in search of further evidence to support his great theory, Charles Darwin dissected mussels, generation after generation of mussels. Barrels of mussels were delivered to his home, for he dissected them at home, in a room sacred to mussels. A new family moved into the neighborhood, and the small son of the new family made friends with Mr. Darwin's little boy and showed him the new family's house. "All very nice," Mr. Darwin's little boy said at the end of the tour of inspection, "but where does your papa do his mussels?"

If Cyril and Vyvyan were to be taken around some little friend's house, they would ask, "Where does your papa pick his oakum?"

That was not amusing, and it was not true. Cyril and Vyvyan would never know that their father had been put into the shameful arrow-marked clothes and made to tear the tarry rope.

No? Unless they were blind and deaf, how could they avoid at some time in their lives reading or hearing the story of their father's fall? In his conceit, his wicked pride, he had failed those darling boys and their mother, who was so much wiser than he.

Oscar bent his head, and the easy tears fell. Was the fault all his? Was there not someone who had stung his pride and taunted him and driven him on until there was no turning back?

The key turned in the lock; the warder opened the cell door and said, "You have a visitor. Follow me; step lively."

One was not permitted to have a visitor until three months had been served. He was not prepared to have a visitor. He could not bear to see a visitor. He was not presentable. He would break down, he would disgrace himself. Who could the visitor be? The visitor must be sent away, must be told the prisoner was not able to see him—was busy. He was picking oakum. He could not be disturbed. What a miserable joke.

"Didn't I say step lively?"

Oscar wrung his hands. Then he got up; the warder's eye was threatening. Oscar brushed at his clothes and rubbed his face on his sleeve. Swaying a little, he followed the warder from the cell and along the gallery past the other cell doors and down a flight of steps, where he swayed dangerously. Perhaps he *should* fall and pretend he could not go on and then they would not be able to make him see his visitor; but then, what if they should bring him to the cell? Whoever he was, he would see the oakum, the bucket. Dear Lord, do not let him be a friend, for I shall die if a friend should see me in my robes of shame, should see my filth, should *smell* my filth, and pretend (as a friend would) that he does not.

It was not a friend. A most distinguished gentlemen, beautifully dressed, waited in a small private room. He dismissed the warder.

"You may not remember me, Mr. Wilde," he began, "although we've met two or three times at the homes of mutual friends. I am Robert Haldane. There has been some concern about you, and I thought I should come to see you, which I could do as an M.P. and member of the Home Office committee investigating prison administration." He put out his hand.

"You are very kind," Oscar said. "No, please do not touch me."

"Why on earth not?"

"I am filthy."

Mr. Haldane put his hand on Oscar's shoulder. "I am very sorry to see you here. Will you forgive me if I say something to you as man to man? You have not fully used your great gifts, and I am afraid the reason is that you lived a life of pleasure and not of dedication to a great subject. You have one now, Mr. Wilde, all around you; you are living it. Life in an English prison. Perhaps this terrible misfortune, as you think it to be, will prove a blessing in disguise."

Mr. Haldane paused. His voice and eyes were kindly. He is waiting for me to speak, Oscar thought. What could he say? Yes, Mr. Haldane, my terrible misfortune may well prove a blessing in disguise? Yes, Mr. Haldane, I now have a great subject, I am living a great subject, and I shall write about it, Mr. Haldane? But with what, Mr. Haldane? With my tears and my blood for ink, Mr. Haldane, and a broken fingernail for a pen?

He was silent.

"I saw the prison chaplain before seeing you," Mr. Haldane resumed. "He tells me that, unfortunately, he has failed to make any way with you. Those were his words."

"He is a stupid man," Oscar said.

"Ah? He is, eh? Why do you say so?"

"He explained to me that I am here, in Pentonville, in all my degradation, as you see me, because we did not have morning prayers at home."

"Ah," Mr. Haldane said in a different tone.

"But I do not mean to complain. Please don't say that I have complained."

"I have not heard you complain. Do you have books to read, Mr. Wilde, and pen and paper?"

"That would be against the rules."

"Perhaps we can manage to get them for you despite the rules."

Tears rose to Oscar's eyes; he put his hands over his face and wept. Again he felt Mr. Haldane's hand on his shoulder. "There, there," the kindly voice said. "I did not mean to distress you."

"I am very weak; forgive me."

"We must make a list of books. What do you suggest, for a starter?"

Oscar wiped away his tears. "Anything by Flaubert, but above all *Madame Bovary*. Oh, yes, please, *Madame Bovary*."

"I rather doubt *Madame Bovary*; the prison authorities, I fear, would frown on her. Flaubert dedicated the novel to his lawyer, you know."

"I didn't know. Then mustn't one dedicate one's novels to one's lawyer?"

"Not if one's lawyer has defended one, as Flaubert's did, successfully, against a charge of obscene publication. It is a very rare prison authority, Mr. Wilde, who believes that any author should be successfully defended against a charge of obscene publication, ever."

Oscar gave a laugh. "Oh, dear me," he gasped. "I am laughing. Do you know that I haven't laughed since—oh, good heavens, since an eternity ago. But Mr. Haldane, dear, kind Mr. Haldane, I should not be talking to you about books to get for me; there is something far, far more important. Will you see my children, please, and my wife, and my mother, and if you cannot come here again—and I could not expect you to—will you write to me and tell me how they are? Because I have had no news. No news of my little boys in all this time."

"I shall, Mr. Wilde."

"But," Oscar said, putting his hand on the other's arm, "you must not tell my boys that their father wears these clothes or that he—that he—"

Mr. Haldane said with a grave smile, "I do not think it would have occurred to me to tell them."

Though Oscar was not yet qualified to receive a letter, Mr. Haldane's was privileged. He wrote that Mrs. Wilde and the two boys had gone to Europe, exactly where he did not know. He had, though, seen Mr. Wilde's mother, and she seemed to be in reasonable health and sent her love.

Surely this was *good* news? Surely it was foolish to weep over the letter? In Europe Cyril and Vyvyan would be spared any chance of seeing the beastly English press, hearing the vile gossip. Wouldn't they?

By his own reckoning Oscar had been in Pentonville for a month and some days when he was moved to another prison—Wandsworth, in London, south of the Thames. He did not know why. The cells were the same, precisely, to the last half inch, to the very muck that clogged the ventilator. The food was worse. Half a cup of a bitter, astringent medicine was served with the midday meal; one was required to swallow the evil draft.

There were more floggings; there was a special flogging place in the basement; the sucking, moist *smack* of leather on flesh and the shriek and groan came from directly beneath Oscar's cell. Discipline was stricter and punishment quicker.

In Pentonville, to sleep had been to fall into erotic dreams, and to dream had been to construct for oneself once again the little cold hell of waking up; but in Wandsworth Oscar yearned, he prayed, he sobbed, for sleep; he could not sleep—he lay wretched and aching on the plank bed, listening to children crying in the night.

There were several child prisoners in Wandsworth. Oscar saw them in the exercise yard. The youngest was perhaps five. He had small sad eyes and a dirty face, and on his feet he wore tight, torn shoes. He tripped again and again over his flapping soles as he trudged in the dust of the yard.

The key turned in the lock. A letter was tossed into the cell.

Carefully Oscar opened the envelope. His hands shook; he had grown quite weak since moving to Wandsworth. The letter was signed "Otho Holland Lloyd." For a minute or two Oscar had to think. Otho Holland Lloyd was Constance's brother. Oscar had had very little to do with him, but Otho Holland Lloyd *was* his brother-in-law and should have been identified at once.

He wrote that Constance and the children were with him, at his home in Bevaix, in Switzerland. They were well. The boys' education had been interrupted but now was being resumed. In future, their name was to be Holland; the reason for the change would be appreciated, he felt sure. His sister had been advised by her solicitors to institute proceedings for a divorce, but Mr. Lloyd thought if Oscar would write to her only once, she would not.

How could he weep when he had wept so much? Surely his body was drained dry! "If you would write only once." Didn't they know? He would have written every day, every hour, poured out his love for his boys, asked a thousand questions, if he had been allowed to write and if he had been given pen and paper.

Otho's letter was a *private* letter. That meant that the three months were finished. Mr. Haldane's promise to send pen and paper had not been kept. Not through fault of his, Oscar was sure; the rule was too strong.

It was his right as a prisoner of three months' standing to receive a private visitor. He would *ask a visitor* to ask the prison authorities for pen and paper, since he himself could not speak unless spoken to. Surely a friend, a score of friends, would be clamoring to see him soon.

What if his first visitor should be Bosie?

Oscar trembled at the thought. If it had not been for Bosie, there would have been no trial. He could not bear to see Bosie.

Was it that he could not bear to have Bosie see him in his filth and ugliness? Would Bosie shudder to see the havoc he had wrought? No, the true reason was that should he see Bosie, Oscar was afraid he would try to do him some harm. By so much had his love changed.

The key turned in the lock and the warder said, "You have a visitor."

It was probably against the rules to refuse to see a visitor once the warder had brought you to the visitors' room. He could not ask who his visitor was. Then he thought: the visitor *can't* be Bosie. Bosie had gone to France after the first trial, on the advice of the lawyers, who had said that his presence might hurt Oscar in the following trial.

He might have returned, though.

"Step lively," the warder said.

Oscar wiped his face and followed the warder from the cell.

He had assumed that he would be taken to the same room in which Mr. Haldane had waited to see him. That had been foolish. That room was for the privileged. The prisoner was not left in seemly privacy with his visitor; he was *exhibited* to him—the prisoner was put in an iron cage, his visitor sat in a box facing him, four feet away. A warder patrolled between, in a great vaulted room.

Oscar made to turn back from the cage once he realized its purpose. Then he saw who was waiting in the visitor's box. It was a dear face, still as young, it seemed, as it had been, all those years ago, in Paris. It was Robert Sherard.

Oscar clambered into the obscene cage, pressed himself against the bars facing the visitor's box. "Robert," he said. "Dear Robert."

Robert made an effort to keep his face from revealing his shock.

"You have twenty minutes," the patrolling warder said. "You had better get on with it."

This was a rare act of Wandsworth kindness. Oscar became aware, though, of the headlong rush of time. From the wall at the nearer end of the room a huge clock stared down at him. Because its home was Wandsworth, the clock did not behave like a normal clock. Wandsworth had driven the clock mad; Oscar could *see* the minute hand move. The minute hand gulped down time with a crazy thirst. In two movements five minutes were gone.

"Robert," he said, forcing his eyes from the clock, "it was kind of you to come to this dreadful place. You must forgive me; I am not quite myself. And I am not—not very presentable."

"Are you writing, Oscar?"

"Ah, no. I have had nothing to write with, you see. You might mention this to some kind person before you leave, Robert. It is not an unreasonable request—I am supposed to have pen and paper, since I have served my three months. And it *is* three months, Robert, or you would not be permitted to be here."

"Yes, it has been three months, Oscar. Oscar—are they mistreating you?"

"Oh, no, Robert, they are most kind." Oscar felt the familiar hot stinging in his eyes, the tears on his cheeks. "My tears mean nothing. Ah, but I am deceiving you; they mean a great deal. They are tears of affection, of friendship, they are the pure, pure essence of friendship, Robert." Oscar clutched at the iron bars; he felt giddy. "Robert, tell me about the new books and new plays; I am most lamentably out of touch, I am really little more than a barbarian, my dear boy."

Robert looked odd; he was trying not to cry. "Hichens has a new novel—Henry Arthur Jones has a new play—"

"Poor dear Henry Arthur. At my very last rehearsal—we were

rehearsing at the Haymarket, where one of Henry Arthur's lamentable effusions was running—there was a loud thud from somewhere or other, and all my people gave a start. 'Pray compose yourselves, ladies and gentlemen,' I told them. 'The noise was merely some of Mr. Jones's dialogue falling flat.' "

Robert laughed; Oscar laughed. Robert wept tears of mirth; they were both weeping.

Soon after Robert's visit, Oscar had pen and paper. He wrote to Constance when the day's oakum-picking was done, and continued writing early in the morning; even so he needed several days to finish the letter. Writing was difficult; his fingers, accustomed to tarry rope, had trouble holding and guiding the pen; and the miserable tears would not cease. He *would not* send to Constance a letter blotted with tears; he *would not* make such a shameful-seeming appeal for pity. His letter would be beautifully written; not a line, not a word crossed out, not a stain on the page. It was impossible, though, to keep the page altogether clear of tarry smudges.

He begged Constance not to divorce him. There were no excuses he could offer for the shame and grief he had brought into her life; he must have been mad, he wrote, to have behaved as he had for the past three years, ever since *Lady Windermere's Fan* opened the floodgates of success; but that was not an excuse. His only solace now was to remember the times of happiness he had known with her and with the children. Though his sins merited any punishment, he prayed that her mercy and compassion would spare him the only one he did not think he could endure—to be deprived of any further sight of Cyril and Vyvyan through a divorce the terms of which would leave them entirely in her care.

Three weeks after his letter was mailed, the key turned in the lock and the warder said, "You have a visitor."

How could he have another visitor, so soon? Someone of importance it must be to have got around the rules.

Oscar was absurdly weak by now; the arrow-stamped clothes hung on his stooped, thin body. Soon he would not be able to do his oakum; then he would be flogged. He followed the warder in a strange, floating way. He was *skimming*. He skimmed down the stone steps and had some trouble getting around the corner—skimmed into the wall and went down on his hands and knees and had to rest before he could get up and resume skimming. The warder did not rebuke him for the fall. That was decent of the warder.

The warder continued on to the same large vaulted room with the dreadful clock. Oscar felt deliciously light-headed and did not really care who was there. He got into the iron cage like a tame ape on display. Then he looked across to the visitor's box and saw a pale, beautiful face. It was Constance.

His heart sank sickeningly; his false euphoria was gone. He closed his eyes. *Oh, Constance, why did you have to come here and see me as I am?*

Desperately he looked around. He must get out. She must not see him a second longer. He could not get out. He should not.

She had come here out of pity. She had come—all the way from Switzerland—in response to his letter. Her coming to this hell had been the best possible answer—so she must have thought—to his letter.

Oscar clung to the iron bars. Tears rolled down his cheeks; he became aware, when he tasted his tears, that his mouth was hanging open. With an effort he closed it. He whispered, "Forgive me."

She was crying.

"Don't cry."

She put a handkerchief to her face. He said, "I am not worth your tears."

Her face was averted. She said something that he could not hear. His hearing had been bad lately. He said in a louder voice, "Do the children know?" She would not know what he meant, though. He added, "Do they know about me? Where I am? The trials, and—and—all that?"

He saw her lips move again. He could not hear her.

"Constance, I am sorry, it is my fault, but I can't hear."

He watched her anxiously. She turned her head toward him but kept her eyes averted and the handkerchief in her hand close to her face, as a shield, perhaps, against the noxious air. Now when she spoke her voice reached him.

"I tried to hide it from them, but Cyril knows. He saw the newspaper placards, and then when we went to Ireland—"

Her bosom and white throat swelled as she took new breath. "We went to Ireland before we went to Switzerland; when we were in Ireland he must have found some old newspapers. He came to me and asked me what they meant. I told him bad people had done this to you, and I told him never to say anything to Vyvyan. He is an honorable little boy and he will keep his promise."

She had not said that radiant, burning word "*honorable*" to hurt him; she had said it simply as the truth; it hurt nevertheless.

Then she added, "It was hard to explain, because—" She caught her breath. "Because *I* didn't know, before. I learned from the papers too. Before that I thought all the gossip and rumors were only the horrible marquess' lies."

"Forgive me!" Oscar cried. He sobbed. The giddy feeling was coming on him again, but there was something more to say. "My sins are scarlet—are scarlet and unforgivable. But not alone to blame. *He* drove me on. Persuaded me to forget my word to you that there would be—would be no trial. I was so weak, so vain. *He* knew that. If I saw him, I—" He said finally, "I would kill him."

"Your time is up," the warder said.

9

ONE MORNING, SOON AFTER CONSTANCE'S VISIT, OSCAR HAD great trouble getting up; once up, he swayed, tried to catch himself, and fell heavily. Later he discovered that he was lying between sheets in a soft bed. Had he, miraculously, got out of Wandsworth? He laughed, to himself: the smell of disinfectant gave Wandsworth away. He was in the prison infirmary.

Everyone was kind; they gave you white bread, meat, and eggs. Oscar had a good deal of pain in one ear, which he thought he must have hit against a corner of the wooden bed when he fell, but that was a small price to pay for remaining here; through gentle and persistent prodding when the lights were out he might encourage the pain to hang on. But when he was hale enough to pick oakum, back he would go to the beastly cell, surely.

The prison doctor, a large, stupid man, of course, was extremely attentive, and two other doctors, who must have come from the outside, since they did not wear the glazed, unlistening, unfeeling prison look, called one afternoon and examined Oscar. Had Mr. Haldane interested others in his case? Was mercy to be shown him? He dared to hope.

The doctors' visits, though, the reports they must have made to higher authority, resulted only in his being transferred to another prison, in the country town of Reading, thirty or forty miles from London. In Wandsworth his cell had been on the second gallery of the cellblock, in Reading it was on the third; that was the sole difference.

Perhaps they reckoned that the country air, struggling through the ventilator's filth, would be better for his health? His labor now was to sew mailbags. To drive the needle through the heavy canvas was a torture at first because his fingertips were still cracked from tearing the tarry rope; and his painful stitching on the first mailbag, a monstrous brute, had to be plucked out and done over. The governor of Reading prison was the strictest man, rumor had it, in all Her Majesty's Prison Service, who did not suffer such faulty stitchings gladly; should they be repeated, a warder said, the prisoner Wilde would feel the sting of the governor's temper.

Oscar was filled with rage. He would kill himself. There was no cutlery in a prison cell, only a spoon supplied for the loathsome porridges and gruels and soups and stews. He would hang, then. To die by hanging, in prison? That would be a contemptible death; what could he use for a noose? If his fingernails were sharp enough to tear rope apart, surely they could tear the soft flesh from the great vein in his wrist. In the morning the warder would find him lying in his blood on the cell floor.

But had he lived through those other hells, Pentonville, Wandsworth, only to be mastered by Reading?

He would survive Reading; he would kill himself on the first day of his freedom. Prisons could not defeat him, but a society that could create them was not worth living in.

He would not die by his own hand, but he would cloak himself in a robe of sorrow as a king cloaked himself in purple. Never again would he smile—he who once had thought that happiness was his by instinct. He would instruct his friends in sorrow; they would learn from him that the true core of life was melancholy.

The thought gave Oscar comfort in the bitter cold. It was truly cold, in Reading. This was his first winter in prison. There was no heat in the cellblock. The cold gripped him, sank into his body like teeth. In the black pit of the endless nights he felt the marrow freeze in his bones. The prisoners stamped their feet in the exercise yard; the frozen earth seemed brittle and sharp as glass. The daytime skies were the color of steel, and a permanent wind moaned around the prison buildings.

One night his mother came into the cell. Her face was sad. She had been traveling; she wore the cloak she had always worn on journeys. Would she not sit down and rest before journeying on? She did not speak, but shook her head. Then Oscar opened his eyes and saw only the night's pitiless face and knew that his mother was dead. He knew more: he knew that she had died brokenhearted.

Constance, with great compassion, came to Reading to tell Oscar of his mother's death, not knowing that he knew. They parted as friends. The children would be in her care, but whatever happened—a divorce or separation, perhaps even life together again —he would never be barred from seeing them.

He reckoned without Constance's lawyers and his friends and their lawyers' efforts to protect his interests. Wrangling over her marriage settlement, a share in which he had, the lawyers fell out; she must have believed that Oscar was at fault and had tried to dupe her; but when he learned this, it was too late. On his leaving prison, she would give him, as the children's father, three pounds a week; but he was not to see the boys. Should he attempt to break that provision or should he again associate with undesirable friends, the allowance too would be stopped.

His plays and books had been banned; creditors had sold up the contents of 16 Tite Street; the trials had bankrupted him. He had no money, no family, no home.

By now he had mastered the craft of talking without appearing to talk; from his place in the trudging circle of men in the exercise yard he could pass on to his fellow in front the ghostly whispers that came to him from his fellow behind.

On the first bright morning of spring, Oscar saw a new man in the yard. He walked by himself, in a lonely, smaller circle: —a good-looking strong young fellow, with chestnut hair and fine red lips, his head well set on the sturdy column of his throat. Why had he been made to walk by himself?

The ghostly whisper came from behind, "That fellow's got to swing."

Oscar stared at the young throat.

The whisper came again, "Them what's got to swing walks by themselves."

Merciful God, that beautiful young man must hang. And he knew it, he knew it. He glanced up wistfully at the blue tent of sky; his fingers, nervously wandering, strayed to his throat.

Morning by morning the whispers circled the young man. He was Trooper Charles Wooldridge, of the Royal Horse Guards. He had got jealous of his pretty twenty-three-year-old wife and in a fit of temper had snatched up his razor and slit her throat from ear to ear. He was not yet condemned to swing, he was on remand, awaiting trial; but he would swing, he would swing.

Soon Wooldridge disappeared from the exercise yard; he was tried and found guilty and brought back to Reading. Now he was in the condemned cell, and two warders guarded him twenty-four hours a day. "Though there's nought in that cell to kill yourself with," the whispering voice added.

He could tear his wrists. Perhaps Wooldridge still hoped,

though. If he could see, every day, the black shed in one corner of the yard, the uprights and crossbar carried into the shed, hear the hammering as they were nailed together to make the gallows— then he would forget hope, for in that shed he was to dance on air.

"He will swing on Tuesday morning," the ghostly whisper ran around the circle of trudging men. On Monday afternoon a grave was dug in the yard. On Monday night Oscar knelt beside his bed.

"Hear my prayer, Father, for the whisperers say that there are hangmen whose clumsy hands condemn their prey to twitch and heave for minutes before the terrible dance comes to an end; but the good hangman, the hangman who has learned his art well, can kill his man in seconds. I beg Thee, for the sake of Thy sweet Son, give young Charles Wooldridge a good hangman."

Early Tuesday morning, in the grimy light, Oscar got up and scrubbed the cell floor. By and by a bell tolled. The prison seemed to sigh. Oscar sighed himself; every prisoner in Reading sighed at the sound of the bell; their sighs rose to heaven in one great sigh as the young man died.

Later, trudging in the exercise yard, Oscar saw that the grave had been filled.

Next day the whisper ran, "He snuffed it quick and easy. Now he's down there in the quicklime, poor young sod." Wrapped in a sheet of flame. Oscar thanked God that Charles Wooldridge had had a good hanging.

As at Wandsworth, Oscar heard Reading's child prisoners crying in the night. One had stolen an apple, another had snared a rabbit. There was a child in the cell next to his. He saw the little thing in the dim light of the cell one morning when the door was open and he was passing on the way to the exercise yard. The face was a white wedge of terror. At Reading the children were not taken to the exercise yard with the men; they were kept to themselves. A child could never understand punishment inflicted by society; the concept of society was beyond its grasp. To be taken away from home and parents by people it had never seen and thrust into a prison cell, to be kept there for twenty-three hours out of the twenty-four, and brought loathsome food by strange men, and ordered about and punished by them—what could the child know but terror? Why would it not cry its heart out?

If I live, Oscar thought, I shall strike with all my power the blind and bestial system that puts these poor innocents here.

In all this time, no letter came from the honey-haired youth whose folly had put Oscar here. He heard from Bobbie Ross, whom he now addressed in his letters as Robbie (*Bobbie* was too close to *Bosie*), that Bosie meant to dedicate a volume of poems *To Oscar Wilde*; at once he wrote to Robbie to forbid the dedication; it would be ludicrous and disgusting. Oscar added that Robbie was to demand all of Oscar's letters to Bosie and seal them away in a safe place; should Oscar die in prison, burn them; should he live, he would burn them himself.

Robbie was to get, too, a pearl chain and enameled locket and a gold cigarette case Oscar had given Bosie for Christmas. It was beyond his power, Oscar continued, to dredge out of his mind the nauseating recollections of the years during which Bosie had been his almost constant companion, and equally impossible to forget how Bosie, simply in order to pursue his feud with his hateful father, had toppled Oscar into the pit; but at least he would *not* have him gloating over his letters or wearing his gifts.

Robbie was to quote the letter freely so that Bosie could be under no illusion. He could hardly refuse to return the letters. He had destroyed Oscar's life: that should be enough to satisfy even him.

10

A NEW GOVERNOR CAME TO READING. PROMISING REPORTS ran around the circle. He was a decent chap, in his thirties, not spoiled by the system. His name was James Nelson. Every man in the prison was to feel free to ask for an interview with him and to state any grievances.

Governor Nelson greeted Oscar cheerfully, expressed his admiration of his plays, and hoped there would be many more. He behaved as though the trials had never taken place, and Oscar's plays had never been banned, his name never denounced as a pariah's.

For the first time Oscar dared to asked, "Has my record in prison been a good one?" The governor sent for Oscar's file, looked into it, and nodded, "Yes."

"Well, then," Oscar continued hesitantly, "will time be taken off my sentence of two years for good behavior?"

"Ah," the governor answered, "didn't you know, have your lawyers never told you—no remissions are granted in sentences of two years and less. But cheer up, the end is no longer *too* far away, now is it? And I have in mind some changes that I venture to think may speed the remaining months. The prison library, such as it is, needs looking after by someone who is on intimate terms with books and could recommend additions; would you accept the post? And unless by this time you have become so attached to sewing mailbags that it would pain you to stop, would you mind instead doing some work in the gardens?" He smiled. "Finally, will you consent to having a jet of illuminating gas installed in your cell so that you can pursue your literary labors at night if you care to?"

Within weeks Oscar had gained pounds. He now slept at night. No more weeping of children was heard in Reading.

He had never finished that lovely thing, *La Sainte Courtisane*. He tried to resume work on it but the words would not come. He knew why. Bosie was on his mind; the years with Bosie. He must rid his mind of Bosie and the scarlet years. He could do so only by writing to him.

One freezing night in the new winter (but each cell was supplied with additional blankets, thanks to Governor Nelson), Oscar began the heavy task.

Since his letter would speak of Bosie's life and of his, he wrote, it would deeply hurt Bosie's vanity. Let him read such passages again and again, until his vanity was dead. And if some of these words made him weep, let him weep as prisoners weep, in the day as well as the night; for only tears could save him.

Why had their friendship, their affection, their love, ended in ruin and disgrace for the man in prison garb who was writing to him? Because he, Bosie, was *so very young* at the beginning of that friendship? Ah, yes, he was very young, but already he knew too much. Youth's innocence had been lost; already he had found pleasure in the gutter, and when the gutter threatened to mire him down, he came to Oscar for help. And out of compassion Oscar gave him help.

For what followed, Oscar blamed himself. Their friendship had never been intellectual, could never have been, for between their minds there was a gulf that nothing could bridge: Bosie an idler, Oscar a supreme artist. He blamed himself for permitting that friendship, of the senses and not of the mind, to dominate him— for yielding to Bosie whenever he came near, for pandering to his whims, for pouring money into his endless and insatiable appetite for pleasure, and thus bringing himself to bankruptcy. And yet he had been warned: Edwin Levy had warned him, Bosie's own mother had warned him, and that unfortunate but gallant and honorable young man Alfred Taylor had warned him; in Bosie and Bosie's appetites and his fecklessness, in his being *all wrong about money*, and in his dreadful feud with his father—in these lay the seeds of ruin. How bitterly he blamed himself now, Oscar wrote, for having ignored the warnings.

Bosie had never been worthy of his love. He supposed, Oscar continued, that Bosie thought he loved him (quite aside from Bosie's delight in being near a person so famous, whose life was charming, fascinating, luxurious); and yes, he felt at heart that Bosie really did love him; but in Bosie there was something stronger than Love. It was Hate. Bosie's hatred of his father conquered everything else. Love could never live with Hate; Love and Hate feed on different foods, Love on the imagination, and Hate— oh, Hate will feed on anything. In Bosie, Hate fed on every rich morsel of food he ate, every sip of wine he took, every cigarette he smoked; Hate fed on all the luxuries in his life and grew fat.

And Hate blinded him. He could never see beyond his coarse desires, his common lusts; they, and his dreadful, driving passion to defeat his father, to have him arrested and tried like a common criminal, to gloat and crow over him. And for two days that passion was gratified; and then, of course, the tables were turned, the trap so cleverly baited by the marquess was sprung—and Oscar took his place in the courtroom dock.

Now, Bosie, listen well.

Had he wished to, Oscar wrote, he could have ripped him apart, could have shown to the world a picture so foul that all seeing it would have shuddered; Bosie himself, seeing his own face, would have drawn back in horror. More! Oscar could have proved that the Crown's three vital charges against him—based on the boys Oscar was said to have been in bed with at the Savoy and his affair with Alfred Wood—in fact should have been placed at Bosie's door. But no, Oscar continued, he would never have done so; he preferred to sacrifice himself.

Was Bosie worthy of that sacrifice? Bosie, who for the meanest of human passions, Hatred and Vanity and Greed, had brought a great artist down to utter ruin?

This might seem to be a merciless indictment; but consider, Oscar wrote, the indictment he could level against himself! What Bosie had done to him was terrible; the crimes he had committed against himself were more terrible still.

He was a lord of language. In the art and culture of his time he occupied a special and significant place, a position that few artists in their times could have boasted to hold. The gods had lavished on him almost every gift—genius, and a proud, ancient name, and courage, and intellectual boldness, and the ability and daring to transform the drama into an art form as beautiful and personal as the sonnet. With his gifts he shook the imagination of this century.

Ah, but he had another gift, a gift for wasting his genius. To waste that genius gave him a peculiar pleasure. He grew bored with the heights; looking for new pleasures, he plunged to the depths. He titillated himself with perverse delights. What the paradox had been to him intellectually, perversity became in the world of the flesh. He had thought that at the critical moment his will-power would always save him; the critical moment came; his will-power was gone, scattered through those scarlet pages; and he was lost, disgraced in the dust—realizing that all that was left for him was utter, unquestioning Humility.

Humility! Humility would nourish and shelter him. He had not a penny in the world, and no home; but with Humility he would gladly beg for a crust of bread; and if the rich would not give it to him, the poor would. With Humility he would sleep in the grass by the side of the road and find rest sweeter than any he had known in his days of senseless and sensual ease.

After many nights Oscar came to the concluding pages of his letter. He knew very well, he wrote, that when he left prison he would find in the world outside many wonderful things waiting for his delight, such beautiful things as *my brother the wind* and *my sister the rain*, in Saint Francis' words. And there would be the dawns and the sunsets—so many glories that, should he make a list of everything that was waiting for him, it would be endless. But he would bring to that enchanting world, which God had created for him, the poorest of poor prisoners, as much as He had created it for anyone else—he would bring to it something that had never been his before he had entered prison. When it was said that someone had become a *better* man, that was unscientific nonsense; but it was possible to become, through suffering, a *deeper* man. And this was what he would bring with him.

Should a friend invite all his friends to come to a great feast, and not ask him, he would not be distressed. He had learned how to be happy by himself. Could anyone not be happy, with such blessings as freedom, and the moon, and books, and flowers, and *my brother the wind* and *my sister the rain?* And feasts, what were feasts? How many feasts had he given in the past, when his table was red with wine and roses? He cared no longer for feasts.

But should some friend refuse to share with him a great sorrow, ah, then he would be hurt! Should a friend bar the door of the house of mourning to him, he would refuse to be shut out, he would return again and again and beg and plead for admission, to share the Feast of Sorrow, to which he was entitled—it was his right to partake of Sorrow in equal shares with all who knew it. The man who could understand equally the wonder of Sorrow and the wonder of the world's beauties was a man who had reached as near to God as anyone could come.

He was to be released from prison, Oscar continued, in May, and his plan was to leave England at once for some humble seaside village in France. Euripides wrote that the sea heals the wounds of the world and washes away the stains; and Oscar found in himself a hunger for the great simple primeval things. There was too much chatter about Nature. See how sane the Greeks were in their attitude. They loved the things of Nature for what they were: the sea for the swimmer, the trees for their gracious shadow, the forest in the high heat of summer for its cool midday hush. Today, in what was called a utilitarian age, people had forgotten the true uses of simple things: that Water cleanses, that Fire purifies, that the Earth is the great Mother, and so the Art of today was a thing that played with the shadows of the Moon; but the Greek Art was the Sun.

He wanted to return to these elemental forces, Oscar wrote, for he knew that he would find purification in them. Of course, as he had said, simply to gaze at the beautiful world would be rapture. To think that on the day he left these hideous prison walls, the lilacs would be blooming! Ah, he trembled with delight to think of the lilacs, and the laburnum—to think of seeing the wind toss the purple plumes and stir that living gold! For him flowers were part of desire; he knew why Linnaeus had dropped to his knees and wept for pure joy when he saw an English heath burning with the flame of furze in blossom; he knew as Linnaeus had known that hidden deep within the rose tears were waiting—his soul was in sympathy with the color of a flower's chalice, with the curve of a seashell.

But he knew now that behind the world's Beauty there was a Spirit. He had to find his way to this Spirit; he had to be in harmony with it. He was weary of men's words. His search now would be for the Mystical—in Art, in Life, in Nature. In Sorrow and in the sea's deeps, perhaps he would find it. But find it somewhere he must. This was absolutely essential.

As for Bosie and the future, perhaps sometime it could be arranged, by Robbie Ross perhaps, for them to meet, perhaps in a month when the roses rioted in all their wanton splendor, in some quiet gray shadowy town such as Bruges. For this brief meeting they would have to change their names—Bosie would have to give up that flowerlike name and pretty title of his, just as he, Oscar, would have to forfeit a name that once fell so sweetly from the lips of Fame.

In the past they had always been separated by the gulf he had spoken of; it was even deeper now, because it was Sorrow, but it could be crossed—for Humility, everything was possible; and Oscar had forgiven him, had *had* to forgive him. He could not permit Bosie to carry through his life the burden of having ruined Oscar Wilde.

A last word. Bosie must not fear the past. All things *are*, as one looks at them. Where one man saw the sun as a disk of fire, another saw the sons of God shouting for joy—so Blake had written. The world thought, and indeed he too had thought, that the future of Oscar Wilde was lost forever when he permitted himself to be taunted into bringing suit against Bosie's father; but now he believed that his future had been lost long before. His future was *past*; his *past* lay before him. He must see it with different eyes, must pray that God would see it with different eyes; and this could never be achieved by pretending that it did not exist—only by accepting it, by accepting with Humility all he had suffered. This very letter revealed how far he was from the true temper of soul that he must come to; but then, he was learning in a terrible school.

Who knew—when he had learned, perhaps he could teach Bosie something far more wonderful than the Pleasure of Life and the Pleasure of Art; he could teach him the meaning of Sorrow, and its beauty.

For some time Oscar pondered how he should end the letter. "Yours sincerely"? "Yours faithfully"?

At last he wrote: "Your affectionate friend, Oscar Wilde."

PART 5

MY BROTHER THE WIND
MY SISTER THE RAIN
AND SOME OTHERS

1 OSCAR WAS DISCHARGED FROM PRISON EARLY ON THE MORN-
ing of May 19, 1897. Newspaper accounts said that he looked
well; according to one reporter, few would have recognized in him
the fat, scented, affected man of two years before. His face was
tanned, the flabby cheeks and pendulous belly had disappeared, his
eyes seemed bright and alert.

After spending the day in London, he crossed the channel that
night to Dieppe, where Robert Ross and Reginald Turner met
him. From Dieppe he went on to Berneval, a seaside village twelve
miles away, where a room had been reserved for Monsieur Sebastian Melmoth. It pleased Oscar to assume this proud, mysterious,
melancholy name; and of course it should guarantee him privacy.

For a time he was content to live with his brother the wind
and his sister the rain. His brother the wind and his sister the
rain filled his soul with rejoicing. Everything was wonderful, above
all the ocean, the mysterious great mother, and the seabirds, tossed
like white flowers by the wind. In the hushed, holy dawns Oscar
walked by the sea at Berneval and under the chaste moon. Sometimes the sea and sky were like an opal, a single luminous stone,
and a fishing boat would pass, moving very slowly, pulling the
wind after it.

He wrote almost every day to Robbie, telling him that he adored
Berneval and the Hotel de la Plage (which seemed to be much
more private home than hotel) and M. Bonnet, the *patron*, and an
old gentleman who was the only other guest, who had come to stay
two days and so far had stayed two years, and whose sole complaint was that Berneval had no theater. M. Bonnet was perfectly
heartless and logical on this point: the old gentleman retired every
night at eight, and so what good would a theater do him? But the
old gentleman swiftly counterattacked by saying that he only went
to bed at eight because he had no theater to go to. M. Bonnet and
the old gentleman argued the issue for hours but reached no decision.

Oscar supported the old gentleman and told him and M. Bonnet that there should be a new political economy in which the
first law would be, Wherever there is a demand, there is *no* supply.
This law would explain the terrible contrast between man's soul

and his surroundings. Civilizations endured because everyone despised them. Today's city was exactly what no one wanted, today's dress was the result of the horror aroused in people by the styles. The top hat would persist so long as men hated it.

Reading Gaol began to turn into an enchanted castle, of which Governor Nelson was the amiable presiding jinn; the ugly turrets, seen from dreamy Berneval, were like minarets; the very warders became figures out of fairy tales. But distance could not erase the memory of children's crying, and one morning Oscar wrote to a London newspaper describing the infamous treatment of children in English prisons. Also he wrote to Governor Nelson to thank him and tell him about the newspaper letter; if anyone could change the brutal system, he was that man. And there were fellow prisoners and a few friendly warders to be remembered, not only with letters, with money; Oscar didn't have much—the three pounds a week allowed by Constance's lawyers and a fund collected for him by friends, administered by Robbie—but he was living so simply that his needs were small.

A letter came from Constance. It enclosed photographs of Cyril and Vyvyan—darling boys smiling in the sunlight.

Oscar replied in a letter filled with penitence. Though he was not ashamed of having been a prisoner, he wrote, he was dreadfully ashamed of the life he had led; no artist should spend himself in the reckless pursuit of pleasure, which withered the soul, and he had not been worthy of his lovely children and his loyal and beautiful wife. But he had learned his lesson, and gratitude, and humility, and prayed that he would be allowed to visit the boys.

Constance answered that they must wait and see. This was probably not so much Constance's voice as it was her lawyers'; it was they who had specified that his allowance would continue only so long as he kept away from dissolute former companions and saw no one but thoroughly respectable people; since thoroughly respectable people (at any rate the English) wouldn't see *him* and his allowance would cease if he saw anyone else, it was apparent that her lawyers intended him to lead a rather sequestered life.

He heard of a small chapel in the neighborhood, the shrine of Notre Dame de Liesse; an enchanting name—Liesse. It turned out to be an Old French word for joy. He made a pilgrimage to the shrine. There he prayed that he and his children would be reunited soon. This same day he felt stirring in him again an idea that went back to the grim morning of Charles Wooldridge's execution —a poem about Reading Gaol. Oscar started to write the next day. He told Robbie in a letter that he thought the poem would be very good.

So the peaceful days slipped into weeks. Oscar had his work and his walks by the sea and through the meadows of the lovely countryside. And he had the company of his brother the wind and his sister the rain.

Soon after Oscar moved into the Hotel de la Plage a letter came from Bosie. It was in his best style; that was to say, revolting. Oscar could almost see him as he had been in those frightful seizures, mouth stretched taut, the screaming voice pouring out obscenities. How wrong Oscar had been to suggest that they might meet under other names in some quiet gray town. The black beast still lived.

That night Oscar dreamt that his mother came into the room and spoke sternly to him: what could this be but a warning that Bosie represented danger, terrible danger? To see him would be to return to hell.

There were other, equally infamous letters from Bosie. And then came a letter so beautiful that all the others might never have been written.

Oscar wept. He saw Bosie as he looked in his sleep—absurdly sweet.

But they could never meet.

To meet, even under assumed names, would mean taking the chance of not being able to part; and who, seeing them, could mistake Bosie? Who could mistake *Oscar Wilde?* Word would spread and get to the lawyers' ears, and his miserable income of three pounds a week would be cut off at once. The fatal thing that could happen would be the loss forever of his darling boys, because the lawyers would tell Constance. Like a dog to its vomit, he has gone back; back to the evilest of all companions, who ruined him, who covered you and your children with shame; and this he has done even knowing what the cost will be. *How little* his children must really mean to him.

One thistledown hair from Cyril's darling head meant more to Oscar than Bosie had ever meant or could ever mean, meant more than all the world's joys and riches. He ached for Cyril and Vyvyan. If only he could see them, the nagging temptation, the thought of Bosie asleep, Bosie slowly waking and turning to him with smiling red rose-leaf lips and open arms, would be gone.

Oscar wrote again to Constance. There was no reply.

There were, however, almost daily letters from Bosie. How ridiculous, that they could not meet, even for an hour! Who would know if Bosie were to come quietly, by a roundabout way, to Berneval, and under a name nobody would ever remember, an old pet name of theirs—Jonquil du Vallon?

If only he could see Bosie, if only for minutes.

Still no reply came from Constance.

Oscar wrote to Bosie suggesting that they meet on the coming Saturday. No sooner was his letter in the post than a letter arrived from Bosie proposing that they meet on Saturday.

Oscar replied at once: *Darling honey-sweet-boy, of course. Have I not already asked you to come then? You are to call yourself Jonquil du Vallon, and here are your directions: go to Dieppe and hire a carriage and tell the driver to take you to the hotel in Berneval-sur-Mer and to drive by the back road, not the main road. Bring with you anything you wish to bring from those who sell dreams and the dust of roses, but most of all bring yourself.*

The next morning, which was a Thursday, a letter arrived from a friendly lawyer in England. It contained a warning: Queensberry had heard rumors that his son intended to resume the relationship with Oscar Wilde, and Lord Alfred was being kept under surveillance by private detectives.

Terror-stricken, Oscar wired to Bosie: *Don't come.*

Oscar heard that young Ernest Dowson, a brother poet, was on the point of being turned out of his hotel at nearby Arques-la-Bataille for nonpayment of his bill. Oscar welcomed the news; here was a distraction that he badly needed. Few things could be more delightful than rescuing a young poet in distress. If only he had enough money *to* rescue him.

Fortunately Ernest's bill was modest. They drank a good deal by way of celebration, and Oscar talked, a trifle sentimentally, perhaps, about the outcast's life, far from hearth and home, that he was forced to lead.

Ernest listened with grave attention. "Your position," he said frankly, "is the result of your tastes, which respectable society regards as unwholesome. Cannot they be changed?"

"I doubt it," Oscar said.

"Surely, my dear Oscar, it would be worth a try."

"I see your point, my dear Ernest, of course. But since the re-formed drunkard is received with hosannas by respectable society, clutched to its breast, wept over, and fed on the fat of the land, might not the reformed—the reformed—"

"Homosexual," Ernest supplied.

"A disgusting word; I prefer 'uranist'—might not the reformed uranist be similarly applauded?"

"Quite so."

"Certainly it is possible," Oscar said. "He might even become a member of Parliament, or Lord Chancellor. This is a horrid thought, Ernest."

"You are frightening yourself unnecessarily, Oscar. Now, here is what I meant when I said that it would be worth a try. There is a brothel in Dieppe. Who knows? You may find that your tastes have changed without your knowing it."

"All brothels are odious," Oscar said. "They are another example of the terrible contrast between man's soul and his surroundings."

"This brothel is not really so much like a brothel as it is like your maiden aunt's sitting room."

"Then it will be overpowering, my dear Ernest, because my maiden aunt lives in an exact replica of Buckingham Palace, which she had built in the middle of an Irish bog to demonstrate her contempt for the English. Did I ever tell you about the party she gave?"

"Oscar, it *is* worth a try, just as an experiment. Please say you will."

"Oh, very well," Oscar said.

The experiment was not a success. It would depress his sovereign lady Queen Victoria, Oscar thought, if word of the fiasco should reach her imperial ear; perhaps, to alleviate the shock and per-suade her that his heart was in the right place, he should honor her Diamond Jubilee, which was to be celebrated on June 22.

The more he thought of the idea the more he liked it. He asked Marcel, the six-year-old grandson of Madame Darcy of the Café de la Paix in Berneval, if he would be interested in attending a Jubilee Garden Party for children to salute *la Reine d'Angleterre*, and

Marcel said yes, he would, provided that *la Reine d'Angleterre* was a reasonable woman who did not insist on one's behaving as if one were in church.

La Reine would attend only in spirit, Oscar explained. Would Marcel supervise the list of invitations and see that all was correct?

When the list was submitted to him, Marcel eliminated five names, observing that he did not like their owners, and inquired what refreshments were to be served at the *Jubilé de la Reine d'Angleterre*. Strawberries and cream, chocolates, cake, and pink lemonade, Oscar replied. *Bon*, Marcel said, and struck off three more guests, remarking that they made pigs of themselves whenever possible and would disgrace the occasion. But since he didn't want any hurt feelings, Oscar managed to smuggle in these and the others whom Marcel considered *declassé*.

On the great day fifteen guests, all the children of Berneval-sur-Mer, assembled in the garden behind the hotel, where a scene of delight met their eyes, a huge table laden with gaily wrapped presents, bowls of strawberries, pitchers of cream, jugs of pink lemonade, and a gigantic cake with *Jubilé de la Reine d'Angleterre* spelled out in pink sugar on top. *La Reine* herself was not here, Oscar explained, welcoming his guests, but had begged His Honor the Mayor of Berneval to represent her, which he was doing in the bar of the hotel. *La Reine* also had asked as a particular favor if the guests would mind accepting their presents immediately, since the sight of wrapped presents made her nervous, even the thought of them. The guests cordially agreed and the presents were swiftly unwrapped. They turned out to be small musical instruments, six accordions, five trumpets, and four clarinets, and were played with tremendous enthusiasm; first the "Marseillaise" was rendered and then "God Save the Queen"; at least the guests said it was "God Save the Queen," and Oscar did not think he should disagree with them.

After the cake was destroyed the guests danced a *ronde* and waved the French and English flags Oscar had supplied. He proposed as a toast the health of *la Reine d'Angleterre* and the guests responded with "*Vive la Reine d'Angleterre!*" Next, Oscar proposed "*la France, mère de tous les artistes,*" and the guests cried, "*Vive la France, mère de tous les artistes!*" Finally, he proposed "*le Président de la Republique*"; he considered it would be diplomatic to do so. With one voice the guests shouted, "*Vive le President de la Republique et Monsieur Sebastian Melmoth!*"

Oscar had never been more deeply moved. The whole thing was an unqualified social success—a triumph. For days afterward, whenever he passed a group of children playing in the streets, they would bow and cry "*Vive Monsieur Melmoth et la Reine d'Angleterre!*" It seemed doubtful that anyone had ever received such an honor.

Soon afterward he had news that Constance was ill. In the confusion of the last weeks at Tite Street with bailiffs and creditors besieging the house, she had tripped and fallen downstairs and injured her back; not seriously, her doctor had thought, but trouble had developed, and she was beginning to find walking difficult.

Oscar asked if he should come to see her. A mutual friend replied: no. Were they so worried, then, that he would see the children too? Apparently that was the reason, for when Constance finally wrote, she said that she had "managed to get the children out of the way for the time being" and Oscar could come for a visit. There were many conditions.

Undoubtedly the conditions were imposed by her lawyers or her doctors, but they sounded like a list of regulations for prisoners. Oscar fell into black despair. That night he drank too much, in the company of some new guests at the hotel—a curious chap whose name seemed to be Byron and an ugly man with golden hair and another man whose hair was *violet*. Oscar asked him if he owed his violet hair to Koko Marikopas; no, he said, he did not know anyone called Koko Marikopas, and his hair had always been violet. How extraordinary, a child with violet hair. Then Oscar thought of his own children, and he wept.

In the morning he had a wretched headache and a cold. He wrote to Bosie: "Please, please, we must meet! If we don't meet, I think I will kill myself. But we must not meet here. Berneval has become horrible to me. We must meet in an old gray town with the sound of church bells in the air and roses climbing wantonly over crumbling stone—"

Bosie replied by wire: "In Rouen, the day after tomorrow."

2

BOSIE WAS WAITING AT THE STATION IN ROUEN. OSCAR CRIED when he saw him, out of pure happiness, Bosie was so good-looking and so charming. He didn't seem a day older than when Oscar had first really known him. Oscar said, "I have never loved anyone else, I *never* could love anyone else. Without you I was empty and despairing, and lonely, lonely, lonely, and I could not work on my poem; I had put my poem aside in disgust. With you I am filled with creative energy, I know I can write again, and remake my world. Unless I have the atmosphere of love around me, I must die. Only you can give me that atmosphere; it comes with your honey breath, from your red rose-leaf lips."

They walked around Rouen hand in hand, like children, and wept, and were happy. Oscar asked, "Why did you never write to me during the horrible years in prison?"

"Oh, my darling, I couldn't, I was so wounded by what Robbie said. Robbie said you never wished to see me again or even hear my name. He said you hated me. He was so fearfully earnest I had to believe him. He is a horrible common little beast, but I had to believe him. And then there was that letter about me. What could I do, my dearest? Could I write to you, if you hated the sound of my name?"

"I was out of my mind. Since leaving prison I've tried to live as my friends wished me to live, and as the lawyers advised me to live, but I could not; I've been lonely and miserable and wretched in a horrible Philistine world, and I had to turn back to you and your love, and we must never leave each other again."

"No, darling Oscar. Never, never."

"But what will we do? Your demon father will try to crush me again, your mother will be furious, *my* friends will be furious too. Constance will be furious, her lawyers will denounce me, my allowance will be stopped. Everyone will be against us."

"I don't care. We will get a little villa somewhere in Italy and live very simply in the sun, and you shall work."

"Oh, I know I will be able to work. I'll finish my poem, and it will be a work of genius, it will reestablish me—will bring in lots and lots of gold. Not that we'll need lots of money. We'll have the sunlight, and a little wine to drink, and the flowers, and our love, and work. A Grecian life."

They went to Naples and found a villa on the Via Posilippo, furnished, with marble steps leading down to the sea. They both loved the marble steps. A man and woman servant came with the villa. Bosie said he had enough money to pay for everything, at least in the beginning, but it turned out he didn't. His allowance from his father had been cut off long ago, of course; his mother paid him eight pounds a week, but Bosie had spent every penny and borrowed ahead too, and so it was up to Oscar to raise the money for the rent of the villa and for the food. He managed to, because no one knew that Bosie and he were together again.

Their first few days and nights were utterly charming. Then they learned that something besides the servants came with the Villa Giudice—rats. They were rats such as Oscar had never seen, extremely rude and casual. A cat would have nothing to do with them. They were told about a professional rat catcher and sent for him. He turned out to be a little old woman with a moustache who muttered incantations and stuffed things down the ratholes in case the incantations didn't work.

The rats disappeared and they were happy again. Oscar worked well on his poem, and Bosie sang and wrote sonnets and lay in the sun. They went bathing together, and did not mind all the letters telling them they were fools. Even Reggie Turner, who had never used such words before, wrote to say Oscar was "a damned idiot." Oscar told him in return "Of course I am an idiot, all lovers are, and whatever my life has been ethically, it is *romantic*, and Bosie is my romance, and even if my romance is a tragedy, it is a romance nevertheless, and Bosie loves me very, very dearly. We have always been meant for each other and will never part again."

They had had quarrels before, there had been frightful scenes without number, but always *in the best of circumstances*. There had always been *money*. When Bosie, in a passion, had thrown his glass on the floor, the glass had usually contained champagne, golden Dagonet, his favorite, two pounds and some shillings the bottle. When he smashed his glass on the floor of the Villa Giudice, the glass spilled forth cheap red wine.

Much of Oscar's time was devoted to writing begging letters and getting refusals, if he got anything. The one great hope was his poem, *The Ballad of Reading Gaol*, which a London publisher, Leonard Smithers, had accepted; but to squeeze a few pounds out of him required endless letters and dreary marches through the heat to the Thos. Cook & Son office in Naples to see if a money order had come. There was no comfort, on returning exhausted from one of these dismal forays, to be pitched into another of the squalid kind of scenes that increasingly dominated life at the Villa Giudice.

"I can't find the cigarettes," Bosie would announce. "Did you hide them?"

"No, I didn't. There weren't any."

"I think it is very petty of you, Oscar, to smoke the last of the cigarettes and go wandering off somewhere or other leaving me without a single one in the house. I searched upstairs and down. You might have left me *one*. But no, not you. I call that disgustingly selfish."

"My dear boy——"

"Please don't call me your dear boy; it sounds revoltingly avuncular. You aren't a very avuncular figure, you know. Besides, any decent uncle would leave his nephew *one* cigarette."

"Bosie, I didn't go wandering off somewhere or other, I walked in the dust God knows how many miles to the Cook office to ask them if a money order hadn't come by cable from London. Do you think I enjoyed it? Do you *really* think I smoked the last cigarette in the house? I haven't had a cigarette since the day before yesterday. I know, because that was the last time you offered me one from the last packet I bought you."

"I suppose you made a note of it, did you, to throw it up to me?"

"No, I didn't make a note of it; I have no time to make notes, I am too pressed writing letters to try to bring in the money to buy you cigarettes. Here, I brought you a packet."

Bosie examined the packet. "I can't smoke this rubbish."

"Then *I* shall."

"It is really *very* petty of you, Oscar, to buy cigarettes you know I can't smoke and then to smoke them in my face."

"I'm not smoking them in your face, am I? Am I?"

"You look absurd when you shout. Your cheeks shake. You are

318

getting awfully fat again, aren't you? Are you eating things on the sly? Heaven knows there's nothing worth eating on the table. Oh, very well, give me the wretched cigarettes. But I shall cough all night." He coughed.

Bosie was proud of his teeth, and deserved to be; they were beautiful pearly little teeth. He would spend ten minutes brushing them after every meal. Often, in prison, picking the shreds of gristly meat from his teeth, Oscar had thought of Bosie's charming devotion to his toothbrush-and-toothpowder ritual. He made such an enchanting picture, brushing away, then daintily rinsing his mouth and bending close to the mirror and smiling, quite adorably, to see how his teeth looked. He had a favorite toothpowder, a French brand, pink and lightly scented.

He had brought a tin of this toothpowder with him to the Villa Giudice—almost empty, Oscar learned, because soon after their arrival Bosie asked him to buy another tin when he next went into Naples. Oscar had had a good long search to find the brand; he knew Bosie would accept no other. The pink toothpowder was far more expensive in Naples than in France, which was only to be expected, considering that it *came from* France.

All this Oscar thought of as he walked back to the Villa Giudice with the toothpowder. He thought also, he could not avoid the thought, it was thrust upon him with every step he took, of the days when a hansom cab had waited for him from morning to night to take him wherever he wished to go, even from one side of the street to the other. He was fortunate now if the passing carriages didn't throw dust and other things in his face. He was even more fortunate, on these damnable walks, if his brother the wind didn't blow steadily in his face going to Naples and mysteriously switch around and blow in his face going back, and if his sister the rain didn't come pelting down from a sky previously cloudless and soak him to the skin.

As for his own teeth, they were in poor condition; they hadn't been brushed at all during the prison years. When he next got hold of a good sum of money he must find a really first-rate dentist and have his teeth attended to. In their shocking state, they were hardly worth brushing. Ah, well, Bosie could do his brushing for him by proxy.

Oscar gave Bosie the tin, and for a while Bosie brushed happily, not stinting himself for toothpowder; he liked to pour a lavish amount into the palm of his hand and smother the brush in the scented little pyramid.

But there came a morning when there was no toothpowder.

Oscar could not believe it. "How can't there be any toothpowder? I bought you a gigantic tin."

"It is gone," Bosie said. He looked at Oscar suspiciously. "Did you think I was using too much of your precious toothpowder? Is that why you hid it?"

"It isn't my toothpowder, it's yours. I bought it for you. Why on earth would I want to hide it? If I wanted to hide it, would I have bought it in the first place? Couldn't I have told you there wasn't any to be had?"

"I'm sure you can't expect me to understand why you do these things; I haven't a devious mind like yours, Oscar. I have no doubt the toothpowder is in your room, tucked away cleverly."

"Then come and look in my room."

"There, you see how furious you are? No thank you, I wouldn't stoop to it."

"I insist that you search my room while I search yours."

"Oh, very well."

After the search Oscar said, "It was my fault. I lost my temper over this ridiculous business. Dear boy, forgive me," he added contritely. "I don't know why I was so upset. Let's forget the stupid toothpowder—I shall bring you more today."

"I am sure I don't know where it can have got to," Bosie said.

"Perhaps a rat stole it."

"A *rat?*"

"Yes, I believe there are rats that are like magpies, with an eye for bright things, and the tin was bright blue, wasn't it?"

"But the rats are gone."

"Well, one might have come back."

"Really, Oscar, I wish you wouldn't. It is too horrible to think about."

While serving afternoon tea the servant, Roberto, inadvertently breathed on Oscar. Roberto's breath was sweet. Oscar knew the scent but could not quite place it. He sniffed cautiously while the tea things were removed, then asked after Roberto's ancient mother. This always involved a long, gloomy answer with many bursts of emotion; Oscar sniffed steadily while Roberto powerfully appealed to the Blessed Virgin to witness his mother's sufferings. The scent was of Bosie's pink toothpowder.

That evening, when Roberto was out, Oscar searched his quarters. There was the bright-blue tin. When faced with the evidence, Roberto admitted all; but he hadn't been brushing his teeth with Bosie's toothpowder; he didn't believe in brushing the teeth, and besides, he had no toothbrush; he had been mixing it in water and *drinking* it. The toothpowder made a delicious drink, he said earnestly. "But not good for the stomach," Oscar said; "it colors the stomach pink, in time."

Roberto was visibly shaken. He begged Oscar's pardon and said it would not happen again.

Bosie wished to sack him, but Oscar said no. "A servant whose only fault is drinking toothpowder is a jewel beyond price. And Roberto hasn't been paid," he added, "in weeks. Indeed, if he had wanted to be nasty, he could have said he was taking the toothpowder in lieu of wages."

To himself Oscar admitted that life with Bosie was proving to be difficult. Not for the world would he have so much as hinted at it to his friends, because they had all condemned Bosie—Robbie and Reggie and More had said he was thoroughly disreputable; the lawyer who had written the friendly letter of warning to Oscar had said that in his opinion *any member* of the Queensberry family was disreputable and, if associated with, would once again ruin Oscar's life.

Once again ruin his life. How many times can one's life be ruined? How many people had rushed forward and offered to live with him after his life *had been* ruined? Someone should start a Society for the Defense of Oppressed Personalities. *He* was oppressed. There was a sort of Grand European Condominium to Exercise a Genteel Tyranny Over Oscar Wilde. To think that after his entire life *had been* wrecked and devastated and shattered by society, by the brutes and hounds who represented society, *to think* that well-meaning people should be doing their utmost to exercise this tyranny over him—should be striving to make him live in solitude. Wasn't that what it came down to, with their warnings of don't go back to Bosie, and now that he had gone back to him, to get rid of Bosie?

He would be damned if he'd give up Bosie.

How difficult Bosie could be, though, when there wasn't all the money in the world.

Once again Oscar sat down to write his begging letters. He sent a desperate appeal to Leonard Smithers.

At heart Smithers seemed to be a decent chap, if erratic. He had praised *The Ballad of Reading Gaol* as a work of genius; but to publish it under Oscar's name would, he thought, be fatal. Oscar agreed. He did not want his beautiful poem, the last great work of his life (he knew there could never be another, the spark was gone) to be banned at once, automatically, as his plays and books had been banned; the public must be given a chance to read it. The poem would be published, then, as by C.3.3.—"C" for the cell block in Reading Gaol, the first "three" for the floor his cell had been on, the second "three" for the cell itself.

But perhaps Smithers thought penury was good for poets? Oscar did his utmost to disabuse him of the idea. "My situation," he wrote, "is appalling. Please cable ten pounds—only ten pounds!—to Thos. Cook & Son, Naples."

The day after Smithers should have received this appeal, Oscar walked to the Cook office and back three times. On his last visit he heard a snicker from the clerks. No doubt he looked sufficiently comic, a rather stout man in elegant but dusty clothes that were much too tight. He tried to seem coolly unconcerned, as though visiting the Cook office three times in one day was purely a matter of whim—nothing else to do between sipping drinks and nibbling pastries, don't you know. While waiting for the clerk's reply to his question, he knew his face was haggard with anxiety.

"No, nothing."

Coolly disinterested again, Oscar said, "Oh, really? Thank you," and strolled out. Behind him he heard another snicker. He would not go back to that office ever, he would not. Oh, he wouldn't, wouldn't he? He would not only go back to that office, and be snickered at, be laughed at, be jeered at—whatever they wished to do to him, in their brutal, careless youth—he would not only go back, he would go back *today*.

He had no choice. The situation *was* appalling. There wasn't a single coin in his pocket. He asked Bosie, "Have you a few coins to spare?"

"But of course you *know* I never have any money."

The toothpowder-drinking Roberto was richer than Sebastian Melmoth, Esq. Esq. had exactly nothing.

For a moment or so Oscar considered asking Roberto for a small loan. "Oh, ah, Roberto, I was wondering—toothpowder frightfully expensive—sank thousands into the last tin—more money expected momentarily from London—until then, do you think you could—" No.

For the fourth time Oscar trudged back to the Cook office, as the sun sank. To enter the office required—was courage too strong a word? The clerks did not snicker. Oscar silently addressed them: Thank you, my dear young men.

"I am sorry, Mr. Melmoth," one of them said, "but a cable hasn't come for you yet. We are closing in half an hour. Would you care to wait until then?"

"That is very kind of you."

"Not at all, sir."

"I think I shall, then—yes."

"Here is a chair, sir."

"Thank you, thank you."

They pitied him.

When he returned to the Villa Giudice Oscar was exhausted; his feet seemed to be on fire. He longed for a good dinner, and some wine, and above all, no arguments.

Bosie was smoking a cigarette in the middle of a litter of papers and magazines. "Wherever have you been?" he asked. "You are a sight."

"For a stroll."

"Terribly hot for that. Or are you trying to take off weight? It should not be difficult here. The fish I had for lunch was shocking. You were lucky to miss it. Were you in Naples, as you always seem to be?"

"Yes."

"Ah. I suppose you had lunch there."

Oscar dragged himself upstairs and bathed his feet.

Dinner was a disaster.

"What *is* this?" Bosie inquired, poking at his plate.

Roberto spoke at some length, apologetically.

"I am sure I don't know what you're talking about. It looks like a cut-up broom."

"Nothing else, signore."

"Are you saying it *is* a cut-up broom?"

"Of course it isn't," Oscar said. "Roberto said it is Pennoni alla Something or other. The sauce is interesting."

"Oh God," Bosie said. "The sauce is not interesting, the sauce tastes like pee. What can one expect if one insists on employing thieves and scoundrels?"

"Not a scunnrel," Roberto muttered.

"You stole my toothpowder, didn't you?" Bosie turned violently to Oscar. "Of course *you* can eat it. *You* had a decent lunch in Naples while I was being made sick by that ghastly fish. Oh, no, I don't have to put up with this, I don't have to. I was told the most monstrous lies; what a beautiful life we'd have, a beautiful life in a beautiful villa, with full staff. God, look at the staff. A thief and an idiot and a scoundrel who steals my toothpowder and *drinks it!*"

"Not a scunnrel," Roberto said again.

"I cannot *bear* it," Bosie cried.

Bosie's face, Oscar saw with a shock, was like that of a shrewish little housewife, all twisted and mean.

Once and for all, finally, Oscar fell out of love.

"Oh, do be quiet," he said. "Really, you are a bore."

3   THE NEXT MORNING BOSIE WAS IN A FILTHY TEMPER; OSCAR
had called him a *bore*. He cabled to his mother for money and left
immediately upon its receipt.

That afternoon the long-awaited ten pounds arrived from
Smithers, and a few days later a check for one hundred pounds
came in the mail. This sudden windfall was due, Oscar learned, to
Lady Queensberry, who had not forgotten Bosie's rash promise
that her side of the family would contribute to the cost of the trial.

One hundred pounds; they made possible the change of scene
Oscar needed to get rid of the taste of Bosie's final departure from
his life. He went to Sicily.

When he returned, Roberto had decamped, taking Oscar's
clothes with him. He was shocked; he hadn't really thought Roberto was a thief, despite the toothpowder, and had meant to tell
him that toothpowder didn't really turn the stomach pink. Perhaps,
though, Roberto had helped himself to the clothes only because
he hadn't been paid all his wages.

Oscar caught a cold. It turned into influenza. He had never felt
more wretched. His life was cursed now; the joy he had known
could never be restored. His friends had deserted him; all they did
was to write letters bombarding him with criticism, which was out-
rageously uncivilized; unfortified places are supposed to be spared
in decent warfare.

Slowly he recovered, but his convalescence was followed by a
dreadful ennui. Not even in his gloomiest moments, however, did
he regret Bosie's leaving; whenever he thought of him he saw not
the beautiful face that had haunted and tempted him in the
past, but those mean, shrewish little features spitting out nasty
words.

Oscar took an apartment in Naples. Then he moved to Paris.
He must pull himself together and make a new effort, follow
up *The Ballad of Reading Gaol* with serious, sustained work. But
how could one devote oneself to serious, sustained work if all one's
serious sustained work had to be devoted to wheedling money
from one's friends and acquaintances and publisher? Occasionally
Smithers would respond with a few pounds. These triumphs had to

be celebrated; the celebrations would leave Oscar without a sou, as all celebrations should, or they wouldn't be celebrations, and he would have to think of where to turn for his next meal or his next drink. He found a restaurant where the meals were only two francs. They were quite inedible, but it was really enormously clever of him to have found a restaurant where the meals were only two francs, and he went there often, to drink of course, not to eat.

Bosie, he heard, was on the Riviera with his mother. He had insisted that they leave a smart hotel because the manager wouldn't give Bosie's name to the press as among recent fashionable arrivals. What an odious little snob he was. Oscar required several drinks to overcome the unpleasant effect of hearing about him; then, in the opulent mood kindly supplied by the drinks, he got into a cab to return to his hotel, although he could not afford a cab, as he well knew. It would be pleasant to move from the hotel into an apartment, a two-room apartment (one room to write in, the other room to have insomnia in; in fact, it wouldn't matter which room he wrote in and which he had insomnia in because it would really come down to his having insomnia in both), but where could he possibly hope to find a two-room or even a one-room apartment as cheap as his hotel—which was to say, an apartment with an owner as easygoing about the rent as was M. Dupoirier, the hotel proprietor?

The horse pulling the cab stumbled. "There would appear to be some confusion," Oscar murmured to himself. "It is I who have been drinking, not the horse. Or has he been drinking too?" The horse stumbled again. "Dear me, he has been, and is not used to it." The horse fell heavily; the cab gave a great lurch and Oscar was thrown forward.

He slowly became aware that he was lying huddled on the floor of the cab and that his mouth was sticky—an absurd position to be in for Oscar Wilde, and one he did not propose to tolerate an instant longer. He sat up, dabbed at his mouth with his handkerchief, and perceived that the sticky substance was blood. Then the cab door was pulled open by a gendarme and he was helped out. The poor horse lay on the street. Oscar turned his eyes away from that cruel sight. He felt in his pocket and found a solitary coin. "Here you are, my dear fellow," he said and gave the staring cabdriver his fare.

For the next three days Oscar did not venture out of the hotel; his lower lip, quite severely cut, pained him a good deal; worse, it had puffed up like a revolting little balloon. He looked preposterous. The whole lower scheme of his face had never been his most winning aspect in any event, and the fact that it was his *lower* lip that had been cut (not the upper, which could sustain a reasonable swelling) served as another proof of his theory that once the world has turned against you, it becomes ever more heedlessly coarse in the methods it finds to wound you.

In those three days his only solace was a letter from Constance. It was a kind, sweet letter, and she had every excuse to write to him hurtfully. Cyril and Vyvyan were in school and doing well. She was afraid she herself wasn't in the best of health but felt sure she would soon improve. Oscar's publisher had sent her a copy of *The Ballad of Reading Gaol* and she thought it was magnificent, at once so powerful and so exquisite that it had moved her to tears. She hoped to hear from him.

He read the letter many times. He thought of her tears, shed over his poem; that she had wept he had no doubt, not because he recalled the poem's power but because he knew Constance's compassionate nature. She would weep for the young man who had died in Reading Gaol; she would weep for the man who had written the poem.

And she hoped to hear from him.

She would hear from him. Ah, he would write her such a letter. It would be a mirror in which she would see the beauty of her soul.

Because he would be satisfied with nothing less than perfection, the letter was difficult to write. It was still not finished two weeks later.

A telegram arrived then from Otho Holland Lloyd, Constance's brother. Her illness had taken a sudden turn for the worse; she had been operated on and had died.

Oscar put the telegram beside his unfinished letter. Then he went out; he did not trust himself to stay alone. Late that night, when he returned, he tried to finish the letter. He could not; he could only weep.

4

I READ, OF COURSE, OF OSCAR'S TRIALS. THEY WERE ELABO-
rately reported in the New York press. Readers of the more sensational journals learned that when he was sentenced to two years
at hard labor, "women of ill fame" danced in the streets, shrieking
their approval. "He'll have that pretty long hair of his cut short
now!" they cried. "And won't go spoiling *our* business no more!"
Perhaps they did kick up their heels and shout these things, and
perhaps it was only a reporter's story; in any event, the general
tenor of public and newspaper opinion was illustrated by an
editorial article in the London *Evening News,* which my New York
paper quoted at length:

> Never has the lesson of a wasted life come home to us more
> dramatically and opportunely. England has tolerated the man
> Wilde and others of his kind too long. Before he broke the law
> of his country and outraged human decency he was a social pest,
> a center of intellectual corruption. He was one of the high priests
> of a school which attacks all the wholesome, manly, simple ideals
> of English life and sets up false gods of decadent culture and in-
> tellectual debauchery. The man himself was a perfect type of his
> class, a gross sensualist veneered with the affectation of artistic
> feeling, too delicate for the appreciation of common clay. To him
> and such as him we owe the spread of moral degeneration
> amongst young men with abilities sufficient to make them a credit
> to their country. At the feet of Wilde they have learned to gain
> notoriety by blatant conceit, by despising the emotions of healthy
> humanity and the achievements of wholesome talent.
>
> Such people find their fitting environment in the artificial light
> and the incense-laden air of secret chambers curtained from the
> light of day. Their pretenses fall from them in fresh air and
> honest sunshine. Light has been let in upon them now in a very
> decisive fashion, and we venture to hope that the conviction of
> Wilde for these abominable vices, which were the natural out-
> come of his diseased intellectual condition, will be a salutary
> warning to the unhealthy boys who posed as sharers of his cul-
> ture. Wilde's fate will teach them that brilliant talent does not
> justify disdain of all moral restraints. It has been the fashion to
> concede a certain amount of immoral licence to men of genius,
> and it is time that public opinion should correct it.

In the face of Edward Carson's savage and ultimately triumphant cross-examination and the testimony given by Charles Parker and others like him at the later trials, no one could expect to hear a voice protesting, however faintly, that perhaps Oscar was innocent of the charges on which he had been tried. The correspondence columns in the New York press were full of letters hailing the verdict; I particularly remember one writer who thanked God that the stalwart virtues handed down by the Pilgrim Fathers had protected us from the debauched Wilde's wicked gospel during his American tour fifteen years ago.

I wrote to the editor asking him to remind his correspondent that Oscar's lectures had been praised by the intellectual leaders of the day and that even in our spotless republic such things as perjurers and frame-ups were not unknown. My letter wasn't printed.

I was convinced of his innocence. Remembering Oscar, I thought the trials were a fraud. The half dozen letters I had had from him, spread over the years, were not those of a "social pest," a "gross sensualist," one who practices "abominable vices"; good heavens, no! In them he talked chiefly about his sons, informed me that Cyril was much plagued by dreams of pigs, that Vyvyan could not eat licorice but hoped to in maturity, when he proposed to eat nothing else and thus confound his older brother, a licorice gourmand. He never failed to ask for news of my own growing family in return.

The Picture of Dorian Gray I regarded as a performance by Oscar the master performer, certainly not as an expression of his philosophy—a performance designed to shock. I thought I could hear him laughing behind the scenes. His plays, I believed, represented the real Oscar, the soul of laughter. To think of him in jail. Perhaps he would laugh the gray walls into gossamer. That, or they would kill him; I didn't think there could be anything in between.

Newspaper stories about the notorious Oscar Wilde continued to appear at intervals: he was in Pentonville Prison, in London; had been moved from Pentonville to Wandsworth, from Wandsworth to Reading. I wrote to him but received no reply. His silence seemed to mean that my worst fears were to be realized.

I read with great relief of Oscar's discharge from prison. Evidently he was in good health. I wrote in care of his London publishers. I don't know if they forwarded the letter; in view of their eagerness after Oscar's conviction to withdraw his books and scrub his name from their roll of authors, I doubt that they did; at any rate, again there was no reply.

My newspaper reported a rumor that the ex-convict Wilde was hiding in the village of Berneval-sur-Mer, near Dieppe, in France. I wondered: would it be a disservice to address him there if the newspaper story was true? But I couldn't believe he *was* hiding, and wrote once more. Again I received no answer.

But in April of the new year a letter came:

My dear Lawrence,

How charming of you to write to me. Once upon a time I am afraid I was prone to judge my friends by their number, not by their quality, but now I know that to the man who has one *true* friend God has given riches beyond the world's reckoning. And since I have *more* than one true friend, I have been given more than I really deserve. But it's always nice, don't you think, to be given more than one deserves?

The prison years, at least until the last months, were quite dreadful because of the hunger, the silence, the degrading conditions in which one lived in one's cell, the stupid, humiliating labor one was forced to perform, and, most of all, the child prisoners whose weeping one heard all night, whose white squeezed-in faces one saw occasionally during the days, and for whom one could do nothing (a warder who gave one of these suffering innocents a sweet biscuit was discharged from the prison service with ignominy); but I cannot say I am ashamed of having been there. There were many good fellows in prison; of course there were brutes too. I learned a good deal, but despite this new knowledge, certainly unobtainable at Oxford (perhaps even at Harvard!), I cannot really recommend this type of education to others (unless they be the Home Secretary of Her Majesty's government and his colleagues), at least not until the accommodations are improved and the bestial system of jailing children done away with.

You are very kind, dear Lawrence, to say in your letter that the trials of *Regina* v. Wilde reeked of perjury on the prosecution's side. Well, yes, there *was* a very considerable reek, but I have to tell you that the verdict was not unjust, not, that is, if the charges laid at my door are thought to be crimes, which of course I do not admit. I hope you are not shocked, but it is better in these things to tell the truth.

330

Your letter would have reached me months ago in Berneval if you hadn't addressed it to Oscar Wilde. On leaving prison I adopted a new name, Sebastian Melmoth, to save embarrassment to all respectable postmen, who would have fits if required by their official duties to transport envelopes marked with the fatal name of Wilde. *Melmoth the Wanderer* was a curious novel written by my grand-uncle the Reverend Charles Maturin (descendant of an ancient French family) in the romantic revival of the early part of the century, most popular in its time, admired by Balzac, among others. And so I was known in Berneval as Monsieur Melmoth, and your letter sat unclaimed in the post office until one day (I assume) the postmistress, an excellent person, dusting it off in her conscientious way, dimly recalled having heard Mr. Melmoth called Oscar by a friend, and determined to forward the letter to the address I had left.

If you should wish to write to me again (I do hope you will), the following will find me:

Sebastian Melmoth
Hotel d'Alsace
No. 13, rue des Beaux-Arts
Paris.

Ever yours,
Oscar

Despite his words concerning the justice of the verdict, I was still unable to think of Oscar as a man of perverted tastes. The companion whose long legs had led me, panting, around the deck of the *Arizona*, who had spotted the dusky gypsy charmer, and drunk dozens of roistering young blades under the table, and plunged to the bottom of western mines—and with whom I had shared goodness knows how many hotel bedrooms—simply could not be reconciled in my mind with the kind of person I thought of as a homosexual, a species of Bunthorne, a posturing, effeminate idiot. It is extraordinary to think of one's naïveté in those days, of the naïveté of New York, for that matter, compared to London and Paris—at any rate the naïveté of the New York I knew. Surely there was some misunderstanding somewhere—judge and jury had been confused and misled, Oscar himself had been confused and mysteriously duped; perhaps was still confused.

When at last I wrote to Mr. Sebastian Melmoth, I said nothing about my continuing faith in his innocence, since in the face of

331

such protestations he only made strange disavowals; I asked about his children and his writing.

Cyril and Vyvyan, he replied in the summer of ninety-eight, were lost to him; he was forbidden to see them. This was the overwhelming tragedy of his life; trials and prison sentence were nothing. As for his writing, he was sending me a copy of *The Ballad of Reading Gaol* and copies of two of his letters to the London *Daily Chronicle* regarding English prisons.

The poem, with its description of the death by hanging of a young man who had killed his wife—he whose wistful eye looked at the little tent of blue that prisoners call the sky—seemed to me unforgettable, a masterpiece. The letters I thought no less magnificent, powerful blows that must certainly shake the British prison system to its roots and bring about its radical reconstruction.

Our correspondence continued, though sometimes with gaps of months, for the next two years, when Dr. Mellish (the son of that same Mellish who had attended my father in his last illness) prescribed a rest and complete change of scene for the headaches that were increasingly bothering me. I knew what I wanted to do, and with the family's blessing I did it. On a late August day, early in the afternoon, I found myself outside the modest Hotel d'Alsace, suddenly in some doubt as to whether I really wanted to see Oscar again—whether I really *should* see him again. The memory of him as he had been was altogether delightful, as were his letters; in them I could hear once more the beautiful voice of so many years ago. Should not things best be left as they were? But then I thought: If you should leave without seeing him, you will always tell yourself that you were afraid to take the chance. And you have come so far. Turn back now?

I almost did, though, at that. But I heard someone laugh. And all the years were gone. I was twenty-two, laughing my head off at his irresistible stories.

He was sitting at a table in the small courtyard with a man who I later learned was the *Ed. Dupoirier, proprietaire* whose name and title I had seen printed underneath *Hotel d'Alsace* on Oscar's letters—that is, when he wrote on hotel stationery, which did not seem to be always available. Even now it is difficult for me to write out M. Dupoirier's Christian name in full: Edouard. A rather grubby little man, with a face like an anxious beaver's. When Oscar wrote to friends seeking a loan, M. Ed. Dupoirier was described as harrying Oscar and hounding him and being on the point of turning him into the street; all this was quite false. M. Ed. knew how he harried Oscar, because Oscar told him and asked if he minded. M. Ed. did not mind; he was content to play the role of villain if it helped his *locataire*, as he called Oscar. M. Ed. had literally taken Oscar in *off* the street rather than tried to kick him into it. No wonder there was not always available a supply of Hotel d'Alsace stationery: M. Ed., with Oscar on his hands, simply couldn't afford it.

As I entered the courtyard, Oscar glanced around and saw me. He couldn't have hesitated for more than a few seconds. "Ah, Lawrence," he said, "how charming that we should meet again." He held out his hands, upsetting a glass on the table as he did so.

He knew from my last letter that I was coming to Europe, and I had changed less than he in the last eighteen years. Even without the setting of the Hotel d'Alsace and his unique laughter, I should have known him—even *with* his flabby face and stout figure and dyed hair and artificial teeth. He had an unmistakable air. One would have recognized Oscar in beggar's rags. The clothes he wore, though, seemed immaculate—a well-cut dark blue suit, a white shirt, a wing collar, and a blue tie. At closer range a little untidiness, a threadbare patch here and there, became evident.

M. Ed. got up, bowed, and withdrew. Oscar took my hands; his were soft and moist. "Dear Lawrence," he murmured, "to see you takes me back to that radiant morning when first with wild surmise I gazed upon the Omaha stockyards. Are you to be here for long? I do hope so."

His skin was flushed, and his breath carried the sweetish licorice smell I later came to know as that of absinthe; the glass he had knocked over had spilled a milky fluid. In my innocence I thought it *was* milk. But he wasn't drunk, or half drunk, or even a quarter drunk, though no doubt he had enough spirits in him even at that hour to set the average man reeling. I remembered him as a truly formidable drinker; the difference was that in those years his youth and splendid constitution kept him on his feet and coherent when others were babbling, whereas now the immediate effect of alcohol was blocked by the swollen organs.

I sat down and asked him please to call the waiter and replace his wasted drink. (Had I known the truth, that the milky fluid was absinthe, that it was killing him, I would have begged him not

333

to have another drink. And graciously he would have obeyed, and drunk twice as much when I was gone.)

I laughed again at the memory of Omaha. Then, to answer his question, I said, "I'm supposed to be back in New York in a month."

"Oh, you must stay longer than that, much, much longer. Otherwise the terrible Mellor might carry me off again and I really could not bear it, since he has now sunk to the point of almost complete abstinence, drinks and talks and thinks nothing but mineral water. I prefer people who drink and talk champagne."

"Who is the terrible Mellor, Oscar?"

"The terrible Mellor is an ancient young man of thirty who suffers horribly over every franc and owns millions of them. Also he owns a motorcar. At first I thought it was charming, but then it refused to go, out of sheer willfulness—like all machines, motorcars are far more temperamental than animals—moody, neurasthenic things. Some day I shall write a learned paper on nerves in the inorganic world. Of course one has to say for Mellor that he was sent away from Harrow for falling in love with the captain of the cricket eleven, and that is the sort of thing that gives one a charm that is never entirely lost no matter into what evil company one may fall." Oscar sipped his drink. "Most refreshing. And one must also say for Mellor that he knows some lovely boys. But dear Lawrence, I forget; I may be shocking you. I hope not. Am I?"

"No, Oscar." His appearance, the unhealthy skin, with a slight rash I had not noticed before, the tainted breath, the casual talk of lovely boys—these were shocking to me; but his charm was greater.

"I am so glad," he said, smiling. "I should not like you to rush away now that you are here. But I seem to be in the mood for talking. Do you mind?"

Thus began those strange, enchanting, terrible weeks; enchanting because of that wonderful voice and the laughter, terrible because one slowly realized that he had abandoned hope and drank not for pleasure but to hasten the final forgetting.

5

THE DRINKS HAD TO BE PAID FOR, THOUGH. EVEN M. ED. Dupoirier, in his almost boundless generosity, could not pay for them all.

Oscar knew I loved to hear him talk. Anyone (even a Queensberry) loved to hear Oscar talk. Moreover, I urged him to talk about his life, and he knew that so long as he went on talking I wasn't going to leave. By now Oscar was, pretty frankly, what the English call a cadger. He floated loans wherever he could, he sold the idea for a play over and over again, and he talked for his drinks and his meals (and ate precious little of them, though he drained every drop of every glass). Of course he didn't cadge or mooch his drinks in a cadging or mooching *way*. One never thought of it as cadging; one was never really aware of it so long as he talked.

"I read with fascination the newspaper accounts of me as I left prison," he said one day (by then he had spoken about the years before). "Of course I read with fascination anything written about me, but in this case there was added a sense of awe. My skin was sunburned, they said, my eyes were clear, my step was firm. One rather had the feeling that I was a simple son of the soil, dressed in simple clothes and smelling divinely earthy, don't you know. I dare say my skin *was* sunburned—I had been working in the prison gardens—and perhaps my eyes were clear, but my step wasn't firm, at least not so far as any newspaper reporter could see, because I didn't walk through the prison gates, I was driven in a carriage my friends had brought.

"Also they had brought some things for me to wear. I wore a suit made by Dore, my old tailor, cut to new, reduced measurements around the waist, and a gray-felt hat from Heath, my old hatter, and a blue-silk tie from Charvet, and gray-kidskin gloves; and in my dressing case, a present from dear Reggie Turner, there were some cakes of *Peau d'Espagne* soap, scent, toothbrush and powder, comb and brushes, and a bottle of a faithful old friend called Koko Marikopas. When I saw that honest bottle's frank, open face, it brought tears to my eyes and a delicious shade of russet-brown to my hair, and I felt prepared to enter the world again. Alas, how soon all this was to fade. No, I don't mean the hair dye, I mean my new hopefulness—with that gilded pillar of infamy who had ruined my splendid life." And Oscar looked at his glass, which was empty; it almost always seemed to be empty. Then the glass was refilled, and he cheered up.

"But I don't know," he mused. "Perhaps in the last analysis it was a necktie that ruined my life. Charles Brookfield's necktie. I haven't told you about Brookfield, have I? No? You are quite sure? Charles Brookfield was an actor who prided himself on his family; a duchess had once spoken quite kindly to his mother, I believe, and it was said that his father had been wished good morning by Thackeray, who mistook him for his groom. I am not quite sure that the last is accurate; some people hold that Thackeray mistook Brookfield's father for the cat's-meat man. At any rate, Brookfield was proud—fancied himself as a writer too. His writing was atrocious. I never told him so, though I was tempted to when he and—who was it now?—Glover, I think; yes, James Glover—when Brookfield and James Glover wrote a parody of me called *The Poet and the Puppets*. A very poor thing indeed. I *did* tell Brookfield that he should never wear a heliotrope necktie. In my opinion, I said, a heliotrope necktie did not agree with his complexion. It is *possible* that I told him his complexion did not agree with a heliotrope necktie, but I am almost completely sure that I put the necktie first. Brookfield, it would seem, brooded over this, made much of it in internal debates and colloquies with the anguished spirits of his ancestors; and when I brought suit against Queensberry it was Brookfield who went to Queensberry's lawyers and told them he could put them on to all the evidence and witnesses they would need—told them about poor Alfred Taylor's rooms and so on. Absurd of Brookfield, wasn't it? I do hope he has profited by the whole thing—no longer wears heliotrope neckties. I fancy not, though."

Another day he spoke of the marquess: "He boasted that he would defeat me, made a bet of twenty thousand pounds in the Orleans Club that I'd fall into his trap. The card was the trap, you see. But in the end I defeated *him*. The very end, for Queensberry, came eight or nine months ago—January of this year. He went mad. Or should one say he *went* mad? He always was, really. As he lay babbling on his deathbed, he thought that he was the victim of a tremendous conspiracy hatched by a group called the Oscar Wilders. The Oscar Wilders had cunningly conspired to lure the marquess into various hotels with beautiful young boys—had ruined him. Even so they weren't satisfied. The Oscar Wilders were still after him, were coming through the door now. And so he died, poor horrible little creature."

He spoke of another death: "My brother Willie died last year. A charming person, and clever too. Willie told me, quite rightly, that my play *The Duchess of Padua* would never have a success. I should turn to comedy, he said. *He* turned to Scotch whisky, and I, in the end, have turned to absinthe, as you see. I remember thinking, once upon a time, how dreadful it was that a great poet should seek to lose himself in his absinthe glass."

And another: "Constance died more than two years ago—yes, more than two years. It was early spring, I remember—April. I suppose it was fitting that she should die in the spring; she was not an autumn or a winter person, though there was winter enough in her life. She looked like spring; her eyes were the misty violet of a spring evening. Her brother, Otho Holland Lloyd, sent me the telegram. I remember writing to friends afterward that I was crushed, that I could think of nothing but this most terrible tragedy —that I wished we had only met once, in a garden, and kissed, just once, and never known each other's name. Our sons were still kept from me. They weren't Cyril and Vyvyan Wilde; they were Cyril and Vyvyan Holland, in the care of a good, kind guardian. I had nothing to say."

He learned later that Constance's illness had grown steadily worse; toward the end she was quite bedridden. "She died in a nursing home in Genoa after an operation that must have been a desperate last attempt to try to give her relief. She was only forty. They buried her in a cemetery at the foot of the Genoese hills. Last year I visited her grave. The cemetery is quite beautiful: a garden, as for her it should be. It is a simple tomb. Her names are carved on it: *Constance Mary.* And then: *daughter of Horace Lloyd.* Not *wife of Oscar Wilde.* Her friends had seen to that. She had good friends near Genoa; she had gone there to be with them. Of course it is better that the legend above her body should not read *wife of Oscar Wilde,* for that would bring shame even in death to one who in life deserved no shame. I put on her grave the flowers I had brought, and I felt all the grief and woe in the world, but also I felt very deeply the uselessness of all regret. *All is vanity and weariness, yet such a weariness and vanity that we shall ever complain of it and love it for all that.* Do you know who wrote those words? Sir Walter Raleigh, near the end of his life."

Oscar stared into his absinthe glass and perceived that it was empty. It was refilled. "Ah, thank you," he said.

"But my trip to Constance's grave was not all sorrow. On one of my walks I met an old peasant who was playing with his rosy-cheeked little grandson, and I asked him the boy's name. 'Aeolus, signor,' he replied. I remarked that Aeolus was an unusual name; how had they happened to give it to the boy? 'Oh well, you see, signore,' the old man said, 'he was born on the night of a very great wind.' Aeolus was the god of the winds, you remember. Isn't that charming?"

Lurid stories have grown describing the dreadful circumstances in which Oscar, a painted, haggard wretch, spent this period in Paris. None of them is true. He was anything but haggard, the only form of cosmetics he used was the faithful Koko Marikopas; M. Ed. Dupoirier looked after him with affectionate care at the Hotel d'Alsace, where Oscar's room was quite comfortable, although to be sure he complained that the wallpaper was killing him; one of them would have to go. He *was* always short of money, but then he had always been short of money, whatever his in-come—it was impossible for Oscar to keep ten francs or ten dollars or ten pounds in his pocket, and he told me that he had grown so accustomed to having the wolf at the door that he often asked the beast in for dinner.

The stories grew up, I dare say, because there were many Ameri-can and English tourists in Paris in that late summer of 1900, more than usual, drawn by the Exhibition that celebrated the new, hope-ful century. Often, in the cafés we visited, I was conscious of shocked whispers and furtive stares; one proprietor asked us to leave because some of his English customers objected to M. Wilde's presence; and quite frequently our entrance was the signal for a group of tourists to get up and walk out once Oscar had been identified. They could hardly be expected to return home and not report that the notorious Oscar Wilde was a shocking sight to see.

"I am a greater drawing card than the Exhibition," he observed. "If only I could think of some way of selling, with immense dignity and at a grossly inflated price, appropriate souvenirs of myself, I should be happy. A picture of me embracing a particularly flamboyant lady of easy virtue would be rather sweet, and it would quite rehabilitate my reputation at home."

But if some people left, others clustered around him, anxious to buy drinks, which he was no less anxious to accept. Indeed, I last saw Oscar in the middle of an admiring group. He was telling them the story of how his Aunt Jane gave a magnificent party but forgot the invitations and then remembered the invitations but forgot the party. Everyone was laughing, and Oscar was laughing too.

ENVOI

I LEFT PARIS EARLY IN OCTOBER. THE CIRCUMSTANCES OF Oscar's illness I learned from the friends who were with him.

He had been bothered by occasional pain in one ear, the ear he had hurt when he had collapsed in Wandsworth. The pain suddenly grew worse, accompanied by fever, and an operation was performed. Oscar did little to aid his convalescence—for the time being he gave up absinthe, but his idea of a nourishing sickbed drink was iced champagne, which he drank, of course, "strongly against the doctor's orders," as Oscar delighted in pointing out. The surgical wounds in the ear refused to heal; suppuration developed, and intense pain; but the doctor (whom Robert Ross described as "a kind, silly, excellent man") said Oscar could go out in the mild autumnal sunshine, that the air and movement would do him good. Instead, the air and the movement (with the help of a couple of glasses of absinthe snatched on the sly) made him giddy, and he had to be helped back to bed.

The nurse who was in attendance told Ross privately that the doctor did not understand that M. Wilde was extremely ill. The doctor was attached to the British Embassy and Ross did not feel that he could question his medical competence; still, Ross implored him to be frank—were things very bad? Not at all, the doctor replied; the patient's progress was excellent and he would soon be up and about. But a word of warning: if in the future he continued his heavy intake of absinthe, the doctor would not give him five years.

This seemed encouraging, but Ross could not persuade himself that Oscar looked like a man who had several years to live; his skin was flushed, his eyes wandered, and he spoke in an agitated way.

Reginald Turner arrived to relieve Ross, and Oscar welcomed him gloomily with the information that the night before he had dreamt he was having supper with the dead. "Dear Oscar," Turner replied, "I am sure you were the life and soul of the party." Oscar was so pleased that he insisted on champagne all around.

The next day he was worse. The pain was so bad that the doctor gave him morphine and Turner called in a specialist for consultation. A good many long words were exchanged in murmurs, but nothing seemed to come of them. As the morphine wore off, Oscar clutched his head in his hands and rolled it from side to side. One of the many things Reggie Turner liked about Oscar was that he never used a vulgar word and never swore, but now he swore, damning the pain, damning himself. He put his hand in his mouth and bit down on it, perhaps to stop the swearing.

Another morphine injection brought relief, and Oscar fell asleep. On waking, he seemed better, but his talk was strange. He asked Turner to hurry out and get hold of a Munster to do the cooking for him, but then said with a shrug that he supposed there was very little difference between one steamboat and another. Reggie Turner did not know what to make of this. He remembered afterward that *Munster* was the name of an intercoastal ship. How ever had it managed to get into Oscar's poor head.

Robbie Ross came back; when he heard Oscar's labored breath and saw the hideously mottled skin, he quickly left, to return with a priest, Father Cuthbert Dunn. Oscar had no formal religion but had asked Ross, a devout Catholic, to bring a priest to him on his deathbed. Father Dunn administered conditional baptism. Ross helped, uttering the responses as Father Dunn gave extreme unction, but Oscar was beyond receiving the Eucharist.

The doctor had placed two leeches on Oscar's forehead in an attempt, he explained, to relieve the brain fever by reducing the pressure of blood. The ugly little bodies grew visibly fatter; soon, satiated, they would drop off and would have to be replaced. Oscar could not take any more morphine, but the pain seemed to have slackened; once he tried to smoke a cigarette, but failed. Then he slept. Turner and Ross went to bed.

The nurse called them early in the morning. Oscar's eyes were open; foam and blood bubbled from his lips; they heard a sound that made them shudder. It was the death rattle, the nurse whispered. The sound went on and on; it was like a rusty crank. Still Oscar lived.

M. Ed. Dupoirier came into the bedroom to keep vigil with Ross and Turner. He wept a good deal.

At quarter to two in the afternoon the sound changed. Ross took Oscar's wrist and felt the pulse flutter. The coiled, hot, aching body seemed to loosen, to lie at ease. Oscar sighed, and was dead.

Reggie Turner set about straightening things in the room so that he would not break down. There were a good many letters wishing Oscar well. One was a kind note from Bosie Douglas, in London, enclosing his check for ten pounds.

Author's Note

FOR THE SEQUENCE OF EVENTS IN OSCAR WILDE'S LIFE I HAVE followed *The Letters of Oscar Wilde*, edited by Rupert Hart-Davis; but no faults or errors of any kind, if they are present in my book, can be attributed to Mr. Hart-Davis' admirable volume. To most of those events (such as Wilde's courtship of Constance Lloyd, their marriage and domestic life, his meeting with Edwin Levy, his visits to Alfred Taylor's rooms, and the scenes with Lord Alfred Douglas at Babbacombe Cliff and the Savoy and the Villa Giudice) I have added details and conversation not to be found in the many biographies and studies, which is one of several reasons that this book is called a novel.

Wilde's prosecution of the Marquess of Queensberry is taken (and condensed) from *The Trials of Oscar Wilde*, edited and with an illuminating introduction by H. Montgomery Hyde. The interpretation of Oscar's conduct during the trial is, of course, wholly mine. The letters are paraphrased or invented.

I can't sufficiently thank Katharine Kidde for her perceptive suggestions and her lucid reorganization of certain chapters.